Between Lost
and Found

Between Lost and Found

Shelly Stratton

KENSINGTON PUBLISHING CORP.
www.kensingtonbooks.com

DAFINA BOOKS are published by

Kensington Publishing Corp.
119 West 40th Street
New York, NY 10018

All Kensington titles, imprints, and distributed lines are available at special quantity discounts for bulk purchases for sales promotion, premiums, fund-raising, and educational or institutional use.

Special book excerpts or customized printings can also be created to fit specific needs. For details, write or phone the office of the Kensington Sales Manager: Kensington Publishing Corp., 119 West 40th Street, New York, NY 10018. Attn. Sales Department. Phone: 1-800-221-2647.

Dafina and the Dafina logo Reg. U.S. Pat. & TM Off.

ISBN-13: 978-1-4967-1115-1
ISBN-10: 1-4967-1115-7
First Kensington Trade Paperback Printing: August 2017

eISBN-13: 978-1-4967-1116-8
eISBN-10: 1-4967-1116-5
First Kensington Electronic Edition: August 2017

10 9 8 7 6 5 4 3 2 1

Printed in the United States of America

PART I

"Man proposes, God disposes."

—Yiddish proverb

CHAPTER 1

Sunday, April 20
Deadwood, South Dakota

Maybe it was a crazy idea. Maybe it was even a *dumb* idea—but only time would tell.

Little Bill wished he had alcohol to blame for coming up with this one. But all he had to drink tonight was a little whiskey—nothing that his seventy-eight-year-old liver couldn't handle. It probably had more to do with the gambling. Having a set of cards or a roll of dice in the waxy palms of his hands always made him take wild chances. The last time he and his girl-friend, Connie, had been at one of those casinos in Deadwood, he had lost five hundred dollars at the blackjack table because he kept doubling down, only to go bust. This time as he played blackjack at the Midnight Star, he had decided to double down yet again—in more ways than one.

It'll work, he had told himself after the nebulous thought floating in the back of his mind finally solidified. He watched the bored-looking dealer turn over the cards, revealing that Little Bill had won, and Bill took it as an auspicious sign. *I know it'll work!*

Later, at the bar, he told Connie his plan and she stared at him like he had just declared himself the king of Siam. She asked him to repeat himself. When he did, her expression morphed from amazement to unease.

"I don't know if I could do that, Bill," Connie said, her dark brows furrowing as she sipped her rum and Coke through a straw. A basket of beer-battered onion rings sat between them. "Why don't you just call her yourself? Talk to her and tell her that you don't—"

"She ain't gonna listen to me! Not while she's out there and I'm back here. I need to see her face-to-face, eye-to-eye."

"But what you want me to do . . ." Connie shook her head as she lowered her drink. "Won't your granddaughter be mad?"

"She'll be mad—at first," he said between chews. He shifted his shot glass aside and rested his elbows on the bar top's polished wood. "But when she finds out why we did it, she won't be mad anymore."

I hope.

"I don't know," Connie said again. "It just doesn't seem right."

"Trust me. All you've got to do is say exactly what I told you."

He had Connie practice over and over again. When she kept stumbling over the words—saying them in the wrong order or not saying them at all—he finally wrote down the sentences on the back of one of the casino cocktail napkins and handed it to her.

"Hi, is this Janelle Marshall?" Connie read aloud, squinting behind her red reading glasses at his jagged script. "Your grandfather's gone missing in Mammoth Falls. We need you to come here and help find him. Get here as soon as you can. Goodbye." She looked up from the napkin to gaze at him. "You . . . you sure that's all you want me to say?"

"Well, what else can you say?"

"It just seems so . . . so cold. Nobody would talk like that to a girl whose grandpa just disappeared. Shouldn't I tell her I'm sorry, or . . . or tell her you were—"

"Just keep it short and sweet. I'm tellin' you, this way is best," he assured before giving her soft hand an affectionate squeeze. He slid his cell phone across the bar top toward her. His granddaughter Janelle's phone number waited on the screen. All Connie had to do was press the little green button.

Connie gazed at the phone warily, like it was a temperamental lizard that could snap at her fingers at any moment. While she dithered, Bill could feel the seconds ticking by. He felt it more at his age, but they seemed to be whipping by him faster tonight, faster than his old eyes could register.

He wondered, *Has it happened yet? Will we be too late?*

Gradually, Connie reached for the phone. Bill released the pent-up breath he didn't know he had been holding. He watched as she slowly rose from the barstool and walked across the room to seek a quiet place that was far away from the ringing of slot machines, the clinking of glasses, and the roar of conversations and laughter. With her long, dark hair pulled back into a braid at the nape of her neck, he could see her face clearly. She still looked uncertain. Connie gave one last hesitant glance at Little Bill over her shoulder before continuing on her path and disappearing behind old-fashioned saloon doors.

Little Bill motioned to the bartender to pour him his second whiskey. That's when the finger tapping started. He started playing a six-beat that he could have hand-danced to in the old days. He looked down at his hands and realized for the first time that he was nervous.

He wasn't worried that Janelle wouldn't come to Mammoth Falls. He knew his granddaughter. If she heard her Pops had disappeared in the mountains somewhere and needed to be found, his baby girl—his little Miss Fix-It—would come running. But he was starting to have misgivings about what the aftermath would be. When Janelle found out he hadn't gone missing, she'd certainly be angry, maybe even furious. She might not want to talk to him for a while. But that was a risk he was willing to take.

He couldn't let Janelle marry that man.

"I want to ask you for Janelle's hand," Mark, Janelle's boyfriend, had said to Little Bill by phone that morning, sounding almost giddy.

"Hand for what?" Bill had asked distractedly as he stood near the gas pump, muttering to himself about the rising price of unleaded.

"Hand in marriage! I plan to ask her to marry me at our housewarming party tonight, but I realized—belatedly—that I should ask you first. You know . . . get your blessing . . . with you being the closest thing she has to a father and everything. It seemed appropriate. Janelle told me you were busy and couldn't fly here to Virginia for the party, so I wanted to give you a quick call."

A quick call . . .

Like asking Bill to hand over one of the most precious things in the world to him was a perfunctory chore.

At Mark's words, Little Bill had fallen silent. He had stared at a U-Haul truck that had pulled up to the pump next to him.

Probably needs a new fan belt, he had thought dazedly as he listened to the truck whine and screech. He had stood silently for so long that Mark had started to wonder if he was still on the phone line.

"Bill? Bill, did I lose you?"

"No, I'm here," Bill had answered before regaining his bearings. "Look, Janelle don't need me or anyone else to give her away. She don't need my permission to get married. She can make up her own mind!"

"Well, I suppose she can," Mark had replied after a pregnant pause, sounding mystified. "That wasn't what I was—"

"There's no *supposin'*. She can and she *will* make her own decisions. I just hope she makes the right one."

"Yes, I expect that she will."

Mark's voice had changed. The boyish giddiness had disappeared. He sounded firm, almost taciturn.

"Well, I'll let you go, Bill. I assume I don't have to tell you not to tell Jay about this since it's supposed to be a surprise. I'll ask her tonight, and we'll let you know when we settle on the wedding date," Mark had said before abruptly hanging up.

Bill couldn't tell Janelle what to do or whom to marry, but it was his humble opinion that she deserved the best—not some pipsqueak mama's boy with a fancy suit and cuff links. Mark wasn't right for her, not by a long shot. A man should be willing to travel miles for his lady love, to scale tall buildings and cross oceans. But Janelle's boyfriend seemed barely willing to walk over a puddle for her.

Little Bill had had similar doubts about his daughter Regina's beau, Carl, almost forty years ago. When he had first laid eyes on that smooth-talker striding confidently through his front door on platform shoes, wearing a pink polyester shirt with a collar as wide as bat wings, Bill had known instantly that he wasn't the right man for Reggie. But he had kept quiet.

"She's a grown woman allowed to make her own decisions, honey. And she's stubborn. It's not like she would listen to you anyway. Just leave it alone," his then wife, Mabel, had said to him as she cleared the dinner table.

She'd handed him a casserole dish filled with half-eaten meatloaf that was already congealing in its ketchup-and-pepper sauce.

"Can you wrap this in aluminum foil and put it in the fridge for me?"

He had done as Mabel asked: wrapped the meatloaf and kept his reservations to himself. Mabel would know best, wouldn't she? She was Reggie's mother, and she had always warned Bill that he was too impulsive, that he "never knew when to leave well enough alone."

Reggie would marry Carl a year later, and with the exception of the birth of Janelle, Reggie's life would become a soul-crushing, backbreaking march of misery for the next eight years before she finally decided to end the pain, sat all Carl's things on her front stoop for the last time, and got a divorce. But Carl had left a permanent stain on Reggie that no amount of joy or love seemed capable of washing out. Never again was she the bright-eyed, cheeky girl that Little Bill remembered.

He refused to let that happen again. He wouldn't keep silent this time around.

He had tried before to talk to Janelle about Mark, about what she really wanted out of life, but she would always deflect and change the subject. And he knew if Mark asked her to marry him, she would say yes. She'd be grateful, maybe even elated, that he asked—like she was winning some big prize on *The Price Is Right*. But the truth was that she'd be selling herself short.

Little Bill thought maybe, just maybe, if he got her away from Mark, from the hustle and the bustle of the big city—if he got her to the silence of the mountains, she would finally *hear* her old Pops.

She ain't gonna like it, but I gotta do it.

Connie returned to the bar a few minutes later. She plopped onto her stool, shoved his cell phone back at him, and glared down at the melting ice in her glass. She jabbed her straw into the glass as if she were stabbing someone.

"Well?" he asked. "What happened?"

"What the hell do you think happened?" Connie mumbled, refusing to meet his eyes. "She sounded scared out her wits, Bill!"

"That's all right. She'll be fine when she sees I'm okay," he said, reaching out for Connie's hand again. But this time she pulled away from him.

"I shouldn't've done it."

For the next hour, Little Bill tried to charm Connie back into a good mood, but nothing worked. Finally, he gave up and finished the last of their onion rings while she sat silently beside him. As he wiped the grease from his hands on another cocktail napkin, he asked her if she was ready to go home. She was supposed to ride back with him to Mammoth, but she shook her head and told him she'd rather stay.

"*Stay?* You mean here? At the Midnight Star?"

"What else would I be talking about? I'll get a ride back later. Some of these folks have to be headed back to Mammoth."

He frowned. "What folks?" He glanced around the bar room at the slim crowd that remained: another couple at one of the bistro tables in the corner, a half dozen loud truckers whose off-color banter would make a sailor blush, and one surly-looking cowboy who had been nursing the same beer at the end of the bar, it seemed, for the past two hours.

Besides the old couple, none of them seemed suitable to escort her home.

"Come on. Don't be that way! Just let me drive you."

"No," she answered firmly before grabbing her leather purse, throwing the studded strap over her shoulder, and walking off.

As he watched her leave and finished the last of his whiskey, Bill couldn't help but worry more about where and in whose bed Connie might sleep tonight than how she would eventually get home.

As he drove alone from Midnight Star in Deadwood back to his cabin in Mammoth Falls, Little Bill restlessly tapped his fingers again—this time on the steering wheel. He was taking one of those side roads that only locals were brave enough to take at night. Even with the help of his high beams, he still had a hard time making out all the details of the winding road in front of him. It was bordered on both sides with melting two-foot-tall piles of snow that had been shoveled by heavy-duty diesel trucks a week ago. On the mountain slopes beyond the snow piles were a seemingly endless army of towering trees— Ponderosa pine, Black Hills spruce, and paper birch. Their pine needles and branches were encased in ice and also sprinkled with snow, making them look like soaring glass figurines that a giant child had left behind. The trees sent up a light dusting in the wake of his passing F-150.

Little Bill squinted out his windshield. The glass was caked with grime though he had given that boy Jesse Eger twenty bucks to wash the damned truck yesterday. Little Bill figured either Jesse had done a shit job (as lazy Jesse Eger was prone to do) or his eyesight was getting worse. Maybe cataracts were finally setting in. But that was part of getting old, wasn't it? If it wasn't one piece of you falling apart, it was the other.

He tore his gaze away from the road in front of him for a few seconds to glance down at the cell phone perched in one of his cup holders on a rattling bed of loose change and discarded gum wrappers. From the programmed chime he knew right away who was calling him. It was Janelle. She had called twice already. This time, like the other times, he did not answer her call. Instead, he reached down and adjusted one of the knobs on his radio. Willie Nelson's voice filled the truck's cab along with the twang of a country guitar. Little Bill hummed along to the old hit and finally stopped tapping his fingers. He began to relax.

Connie will see, he thought.

Because it would all work out fine in the end. Janelle would arrive in Mammoth Falls soon, and he'd talk to her. Then she'd dump her second-rate boyfriend. He and Connie would make up.

Everything will be A-okay, Little Bill thought.

"*Uh-huh,*" his deceased wife, Mabel, said in his head, then grunted.

Mabel often spoke to him at moments like this when he was cloaked in solitude. She also spoke to him when he was about to make a true ninny of himself.

"*Sounds like you still aren't too good at making the right bet, Bill,*" she argued.

He turned up the volume to drown out Mabel's voice, then leaned back against his headrest. Only a few other cars passed him as he drove: a blue Chevy truck, an ancient hatchback, and one RV with a garbage bag taped over one of the rear windows. Each time their taillights disappeared in his rearview mirror, Little Bill gave them a brief wave good-bye.

"*Better slow down,*" Mabel suddenly warned.

He glanced down at his speedometer. He was barely inching above forty. He was fine. Though his vision wasn't quite what it used to be, he still knew to keep an eye out for a spindly-legged deer crossing the road, elk, or—on one occasion last year—an errant, ornery bison who refused to get out of the damned way. He had lived in the Black Hills long enough to know that.

A minute later, he turned the bend and caught sight of a snow pile in the middle of the road, but the pile was small enough that his truck would have no problem driving over it.

"Is *that* what you were trying to warn me about?" he asked his dead wife, then chuckled. "You worry too much, Mabel."

But as Little Bill drew closer, the "snow pile" shifted and turned. When he was only six feet away, he spotted a canine's startled brown eyes in the truck's headlights. The dog, whose matted mane was caked with ice and snow, sent up a mist into the frigid night air when it yelped at the sight of the F-150.

Little Bill didn't particularly like dogs, not since Mabel had brought home a basset hound puppy back in '72 that she had named Doodlebug. The thing had whined and bayed throughout the night—keeping them both up into the wee hours of morning. It had left little bite marks on the wooden legs of all their end tables and in the leather and plush velvet arms of every sofa and chair, and finally—for its grand finale—it had taken a crap in the middle of their four-poster bed. Mabel had had to give the puppy away to a neighbor who already had four dogs and six cats and wouldn't mind the added chaos Doodlebug could bring.

After Doodlebug, Little Bill had never worked up enough energy to own, let alone like, a dog. And he would soon find out that dislike was cosmically justified.

Little Bill's heart leaped from his chest to his throat. He slammed on the brakes and whipped his steering wheel to the right to keep from hitting the dog. His tires squealed as they lost traction on a patch of black ice and the truck started to skid. He whipped the wheel to the left, overcorrected, and the truck began to spin. Around and around it went, and Little Bill saw a flash of trees, road, and mountains . . . trees, road, and mountains . . . trees, road, and mountains. Finally, he let go of the wheel and closed his eyes, praying for the crazy carousel ride to end. It did seconds later when the truck slid off the road, dipped down a steep slope, and slammed into the sturdy trunk of a pine tree. He heard the glass of his windshield shatter. His airbag inflated with a *whomp* and with enough force that it threw him back against his headrest and knocked the air clean out of his lungs.

Then everything went black.

CHAPTER 2

Sunday, April 20
Chantilly, Virginia
Two hours earlier

Janelle Marshall set the Lucite tray of mozzarella and pro-sciutto near the center of the table, between the wine bottles and the platter of roasted carrots and parsnips drizzled with white balsamic vinegar. She shifted the stainless steel tongs to the left by two inches then back to the right another inch. She took a step back and clutched her hands in front of her.

It was a modernist masterpiece on white tablecloth, and like a gallery visitor, she examined the artwork. She appreciated the symmetry and the clean lines of the eggshell-white stoneware and the way the wineglasses refracted the light from the French crystal chandelier overhead. She noted the vibrant red and yel-low of her Mediterranean salad and the understated green and orange of the vegetarian summer rolls she had purchased at the killer banh mi place six blocks from her office but planned to subtly pass off as her own. It all looked so impeccably com-posed, so . . .

"Perfect," she whispered with a grin.

Tonight's housewarming would be seamless. She'd gone over the checklist on her iPad to make it so, reviewing every minute detail—from the lighting to the song selection uploaded to her iPod, even to the dinner napkins she had spent hours folding into fleur-di-lis patterns. Now everything was in its rightful place and she could *finally* relax.

"The guests are starting to arrive, baby. Are you almost done?" Mark said as he strode through the dining room entryway, carrying a silver-lidded platter.

He was wearing a tan Hugo Boss blazer, dark khakis, and a yellow polka-dot bowtie she had gotten him for his birthday. He looked much like he had the first night she had met him, like a black Tucker Carlson.

Janelle had known even back then that Mark was the type of sturdy guy you could build a life upon. He was the stellar boyfriend who came home with the dry cleaning without being asked to pick it up, who took her car to get the oil changed as soon as the odometer shifted three thousand miles. Mark was as reliable as a Swiss watch—and she loved him for it.

Janelle examined their buffet table one last time, then nodded before turning to him and giving a small adjustment to the knot in his tie. "Yep, all done!"

"Great!" He then shoved the tray of mozzarella and prosciutto aside, cramming the silver platter into the now open space.

Watching him ruin her masterpiece, she almost cried out "No!" but she bit it back before the word passed her lips.

It's okay. It's fine. Take a deep breath. It's just a minor imperfection. Only you'll notice.

"Breathe in, breathe out," is what she often told employees at Bryant Consultant Group who came storming into her office, slamming the door behind them, ready to unload some grievance. As HR director, she had to play arbiter and problem solver. She could not, under any circumstances, lose her cool. She would have to do the same tonight.

Trust in the Zen, she reminded herself before giving one last longing glance at the buffet table, resisting the urge to shift around the dishes again to regain the symmetry and balance it once had.

"Mom's here," Mark said as he removed his wire-framed glasses, grabbed one of the linen dinner napkins, and began to wipe his lenses.

"Yes, I heard."

Even over the sound of jazz playing on their surround sound system and the rising murmur of conversation, Janelle could hear Mark's mom, Brenda Sullivan, with her distinct Southern drawl. Though, truth be told, that drawl was as fake as the curly wig Brenda wore. Janelle wasn't sure why the aging divorcée spoke like Scarlett O'Hara considering, according to her son, she had grown up in the projects of Detroit and not on a plantation in Savannah.

"She didn't come empty-handed, either. She brought this," Mark said as he placed his glasses back on his nose and removed the silver lid. He grinned. "Looks good, huh?"

Janelle stared down at the platter.

The dish was displayed in a carved-out pumpernickel loaf with a nest of gourmet crackers and bread slices radiating around it, with shavings of parsley sprinkled on top like green confetti. It looked like it should have been on the cover of one of those gourmet food magazines—*Bon Appétit* or *Saveur*.

"It's crab dip," Janelle said flatly.

"Yeah, it's crap dip. What? What's wrong?"

"What's wrong? Honey, you know I'm allergic to it, and so does your mom," she said, dropping her voice down to a whisper.

Allergic—as in breaking into hives, swelling like the Stay Puft marshmallow man, gasping for air, and ultimately dropping dead—unless she got a quick stab of epinephrine.

"So then don't eat it!" He chuckled in exasperation. "I

mean, come on, baby! Mom just meant to be nice. She didn't mean anything by it."

Janelle glanced at the crab dip again. *Deep breath in. Deep breath out.*

"You're right," she said, patting his arm. "It's no big deal."

She would just have to shrug this off like she had shrugged off the other little digs from Brenda since she and Mark started dating, all of which could be mistaken for (or disguised as) well-meaning though clueless gestures.

Thanks, Brenda! A Weight Watchers subscription is just what I needed for my birthday!

You're right, Brenda! My curly hair does look awfully big. I should straighten it or just cut it all off!

Brenda's assistant, Shana, was another annoyance. Shana would sometimes come through the door trailing behind Brenda, nodding eagerly as she carried boxes like a happy pack mule, taking notes and gushing over everything Brenda said and did. She felt like yet another impediment to Janelle and Brenda truly ever bonding.

But we'll bond—eventually, Janelle told herself. *It* will *happen.*

Because with time and with effort, she could make it work— like she made everything else work.

Mark replaced the silver lid, leaned down, and kissed Janelle's cheek. "That's my girl! Don't sweat the small stuff, baby. Let's just enjoy the night." He glanced over his shoulder. "We should get out there and mingle with our guests. You ready to jump into the fray?" He extended his hand to her.

She nodded before taking his hand, standing on the balls of her feet and giving him a quick kiss. "Of course, honey."

He escorted her into the living room, where there were several clusters of partygoers near the fireplace, the bay windows, and nestled on the sofa and armchairs. It was a microcosm of typical NoVa (or "Northern Virginia," for those recent transplants) types: Beltway political insiders, long-time federal employees who could rattle off where they fell on the government pay scale faster than they could their own Social Security numbers, and pseudo-liberals who donated thousands to the Green Party but would still pull their Michael Kors purse close to their side whenever a hoodie-wearing guy walked nearby.

"Great party, Jay!" someone shouted out to her.

"Your new place looks amazing," someone else called.

Janelle waved and blew a kiss to them, graciously accepting the compliments she had worked so hard to earn.

Brenda spotted Janelle and Mark as soon as they walked into the room. She sauntered toward them with wineglass in hand. Shana skittered after her across the Brazilian hardwood.

Brenda and Shana were wearing almost identical Albert Nipon suits. Brenda's was gray and probably purchased at full price; Shana's was red and likely bought off the sale rack. They looked like mirror images of each other, from their clothes to their petite figures to the plastic smiles on their faces.

"Janelle, there you are! We were wondering where you were hiding." Brenda kissed Janelle, leaving a smear of blood red lipstick on the younger woman's cheek that would have to be discreetly wiped off later.

Shana did a perky wave. "Hi, Janelle!"

Janelle nodded and forced her smile to stay in place. "Brenda . . . Shana, thank you so much for coming tonight."

"And for the crab dip," Mark added, gently nudging Janelle's elbow. "Right, Jay?"

"Of course," Janelle said through clenched teeth, almost tasting the words as they curdled on her tongue. But she was the consummate hostess. She refused to be rattled, even by the likes of Brenda and her deadly appetizers.

"Anything for you, darling," Brenda drawled before playfully pinching Mark's cheek. She turned back to Janelle. "Janelle, I was hoping to finally meet your family tonight." Brenda looked around the living room. "Where is your mother, anyway?"

"Oh, Mom's on a two-week cruise in the Mediterranean. She'd hope to make the housewarming, but I told her to just go and enjoy herself." She waved her hand and chuckled. "She's wanted to do this cruise for years!"

"Is your dad on the cruise with her?" Shana asked with raised brows. "Or is he coming tonight?"

For the first time, Janelle's casual veneer and deep breathing exercises wavered. Her polite smile teetered on its axis. "My dad's . . . uh . . . he's dead."

Shana looked stricken. Her mouth formed into an "O" as she clapped a hand over lips. "I am *so* sorry! I didn't know!"

"No, it's fine." Janelle shrugged awkwardly. "He died more than a decade ago, and he was . . . well, out of my life, for the most part. So when he passed away, I barely even noticed. I-I mean I *noticed*. He was my father! I was sad, of course. But I wasn't . . . you know, devastated."

Her voice shook a little as Shana lowered her hand. The two women stared at Janelle with blank faces. Mark squinted at her like she had all of a sudden decided to speak in French.

Oh, God. I'm babbling.

She always did that whenever she spoke about her dad, which is why she preferred not to talk about him, let alone think about him.

"I just meant it wasn't like I missed out on much because my mom was . . . was *really* great and—"

"Her grandfather raised her," Mark interjected, saving her. "He was like her dad. Too bad he couldn't make it tonight either, huh, baby?" Mark swept his hand around him before throwing an arm around her shoulder and giving her a squeeze. "It would have been nice for him to see how well it all turned out. I bet he would have been impressed!"

"Oh, absolutely!" Janelle gushed, though, in truth, she highly doubted Pops would find any of this impressive.

When she had given him a tour of their new home more

than a month of ago, she had proudly shown him the Phillip Jefferies stitched-linen wallpaper that she and Mark had chosen to hang in their living room: a sumptuous chocolate interlaced with gold thread. All Pops had said was "Jeffries *who?* You'd think I'd at least heard of the man if he's gonna charge people two hundred dollars for one sheet of wallpaper!"

If he saw their home now with all its expensive details and finishes, he probably wouldn't have anything nice to say—much as he had very little nice to say about Mark.

"Well, I'll let you two get back to your other guests," Brenda said. "Maybe there will be another special occasion where I can finally meet your family, Janelle."

She gave an exaggerated wink at Mark, causing Janelle to furrow her brows in mystification. Brenda wiggled her fingers in good-bye, making her many rings twinkle underneath the glare of the recessed lights. She then strode away with her human puppy, Shana, trailing after her.

"That was odd," Janelle muttered, staring after Brenda.

"No, it wasn't," he said, clutching her hand again. "That was just Mom being Mom."

"If you say so, honey."

He gave her hand a squeeze. "Don't worry about her. Besides, tonight is about you and me, right? Not Mom!"

"You're right. It is about us," she said, her chest warming at the word "us."

He leaned down to give her a quick kiss, and they held eyes.

How could Pops not see what she saw right now in this man's adoring gaze?

"Come on. Let's mingle," he said, abruptly ending the moment.

And for the rest of the night, Janelle and Mark charmed their guests. They looked good together; she looked like the black Ann Coulter next to his black Tucker Carlson. They filled in the gaps in each other's conversation, reminding the other of a name, place, or date the other had forgotten.

"I'm so glad you made it, Don," Mark said to one of their guests and shook his hand. "So where is your darling wife . . . uh . . . uh . . . ."

"Celeste," Janelle said in a voice only loud enough for him to hear.

". . . Celeste?" Mark asked, not breaking stride. "How is she?"

It was a delicate dance, and as a couple, they performed it wonderfully. She felt like a seasoned tennis player on the court engaged in a game of doubles. Janelle knew instinctively when to hit the volley and when to back off and let her partner, Mark, take a backswing.

This seamless synchronicity was something Janelle had never witnessed between her own mother and father before their divorce. Her parents' marriage was less like a game of doubles and more like a mixed martial arts death match some nights. ("Get the hell off my back, woman!" her father would yell. "I wish you would just walk out that door and never come back, Carl! Never . . . come . . . back!" her mother would shout in reply.) But Janelle had learned a different way, a *better* way, after years of trial and error, after watching other couples interact, and after trying her best and failing miserably with ex-boyfriends. Practice makes perfect and with practice, she had become a pro at this.

Even when she and Mark were separated, Janelle felt an imaginary tether between them—something to let her know that they were always connected. She felt the tug at that tether mid-conversation with one of her new neighbors. She turned to find Mark standing near the fireplace, tapping a knife against the side of a wineglass.

"Excuse me!" Mark called out as he pressed a button on a remote to lower the volume of the music playing in the living room. The sound of tinkling piano keys and Coltrane faded. "Excuse me, everyone!"

Suddenly, her cell phone began to chime.

Janelle shoved her hand into her skirt pocket to silence it, but the peppy ringtone continued to play. She yanked out her phone just as she heard Mark say, "If you guys could just quiet down for a few minutes, I have an announcement to make."

Huh? What announcement? She stared at her phone's glass screen, prepared to send the call to voice mail.

But when she spotted the name on her caller ID, she beamed. It was Pops.

She had wanted him here with her tonight but he had made a half-hearted excuse about why he couldn't come.

"Sorry, baby girl," he had said. "Got too much to do back here."

She knew the truth. Rather than standing around sampling brie, crackers, and Chardonnay at a housewarming party, Pops would rather be off playing cowboy in the small mountain town in South Dakota that he went to eight to nine months out of the year. She suspected that's where he was happiest.

"Hey, Pops!" Janelle said in a voice barely above a whisper so as to not disturb whatever speech Mark was making. She began to walk toward the kitchen. "I didn't expect to hear from you today. This is a nice surprise!"

"Hi . . . uh, hi . . . is this J-Janelle Marshall?" a woman answered.

Janelle paused. Her grin and stride faltered. That wasn't the voice she had anticipated hearing. "Yes, this is she."

"Umm . . ." The woman cleared her throat. "Your . . . your grandfather has gone missing in Mammoth Falls. We need you to come here and . . . and help find him. Get here as soon as you can."

"What?"

The woman's tone was stilted, like she was reading off of a

teleprompter. She sounded so strange that Janelle wondered if she had heard her correctly. It sounded like she said Pops had gone missing, but that couldn't be right.

"I'm sorry. What did you say?"

"Uh, I-I said that your . . . your grandfather is missin'." The woman cleared her throat again. "I thought . . . I thought you should know."

Janelle's stomach took a nosedive straight to her knees. Her grip on her iPhone tightened to the point that she could swear she heard the plastic-and-metal casing crack.

"What are you talking about? What do you mean he's missing?" she cried, now frantic.

She turned to look at Mark, who was talking, smiling, and gesticulating in front of the fireplace. He must have made a joke. Several partygoers around her began to chuckle. A man standing next to her hooted and slapped his thigh.

Janelle rushed across the living room and reached the kitchen, almost stumbling into the corner of the center island. She gripped the edge of her marble counter to steady herself. Her legs felt weak.

"What happened?" Janelle asked. "Wait! Who is this? Why do you have his phone?"

"Uh, I can't tell you who it is. You don't . . . it ain't something you need to know. He's missing and . . . and if you're any decent kin, you'll . . . you'll come looking for him. You'll come to Mammoth Falls!"

"Looking for him? What?"

"Come and find your grandfather! If you're really worried about him, you'll come here," the woman insisted.

As Janelle listened, she told herself to remain calm, to not become hysterical.

Breathe in, Breathe out.

But it wasn't working in the slightest.

"Are the police searching for him? Wait . . . did you call the police? Did you tell them that he's—"

The caller hung up, and Janelle was left staring at her phone, dumbfounded.

"Jay!" someone shouted from behind her, making her jump. Her phone fell from her hands and clattered to the floor.

Janelle whipped around to find one of her old sorority sisters, Melanie, standing in the entryway, flapping her arms wildly as if she were trying to take flight right there in the kitchen.

"What are you doing hiding with the pots and pans?" Melanie cried, rushing across the room. "Get out there, girl! He's looking for you!" She then grabbed Janelle's arm and pulled, running across the room with high heels click-clacking over the tiled floor.

Janelle was too dazed to ask why she was being dragged out of the kitchen or who exactly was looking for her. She allowed herself to be pulled along like a limp ragdoll. When she entered the living room, she was greeted by more than two dozen pairs of eyes. All of them stared at her with a feverish intensity and palpable anticipation that made her anxious and even more confused.

What the hell is going on?

"There you are!" Mark exclaimed as he stepped away from the fireplace. His shout sounded like a thunderclap in the hushed room. The crowd parted to clear the path for him as he strode toward her.

Brenda stood behind Mark, dabbing at her reddened eyes with one of the linen napkins from the buffet table.

"I thought you were in here," he said, grinning ear-to-ear. "You missed my whole buildup. I did a speech and everything!"

"A s-s-speech about what?" she sputtered.

"It doesn't matter. I'm sure someone in here got it on their phone. You can watch it later. Besides, the only part that *really* matters is this." He then reached into one of the inner pockets of his suit jacket and pulled out a black velvet box. She watched as Mark slowly, almost dramatically flipped the box lid open.

He revealed a solitaire diamond set against a simple white gold or platinum band. A collective gasp filled the living room. Someone let out a girlish squeal.

"Janelle April Marshall, you are everything I've ever wanted in a woman: beauty, brains, all in a no-nonsense package. You're my other half, my perfect fit, and I couldn't imagine a day without you. Janelle, will you marry me?" Mark asked, holding out the ring to her. She gazed at it dumbly while everyone in the room fell silent, waiting for her reply.

The spotlight was on her. She tore her eyes from the ring and met Mark's dark irises.

"Well?" Brenda said, leaning forward.

Someone coughed.

A myriad of thoughts jostled around in Janelle's mind at that moment. She uttered the one that shoved the hardest, that shouted the loudest.

"Pops is missing," she said.

CHAPTER 3

Janelle sat on the edge of the bed and rubbed lotion—or "body rescue cream," according to the bottle label—onto her hands and forearms. She raised the hem of her silk nightgown and stared down at her feet, which were now sporting reddened soles and budding calluses thanks to the dainty sling-back heels she had worn during the housewarming. She decided her feet could use some "rescuing," too. She grabbed the bottle to squeeze more into her palm.

Her hands moved ceaselessly, massaging the scented lotion onto her feet. It helped her stifle the urge to wring her hands.

Pops is fine, she told herself. *There's no reason for alarm. That woman was playing some horrible prank, that's all.*

Janelle then glanced at her cell phone. It sat on her ebony night table between her alarm clock and a box of Kleenex. She wanted to keep it within arm's reach because even though she had left messages on both Pops's cell and home phone, he still hadn't called her back, which wasn't like him.

He's just busy.

The sound of the evening news droned in the background on the wall-mounted flat-screen television. Through the closed door, she could hear Mark shuffling around in their master bath—opening and closing cabinets, turning on the faucet, and banging his toothbrush against the rim of one of the vanity's double sinks.

Pops hasn't disappeared. Don't leap to any irrational conclusions. There has to be a reasonable explanation for this. You know . . . Occam's razor and all that.

But with each passing minute, her anxiety ratcheted up higher and higher. She felt jittery, like a soda bottle that had been shaken too hard and all it would take was one twist of the lid and she would explode in a frothy mess.

Janelle nearly jumped when she heard the toilet flush. She heard Mark turn the water on and then off before opening the door and striding into their bedroom wearing only his t-shirt and boxer briefs. He yanked back the gray silk duvet and climbed in bed beside her.

"Well, tonight was interesting," he muttered.

"Huh?" she asked absently, still rubbing on lotion.

"The housewarming party that I thought was going to turn into an engagement party but didn't." He punched the stack of pillows behind him, leaving an indentation in the down feathers. He then braced his pillows against their leather headboard and leaned back. "I said it was interesting."

She winced and lowered her foot back to the floor. "I'm sorry, honey. You just caught me off guard. It was the worst case of bad timing."

"I didn't know me choosing to ask you to marry me in front of all of our family, friends, and neighbors was bad timing."

She loudly sighed as Mark grabbed the remote from his night table. He pointed it at the television across the room and started flipping channels, refusing to look at her.

The two fell into strained silence.

She knew she probably should feel bad that his proposal had gone so horribly. Instead of gushing over the ring and shouting, "Yes! Yes, I'll marry you," followed by applause worthy of any stellar Broadway performance, she had railed about the mysterious phone call and her grandfather disappearing somewhere in the Black Hills. Mark had had to ask her to repeat herself three times before he finally figured out what she was saying.

All of the guests left soon after, whispering among themselves or exchanging bemused expressions. Janelle Marshall . . . raving like some lunatic? *Her* of all people?

"Shana, let's go," Brenda had barked before glaring at Janelle almost with disgust, as if she blamed her for ruining Mark's proposal. She had then stomped out the front door and down the walkway to her Jag.

" 'Night!" Shana had shouted over her shoulder before scuttling after Brenda.

But what was I supposed to do? Janelle thought.

This could be a serious emergency—an elderly man may have disappeared in the cold, lonely terrain of the Black Hills. That took precedence over anything else, including an elaborate proposal. But she realized Mark had put a lot of effort into this. She knew he must be disappointed in how it had all turned out.

"Mark, honey," she began tentatively, turning toward him, "I really am sorry about what happened. You know I don't normally act like this. I mean it . . . if I could do it all over again, I would—"

"I just don't understand why you didn't say yes. You just left me standing there, holding the ring like some . . . some jackass!"

"I couldn't say yes because I was shell-shocked! I went from being stunned to being worried about Pops. I'm *still* worried about him!"

He furrowed his brows. "Why? You said yourself that that woman who called was probably playing a joke on you."

"Yes, but . . . I don't know that for sure. I mean he still hasn't—"

"She was probably one of his drinking buddies or something," Mark said, not hearing her. He finally landed on MSNBC, where Lawrence O'Donnell sat in front of a fake backdrop of the New York City skyline while talking about the auto industry. "They got sauced off their asses and thought it would be great to steal his phone and tell his granddaughter he got lost somewhere," Mark continued. "I would imagine that for people in the sticks, you find your entertainment wherever you can get it."

She set down her lotion bottle. "I know, honey! But that still doesn't keep me from worrying about him." She glanced again at her silent cell phone. "I hate that he hasn't called me back. It's just letting all these paranoid fantasies run wild in my head. What if he really is missing? What if that lady and her friends kidnapped him and are holding him for ransom in some—"

"Are you serious? *Kidnapping?*"

"I know it sounds crazy!" She shrugged helplessly, feeling very worn and very tired. "But I told you, until I talk to Pops, I don't know anything for sure."

"Yeah, well, I know a few things for sure," he said with widened eyes. "I know that I now have an engagement ring in my drawer that I thought would be on your finger. I know a random stranger halfway across the country completely ruined our evening with some dumb joke!"

"But it might not be a joke! It could *really* be something serious. Pops could be—"

"I also know I'm tired of talking about this!" he shouted.

Janelle's cheeks flushed with heat. She bit down hard on her bottom lip.

"Fine," she said, making Mark roll his eyes in exasperation. "Then we won't talk about it anymore."

"Jay, come on . . ."

She reached over and turned off her night table lamp, dropping her side of their bedroom into darkness. She pulled back the duvet and climbed beneath it. She turned her back to him and burrowed under the sheets until they were up to her shoulders.

The drone of O'Donnell's voice filled the gap that the couple's silence left behind. Mark slowly exhaled then placed a hand on her shoulder.

"Look, I'm sorry I yelled at you."

She didn't answer him and raised the sheets to her chin.

"I know you're worried about your grandfather. I just don't think you have anything to worry about, baby. I spoke to him today. I called to ask him for permission to marry you, and he . . ." Mark paused. "Well, anyway, I'm sure not *that* much has changed between this morning and this evening. It's not even twenty-four hours. How would they even know he's missing? He doesn't need your help. He'll call you back tomorrow. Just . . . just get some sleep, okay? Stop worrying."

Mark's hand disappeared, and all she could feel was the warmth his imprint left behind on her skin. Janelle listened as he turned off the television then flicked a switch, making the entire room go black save for the blue, ghostly glow from both of their alarm clocks. She heard the soft clatter of his glasses landing on his night table. The bed dipped as he shifted, adjusted his pillows, and lay on his side.

"Good night," he whispered before leaning over to sweep a kiss as dry as crepe paper across her cheek. It was so quick that she barely registered it.

Within fifteen minutes, she could hear Mark's rhythmic snores.

She groped in the darkness for the edge of her night table, then felt along the surface until she found her cell phone. She shoved down the sheets and checked her screen. She still hadn't gotten a call from Pops. She checked the volume on her ringer. It was at the highest setting. If her grandfather called, she would hear it. She slid the phone back onto her night table.

Janelle closed her eyes. She raised her wrist to her nose and sniffed, inhaling the "body rescue cream." It smelled like lavender and vanilla—a scent that was supposed to be calming but seemed to have no effect on her. She couldn't be calm. She couldn't quiet her thoughts. They were like wailing infants, screaming for her attention.

Pops is missing!

You need to go to Mammoth Falls to find him!

Pops hasn't called you back!

Maybe something is wrong!

Waaaaaaaaa!

She opened her eyes, pulled back the covers, and eased out of bed so as to not wake Mark, though disturbing him wasn't likely. Mark's snores were louder now. They sounded like a buzz saw, like a hog with nasal congestion. His snoring, which she usually ignored, annoyed her tonight. At least the noise would drown out any sound she could possibly make.

She found her phone in the dark and used the glowing screen to guide her way across their expansive bedroom. She was careful not to bump into the armchair on her side of the bed or trip over the Brooks running shoes that Mark had left in the middle of the floor yesterday and still hadn't put in his closet, even though she had asked him twice to do so. She slowly opened the door and stepped into the hallway, shutting the door behind her with a soft click.

As she walked down the hall to their home office, she speed-dialed the number to her grandfather's cabin, the cabin she had seen only in pictures because she had never set foot in Mammoth Falls.

"I am *not* going to Mammoth, Pops! I don't fish. I don't hunt," she could remember proclaiming once as she counted the "don'ts" off on her fingers. "You really expect me to go to a place with moose and geese and mountain people? What in the world is a person like me supposed to do in Mammoth Falls, South Dakota?"

Once she got Pops on the phone, her worry would disappear. She told herself this as she walked into the twelve-by-twelve-foot room that was filled with two matching desks facing opposite walls. Opened laptops sat on both desks, and in front of each were identical leather rolling chairs. More unopened cardboard boxes sat near the room's only window, waiting to be unpacked.

Janelle sat in one of the chairs and listened to the phone ring in Pops's cabin. The phone rang . . . and rang . . . and rang.

"Hey! This here is Little Bill," her grandfather answered jovially in his voice mail greeting in the raspy voice she knew all too well. "I can't come to the phone right now! So you go on and leave your name and phone number after the—"

Janelle hung up. She then quickly dialed his cell phone—the one she had bought him for Christmas, along with a charger. She had made him swear to keep his cell on him at all times, though considering that woman had called from his phone hours ago, it didn't seem like Pops had kept his promise. Janelle leaned forward with her elbows on her knees as she listened to it ring over and over.

"Pops, where are you?" she whispered desperately. Again, she hung up before the voice mail greeting ended. She set her cell phone on the desk beside her and slumped back into her chair.

Janelle sat in her office for several minutes, staring at nothing in particular, not moving. She listened to the soft hum of the AC unit and the *tick-tock* of the vintage grandfather clock in the hallway. Finally, she turned around and booted up her laptop. She told herself that she would get some work done for an hour or two if she wasn't going back to sleep immediately. Work was drudgery to some, but it was always calming to her. There were emails she could draft, staff evaluations to review. She didn't realize what she was *really* doing until she closed the screen on one of the HR documents she had opened and pulled up a travel web site. She started researching flights from Reagan National, BWI, and Dulles International to see what carrier had the cheapest and earliest flights to airports in western South Dakota.

"*What are you doing?*" a little voice in her head asked. It sounded a lot like Mark's. "*You aren't really considering going out there, are you?*"

She dragged her finger across the keypad and scrolled down the page. There was a flight leaving BWI at noon tomorrow. There was another leaving Reagan at 10:35 a.m.

"*Oh, Jesus, you really are considering going there!*" the voice in her head lamented. "*He isn't missing! This was just some asinine prank and now you're going to travel hundreds of miles across the country because of it?*"

"One seat left!" the screen taunted in bright red letters next to the Reagan flight listing. Janelle gnawed her bottom lip as her finger hovered over the keypad.

"*Are you insane? You can't disappear to Mammoth Falls on a wild goose chase!*" Mark's voice yelled frantically in her head. "*You have to go to work tomorrow! You have that PowerPoint presentation on sexual harassment to review, and the two new hires are starting their orientation. You have a mountain full of boxes to still unpack. You were supposed to meet Allison for dinner Thursday so that you guys can plan Crystal's baby shower. You made a whole color-coded binder of Pinterest baby shower photos! Those are your priorities! Not some silly phone call from a woman who wouldn't even give you her name. Just go back to bed, go to sleep, and give up this ludicrous idea!*"

Janelle glanced at her silent phone yet again. She had now called her grandfather more than a half dozen times and left messages, but he still hadn't called her back.

The last time something like this had happened, it had been her father, not her grandfather who had gone missing, and she had continued to wait for him—letting one day turn into two, and two into three, and three had finally stretched into a full week.

"I still haven't heard from him, Mom," she'd told her mother all those years ago while sitting on her college dorm room bed, dangling her feet over the bottom bunk. "I know Dad's gone MIA before—"

"You mean like the time he didn't show up to your high school graduation and didn't call you back until two days later?"

"—but his friend said he hasn't seen him in a while. I'm starting to worry that something really is wrong!"

Janelle had anxiously twisted one of her long braids around her finger as she spoke on the phone, finding some perverse comfort in the way the hair tightened around her skin, making the tip of her index finger turn red.

"I wouldn't worry about it, honey," her mother had said on the other end of the phone line, sounding tired. She'd yawned. "You know your father. He's a little boy trapped in a grown man's body. He doesn't know how to be a responsible adult. I'm sure he got your messages. He'll call you back whenever he feels like it."

"I know, but I'm wondering if we should call the police and—"

"Honey," her mother had said, "I spent almost a decade worrying about your father, chasing after him. I remember spending nights awake wondering why he hadn't come home. Did he get so drunk that he drove off the road and hit a streetlight? Did he get high with one of his old buddies and OD? I'd leave you alone in the house asleep, throw on a coat, and go hunting for him in the middle of the night, driving to any place I knew to track him down, only to find him passed out in some bar or in some other woman's bed. I can't do it anymore. I *won't* do it anymore! You understand? I suggest you don't do it, either. Your father hasn't spoken to you in *months*. He doesn't want to be part of our lives, baby. He isn't worth the time and effort."

Janelle had closed her eyes and released the braid around her finger. Grudgingly, she'd nodded. "You're right, Mom.

You're right. I should get back to studying. I have a chemistry exam tomorrow. Those isotopes are kicking my butt."

Her mother had laughed. "You'll do fine, honey. And don't worry. Dad will show up somewhere eventually. He always does."

Her mother had been right—Janelle's father *did* show up. The police found his body three days later in an abandoned row house in their old neighborhood. He had been slumped against the wall in one of the upstairs bedrooms with a needle still in his arm and a half-empty bottle of whiskey at his side.

Despite her mother's insistence that there was nothing they could have done to save him, Janelle would always wonder if she should have done more than just leave phone messages. Could she have tried harder to find him—to save him?

Janelle's gaze now returned to her laptop screen.

"Come and find your grandfather," the woman had said. "If you're really worried about him, you'll come here."

"One seat left," she whispered.

Finally, she lowered her finger and pressed the on-screen button to purchase a ticket on the 10:35 flight to South Dakota.

CHAPTER 4

**Welcome to Mammoth Falls . . . the Gold Nugget
of the Black Hills!**

Hunters, fishermen, and lovers of natural beauty, feast
your eyes on Mammoth Falls, South Dakota! Set in
the heart of the Black Hills and named after the mam-
malian creatures that once roamed North America,
the town was founded in 1889, soon after gold was discovered in the Homestake mine in neighboring Lead.
But while the gold rush brought both outlaws and law-
men to nearby towns like the infamous Deadwood,
Mammoth Falls was populated by simple, gentle folk
from the South and West. And simple, gentle folk still
live there to this day.

Visit this fair hamlet to witness nature's majesty
and the history of the Old Wild West all in one. Fish
on beautiful Pasque Lake and tour the magnificent
mountains the Lakota Indians once called home. Learn
more about the gold rush at the Black Hills Mining
Museum in Lead. Enjoy a game of poker and watch a
real Wild West shootout in nearby Deadwood. Bring

the family. Heck, bring the dog, too! Come to Mammoth Falls today!

—from www.cityofmammothfalls.com, *last up-dated August 2012*

Did it really require a whole *six* hours to fly from D.C. to Minneapolis then Rapid City? With all the developments in modern aviation, this was the fastest she could go on a commercial jet?

These were the questions Janelle kept asking herself during her flight across country as she glanced at her watch, watching the minutes tick by. It had taken all her restraint not to climb out of her seat, storm the cockpit, and commandeer the airplane so that she could move the Boeing 717 along a lot faster. Instead, she buried her growing anxiety and impatience under bad in-flight movies and a stack of glossy magazines with mind-numbing articles about silicon-enhanced, Botoxed celebrities that she had picked up at one of the airport magazine kiosks.

"Does Beyoncé Really Rule the World?" one intrepid headline read.

"KHLOE KARDASHIAN'S SECRET HEARTBREAK IS REVEALED!" said another in superfluous all caps.

When Janelle wasn't doing her deep breathing exercises, reading, or staring vacantly at the drop-down television screen above her head, she was surreptitiously making phone calls in the airplane bathroom, hoping that her phone signal wouldn't make their plane crash into a farm field or Lake Michigan.

First, she called her mother.

"No, Mom, Pops isn't dead," Janelle assured her mother, who became hysterical when Janelle told her about last night's cryptic phone call. "He's just missing . . . That's the most I can tell you right now. Yes, I know . . . I know! Don't worry . . . No, you don't have to take the first flight back home. I'm taking care of it. I'm flying out there, and I'll find out what's going on. I'll tell you as soon as I get this straightened out."

Next, she checked in with her assistant human resources director, Lydia.

"Uh-huh . . . Uh-huh . . . I know we were supposed to review that presentation today, but it's a family emergency . . . I had no choice, Lydia." She rolled her eyes as she listened to Lydia rant on the other end of the line. "Yes, I am aware that it's important, but again, I had no control over this. . . . Look, there is no need to freak out. I completely trust you. You're totally capable of taking care of everything in my absence and, if you need anything, you can always reach me by email or on my cell. I'm a phone call away . . . I told you, I should be back in a couple of days . . . Yes . . . *Yes!* . . . Look, I have to get off the phone," Janelle whispered, wincing at the pounding at the bathroom door. "There's a line three deep to get in here, and they're probably going to try to batter the door down."

The only person she hesitated in calling was Mark, mainly because he had taken the news about her decision to fly to South Dakota to find her grandfather as well as she thought he would.

"You can*not* be serious, Janelle!" he had said that morning as she prepared for her flight. His mouth had hung agape as he watched her rush around their bedroom.

"Yes, I'm very serious. I'm going to find him." She had hurriedly shoved clothes, toiletries, and a few other choice items into the carry-on suitcase she had dragged out of her walk-in closet.

Wanting to be prepared, Janelle had checked the weather forecast. Though it was late April and light sweater weather in the Washington, D.C. suburbs, it still seemed to be wool coat and parka central in the Black Hills. Normal temps in April usually ranged between the thirties and fifties, but western

South Dakota seemed to be going through a long winter this year. Yesterday was a high of twenty-six degrees.

Just my luck, she had thought before adding another turtleneck to the growing pile in her suitcase. She hated the cold.

"Baby, this is ridiculous! Seriously, what is going on with you?"

She had ignored him and tossed in another sweater and a pair of wool gloves.

"I mean, just . . . just stop and think about this for a sec! You're going to pack up and fly across country because of one phone call? *Just like that?* If you're so concerned, why not call the cops and have *them* find your grandfather?"

"I did that already," she had muttered, grabbing her suitcase zipper and yanking it closed.

She was fretful but not completely irrational. *Thank you very much.*

"They told me to call the police in Mammoth Falls. Their office opens at eight a.m., but they're Mountain Time . . . two hours behind us. I planned to call them when I—"

"Then why still fly out there? At least let the cops investigate it first. You're not a detective!" He had stared at her as she started to lug her suitcase off the bed. "None of this makes any sense, Jay! I can't believe you would—"

"Believe it because I'm going!" she had snapped as she let her suitcase fall to the floor with a thud. She had winced reflexively at her tone. She hadn't meant for it to come out like that. "I'm sorry, Mark, but I . . . I can't wait around here and keep making phone calls. I have to *do* something. For my own peace of mind, I have to go. I have to see that he's okay. Please try to understand."

"You're usually so supportive . . . so understanding. Why not now?" she wanted to add but didn't.

Mark hadn't responded. She had watched instead as his jaw tightened and his Adam's apple bobbed over the collar of his crisp white shirt. He had grabbed his briefcase and tossed his suit jacket over his forearm.

"I have to get to work," he had said quietly, walking across their bedroom. He had paused in the doorway and opened his mouth as if to say something else but had clamped it shut and shook his head in frustration before walking out.

As Janelle hid in the airplane bathroom, she stared down at Mark's cell number on her phone screen. She stared at it for a long time. Finally, she tucked her phone back into her purse, telling herself that she would call him when her flight touched down in Rapid City.

But it was two hours later, and Janelle still hadn't called him. Instead, she was listening to her grandfather's phone ring while she drove a lonely stretch of two-lane highway as the sun continued its descent over the Black Hills. The mountains, which were haloed by the dying light, loomed so high around her that they seemed to lean toward each other drunkenly. It was as if they were on the verge of toppling over and crushing her Volkswagen.

When she got his voice mail, she pressed a button on the glass screen to hang up and hurled her phone onto the leather passenger seat in frustration.

For the past hour, Janelle had alternated between calling his cell phone and his home phone. She still had no luck in reaching him.

Something was wrong. Something was definitely wrong. She was sure of it now.

The miles were clicking by, at least, but still not fast enough for her liking. Janelle was on the last leg of her trek to Mammoth Falls. She was all alone in a rental car—a green Jetta—and she had no distractions. It was a recipe for disaster. It was a recipe for a full freak-out.

Pops could be stranded in the middle of the forest somewhere, she thought as she frowned at yet another slope of pine trees covered with a blanket of week-old snow and bordered by craggy rock. Beyond that was an old mining quarry. Her gaze was magnetically drawn to the quarry's dark depths.

Pops could have fallen into some pit. Oh, God! What if he's dead?

"He's not dead," she whispered firmly as she drove. "Don't be ridiculous. He's fine. He's just . . . just lost, and I'll find him—somehow."

But even saying those thoughts aloud didn't help temper her burgeoning panic. Her hands still tightened around the steering wheel, and she fought the urge to floor the accelerator for fear of falling off the winding road and plunging down the side of the mountain. Besides, there was no need to rush.

"I'm almost there anyway," she told herself.

She had passed the borders of Deadwood and Lead miles back and should be nearing Mammoth Falls soon, according to the dashboard navigational system. She squinted as the car passed a green highway sign that stood on the shoulder.

"Mammoth Falls, five miles," she read aloud. She sat upright in the driver's seat. After driving for more than sixty miles, she was finally getting close to her destination, and her first stop would be the police department.

She had tried calling the Mammoth Falls cops while at the airport waiting to board her flight, but the hicks in that mountain town had been of absolutely no help.

"Mammoth Falls Police Department," a woman had chirped into the phone. "How may I help you?"

"I'd like to report a missing person."

"Oh, gosh! *A missing person?*"

Janelle had heard the rustling paper, a dropped phone, and then a *thunk* that sounded like a coffee cup being knocked over.

"Hon," the voice had said after the shuffling stopped, "the

chief and his officers have stepped out. I'm going to have to take down your information. Now . . . now speak slowly. Okay?"

"Okay."

"Now go right on ahead! Who's missing?"

"My grandfather, William Marshall."

"William Marshall? You mean *Little Bill?* Is this . . . Is this some kind of a joke?"

"No, it's not a joke! I got a phone call yesterday saying that he was missing. I asked them her they she called the police and—"

"Well, then that person must've been playing a joke on *you,*" the voice said with a laugh. "Little Bill isn't missing!"

"He isn't? Oh, thank God!"

Janelle had been filled with relief. She wouldn't have to fly to South Dakota after all. Mentally, she calculated if she had enough time to grab a quick breakfast at one of the eateries in the airport before she caught the next metro train back home.

"I've been so worried," she had gushed to the woman on the phone, feeling her heart rate slow. "You would not believe! So you've seen him? You've seen him around town?"

"Well . . . no."

"No? So how do you know for sure he isn't missing?"

"I think I would've heard about something like that, hon." A giggle had filled the phone. "He's called Little Bill but he's got a big enough personality that you'd notice if he was gone! And on account of . . . well, you know . . . him sticking out a little."

"Sticking out" as in being one of the few if not only black men in town.

"Well, he's not answering any of my phone calls or texts. I've called him at least a dozen times and—"

"Maybe he just doesn't wanna talk."

Janelle had loudly sighed on the other end, trying to hold on to her patience. "Can someone just . . . I don't know . . . stop by his cabin and do a welfare check? That's what you do in these situations, correct? Make sure that everything is all right?"

"I'm afraid the chief and officers here got plenty to do besides check on a man who isn't missing."

Like what? What the hell do the boys in blue in Mammoth Falls have to do that's more important than look for a missing elderly man?

"Yes, I understand that, but if he really is missing, then wouldn't it be—"

"If I run into Little Bill, I'll tell him his granddaughter is looking for him. Okay?"

"Wait, I—"

"Thanks for calling!"

The person had hung up soon after, leaving Janelle with the strong desire to chuck her phone at the wall like she was throwing the opening pitch at a Nationals game.

Breathe in. Breathe out, she had told herself.

Instead of throwing her phone, she had dropped it back into her purse.

The cops couldn't ignore her when she was standing right in front of them.

I won't let them, she now silently resolved as she drove to Mammoth Falls.

She'd be damned if she'd let some old blue-hair from a podunk town dismiss her again. She'd get someone to take her grandfather's disappearance seriously.

After a short while the trees lining the shoulder gradually reduced in number and buildings began to appear in their place. Janelle gazed through the windshield at Mammoth Falls.

Built in the mountains, the town more resembled a tiered wedding cake than a straight boulevard of municipal and industrial buildings and houses; everything was covered in last week's snowfall and set on an incline. She passed a few stores with simple log-and-brick fronts and signs in their windows or hanging under their awnings. None of the names looked familiar. Painted on the side of one building was a faded 1940s Coca-Cola advertisement that showed a dark-haired woman with a yellow bonnet holding a coke bottle and gazing into the eyes of a man who looked like an old matinee idol.

"Try Coke! It's delish!" the advertisement proclaimed.

She slowed down at an intersection where two men were hanging a banner from old-fashioned, cast-iron street lamps on opposite sides of the roadway. One man stood at the top of a steel ladder while the other was at the bottom, motioning for him to raise the banner up higher, to shift it slightly to the left. Finally, he gave the thumbs up and the other man knotted a rope, securing the banner into place.

Janelle squinted as she peered overhead.

Twisting in the high winds were the words, "The First Annual BLACK HILLS WILD WEST FESTIVAL," spelled in big copperplate script with spurs and a lasso in the background. "Two Weeks of Fun! April 21–May 4," was printed in smaller script beneath it.

As Janelle read the words, she sucked her teeth.

No wonder the police are too busy to worry about Pops, she thought as she lowered her eyes and continued to drive down Main Street. *Why be concerned with a lost old man when "two weeks of fun!" is headed to town?*

Several people were on Main Street, walking along the sidewalk and even spilling into the roadway. Some were unloading trucks and trailers for the festival, she presumed. Their vehicles took up both sides of the street for a stretch of three to four blocks, making a path so narrow that she worried her mirror might sideswipe someone's car. A bearded, white-haired man pushed two beer kegs down a ramp before trudging back up the ramp again. A woman stood underneath a white tent, setting up a table and unloading two plastic crates filled with t-shirts.

Those who weren't preparing for the impending festival

seemed to be going about their everyday business. One woman talked avidly on her cell phone as she shoved along a blond little girl who seemed to be trying to get the woman's attention by yanking her coat sleeve. A guy wearing a red "Make America Great Again" cap stepped out of a glass door onto the sidewalk with two paper grocery bags in his arms and paused to spit a black stream of chewing tobacco from the side of his mouth onto the sidewalk, making Janelle cringe. A group of teenagers laughed before hopping into the cab of a navy blue pickup truck with a "NOT A LIBERAL" bumper sticker in the blacked-out rear window.

As Janelle drove, it sank in that she was a stranger in a strange land. Many of the townsfolk must have agreed that she didn't belong, because no one smiled when cracked a polite smile in greeting through the car window. She wasn't sure if she had imagined it, but it seemed that some even narrowed their eyes at her with suspicion as she drove by. She guessed she didn't look like the average tourist coming to town.

Don't worry! Just passing through. As soon as I find Pops, I'm out of here!

She quickly spotted City Hall, where the Mammoth Falls Police Department was located.

It was an unassuming two-story, brick building near the second intersection on Main Street. A simple "CITY HALL" in stark, black metal letters sat above the double doors.

She parked her Volkswagen in front, in a parking space labeled "For Visitors" between a Chevy truck and a police cruiser. Janelle climbed out and took a fortifying breath before striding through the building's entrance.

"I am capable of doing this. I can do this. I *can* do this," she chanted softly to herself.

She walked down a series of hallways with placards along the walls. When she finally found "Police Department," she stepped through the doorway and was met by an open room with a reception counter and several office desks in a bullpen arrangement. All of the desks but one were empty.

Janelle had hoped the universe would cut her a break and she'd stumble upon a friendly face as soon as she stepped through the doorway—maybe the Mammoth Falls version of Barney Fife. But instead she found a surly-looking, hefty old man in a navy blue police uniform. He was hunched over his desk, reading a newspaper and drinking from a mug with a deer carved on the front. She got a clear view of his pink scalp through the few graying strands he had shellacked across his crown. Janelle pitied him for having such a horrible comb-over.

When she loudly cleared her throat to get his attention, he slowly looked up from his newspaper.

"Can I help you?" he drawled. His mustache bristled. He raised his puffy white eyebrows. His name tag read "Sgt. Bachmann."

Think Zen. Think Zen, she told herself. She was trained to deal with delicate situations. She could do this.

"Well, I hope you can," she said with a forced laugh as she lowered the zipper of her coat. "I need help finding my grandfather."

His mustache bristled again. "Pardon?"

"My grandfather," she said, taking another step toward the counter. "He's missing . . . I think."

"You *think?*"

"I know it sounds crazy, but someone told me he was missing, and he isn't answering my phone calls, which isn't like him."

Sergeant Bachmann rose from his desk with a long, loud sigh—like he was being severely put upon, like she had just stopped in and asked for directions to Mount Rushmore. He walked toward the counter, grabbing a yellow steno pad, and brought it with him.

"And you stopped by his place, and didn't see him there either?" he asked, licking his thumb and flipping the first page of pad over. "Was the door locked?"

"Well . . . no, I didn't stop by," she said.

Janelle hadn't considered going to Pops's place first. From what Pops had told her, his cabin was in one of the more remote parts of Mammoth Falls. It wasn't something she could plug into her Google maps app. It didn't even have an address— just one of those weird postal descriptions you only saw on envelopes going to rural and far-flung places.

"No, I didn't go to his cabin because I'm from out of town and I . . . well, I don't exactly know where it is," she conceded.

She could tell from the way Sergeant Bachman looked her up and down that her being an out-of-towner was plainly obvious.

"It would be too hard to find on my own anyway."

"So let me see if I'm hearing you right," he said, leaning one of his thick forearms against the Formica countertop. "You think your grandfather is missing because he didn't answer his phone. And . . . how long have you been calling him?"

She cleared her throat. "Since yesterday."

"Uh-huh. You've only been calling for *one day* and you haven't been to his place, either?"

Grudgingly, she nodded and watched as he flipped his notepad closed.

"Well," he said, tapping his pen against the counter, "I suggest you go and pay your grandfather a visit *first* and then—"

"All right, Hank!" a woman shouted from behind Janelle. "They didn't have your bacon bison burger so I had to get you just a plain ol' double bacon burger."

Janelle turned around to find a petite blonde shoving her way through the door, carrying two plastic bags filled with Styrofoam trays. The woman blew a gust of air out of the side of her mouth, making her bangs flutter.

Sergeant Bachmann slapped his pad and pen on the counter in outrage. "But I wanted the bison, Rita!"

"Well, there's no point in pouting about it!" Rita argued, glaring back at him.

Janelle thought the woman sounded vaguely familiar.

"That's what happens when you order off the lunch menu when it's almost four o'clock in the afternoon," Rita countered. "I tell you that every time!"

She dropped the bags on the counter in front of Janelle and yanked off her wool coat and rainbow-colored gloves that were so small that they looked like she could have stolen them from a five-year-old. She shoved the gloves into the coat pockets. She then tossed her coat onto a nearby metal rack, standing on the balls of her feet to reach one of the pegs.

Rita turned and looked up, finally acknowledging Janelle's presence. She smiled. "Have you been helped, hon?" she chirped.

Hearing the woman's voice again, Janelle realized this was the same woman she had spoken to on the phone when she called the police from the airport.

Sergeant Bachmann nodded before reaching for one of the Styrofoam containers and turning back to his desk. "Yep, she has," he muttered, flipping the lid of the container open.

"Actually, *no,* I haven't," Janelle answered tightly. "I'm looking for my grandfather, and I would like police assistance if it isn't too much to ask."

Rita pointed up at her. "Hey! Are you the lady who called this morning asking about Little Bill?"

"Yes! Yes, that was me, and I—"

"Still haven't found him, huh?" Rita shook her head, sending her blond ponytail swinging. She raised a partition in the counter so that she could step behind it. It landed with a *thwack*, startling Janelle. "Well, I'm sure you'll wrangle him up soon enough. Can't think of why he won't answer his phone.

He might be busy or his phone died. I know I never remember to keep my phone charged. And I'll tell you . . . that thing goes through a battery faster than salmon through a river."

"He has a charger," Janelle said through gritted teeth.

Rita snapped her fingers. "Or maybe he's in a place where he can't get reception. He could be up at Pasque Lake doing some ice fishing before the thaw." She tilted her head. "Or he could be over at Connie's place. Sometimes, I can't get a signal up there too good, either. Did you try Beaver Lodge?"

"She hasn't even tried his cabin yet," Sergeant Bachmann mumbled between bites of bacon burger.

He was back at his desk and flipping through his newspaper again. Bits of medium well ground beef and sourdough bun tumbled out of his mouth to the broadsheet's pages. Some of it commingled with his mustache.

Rita let out a high-pitched laugh. *"What?* Here I was thinking you looked all over for him!"

Think Zen, Janelle told herself again. But she was losing her battle of tranquility. She balled her fists at her sides then unclenched her hands.

"I can't go to his cabin," she said slowly, trying to keep her voice even. "Because I don't know where it is. That's why I need your help. I—"

"Oh, finding Little Bill's place won't be that hard!" Rita assured with wave of her tiny hands. She pointed to one of the adjacent windows overlooking the scenic thoroughfare. "You just head out here and make a left. Then you go straight down to corner of Jasper and Big Tree. You can't miss it. The post office is right there on the corner. It's been there since '06."

" '02," Sergeant Bachmann corrected between munches.

"The post office moved there back in '06," Rita repeated firmly. "So you make the right turn there and then you—"

"It was 2002," Sgt. Bachmann corrected again.

Rita's hundred-watt smile dimmed. She pursed her lips and turned to glare at the officer. "It was in 2006, Hank!"

Janelle closed her eyes. She had officially lost the Zen battle. She wanted to thump her head on the counter in defeat. The only thing that kept her from doing that was it would make her budding headache worse.

"Hank, I remember that they built the new post office back in June 2006 because it was back when I was getting a divorce from my first—"

"Good afternoon," a booming baritone rumbled behind her. "What I miss?"

Great, Janelle thought.

Here was yet another interruption, yet another Mammoth Falls resident who would probably add to the meandering conversation about cell phone reception and the ground-breaking at the local post office. And none of it would bring her closer to finding Pops.

Janelle turned and opened her eyes. When she saw who stood in the doorway, her breath caught in her throat.

It's the Marlboro Man!

Well, not really. The Marlboro Man of her memory wore chaps, sat astride a stallion, and held a lasso while a cigarette dangled from the corner of his mouth. The towering human colossus in front of her wasn't riding a horse or wearing chaps or smoking, but he did have the cowboy hat—a tan Stetson with a brown leather band around it. In fact, he was in full Wild West regalia, from the leather vest to the snug fitting brown pants and cowboy boots to the silver star on his chest with the word "Sheriff" stamped on it.

He pushed back the brim of the hat and glanced down at her with striking blue eyes—a cerulean flecked with green and gold. When his gaze settled on her, the openness of his expression disappeared. His blue eyes went flat. He flinched, like someone had pinched him or jabbed him with a salad fork. Janelle became overwhelmingly self-conscious, wondering why he had reacted to her that way.

I don't look that bad, do I?

She turned and gave herself a quick once-over in the reflective surface of a display case filled with award plaques from the Kiwanis and Lions clubs and photos of smiling police officers striking poses with gangly, bespectacled Cub Scouts.

Janelle's curly hair—which she usually painstakingly styled, brushed, and gelled into some semblance of order—was now haphazardly held back by a cloth headband. The rest was an unruly mess that would probably make Brenda faint. Her outfit wasn't one of the carefully chosen ensembles she usually wore, either. She'd had to grab the first thing that looked clean and comfortable, and she hadn't changed her outfit since she boarded the plane back at Reagan National. Her slacks now had more wrinkles than Methuselah. She winced when she realized she also wasn't wearing any makeup. The dark circles of fatigue that were under her eyes were clearly visible.

You're a hot mess.

"Hiya, chief!" Rita gushed, tearing Janelle's attention away from her own reflection. Rita's face went brighter than a Times Square sign. "Don't you look handsome? That getup turned out nice!"

He slowly turned away from Janelle, though his uneasy stare lingered on her a bit longer than she would have liked. His lazy smile finally returned as he rolled his eyes at Rita. "I guess. Personally, I'd prefer to be wearing my uniform, but the mayor wants us to show up in costume, so . . . ." He patted his vest and looked down at himself. "At least I only have to wear this monkey suit tonight for the festival kickoff at the Legion."

"The Wild West Festival was a dumb idea and everybody knows it," Sergeant Bachmann grumbled, licking barbeque sauce off his fingers. "It's one of the *dumbest* ideas Mayor Pruit's had in quite a while. Who ever heard of having a festival when it's cold enough to freeze snot?"

"I don't think it's dumb! Pruitt probably didn't want to have to compete with Wild Bill Days over in Deadwood or the Sturgis Motorcycle Rally. And this festival isn't the only thing we have when it's cold outside. What about the Black Hills Stock Show and Rodeo in Rapid City? They have it in February. This is no different!" Rita argued. She inclined her head thoughtfully. "I kinda like the idea of a festival. It adds a little fun and excitement to town! And it could bring in tourist money. We aren't hurting for it, but it could certainly help the town. There are plenty of places around here that could use some sprucing up."

"The stock show and rodeo are at the Civic Center—*indoors!* This isn't," Sergeant Bachmann said, slapping shut the lid of his Styrofoam container like he was slapping aside all the other valid points Rita had made. "No one wants to freeze their tail off while they stand in line for popcorn and cotton candy."

Rita tiredly shook her head. "I swear you are such a curmudgeon, Hank. Look to you to bring the storm clouds on a clear blue—"

"Excuse me," Janelle said, holding up her hand. "I hate to interrupt your little debate, but can we please return to the topic of my missing grandfather?"

The chief's expression abruptly changed again. His dark brows knitted together with concern. "Your grandfather's missing? Was he vacationing here in Mammoth?"

Janelle hesitated under the intense gaze. She opened her mouth to answer but wasn't fast enough.

"She's talking about Little Bill. I was just giving her directions to his cabin so she could see for herself that he's all right. But Hank here"—Rita glanced over her shoulder in annoyance at Sergeant Bachmann—"had to poke his big nose in and interrupt me."

"Just pointing out that you got your facts wrong, that's all," Sergeant Bachmann said as he flipped another page of his newspaper and shifted, making his rolling chair emit a loud, painful squeak.

"I do *not* have it wrong! The post office was built back in '06. Tell him, Chief!"

The chief bit back a laugh. "Actually, it was '04, and I'll take it over from here, Rita."

Sergeant Bachmann chuffed through his flared pink nostrils like a dog that had grown bored with listening to the humans' conversation.

The chief had been shrugging out of his camel wool coat while the officer and Rita argued, but now he tugged it back on. Seeing him standing there with his Stetson, cowboy boots, and sheriff's star, all the stereotypes Janelle held of the Wild West came rushing forward. She expected the chief to stride to the door, kick it open so hard that it slammed against the wall, walk through City Hall and out the double doors before hopping on the back of a calico horse. He'd then go thundering off with clomping hooves and a twelve-man posse to rescue her grandfather.

"You can come with me, Miss . . ."

"Marshall," she finished for him. "Janelle Marshall."

He nodded and tipped the brim of his cowboy hat in greeting as she stepped in front of him, but the wariness returned to his face. She wondered what it was about her that kept making him look at her like that, like she was on the verge of speaking in tongues or sprouting a second head.

Was it the out-of-town thing? The black thing?

It's my hair, isn't it, she thought, smoothing her curly tresses.

"So when's the last time you talked to Little Bill?" he asked as soon as they stepped outside.

Janelle raised the zipper of her coat just as the blast of cold air hit her, making her duck her head and raise her fur-trimmed hood. She watched as he shoved his hands into his pockets after raising the collar of his coat around his ears, which were already turning pink from the biting chill.

"I talked to him about three days ago," she said.

Where are we going? Janelle thought as she shuffled beside him, watching the few people who milled about on the sidewalks and in front of storefronts. They passed more vans and trailers where vendors were unloading their wares for the festival—cowboy hats and boots, plastic pistols, and beaded jewelry. Two blocks down, a crew was adding the finishing touches to a small stage that looked like it had been borrowed from a high school gym. A few men were unloading speakers and mike stands. Another adjusted lights on the scaffolding overhead.

"Did Bill say anything out of the ordinary?"

She thought back to her last phone conversation with Pops. Her grandfather had asked her about her plans for the weekend. She reminded him that she was having a housewarming party. He mentioned that he was going into town to get more deicer. The conversation had seemed so bland and inconsequential. No warning signs. Nothing that screamed, "This may be the last time you talk to me!"

"Not really," she said.

She sniffed, feeling a trickle form under her nose. It always did that in blustery weather. She tried to discreetly wipe it with her gloved hand.

"Well . . ." He paused. "I'm sure he's all right."

The chief licked his slightly chapped lips, keeping his eyes focused forward on a destination that still was a mystery to her. She studied his face in profile—the pointed nose, slightly hooded eyes with the first signs of crow's feet at the corners, the downturned mouth, and his cleft chin. Ruggedly handsome was the description that came to mind when she looked at him. She didn't know faces like his existed in real life outside of movies or print ads.

"Little Bill has been around these parts long enough to know how to take care of himself," the chief continued. "I wouldn't worry."

"I'll try not to," she mumbled, though she could feel her anxiety growing with each step they took. She silently willed the cell phone in her purse to ring. She willed her grandfather to finally call her back.

"So what's the . . . you know . . . procedure for something like this, if you don't mind me asking, Sheriff?"

"Chief," he said, making her pause.

"Pardon me?"

"I'm police chief. Not a sheriff," he corrected. "The sheriff's star is just part of the costume," he said, tapping his breast through his coat. "The *real* sheriff is over in Deadwood. It's just lowly police chief down here in Mammoth."

"Oh, I'm sorry! I didn't—"

She was stopped midsentence by her own clumsiness. She stumbled on an ice patch the size of a large snow boot that was in the middle of the sidewalk. Her arms windmilled wildly, and the chief grabbed one of them to keep her from falling to the ground and face-planting in a patch of snow that was gray from exhaust and yellow with another substance she suspected might be urine. As a reflex she grabbed onto him, too, to steady herself. With a strong tug, he lifted her upright, and she stared up at him, feeling the warmth of his hand even through the thick lining of her coat. Her stomach did a little flip-flop, catching her by surprise.

"Thanks," she said, meeting his eyes as he released her. She realized she was still holding onto him, so she let go. "I told my grandfather Mammoth Falls was too dangerous for a girl like me. I can barely walk around without falling down."

She gave a self-deprecating laugh. The chief didn't join her in her laughter or even crack a smile. Instead, he turned and started walking again, bunching his shoulders against the chill. Her cheeks warmed as she rushed to catch up with him.

"Were you actually flirting *with him?"* a bemused voice in her head chided.

No, I wasn't flirting, she thought defensively as she and the police chief walked in silence. *That's just . . . just insane!*

Flirting was the furthest thing from her mind. She loved Mark. She was just admiring the South Dakota scenery, so to speak. She wasn't blind, and her androgen levels were in good working order; of course, she was attracted to the chief. Just like she knew Mark was attracted to other women: the buxom jogger on the bike trail in their neighborhood whom he tried to slyly watch as she passed, or the pretty waitress at the Italian bistro they liked with whom he always joked and flirted. Mark was a red-blooded man, and she wouldn't resent him admiring the opposite sex occasionally.

No harm, no foul. We're all human.

"What do you mean by procedures?" the chief asked.

"What?" She stared dazedly into his to-die-for blue eyes.

"You asked about procedures," the chief reminded her, speaking slowly.

"Oh, yes! Yes! Right. Procedures," Janelle said, forcing herself to focus again on the topic at hand. "What's the procedure for searching for a missing person? Do I need to file paperwork? Do you guys go to his cabin first? How does this work?"

They crossed the street and passed a clapboard storefront with a wagon wheel and chalkboard in front advertising biscotti and "The Finest Cup of Joe in the Black Hills." Two women in reenactment costumes walked by them holding paper cups. One had on a blue bonnet and a long, drab gray dress under her shearling-trimmed wool jacket. Janelle could spot the lace hem of a saloon girl costume under the other woman's parka.

"Well, we would probably check his cabin and then try to

locate his truck," the chief said, glancing at her. When their eyes met, he looked away again. "We'd also want to talk to anyone who was last in contact with him—probably his buddies and his girlfriend."

Janelle's brows raised a few inches. *Pops has a girlfriend?*

"We'd also do a search of the surrounding forest and the lake. We partner with the state police, the Lawrence County deputies, and the police departments in neighboring towns. They would bring in the search dogs. Then, if the weather cooperates, the county would even break out the helicopters for the search. That's what we had to do for that one hiker who got stranded in the woods a couple years back after a bad hailstorm."

"Oh, you did? Did you find the hiker?"

"Yeah, we found him."

"And he was okay?" Janelle asked, feeling her first glimmer of hope since she arrived in Mammoth. They crossed another street.

"Hey, Chief!" someone called out, and Janelle turned toward the roadway.

She spotted a young woman who looked to be in her mid-twenties with almost iridescent lime green hair in two pigtails, waving at them. At the sight of her hair, Janelle did a double take. The woman paused midway in climbing on the back of a Harley that was splattered with mud and drying snow slush. A guy whose face was obscured by a helmet and aviator sunglasses sat waiting on the motorcycle for the woman to board. He waved absently at the police chief.

The green-haired woman was wearing an orange wool jacket and a short denim skirt, revealing black-and-white-striped wool tights that made her look like a witch or a marauding pirate. She finished the ensemble with yellow combat boots. When she saw Janelle, her brown eyes widened with interest.

"Hey, Yvette!" the chief shouted back. "You staying out of trouble?"

The woman laughed. "Don't I always?" she asked, giving full indication that she was a woman who most certainly found her way into trouble.

"Don't worry, Chief!" the driver assured. "I'll watch out for her."

"You two watch out for *each other!*" the chief called back.

Janelle and the woman held gazes a bit longer before the woman slapped on a plum-colored helmet the driver held out to her. As soon as she finished securing the helmet strap, the motorcycle pulled off with a thunderous roar. Janelle turned back to the chief.

"So the hiker was okay?" Janelle repeated.

"Huh? Oh, yeah, well, he was . . . alive."

"Alive?" She squinted. "Alive? What does that mean?"

The chief cleared his throat. "The hiker's left arm had to be amputated because of injuries from his fall and being stuck in the elements for a few days, but he was just happy that we found him before . . ." His words drifted off. His chapped lips formed a grim line.

"Before what?"

"Before the animals got to him."

Janelle gulped audibly. For all she knew, Pops was lying on the side of the mountain being eaten by a vulture or his body was being dragged into the burrow of some she-wolf that would use his decaying flesh to feed her young.

"Chief, we have to start looking for my grandfather now— *right now!* We've wasted enough time already!"

He nodded in agreement. "We *are* looking for him."

"No, we're not! We're taking a stroll along Main Street where people are setting up tents and walking around in costumes," she exclaimed, pointing up at the three- and two-story build-ings around them and the passersby. "I'm expecting someone to walk up and show me where Wild Bill Hickok was shot!"

At that, the chief chuckled and continued his long strides beside her. "That would be the Saloon No. 10 back in Dead-wood."

"Chief," she said firmly, not finding the humor in any of this, "I'm being serious."

She wrapped her arms around herself as a gust of wind sent her hood flying back and off her head. She looked around Mammoth Falls. It appeared just as you would expect a quaint, sleepy mountain town to be, but she couldn't ignore the over-whelming presence of the Black Hills—those dark granite slopes that looked like they could spring to life at any moment and shake off the town and all its residents like an annoying fruit fly. And her grandfather was somewhere lost out there.

She watched helplessly as the chief paused in front of a door with the sign "Toby's Bar & Grill" hanging over the entrance.

"I don't care what you have to do, who you have to talk to, or where you have to look. Just . . . just . . ."

He shoved the bar door open and stepped inside. The bar was mostly empty, save for one person sitting at the counter and a few of the tables where one or two diners loitered over half-eaten plates. A haze of smoke lingered in the air, catching Janelle by surprise. She hadn't smelled smoke in a bar in al-most a decade. It was definitely verboten back east.

Despite her watery eyes and instant hacking, she angrily marched in after the police chief.

"Just find my grandfather, *please!*"

"Will do," the chief said as he strode across the smoky bar room toward a dark-haired woman who was hunched over a beer and biting into a sandwich. The woman gazed up at the TV hanging over the bar where a baseball game played.

"Hey, Connie. I hate to interrupt your meal here, but uh . . . have you seen Little Bill anywhere?"

The woman slowly turned to them and lowered the Rueben sandwich from her mouth to her plate. Her eyes zeroed in on Janelle. She smiled timidly. "You must be Bill's granddaughter."

CHAPTER 5

Janelle stared down at the woman in confusion. How did she know who she was?

"I'm the one that called you yesterday," Connie said, answering the question Janelle hadn't voiced aloud. Connie's cheeks flushed crimson. Her neck erupted in streaks of red. She lowered her gaze to the scuffed wooden table. "I'm the one who told you Bill was missing."

The chief took a step back, tipped back the brim of his Stetson, and stared at her. "What are you talking about? So Little Bill really did disappear somewhere? Well, why the heck didn't you report it?"

"I didn't because there was nothing to report, Sam. Bill is fine."

"*What?*"

"He didn't disappear."

"Wait, so he's not missing then?" the police chief asked.

Connie shook her head, making her long, dark hair sway like a lush velvet curtain behind her. "No, he's not missing. That's what I've been trying to tell you!"

The police chief and the woman continued to go back and forth. Now Janelle was even more confused. She was trying her best to orient herself to the bar with its smoke haze and base-ball game playing loudly on the television. The announcer shouted that one of the Dodgers had just hit a home run and the crowd on TV erupted into a roar. One of the diners started to clap.

"All right! Don't make a liar out of me, fellas!" he shouted before shoving a forkful of coleslaw into his mouth.

She tried to orient herself to the paradoxical conversation between the police chief and this woman whom Janelle had never met or heard of before—but she couldn't.

She felt dizzy, like someone was swinging her around and around in a maniacal game of ring o' ring of roses. "And we all fall down!" they would shout, and she would fall to the floor in a heap.

"So then why'd you tell his granddaughter that he disap-peared?" the chief persisted. "Are you saying you lied to her?"

Connie looked shamefaced, and it was all the answer they needed. "It's . . . it's complicated, Sam."

"It's not complicated; it's crazy! What were you thinking?" he asked, his voice rising almost to a shout. Several diners' eyes swiveled in their direction. "What got in your head to—"

"I know it was wrong, Sam! I don't need you lecturing me like I'm some high schooler who decided to whip-cream some-one's car."

He sighed gruffly. "I'm not lecturing you, Connie. I'm just saying that you can't—"

"Look, I'll explain everything to you. I promise. I know it wasn't the right thing to do. I know that now. But like I said, it's complicated." Her eyes locked with Janelle's again. "Just let me talk to her first. Okay?"

Sam looked between both women, as if contemplating whether he should stay or go. Finally, he took a step away from the table and held up his hands in surrender.

"All right. Fine. I've got work to do anyway. I'm interested in hearing the backstory on this one, but I'll wait—for now. You know where to find me."

He then turned and walked back across the bar. A few people shouted their hellos to him, and he waved and greeted them back. Janelle watched as he pushed open the door and stepped into the cold.

"He's a good man," Connie volunteered, making Janelle turn back around to face her. "His father was police chief too, before he died last year. Sam comes from good people, though his father rode him a bit too hard when he was alive."

Janelle nodded absently. Frankly, she didn't give a damn about the Mammoth Falls police chief's lineage or the relationship he had with his father. She was more concerned with why this woman had lied to her.

Connie pulled out an empty chair beside her, dragging it over the bar's hardwood floor. She patted the seat. "Go on and have a seat."

Janelle stared down at the seat. She didn't move.

"Go on! I won't bite," Connie said, her smile widening.

Janelle finally lowered herself into the chair Connie offered her. She took off her coat after yanking down the zipper with enough ferocity she almost ripped it off its track. She balled her coat in her lap, holding its unwieldy bulkiness in her arms.

"Hiya! What canna get ya?" a waitress asked in a "Gosh darn don'tcha know" accent that made Janelle look up. The young woman held a notepad in her hand and chewed gum with loud pops as she looked at Janelle expectantly. "If ya'd like to know today's specials, it's the—"

"No. No, thank you," Janelle said. "I don't want anything."

I just want to find Pops and go the hell home, she thought, furious that she had turned her life upside down for a lie—a stupid lie. Mark had warned her, but she hadn't listened.

The young waitress shrugged, stuffed her notepad into her jeans back pocket, and walked away.

"Where's my grandfather?" Janelle couldn't keep the accusation out of her voice. She was too angry to mask it. It sounded like she was accusing Connie of hiding him, and deep down, she probably was. "Is he here?" she asked as she looked around the bar room.

"No, he's not here. We usually meet for an early supper after I close down the shop for the day, but we . . . well, we had a fight last night when he asked me to call you, and I guess he thinks I'm not speaking to him."

"He asked you to call me?"

"Uh-huh. He told me what to say to you."

"So he told you to make up that . . . that . . ."

Janelle struggled to find the right word. Her anger made her thoughts flit around in her head like frenzied bumblebees. The thoughts landed long enough for her to grapple with what she was trying to say but flew off again before she got the chance to articulate them.

"He told you to make up th-that *ridiculous* story about him disappearing?" she finally sputtered.

Connie nodded.

"And why the hell would he do that?"

"He didn't want you to get engaged to that man of yours," Connie answered plainly before taking a sip of her beer. "That Mark guy. Mark called and asked him for your hand in marriage that morning—the day of your party. Bill doesn't like him and said he had to stop it, so he roped me into it." Connie then spread her hands in a helpless *"What can you do?"* gesture.

Janelle stared at Connie in astonishment. How did this woman know more about what was going on in her life than she did? What other details about her life had Pops discussed with Connie, a woman whom he had never mentioned once to his own granddaughter? Janelle doubted even her mom knew about Connie.

"So I guess you're his . . ." Janelle grimaced. She struggled again with the right word, not because she didn't know what to say, but because she was reluctant to say it. "You're his girl-friend?"

Connie's face reddened again. She lowered her beer back to the table. "Yes, we've been friendly for quite a while. About five years now."

Friendly? For *five* years?

Longer than some marriages, Janelle thought with disbelief. But again, Pops had never mentioned Connie or their relation-ship.

But why?

She let her eyes scan over the woman sitting across from her. Maybe Connie's appearance was the explanation for this quan-dary. Though Pops was in his late seventies, Connie looked a lot younger. Janelle surmised that maybe Connie was in her fifties, judging from the vague etching of wrinkles Janelle saw on her olive-toned skin and Connie's glossy black hair that had only a few patches of gray. That would make her . . . what? . . . only a few years younger than Janelle's mother.

Embarrassed about robbing the cradle, Pops?

Connie also didn't look like someone you would expect to find on an elderly man's arm—that is, unless said elderly man drove a gleaming sports car, belonged to Hair Club for Men, and popped Viagra like the pills were Tic-Tacs.

Because it was freezing outside, Janelle had donned a thick cable-knit sweater that had a collar so high it was almost a turtleneck. In contrast, Connie had on a plaid flannel shirt that was rolled up at the sleeves and unbuttoned to the navel. She wore a blue tank top underneath that showed a great deal of cleavage, and on her left breast was a heart with the name "Buddy" written in the insipid curly script that only seemed to be used by women who get those types of tattoos. Silver-and-turquoise chandelier earrings dangled from Connie's earlobes. Two silver bracelets were on her wrists. She wore black eyeliner and ruby red lipstick. Janelle looked down at the woman's feet, bemused to find her wearing suede Uggs—something that the teenage girls would prance around in at the suburban malls back home.

Mom would not approve of this . . . of any *of this*, Janelle thought. And frankly, she wasn't sure if she approved of it, either.

Why couldn't Pops have chosen a woman more like her Nana?

Involuntarily, she fingered the gold-and-diamond pendant necklace at her throat—the necklace she always wore, whether it complemented her outfit or not. It had once belonged to her grandmother.

Janelle still remembered Nana even though she had been dead for almost twenty years. She remembered her smell—a mix of talcum powder, cocoa butter, and a Fendi perfume that had long since been discontinued. She remembered her voice: a *real* North Carolina drawl unlike the manufactured one Brenda used all the time. The retired schoolteacher had always worn silk blouses and matching scarves with gold pins in the shape of butterflies, parakeets, or turtles. On Sundays, she wore wide-brimmed, elaborate hats to church, and she donned dainty garden gloves with bows on the wrists whenever she fiddled around in the garden that Pops had set up for her in their back-yard.

Nana had been the perfect mix of refinement and down-home warmth—just what someone like Janelle had needed the most back when she was a shy, somewhat uncertain little girl. The old woman had been one of few solid anchors in Janelle's chaotic childhood. On some level, Janelle knew she had even modeled herself after her grandmother, trying her best to al-ways be composed and polished—the sturdy shelter against the strong storms of life.

Janelle's eyes now traveled over Connie again. She had no idea what Pops saw in her. How could he possibly have loved and been married to Nana for almost four decades and now date a woman like *this?*

"Bill talks a lot about you," Connie continued, still smiling. "He's very proud of his 'baby girl.' That's what he calls you, right?"

Janelle nodded absently.

"I think that's why he did it. He said he only wants the best for you."

"Yeah, well, his ruse worked. I'm here!" Janelle's eyes went wide with sarcasm. "Like a fool, I came running to the rescue."

"You weren't a fool. You did it because you love him. Bill would appreciate that."

Oh, what the hell would you know?

Janelle looked away, annoyed to be having this conversation with a total stranger, with Pops's clandestine lover. She'd rather talk to the man himself.

"So where is he?"

"If I had to guess, back at his cabin. The last time I saw him, he was—"

"I've called his cabin five hundred times, he's not there," Janelle snapped.

Connie tilted her head, a patronizing gesture that made Janelle want to smack her.

"Well, honey, he wouldn't answer if he knew you were calling. He wanted you to come. I guess he figured if he didn't answer, you'd get riled up and check on him yourself. Which is what you did, right?"

Janelle paused. Connie did have a point. She watched as the older woman pushed her sandwich plate and beer aside. She rose to her feet.

"That's all right, though. Bill can't hide from me. I'll track him down and end this nonsense. It's about time you two hashed it out." Connie did a little shimmy and tugged her hip huggers back up her curvy hips. She grabbed a wool coat slung over the chair behind her and motioned to Janelle. "Come on. Put your coat on. We better get going before it gets dark."

Janelle bristled at Connie's tone. Who was she to be ordering her around? But Janelle had to admit that she didn't have much of a choice. She didn't know how to get to Pops's cabin. Connie did, and she seemed to be one of the few people in town willing to take her there. Reluctantly, Janelle also rose from her chair and put on her coat.

A few minutes later, Janelle was trailing behind Connie's beat-up Silverado down Main Street. The major thoroughfare that had been teeming with people less than an hour earlier now seemed to be all but deserted. Only the ghostly shell of empty tents and stalls remained.

Janelle made a left when the older woman made a left, then another left, then a right before turning onto a quaint street bordered by Victorian and Craftsman-style houses with small front yards and white picket fences. A wind chime hung underneath one of the porches, a series of dangling ballerinas pirouetting frantically in the wind that was picking up ferocity. A "Trump/Pence 2016" yard sign caked in a layer of ice was in a neighboring yard, dipping toward the ground.

Behind the silhouette of the houses, the sky had darkened even more and not just because the sun had almost finished its descent behind the mountains. It looked like a storm was coming, bringing either heavy rain or more snow.

As they drove, Janelle saw the first drop hit her windshield, then the second. They looked like ice chips. Suddenly, it seemed like the sky was ripped open. The car was pelted with freezing rain.

The houses disappeared. It was harder to see Connie's truck in front of her now. Janelle turned on her headlights and windshield wipers and leaned forward to peer at the road, or at least what part of the road she could make out around the Silverado's rear end.

She felt the pavement give way to snow and mud before she realized that they were no longer on the main road through town. The car began to bump over the rough terrain, and Janelle got the sensation of riding a bucking horse. It looked like some-one had created a makeshift road back here years ago—carving a path just barely wide enough for a truck to fit through. The pine branches scraped at the windows as they drove, like prying fingers begging to be let in. The headlights of the Silverado and her Jetta danced off the canopy of trees above them, casting gloomy shadows in the branches. Janelle still didn't know what she thought of this Connie woman, but she was at least grateful to have someone driving the path with her. At least she wasn't alone out here.

Janelle said a prayer of thanks when they finally drove through a clearing and pulled onto the snowy gravel driveway leading up to her grandfather's cabin. But her shoulders fell and her spirits plummeted when she realized that none of the cabin lights were on. Pops's truck was nowhere to be found. It looked like Connie had been wrong; Pops wasn't home.

She shifted the car into park and gazed through the rain-splattered windshield at the cabin that loomed in the car's headlights.

"You've gotta be joking," she murmured, her voice barely audible above the squeak of the windshield wipers, the steady hum of the car's heater, and the patter of rain on the car windows and roof. "Pops, you live *here?*"

The few pictures she had seen of his home hadn't done it justice—and not in a good way. It was, in fact, a *real* log cabin, unlike the Victorians and old Craftsman-style houses they had passed on their brief ride through town. It was one story with a brick chimney that towered over a roof that looked like it was made out of galvanized sheet metal. The cabin seemed less like a welcoming vacation retreat and more like it should be on the set of *Friday the 13th*. Paranoid, Janelle felt like at any moment a guy with a hockey mask would come charging at her through the front door.

The driver's-side door to the Silverado flew open. Janelle watched as Connie tugged her jacket over her head, hopped down from her pickup truck, and raced toward the cabin, getting doused with rain as she did it. Janelle realized with dismay that she would have to follow her. She turned off the headlights, plunging the world around her into momentary darkness. She quickly tugged her key from the ignition and opened the car door, making the overhead compartment light come on. She was no longer lost in pitch black, but now she was being pelted with stinging rain. She let out a girlish squeal as the icy cold water soaked her shoes and then her pants within seconds. Janelle tugged the hood of her parka over her head and slammed the driver's-side door shut. By the time she climbed the steps of the porch, her parka was a wet, soggy mess.

A motion-detection light burned bright. It had clicked on soon after Connie climbed on the porch. Janelle looked around them. From this vantage point, the cabin looked a lot less menacing. Her grandfather's rocking chair sat a few feet away from the front door. She could see light blue gingham curtains in the window.

Beside her, Connie dug into one of her coat's pockets. She pulled out a key.

She has a key to his cabin, Janelle realized, slightly irritated. When did Pops give her a key to his cabin?

Connie pushed open the front door and stepped inside. Janelle followed. She was hit by a familiar smell that made her smile despite her unease: the warm, reassuring scent of her grandfather's cologne. It calmed her.

Connie reached along the wall and turned on the light switch, revealing a tidy living room with a chartreuse-and-gray plaid couch, a leather recliner, a scarred wooden coffee table, and two end tables that featured old Tiffany-style lamps. Janelle frowned at the deer head over the brick fireplace mantle and the line of cowboy hats hanging on the other side of the living room.

"Bill!" Connie shouted before marching from room to room.

As Connie did what was bound to be a fruitless search, Janelle shut the front door behind them and removed her soaked coat. She hung it on a hook, hoping that it wouldn't leave a puddle on the floor. Then she walked into the eat-in kitchen, which was small, but clean, with oak veneer cabinets and two bar stools at the Formica breakfast counter. The oven and refrigerator looked like they had seen better days. They were tan, instead of black, white, or stainless steel like most modern appliances. She opened the refrigerator and gazed at the minimal amount of food on the shelves: a loaf of bread, bologna, horseradish mustard, and wilting lettuce.

Typical bachelor fare, Janelle thought before shutting the fridge door.

"Bill!" Connie shouted again, making Janelle roll her eyes.

He's not here! Can't you see that? Where would he be? Hiding in a closet?

She watched as Connie marched down the hall and pushed open another door, revealing what looked like Pops's bedroom. Connie didn't hesitate before walking inside, like she had been in his bedroom hundreds of times before.

That fact irritated Janelle even more.

"Bill, where the hell are you?" Connie muttered before walking back into the living room. She flapped her arms. "He's not here."

"Obviously," Janelle mumbled under her breath.

"He *should* be here! He was leaving Deadwood last night so he could get back here and be up bright and early. He said so. He was meeting some guy who was supposed to come and fix his generator."

The two women fell silent. Janelle surveyed the cabin again with a sweeping glance.

"Maybe this was the rest of his 'plan,'" she said, making air quotes, ". . . you know, to disappear for a few days."

"But that doesn't make any sense!" Connie shook her head and crossed her arms over her chest. "If it was part of it, he didn't say a damn thing to me."

Connie sounded angry, but she looked far from it. She seemed to be gnawing the inside of her cheek. Her dark brows were knitted together. She looked . . . worried. Finally, someone else besides Janelle was worried about Pops. It gave her some sense of relief. It thawed the iciness she felt for Connie, at least temporarily.

"Frankly, none of it makes sense, but it doesn't seem like Pops was being very rational yesterday."

He had made up a lie about disappearing in the mountains to keep her from marrying Mark, to get her to finally come to Mammoth Falls. It seemed so absurd and far-fetched, but within the context of the Pops she knew and loved, it made perfect sense. This was the same man who had proposed to his wife only three months after meeting her. This was the same man who started a furniture store that specialized in Mennonite handcrafted furniture simply because he had purchased a bed from the local Mennonites and liked it more than any piece of furniture he had ever owned. And this was the same man who almost twenty years ago just decided to travel to South Dakota on a whim and disappear there for almost a year. Pops would later return to D.C. and in the same dramatic fashion announce that Mammoth Falls was his new home.

Needless to say, Pops had a reputation for impetuousness. Janelle thought he had tempered those impulses in his old age, but she guessed she had been wrong.

"Look, I'll . . . I'll wait for him. Maybe he'll come back home tonight or tomorrow. I'll wait, and if he still doesn't come home"—Janelle hitched her shoulders—"we can go back to the police chief and tell him that maybe something really is wrong."

Connie slowly nodded, now looking as lost as Janelle felt. She pushed her dark hair back over her shoulder. Some of it was wet and clumped together, thanks to the rain.

"All right," Connie said. "I'll check in with you tomorrow if he doesn't call me first. Bill keeps a spare key to the cabin in the kitchen drawer if you need it." She walked toward the front door then paused. "Are you going to be all right out here by yourself? I can stay here with you if you—"

"No, I'll be fine," Janelle said quickly.

The last thing Janelle wanted was for this to turn into a sleepover. Besides, she was still reeling from the punches she had endured today. She desperately wanted . . . *needed* some time alone to mentally process this mess.

"Have you ever been alone in a cabin in the woods before?"

Janelle almost laughed at her question. Connie made it sound so dire, like she was asking Janelle if she had ever ridden a motorcycle without a helmet or jumped out of a plane without a parachute.

"No, but there's a lock on the door. There's food in the fridge. That's all I need. I'll be fine."

She could tell from the look on Connie's face that she didn't believe her.

"Okay, if you swear you'll be all right, I'll go. But if you need anything, and I mean *anything* . . ."

Connie dug into her coat pocket and pulled out a business card. She handed it to Janelle.

Janelle gazed down at the laminated card and read the bubbled script aloud. "Hot Threads & Things Boutique?"

"That's the number to my shop, and my home number is on the back. Call me anytime."

Janelle tucked the card into one of her pants pockets. "Don't worry. I will."

Connie walked toward the front door and swung it open. "I swear when I get my hands on that little man," she muttered, her voice barely audible above the roar of the pelting rain. She then shut the door behind her.

A minute later, Janelle held open one of the gingham curtains as she watched Connie's taillights get smaller and smaller, then finally disappear behind a line of trees. She let the curtains fall closed and strolled across the living room where the muffled sound of falling rain echoed all around. She fell back onto the plaid couch and stared at her cell phone, which now sat on the scuffed coffee table in front of her.

She was exhausted and jet-lagged. Her adrenaline high had long ago disappeared, but her headache remained. She wanted to take an aspirin and sleep a thousand years. She wanted to save all her energy for the tirade she would unleash on Pops when she finally saw him either later tonight or tomorrow morning, but before she collapsed, she had one last task. Janelle took a long, deep breath, picked up her phone, and dialed Mark's number.

"*Jay?* Baby, you finally called!" he shouted, picking up after the first ring. "I was worried about you!"

The elation and concern she heard in his voice was almost painful. It made her wince.

I should have called him on the plane. I should have called hours ago.

Why had she avoided calling him? What had she thought he would say? She had read too much into their argument. Mark obviously missed her. The same loving, supportive man she had known him to be still was there—thank God!

"Hi, honey," she said. "I'm okay. I'm sorry I didn't call you sooner."

"That's fine. It's just good to hear from you."

At his words, she placed a hand over her heart. She instantly felt a soothing heat spread across her chest.

"So are you in South Dakota? Did you find out what's going on with your grandfather?"

Janelle hesitated, not quite sure how to explain what she had discovered today. How could she tell Mark that her grandfather had made up a lie about disappearing in the mountains to sabotage his proposal? That wouldn't exactly endear him to his possible future in-law.

She cleared her throat and began to fiddle with a loose thread in one of her sweater sleeves, mentally imagining the invisible thread that tethered her to Mark. "Well, I know that Pops isn't missing," she began.

"See, I told you, baby! Didn't I tell you?"

"Is that Janelle?" she heard Brenda squawk in the background, cutting into their conversation with all the subtlety of someone wielding a hatchet. "Is she with those hillbillies?"

The warmth in Janelle's chest went cold. Janelle let go of the thread. "Your mom is there?"

"Yeah, she came over to cook dinner." Janelle could suddenly hear the banging of pots and pans and the opening and closing of her kitchen cabinets. She heard a door slam. Her refrigerator, maybe? "I told her you were out of town and I was in the house by myself with nothing in the fridge but party leftovers. She decided to cheer me up with a home-cooked meal."

"Hi, Janelle!" Shana piped.

"Shana's here, too," he added. "She's helping mom. They're making—"

"*Ceviiiiicheeee!*" Shana sang in an exaggerated Spanish accent.

"Ceviche. We're having ceviche. They thought it would be nice to make it since . . . uh . . . since I don't eat much seafood anymore because . . . well, because you can't eat it."

"Oh."

Janelle took another deep, steadying breath. She told herself that they were just having dinner.

No big deal.

"That was n-nice of your mom and . . . and Shana."

"Yeah, I know. Anyway, so when are you coming home? Are you going to try to catch a flight out tomorrow?"

"Uh, probably."

"Probably? What do you mean probably?"

"Well, I still haven't actually spoken to Pops. I'd like to talk to him before I leave here."

There was a long pause, and Janelle could hear Brenda shouting for lime juice and Shana asking how to use the "blender"—more than likely the new Cuisinart food processor Mark and Janelle had gotten as a housewarming present.

"So when exactly are you coming home?" He laughed, but there was no levity in his tone. His voice sounded tighter than a violin string.

"Soon."

"Soon?"

"I will definitely, *definitely* leave soon."

"But what is 'soon'? Tomorrow? The day after tomorrow? *Next week?"*

She closed her eyes and rubbed her forehead. Her headache was getting worse. A dull throb was making its way across her temples like a slow-moving weather front.

"No, not next week. Maybe in a couple of days, but I just can't . . . well, say anything definitive right now."

Silence greeted her again on the other end, making her stomach twist into knots.

"Okay," Mark finally said, catching her off guard. He had sounded frustrated only seconds ago. Now his tone was calm, eerily so.

"*Really?* You aren't . . . you aren't upset that I'm not coming home right away."

"No, I'm not upset. You take as much time as you need to talk to your grandfather."

She furrowed her brows.

"Let him know that we're a *serious* couple now—and he has to accept and respect that. No more pseudo-emergency calls. No more fake disappearances."

She shifted uncomfortably on the sofa. So Mark had rightly guessed Pops was the mastermind behind this fiasco. She could deny that he was, but she didn't think she would be very convincing.

"And when you come back home, I want to do the proposal all over again. It'll be just us at our favorite restaurant at our favorite table. No big production. No public announcement. I want the focus to be on *us*. All right?"

"Of course!"

"Because that's what this is about, Jay. Not our friends or families, *especially* not your grandfather. It's about you and me, baby. And when I ask you this time, you won't feel any pressure. You can just speak from the heart. You can say yes." He paused. "You *will* say yes, won't you?"

"Of course!" she said again.

"Dinner's almost done, sweetie," Brenda cooed in the background. "Come into the dining room. You've got to see this table that Shana made. It's *gorg*eous!"

"Look," Mark said tiredly, "I've got to go."

Janelle sat upright. "Sure, I understand."

"You get some rest. Like I said, have a good, long conversation with your grandfather. I'll see you in a couple of days . . . hopefully."

"You *will* see me, honey. I promise! I'll take care of this."

He chuckled. "I know if anyone can, you will, baby. Talk to you later."

"Mark?" Brenda shouted again.

"Talk to you later!" Janelle repeated back to him, trying her best to be heard over his mother. "I love—"

He hung up before she could finish. Janelle stared down at her cell phone.

"I love you," she muttered to the empty cabin.

CHAPTER 6

Missing Hiker Found After Helicopter Search
Hiker Says He's Just Happy to be Alive
Sept. 17, 2014
By Bob Eunice, Special to the *Rapid City Journal*

There are few things more terrifying for a visitor to the Black Hills than being stranded on one of the many peaks that make up the scenic mountain range. But that is the situation in which 28-year-old Portland, Ore., resident Kurt Abramowitz found himself last week while hiking along Overland Trail.

Abramowitz gave an exclusive interview to the *Rapid City Journal* after he was found and rescued by Lawrence County Sheriff's Office helicopter on Sept. 14 at 5 a.m.

Abramowitz is now recovering at Lead-Deadwood Regional Hospital after amputation of his left arm due to injuries he sustained prior to his rescue. He is also being treated for acute dehydration.

Abramowitz said he was originally headed on a road trip to meet up with friends in Austin, Texas, when he decided to make the impromptu stop and go on a hike in the Black Hills to "check out the views."

"I never should have had that last beer," Abramowitz said, thinking back to his first night on the trail. "I was going to head back but I thought I'd break open a quick one and watch the sunset. You know, chill out after a hard climb. But then it got dark and then the rain came in and well, you guys pretty much know what happened after that."

Abramowitz said the rain and subsequent hailstorm disoriented him and he accidentally wandered off the trail on the way back to his campsite. He fell, was injured and ended up stranded on a steep ledge.

"I was freaking out," Abramowitz said. "No one knew I was up there. I was all by myself. I sat alone for two days watching the sun come up and go down and I wondered, 'Am I going to die up here? Will anyone ever find me?' By the third day, I pretty much figured I was toast."

But friends alerted local police that Abramowitz hadn't arrived in Austin and had last posted photos of his hike on Facebook and Instagram.

After the rain ended and the fog abated, authorities conducted an air search. A helicopter located Abramowitz three miles from the trailhead.

Thanks to the joint efforts of the Lawrence County Sheriff's Office, the Lead Police Department, the Deadwood Police Department, and the Mammoth Falls Police Department, Abramowitz was rescued.

"I wouldn't wish what I went through on anyone," Abramowitz said. "That's a lot of alone time to be stuck in your own head, thinking about your life and stuff. You think about everything, and I mean everything. And I didn't know how long I would be up there. Besides the

> pain, that was one of the worst parts. If the cavalry
> didn't come when it did, I think I either would have
> died—or gone nuts."

It was a weird dream—the type of dream that usually only came when Janelle drank too much Pinot Grigio on an empty stomach or when she fell asleep with the television still on in her bedroom, only to wake up and find some existentialist foreign film or slasher flick on the screen.

She dreamed that she was in a wedding gown—a beautiful ivory sheath of French lace with capped sleeves and a lavender satin belt at the waist held together with a delicate diamond broach. She was at an antebellum mansion, wandering from room to room searching for Pops. He was supposed to escort her down the aisle. A violin trio played the wedding march, signaling the start of the ceremony. Janelle could hear a woman shouting that the ceremony was about to begin as she rushed down the corridor, tripping over the hem of her gown and dragging her cathedral-length veil behind her. She yelled for her grandfather as she ran.

"Pops! Pops, where the heck are you?" she cried, almost out of breath.

Finally, when she reached the end of the corridor, she flung the last door open. *"Pops? Are you in here?"*

She found herself in a sitting room where the ceremony was taking place. She stepped inside and saw the room was decorated with rose, calla lily, and gladiolus freestanding arrangements along each floor-to-ceiling window. A canopy of ivy and silk was at the front of the room, waiting for the bride and groom to stand underneath it. All the guests were seated in the gilded Chiavari chairs. A smiling Mark stood in his single-breasted tuxedo next to the minister. And as the violins played their last note, Janelle realized that another woman in a wedding gown was already walking toward Mark. He offered the woman his hand, and she eagerly grabbed it with her white-gloved one.

Janelle came to a halt right there in the center aisle. This was her and Mark's wedding, wasn't it?

"What's going on?" she cried.

Brenda rose from her chair in the front row and fixed Janelle with a smug grin.

"You snooze, you lose, honey! Mark got tired of waiting on you," Brenda said proudly. "He decided to marry someone else."

Janelle dropped her bouquet limply to her side. "Someone else? *Who?*"

She never got to find out who the bride was. She opened her eyes seconds later to the beep of her cell phone alarm and the rays of sunlight coming through the cabin's bedroom blinds.

Janelle had taken enough college-level psychology to know her besieged subconscious was the culprit for what could be only described as her worst nightmare. She was worried about Pops. She was anxious about the state of her relationship with Mark. The dream had been the manifestation of all of this.

I'll talk to Pops and be home in a few days, she reminded herself. *Mark and I will pick up where we left off. No big deal.*

Yet she couldn't shake her sense of worry that some impending doom lurked around the corner. She couldn't shake it even as she showered, dressed, and did a few haphazard strokes with a hairbrush before giving up any hope of taming her frizzy, unruly curls. She was in desperate need of a deep leave-in conditioner and a good detangler but knew there was no hope of getting either here in Mammoth. Later, she wandered around the cabin, assessing it in the light of day, hoping that would settle her mind.

Pops's cabin was clean, though it showed its age. It was obvious that he hadn't redecorated since the early 1980s judging from the sofa and armchair that looked like they should be encased in plastic. The periwinkle laminate flooring in the kitchen had been swept and mopped, but it was starting to peel around the edges. The particleboard was flaking under the veneer of some of the cabinets. She slid the toe of her boot along the hardwood floors in the living room.

"Could use a polish," she whispered as she stared at the nicks and scratches in the wooden planks.

She raised her eyes from the floor at the sound of a car engine and peered out the window, expecting to see Pops's truck bumping toward the cabin. But she saw nothing but pine trees and the last bit of gray clouds from last night's storm. She glanced at the clock on the fireplace mantel.

6:39.

It was still early. The sun had risen not too long ago. Maybe he hadn't left Deadwood yet. Maybe he was just now checking out of a hotel, or he had decided to grab a quick breakfast before his drive home.

He'll be here soon.

While nibbling on a piece of stale toast, Janelle decided to do a bit of snooping. It was something she had done a lot when she was younger, when she spent the night at her grandparents' house or was stuck inside on rainy days. In her boredom, she would entertain herself by playing detective or pretending to be a pirate hunting for buried treasure under old coats, comforters, and dusty board games stacked in the attic.

Today she planned to rummage through the cabin's closets, dig through drawers, and peek underneath the bed. What else could she find out about Pops that he hadn't told her? What other secrets did he have besides a girlfriend of five years Janelle hadn't known existed?

She looked under the bed first, then searched the closets. Pops was fastidiously neat. She noted this as she pushed aside a rack of shirts and jeans and examined the orderly stack of hats on a shelf and line of cowboy boots at the bottom of his closet.

She shifted her attention to his night table. When she saw an opened box with a half dozen metallic packets inside, she cringed.

"Ultra thin . . . for ultimate sensitivity," she read aloud before tossing the box back inside the drawer in disgust. "Some things can't be unseen," she said drily.

She slammed the drawer shut, then walked across the room to his pine dresser. She opened the top drawer, yanking hard to free it; the bracket seemed to be broken. She didn't see anything particularly eye-opening or shocking inside of the drawer. She opened a second drawer and discovered a pile of athletic socks and underwear—also unexceptional. She was about to slam that drawer shut, too, when she noticed the bright yellow edge of a manila envelope beneath the pile of white cotton. It practically beckoned her. Janelle pulled it out. She slowly opened it and found a sheet of paper inside. She began to read. When she did, she took a step back, almost bumping into the bed behind her and dropping both the paper and envelope to the bedroom floor. She stared at the paper in shock.

It was a marriage license issued by Lawrence County, South Dakota, in July of last year. Her grandfather's name was on the license, along with Connie Marie Black Bear.

Janelle clamped her hand over her mouth, holding back her cry of surprise.

Her grandfather and Connie were married? Why hadn't Connie said anything? Why would she keep a secret like that? Why wouldn't he . . .

Her rapid thoughts came to a screeching halt as her eyes scanned the document again before landing on the spot that was supposed to be signed by the officiant. It was blank. Neither Connie's nor Pops's signatures were on the document, either.

So did they get married?

Not on that day, judging from the marriage license.

But did they get married after?

Janelle's brows furrowed as she collapsed back onto the bed, still clutching the license. Her sweaty fingertips left imprints on the paper. What did all of this mean? Now she had even more questions for her grandfather to answer.

After some time, she finally rose to her feet and returned the license to its envelope and the envelope to its drawer, careful to cover it with the pile of socks and boxers again. She left the bedroom, no longer interested in snooping, afraid of what else she might find.

Janelle returned to the quiet living room, rubbing her shoulders. She adjusted the thermostat—raising the cabin's temperature by another two degrees—and glanced at the mantle clock again.

7:26 . . . still too early.

She turned away from the clock face. She hadn't wasted much time.

Damn it, where are you, Pops?

The problem was Janelle was restless. Her body was still on East Coast time. Her mind was still set to the schedule of the city with its early rising, quick jog on the treadmill before breakfast, racing for trains, and trying to make it through busy intersections before the light changed from yellow to red. If she were back at home, she'd be literally running from the parking garage to the nearby Starbucks to grab a cup of iced mocha latte before her nine-thirty department meeting. She'd be dodging past fellow morning commuters on the sidewalk—bouncing back and forth erratically like a chrome steel bearing in a pinball machine—while she scrolled through her phone checking text messages and emails from Mark, work, and friends. It seemed strange to be sitting on her hands doing nothing. It felt odd to not get some job, *any* job done. She was waiting for something to happen, and that sensation unnerved her.

I've still got résumés to review, she told herself. She still had a baby shower to plan. With an iPad and a 3G wireless connection, there was no reason why she couldn't work on that stuff out here.

Janelle sat on the couch, grabbed her iPad, and scrolled through her emails. She felt a rush of bliss, like a junkie getting a badly needed fix, as her index finger swiped across the glass screen and furiously clicked digital keys. She spotted a message from Mark with the subject line "Morning" She opened it eagerly.

Hey Jay,

Sorry, if I sounded off last night, baby. I just want you back home. I'm lost without you—literally. I can't find a damn thing in this house! I'm constantly opening boxes in the guest room and office, looking for stuff I know you wouldn't have any problem finding. I need you back.

I know you said it may be a couple of days before you can book a flight back home, but I saw a few good deals with US Airways. Maybe you could book one of those flights. Only one was a single transfer through Minneapolis for Wednesday. I'd book it soon and take advantage of the discount.

Can't wait to see you, baby! Call me when your flight touches down.

—M

BTW, speaking of not being able to find things . . . Mom wants to know what you did with the vase she put on the

entryway table. You know, the one she gave us as a gift.
It's disappeared and I told her I don't know where it is.
Any ideas?

Janelle grimaced. In fact she did know where the vase had gone. She had given it to an elderly neighbor who had said how much she loved it when she stopped by two weeks ago with a green bean casserole to welcome them to the neighborhood. Because Janelle had thought the vase belonged in an exhibit case of the Mütter Museum, along with the other oddities—not in her foyer—she had happily given it away. She should have known Brenda would notice its absence.

Janelle's fingers hovered over the screen for a beat before she began to type.

Janelle Marshall <jayjaymarsh@yahoo.com

April 22 at 7:38 a.m.
To: Mark Sullivan Jr. <Sullivan.MarkJr_113@gmail.com>
Re: Morning

Hi,
Thanks for the telling me about the Airways deals, luv.
You're amazing!

She paused. Was she gushing too much? "You're amazing." Did it scream inadequacy and a feeling of desperation? "I hope you still love me despite all this," is what she really wanted to say. She pursed her lips, rapidly clicked the delete button, and resumed typing.

Hi,

Thanks for the telling me about the Airways deals, luv. I miss you too and can't wait to get back home in a couple of days. I can't get there soon enough.

—J

She paused and started typing again.

Oh, and no idea where your mom's vase is. Guess it got moved during the housewarming. Did you check the garage?

She slid her fingertip along the keypad and hit the "SEND" button on screen, feeling guilty about lying to Mark—but only slightly.

"It was an ugly vase anyway," she mumbled.

For the rest of the morning, Janelle read and answered emails: a panicked query from Lydia about the PowerPoint presentation, one from Bryant Consulting Group's vice presidents, who had a complicated 401(k) question, and a two-page rant *with* diagrams from one of the employees who swore there was a conspiracy to have him fired from the company. She reviewed work files, scanning over spreadsheets until her eyes blurred. All the while, her anxiety remained in the background, like an ongoing backbeat of a song that kept an ever-increasing rhythm. She couldn't resist looking up every time she thought she heard an approaching car or the thump of footsteps on the front porch. More than once she peered out the window, willing her grandfather's mud-splattered F-150 to pull into the driveway—only to turn away in frustration when it didn't manifest.

A little before noon, she heard the sound of gravel crunching under tire wheels, but Janelle didn't look up from the email she had been drafting for an applicant. These phantom sounds had been toying with her all morning. She wasn't going to get her hopes up again. So when she heard the sound of a key unlocking the door soon after, she almost leaped from the couch in surprise. Her iPad clattered to the floor and slid across the room. She stumbled to the welcome mat, tripping over the knitted quilt she had slung over her lap to keep warm. Her body tensed as the door swung open.

"Pops?" she cried, no longer angry at him. She was too happy to finally see her grandfather again. He was alive and well; that was all that mattered.

But her elation quickly deflated and her smile disappeared when she realized it was Connie, not her grandfather, standing in the doorway with the sun silhouetting her.

"I'm guessin' he's not back yet, then," Connie said, raising her brows.

She was wearing hip huggers again, but this time there was a winding pattern of gold sequins along the side seams and hem. She also had on another pair of Uggs—purple and suede with a faux-fur trim that looked like it had been shaved off of a Muppet. The woman was in her fifties but for some reason insisted on dressing like she shopped exclusively at Forever 21 or some other teen store with bright lights and booming sound systems.

How could you marry this woman, Pops? And if you didn't marry her, how could you have even considered doing it?

"No, he's not back," Janelle muttered, not hiding her disappointment. "I thought you were him."

Connie stared over her shoulder at the driveway and her Silverado and stomped a foot like a sullen four-year-old.

"Damn it," she murmured. She then dropped her hands to her hips and turned back to Janelle. "Well . . . have you eaten lunch yet?"

Janelle frowned, confused by the subject change.

"I bet Bill doesn't have a lot of food in there. That man has never been much of a cook. You want to grab something to eat in town? I've got some fixings back at the shop if you're hungry."

Janelle hesitated. Connie had been right. Janelle wasn't looking forward to the limited sampling of food Pops's fridge and cabinets had to offer, but she wasn't sure if she wanted to have lunch with Connie, either.

"You need to get out of this house," Connie urged.

Janelle's frown deepened. Why did Connie insist on talking to her like she was a child?

"You've been cooped up in here all morning probably waiting on Bill, am I right?" Connie nodded in reply to her own question before Janelle could respond. "Have lunch with me and my pain-in-the-ass daughter. We'll have ourselves a Girls' Day."

Janelle eyed the older woman. "What did you say?"

"I said we'll have ourselves a Girls' Day." Connie paused. "What? You're telling me that you've never had one of those?"

"Well, yes, but . . . not for a long time."

The last "Girls' Day" Janelle had had was twenty-seven years ago. She was supposed to meet her father for a scheduled weekend visit. It had been a fifty-fifty chance (well, closer to seventy-thirty) that he would be a no-show, but a naïve nine-year-old Janelle had excitedly sat on the windowsill and peered out her grandparents' living room window, scanning the roadway for her father's cream-colored Lincoln Continental with the fuzzy pink dice hanging from the rearview mirror and the rust stains on the passenger door. She had pressed her forehead against the cool glass, her hot breath forming a two-inch circle of condensation by her lips. She kept her skinny rear end on that wooden ledge long after it started to hurt. But she kept looking and kept waiting despite the muscle soreness and a stinging bum because she was certain her father would come like he promised, like he *always* promised. Of course, she didn't see his Lincoln at nine a.m. when he was supposed to arrive. Nor did she see it hours later. By noon, Janelle had been almost in tears.

"I say we have a Girls' Day," Nana had whispered into her ear, making Janelle pull her reddened eyes away from the window. The old woman had wiggled her perfectly arched gray brows and squeezed Janelle's narrow shoulders. "No stinky men. Let's just go out and do the things that girls do!"

That day, Nana had taken her to a local nail salon for the first time to get her toenails painted bubblegum pink. She had bought her a taffeta dress that was both girly and impractical with its wide, poufy skirt, flouncy bow at the waist, and lace trim around the bottom. They had ended the day at the local bakery, feasting on lavender-and-orange-flavored petit fours that had been ignored thanks to the apple fritters and colossal donuts beside them. Nana had sipped tepid Earl Grey tea and Janelle had drunk ginger ale out of a real porcelain teacup.

It had been a lovely day, so lovely that it had almost erased the memory of Janelle's father ditching her for either the warm embrace of one of his girlfriends or the siren call of Jim Beam and Crown Royal.

To have Connie make the same offer that Nana had made twenty-seven years ago was . . . disconcerting.

"So are you coming?" Connie asked, turning back toward her truck and striding down the cabin steps.

"Uh, yeah. Sure." Janelle gestured over her shoulder. "Just let me grab my coat."

CHAPTER 7

"I've got Lean Cuisine chicken paninis!" Connie yelled over a strumming of a guitar and banjo and banging of drums. "I've got some microwaveable flatbread pizza, too, if you wanna try that instead."

"Either's fine!" Janelle shouted, trying her best to be heard above the crooning voice on the loudspeaker.

The voice and the music were coming from the stage several blocks down on Main Street where a band Janelle had never heard of played. A group of twenty or so people gathered around in front of the stage. Some were dancing; a few couples were even doing the two-step.

Janelle and Connie passed a line of Porta-Potties that gave off a faint aroma that Janelle knew from past experiences with county fairs and carnivals would only get worse when the temps increased. The line in front of each potty was at least five deep. But as she gazed around her, she saw that the rest of Main Street was almost entirely vacant. She had seen more people in downtown D.C. at noon on a Sunday than seemed to be here today in Mammoth Falls. Several of the vendors stood at their tables, looking keenly at the few passersby, holding out coupons and flyers. Some didn't even bother to look up and instead read magazines or stared down at their cell phones. Even the horses hitched to a post near Toby's Bar & Grill looked bored.

Maybe Sergeant Bachmann had been right. It was just too damn cold for popcorn and cotton candy. It looked like the first annual Black Hills Wild West Festival was going to be a bust.

As Janelle and Connie walked toward the shop's entrance, Janelle tried her best to avoid the vendors' eager gazes. Instead, she focused on taking careful steps to avoid any falls on the icy sidewalk. Connie seemed oblivious to the snow and took long, purposeful strides in front of her.

The older woman tugged a set of keys out of her coat pocket. "We've got a microwave in the stockroom. A fridge, too."

Janelle was barely paying attention to what Connie was saying. Instead, she gazed up at the "HOT THREADS & THINGS" sign painted over the shop window in cursive letters. The silhouette of a curvy, naked woman was drawn leaning seductively against the last "S," like the naked woman that appeared on the back of tractor trailer tire flaps.

Tasteful, Janelle thought derisively. She guessed she should have expected as much of any shop Connie owned.

"Well, this is my baby!"

As Connie made the proud declaration, she unlocked the door and shoved it open with a flourish. A bell jingled overhead. Janelle stepped inside the boutique as Connie flipped the "CLOSED" sign hanging in the door window to "OPEN." Connie flicked a switch and series of track lights overhead blazed bright.

"Go on! Look around," Connie urged.

Janelle took off her coat, happy to be rid of it. Thanks to last night's dousing, it now had the musty smell of rotting books in abandoned libraries. She hung the parka on a hook near the entrance and discreetly sniffed her turtleneck, relieved that it didn't smell like mildew, too. She then wiped the palms of her hands on her jeans and did as Connie said. She looked around the shop.

Toward the front of the store was a six-foot-long display case/checkout counter that had a mix of costume jewelry including rings, necklaces, and bangles on the shelves inside of it. A bust sat near the cash register wearing a ruby red cowboy hat with silver sequins along the brim.

Beyond that were several racks filled with clothes, most of which Janelle could never see herself wearing: lots of low-cut tops, plenty of short Lycra dresses, and of course, bedazzled hip huggers. Several mannequin torsos hung along the walls, featuring ensembles that Janelle fought the urge not to gawk at openly or burst into laughter at.

"If you want to buy anything, I'll give you a discount," Connie said before taking off her coat and hanging it on a hook beside Janelle's parka. Connie adjusted the front of her royal purple, cowl-neck sweater, revealing the "Buddy" tattoo on her left breast again. "Just let me know."

Janelle glanced at a quilted pleather jacket with an orange mohair collar that was hanging on one of the sales racks. "Oh, I will," she replied, barely masking her sarcasm.

The store bell jingled again. Janelle turned to find a woman with bright green hair standing in the doorway—the same woman Janelle had seen on Main Street yesterday while she was walking with the police chief.

"Well, look who finally showed up at the crack of noon," Connie muttered. "Yvette Black Bear, where the heck have you been?"

"Does it matter?" Yvette croaked, tugging off her dark sunglasses and lowering the zipper of her leather jacket. She had the bleary eyes and wrung-out look of someone recovering from an epic hangover. "I'm here now, aren't I?"

And then she walked across the shop toward them. Well, more accurately, Yvette *strutted* across the shop. Janelle had always admired women who could walk like that, like they were on a Milan runway or like they came accompanied by their own sound track of heavy bass and guitar riffs. She watched in bemused awe as Yvette yanked her jacket off her shoulders and tossed it on the jewelry counter, making its metal buckle ricochet off the glass top in such a forceful way that Janelle was sure a crack might appear on the glass.

"Yes, it does matter," Connie answered, her lips tightening. "I expected you here at eight a.m.!"

"I had something to do this morning. I told you'd I'd be a little late. So now I'm a little late. What do you want me to say?" She glanced around her. "You got any coffee around here?"

"You know it's in the back room!" Connie barked. "And 'a little late' in my book is fifteen minutes . . . maybe thirty. It sure as hell isn't four hours!"

Yvette groaned in exasperation before turning her focus on Janelle. A smile crossed her maroon-painted lips as she pointed at her. "Hey, don't I know you?"

Janelle watched as Connie's anger dialed down from a boil to a simmer. The older woman sucked her teeth in exasperation, walked behind a counter, opened a drawer, and tossed her purse inside. She locked the drawer with a key connected to a lanyard that she threw over her head. She tucked the dangling key between her bosoms.

"I saw you around town yesterday, didn't I?" Yvette persisted.

Janelle nodded and extended her hand for a shake. "Yes, I'm Janelle Marshall. I'm Bill Marshall's granddaughter. It's a pleasure to meet you."

"Aren't we formal?" Yvette glanced down at Janelle's hand and laughed. "You can save the curtsies and the handshakes, honey. I'm not the first lady."

Janelle's face warmed as she slowly lowered her hand back to her side.

"So when we have the festival fashion show next week, you *are* going to show up on time to help me, right?" Connie asked.

"Oh," Janelle said, forcing a smile, "you're having a fashion show?"

"Yeah," Yvette murmured drily, "some overweight house-wives and flat-chested teenagers in too-tight dresses prancing around on stage like they're in the Miss America pageant."

"That's not how it's going to be at all," Connie insisted. She turned to Janelle. "I'm going to have my prettiest gowns and dresses. We're going with a rodeo queen theme with cowboy hats and—"

"Which is boring as hell and something people have seen a hundred times before," Yvette argued. "I thought it would at least be cool for them to rip off their clothes and unveil a banner at the end. It would be in support of the NoDAPL protests in North Dakota . . . you know, the one against the pipeline going through tribal land. And then the models could all give the finger at the end," Yvette said, shoving her middle finger into Janelle's face, revealing her chipped black nails. Janelle took a step back. "Like a 'Fuck you!' to the whole Wild West Festival and all that fake bullshit." She lowered her finger and shrugged. "But Mama shot down that idea."

"I shot it down because it doesn't have anything to do with a fashion show."

"But it's for *our people*, Mama! Come on! It's about more than some stupid dresses and—"

"Evie," Connie said tiredly, "when you have your fashion show, you can do it whatever way you want. But this is *my* show, all right?"

Yvette crossed her arms over her chest.

"Can't you just do what I ask you to do?"

Yvette turned on the heel of her combat boots and glared at her mother. "I said I would, didn't I?"

"You say a lot of things," Connie grumbled before angrily

marching to the stock room. "Come on. Let's eat," she said over her shoulder.

"Man, what a bitch," Yvette muttered under her breath. She then followed her mother.

So this is Girls' Day, Janelle thought. *I should have stayed at the cabin.*

"Damn! These are good," Yvette said with a mouth full of panini. She then leaned on the back legs of a wooden chair with one booted foot propped up on the stockroom table, revealing thick layers of dirt and pebbles embedded in the sole of her shoe.

"They're low cal, too," Connie said as she finished pouring a cup of coffee, then handed her daughter the mug.

"Oh, caffeine goodness," Yvette mumbled before taking a sip. "I needed this! Thanks, Mama!"

In response, Connie smiled and ran her hand over the back of Yvette's green head, a tender gesture that reminded Janelle of her own mother.

I guess they aren't that bad, Janelle thought as she watched the duo.

But Connie's maternal caress abruptly switched to swatting Yvette's thigh—making both Janelle and Yvette jump.

"Oww!" Yvette yelled, then winced. "What the hell did you do that for?"

"Get your feet off the table," Connie ordered.

Yvette grumbled and lowered her boot back to the floor. She then turned her withering gaze onto Janelle. "So why were you hanging all over Sam yesterday?"

Janelle almost spit out her spongy French bread pizza. "Excuse me? I wasn't *hanging all over him,*" she clarified, not liking Yvette's use of words or tone.

"I saw you leaning against him on the street. Looked like you were hanging onto him to me."

Connie raised her brows with interest as she slammed shut the microwave door and took out a tray of linguine.

"I almost slipped on the sidewalk, and he was keeping me from falling down. That's all! The only reason why I was with him at all was because he was trying to help me find my grandfather."

Yvette snorted. "Oh, yeah, because mom lied and said Little Bill was missing."

They had already told Yvette about Pops's plan to pretend he had disappeared to get Janelle to come to Mammoth Falls and how it looked like he was following that plan to its fullest. Instead of being shocked by the news, Yvette had found it hilarious.

"Oh, Bill! You crazy ol' bastard," Yvette had hiccupped before clapping her hands gleefully.

"I only lied because he asked me to!" Connie now argued as she turned to Janelle. She took the remaining chair at the table. "I didn't want to do it, but Bill talked me into it. Now I wish I would have stuck to my guns and said no."

Janelle gazed at Connie, whose dark head was bowed. Connie looked grim—daresay guilty.

But what do you feel guilty about? Janelle wondered as she watched Connie swish her fork around her tray of microwave linguine. Did Connie feel remorse for lying about Pops's disappearance, or was there something else, something more that she wasn't telling Janelle?

Since finding the wedding license in Pops's drawer this morning, Janelle was starting to have her doubts about Connie. Those doubts had started off small but, like an annoying mosquito bite, they were growing larger and harder to ignore each time she scratched at them.

Do you know where he is, Connie?

Scratch.

Do you know what really happened to Pops?

Scratch. Scratch.

Did you just tell everyone that he pretended to disappear but something truly horrible has happened to him?

Scratch, scratch, scratch, scratch!

But she tried to keep her meandering thoughts and doubts in perspective. Connie obviously hadn't told her everything about her relationship with Pops, but a few omissions didn't make her a criminal mastermind, and Pops could very well show up back in town at any minute.

I'm just being paranoid, she told herself. *I need to get back home. I'm going crazy out here!*

"When I saw you with Sam, I thought Police Chief Stud Muffin had gotten back with his wife," Yvette said as she bit into her sandwich. "You look a lot like her."

Janelle tore her gaze away from Connie's bowed head and stared at Yvette, reorienting herself to the conversation in progress. "I'm sorry. What?"

"I said you kind of look like his ex-wife." Yvette lowered her sandwich from her mouth, sucked melted cheese off of her fingers, and scanned her eyes over Janelle. She nodded thoughtfully. "Yeah, with that dusky skin, curly hair, and big eyes . . . you're almost her twin. She was some Mexican waitress or Puerto Rican model or some shit like that. He met her back east. They got divorced a couple of years ago."

Janelle sat back in her chair. For some reason, she could never envision the police chief married to a Mexican waitress or Puerto Rican model. He was still a sheriff from the Old Wild West in her mind. This didn't fit that image at all.

"Sam took their breakup pretty hard," Connie elaborated, sadly shaking her head. "He's never gotten over that divorce from that gal. I think that's why he hasn't stepped up and started anything serious with anyone." Connie raised her eyes and finally started to eat her linguine. "Though it's not like any of the women around town haven't tried. He's a hot ticket around these parts."

"That's for damn sure!" Yvette finished the last of her sandwich and pointed at Janelle. "You probably stand a better chance than anybody else with him, looking so much like her and all."

"I don't know what your type is, Janelle, but you wouldn't do bad hooking up with Sam," Connie insisted. "Like I told you before, he's a good man."

Janelle cleared her throat, feeling very uncomfortable with the course of this conversation. "Look, the police chief didn't seem remotely interested in me."

She thought back on how he flinched when he saw her for the first time and how he barely seemed willing to look at her after that. Whatever he thought about his ex-wife, Janelle's presence didn't seem to bring back any good memories for him.

"Besides, I'm in a serious relationship. I live with someone. We're practically engaged!" she gushed.

Yvette and Connie stared at her, not looking at all dissuaded or impressed.

"Oh, honey," Yvette said before gulping down coffee, "that doesn't mean a damn thing! I've seen men who were married for twenty years dump their wives and kids for girls covered in baby oil who shake their tits for a living."

"Well, that's not me," Janelle said primly, raising her chin. "I would never cheat on Mark. He and I are . . . happy."

She regretted pausing before the word "happy" as soon as she did it. It was like a poker tell, and Yvette immediately pounced on it.

"Uh-huh," Yvette uttered—sounding and looking doubtful. She leaned back in her chair again and snorted. "The people who say they would never do something are the ones I know for sure will do it."

"Evie, leave her be," Connie warned. "She already has a man. Let it go."

"Well, why don't *you* go after Sam," Janelle said indignantly, now more than slightly annoyed. What was it about these people that made her forget all her conflict resolution and role-playing training? "If he's such a hot ticket, then why haven't you dated him?"

"Believe me, I'd jump on him like he was a pogo stick, but he won't have a girl like me. He likes them cleaner, and I like my men dirtier," Yvette said, giving a little saucy wiggle in her chair.

"By dirty, you mean that no good Tyler Macy?" Connie asked, not looking up from her linguine.

Yvette's smile disappeared. "There is nothing wrong with Ty."

"There's nothing right with him, either."

"Don't start, Mama," Yvette said through gritted teeth.

"That guy is just like your father, Evie. You're just setting yourself up for—"

"I said don't start, damn it!" Yvette shouted, leaping to her feet and sending her chair careening to the floor. Janelle jumped in alarm. "Why do you do that? Why can't you just . . . just keep your mouth shut for once?"

"Do you want me to lie? Is that what you want me to do? To tell you I think Tyler Macy is a great guy and I'm happy for you?" Connie shook her head. "I'm sorry, but I can't."

"Oh, and you're fuckin' perfect? You've dated guys a lot worse than Ty! How many piece of shit truckers and bikers did you bring home in the last forty years? Huh?"

Janelle's eyes nearly bulged out of her head. *Truckers and bikers? Does Pops know this?*

"And I learned from my mistakes. I'd hoped that you finally would, too."

Yvette took a slow, deep breath that made her shoulders tremble and her chest shudder. Janelle winced, preparing herself for the verbal onslaught that Yvette was about to unleash, but the younger woman instead coolly licked her lips and turned on her heel.

"I'm not taking this shit," Yvette mumbled before marching across the room and throwing open the stockroom door. "I'm outta here."

"You said you were going to help me today, Evie!" Connie shouted after her.

"Not if you're going to be the world's biggest bitch!"

Janelle leaned forward and watched through the doorway as Yvette grabbed her leather jacket off the sales counter and, in her haste, knocked the bust with the ruby red cowboy hat to the floor.

"Typical," Connie muttered under her breath, shaking her head.

"To hell with you, you old hypocrite!" Yvette shouted over her shoulder. "Nice meeting you, Janelle!"

"Umm, n-nice meeting y-you, too," Janelle stuttered just as Yvette swung open the store door and slammed it shut behind her. The bell jingled again. The mannequins near the window shook and shimmied like they were partygoers at a disco.

Janelle watched as Connie slowly rose from the table and walked back into the store. She stared out the shop window, seeming to look at nothing in particular.

Janelle set her now half-eaten pizza back onto its grease-covered paper plate and followed Connie. She bent down and picked the bust off the floor, carefully set it back on the jewelry counter, and placed the fallen cowboy hat on its plastic head.

"Sorry about Evie," Connie said absently, still looking out the shop window.

"It's . . . all right," Janelle said, unsure of how else to respond to what she had just witnessed.

"I gave her my temper—and my mouth," Connie continued, as if not hearing her. "Looking at that girl sometimes is like looking at my own reflection—at the *worst* angle. But Evie's right about one thing: her mama's a hypocrite. Before Bill, I didn't make . . . well, good choices when it came to men . . . when it came to life, either." She turned back to Janelle and shrugged. "I didn't know any better, though."

Janelle didn't say anything, having exhausted all polite responses. Instead she stood awkwardly in the center of the shop.

"I grew up on Pine Ridge Reservation with a drunk for a daddy and a mama who wanted to do right, but didn't know how to," Connie said, her gaze still unfocused. Janelle finally realized that Connie was staring at the silhouette of mountains. "Mama was just a baby herself. She got pregnant with me when she was fifteen and dropped out of school. She was stuck with a drunken husband and four rowdy kids. He was stuck with a marriage and a family he didn't want. So they both made us all miserable. I only ended up leaving when Social Services came and farmed us out to foster care. They thought we'd do better living with the white families, but some of them were worse . . . a helluva lot worse." She dropped her hand to her hip. "It's not a good way for a young girl to grow up, you know? You make lots of bad decisions and look for love in all the wrong places." She gave a sad smile. "You're lucky you didn't grow up like that."

Janelle recalled her own alcoholic father and his philandering ways. Before her mom divorced him, Janelle could remember the women her father would sneak inside the house while her mother was at work and dad was supposed to be watching her after school: the chubby girl in the horizontal-striped halter dress, the buxom cashier from the Quickie-Mart down the street who wore velour tracksuits with white piping, and the skinny chick with the blond wig and high-pitched laugh who drank martinis like they were water.

Janelle also could remember hearing her mother weeping alone in her bedroom at night after kicking her father out for the umpteenth time, only to open the door and let him back in the next morning when he returned home shamefaced and contrite.

But that last night—the night her mother would never let him back in again—stood out in Janelle's memory like a gleaming diamond on a bed of coal. Her father had gotten so drunk that he could barely stand. Her mother—tired of all the empty liquor bottles littering their house, the phantom scent of women's perfume on his clothes, his extended and unexplained absences, and the laundry list of disappointments—finally couldn't take it anymore. She had hit him over and over again. She had screamed and kicked.

"How much can I take, Carl? How much do you want from me? Haven't I given you enough? What more can I give?"

Her father had lunged for her mother, and Janelle had watched, petrified, as he had wrapped his hands around the woman's throat and squeezed until her mother had clawed at his fingers, until her eyes went pink and began to water.

Janelle had yelled for him to stop, punching her small fists into his shoulders, and he finally had released her mother, who gasped and wept on their living room floor.

When the police arrived an hour later, her mother had looked more embarrassed than anything else.

"I shouldn't have let this go on for so long," she had kept muttering as she rubbed dazedly at her throat, which was already darkening with hand-sized purple bruises. "I shouldn't have let it get this bad," she had mumbled as Janelle's father was placed in handcuffs and escorted past the broken coffee table and tipped-over dining room chairs to their opened front door.

"You're a classy woman with a college degree," Connie said, now gazing at Janelle. "Bill told me you live in a big pretty house in a nice neighborhood back there in Virginia. I bet you always make good decisions, don't you?"

"I try to," she answered honestly.

Pragmatism and order were the compass points by which she navigated her life. Janelle had seen the bedlam that could come with flying by the seat of your pants, following your impulses, and getting swept up in passion and emotions. Her parents had been perfect examples. Watching Connie and Yvette was yet another reminder of how messy her life could be if she had followed that path and let those ghosts from the past take over.

She jumped, startled by a sharp knock at the window. She and Connie whipped around.

The police chief stood in front the shop window with his hands cupped around his eyes. He peered through the glass and between the line of mannequins. When Connie waved, he lowered one of his hands and waved back.

"Well, speak of the devil," Connie said, beaming. The heavy exchange they had had seconds earlier seemed to be forgotten. "Hey, Sam! Come on in!"

Please don't, Janelle thought desperately, though she wasn't quite sure why. She watched with dismay as the chief wiped his feet on the welcome mat outside the shop door and stepped inside the boutique.

He wasn't wearing a Stetson and costume today, but a police uniform and black nylon bomber jacket with the police department emblem on the breast and sleeve. He smiled openly at Connie, then glanced at Janelle, flinching only ever so slightly this time.

"Good afternoon, ladies," he said with his cowboy bravado, taking off his cap and gloves and running his fingers through his hair to comb his matted locks back into place. His cheeks and ears were pink from the cold again, along with the tip of his nose. He sniffed. "What have you been up to?"

Janelle bit down hard on her bottom lip. Her cheeks burned, and her throat went dry. She glanced down at her palms. They were actually *sweating*.

"Not much," Connie answered while Janelle remained conspicuously silent. "We were just finishing up lunch, and I was showing Janelle here my shop."

"Hear from Little Bill yet?" he asked, stepping farther into the boutique.

Connie shook her head. "No, not yet . . . and between you and me, it's starting to piss me off. He's taken this thing way too far!"

The chief nodded. "So you mind telling me what 'this thing' is?"

Connie blew air out of her puffed cheeks then unloaded, telling the chief the story of how Bill came up with his plan to get Janelle to Mammoth Falls while they were on a date at the Midnight Star in Deadwood. She also told him about the phone call she made.

"But why would he do all that?" The chief glanced at Janelle again. "Did he tell you why he wanted her to come here? Was something wrong? Is that why he's gone?"

Connie shook her head. "There wasn't anything wrong. He just didn't want her to—"

"Miss out on the chance to see Mammoth Falls!" Janelle loudly interrupted for the first time, making Connie frown at her.

Janelle didn't want the chief to know about how her grandfather was trying to thwart her engagement. If Connie told the chief that, it would require an explanation, and Janelle didn't want to have to explore Pops's low opinion of her relationship with Mark in front of the small-town cop. He was practically a stranger. Connie and Yvette had already prodded into her personal life past the point of comfort. She wasn't about to let someone else wedge his way in, too.

Janelle finally stepped forward. "He's been trying to get me out here for years. I guess he was getting desperate," she said, hitching an awkward laugh.

The chief's gaze shifted between the two women. "Is that right?"

He could sense something was amiss, that they weren't telling him everything. Janelle could see it on his face and in the way he eyed them both suspiciously. His keenness to know the truth made her even more desperate to get out of there.

"Well, Connie, thank you for the lovely lunch," she said, sounding a lot more proper than she intended, like she was thanking Connie for inviting her to high tea instead of giving her microwaved French bread pizza. "But I really should be getting back to the cabin. Maybe Pops is back already."

Connie blinked. "Oh, well, uh . . . let me grab my coat and keys and—"

"I could take you back," the chief volunteered.

The instant he did, two female heads pivoted in his direction. Connie grinned, and Janelle's face morphed into a look of sheer horror before she caught herself and toned it down to a smile that seemed more like a grimace.

"Why that'd be mighty nice of you, Sam," Connie said just as Janelle rushed out, "No, you don't have to do that!"

Sam looked between the two women again with brows raised. "It's no trouble. It'll save Connie from having to leave the shop to take you back."

"Yes, but you've probably got work to do, being police chief and . . . and all," Janelle stammered.

"I've got a meeting at City Hall, but I'll be back long before then. This'll only take fifteen, maybe twenty minutes. I could spare that."

A fifteen- to twenty-minute car ride alone with the police chief. *Oh, joy,* Janelle thought, swallowing loudly.

She stared at Connie, hoping that the older woman could sense her desperation and insist that she take her back instead.

But Connie didn't utter a word. She was either completely oblivious or intentionally ignoring Janelle's silent plea for help.

"Thank you, Chief," Janelle said almost grudgingly, accepting defeat. "I would appreciate the ride. It's . . . It's very kind of you."

He tugged his cap back onto his head and nodded. "No problem. And call me Sam."

Chapter 8

Janelle sat in the passenger seat beside the chief—or Sam, as she was supposed to call him now—wedged between a laptop and so many electronics that she was terrified of touching anything. So she sat ramrod straight with her arms at her sides at ninety-degree angles and her hands firmly on her lap. Her shoulders and back were starting to hurt. She stole anxious glances at Sam, trying her best to do it inconspicuously but not quite succeeding.

She missed his Stetson no matter how cheesy that admission made her feel, but even without it, he didn't look any less rugged. His hard jaw was already starting to show the first signs of a five o'clock shadow. She wondered if he was one of those guys who had to shave twice a day to keep the beard stubble at bay. She wondered if she reached out and ran her finger along his cheek if it would feel like sandpaper, or would his whiskers be silky smooth.

Janelle cringed at the thought. *Where did that come from?*

Why was she wondering about running her fingers along any man whose name wasn't Mark, let alone the man sitting beside her?

"So you're from back east?" Sam asked as he drove, finally breaking the silence that had settled between them.

"Um, yes, I'm from Washington. . . . Washington, D.C., I mean."

She stared at his right hand. It was clutched around the steering wheel. It seemed much safer than staring at his face. Her eyes traced the line of his hand from the blue veins along his wrist to the tufts of pale blond hair on his knuckles to the white crescents under his nail beds.

"Actually I live in the burbs of D.C. My boyfriend and I just bought a house in Chantilly. You've probably never heard of the place, but it's—"

"I've heard of it." He still hadn't torn his gaze from the windshield. "You mean Chantilly, Virginia. Right?"

Her eyes jumped from his hand back to his face. She slowly nodded, totally surprised. "Right," she answered softly. "How did you—"

"I've been there a few times. I had a friend who lived there when I was back east. I used to live not too far away from him, out in Vienna."

Her mouth fell open. When she realized she was gaping, she snapped it shut.

"We had a condo there. We'd eat at this Thai place down the street at least twice a week," he continued, seemingly oblivious to her shock that he not only knew the city where she lived but had once lived less than twenty miles away, in a setting very similar to her own.

But he was a cop from a small town in the Black Hills of South Dakota. She tried to imagine Sam instead at one of the dinner parties she and Mark always attended back home. She tried to envision Sam standing in a brownstone with a view of the Potomac, sharing polite conversation over a glass of red wine, talking about the latest appointee within the Obama administration or the merits of using ginkgo biloba versus fish oil as a supplement. She couldn't see it. She couldn't see it at all.

Sam chuckled, oblivious to the mental earthquake he had just given her. "It got to the point that he knew us by name."

"He?" she uttered vaguely.

"The kid who used to answer the phone at the Thai restaurant," Sam elaborated. "He even knew my order—drunken noodles and spring rolls. We'd get there and I swear they had those plastic containers waiting for us in the back."

"By 'we' you mean you and your ex-wife?"

Sam whipped around, finally turning away from the windshield. He stared at her as if she had just shouted a string of obscenities at him.

She immediately regretted asking him that question. Why had she mentioned his wife? She guessed she had caught a case of verbal *vomitus* from plain-spoken Yvette.

"I'm sorry. I didn't mean to . . . I mean, Yvette and Connie mentioned that you were . . . that you had once been . . . well, married before. I didn't know that—"

"It's fine," he said, raising one of his hands off the steering wheel and silencing her. "It's not like it's a secret or anything. Everyone around Mammoth knows I'm divorced. I have been for a couple of years now." He sighed. "And yes, I lived out there with my ex-wife, Gabriela. I guess she still lives there, too."

"You guess?"

"Well,"—he paused and inclined his head—"Gabby and I aren't exactly on speaking terms. I wouldn't expect to get any Christmas or birthday cards from her any time soon."

"Oh," she said quietly.

The conversation petered out after that. They finished the rest of the ride to her grandfather's cabin in mutual silence, listening to the police radio chatter while Sam drove and she gazed out the passenger-side window, taking in the monotonous scenery of trees, rock, and blue skies once they made it out of downtown Mammoth Falls.

The awkwardness between them felt even more elevated now, and it was all her fault. She could tell that she had crossed some unseen line with Sam that she should not have. Sam claimed that he didn't mind talking about his marriage or about his ex-wife, but she could sense that was untrue. He still cringed at the sight of a woman who vaguely resembled his ex-wife, for God's sake! If that wasn't an example of "not getting over the past," she didn't know what was.

Janelle suspected that there was some intriguing story there with Sam, his ex-wife Gabriela, and their days back east. It might even be a heartbreaking one. But she wouldn't pry. She may have had verbal *vomitus* earlier, but she wouldn't have it again. Her lips were bolted shut. The lock was in place. She wasn't asking any more questions. The chief could keep whatever secrets he wanted.

A sense of relief washed over her when he pulled into the clearing leading to her grandfather's driveway. Janelle fought the urge to immediately reach for her seat belt and the door handle when the cabin's metal roof came into view. She didn't want to look too impatient to get away from Sam, though she wanted nothing more than to escape his truck and get back to the solitude of the cabin's interior.

"Thank you for the ride," she said as he drew to a stop.

"No problem." He glanced around the yard. "Looks like Little Bill still isn't back yet."

Her hands paused midway in removing her seat belt and grabbing her purse. During the car ride, she had somehow forgotten completely about her grandfather's absence. She followed Sam's gaze. He was right. Her grandfather's truck wasn't there. He still had not returned. Unease crept into her again.

"You mind if I look around?" he asked, turning to her.

"Why would you look around?"

"Maybe I can spot something. Maybe he left a note or some sign that he's been here already, but you might not have noticed."

That wasn't likely. Connie had already looked throughout the cabin last night, and Janelle had examined it from top to bottom only hours ago. What would Sam find that they hadn't? Besides, she didn't want him in the cabin with her.

"Why?" a little voice in her head asked. *"Connie said he's a good guy. It's not like he's going to try anything."*

That's not what I'm worried about.

She didn't want to be alone with Sam any longer than she had to be. She didn't like the way he made her feel—awkward and feverish, silly and feminine. She was not that woman back home—not at work as she walked from office to office, introducing new hires, and not at dinner parties while she stood at Mark's side—and she refused to be that woman here in Mammoth Falls.

"I just wanna help," he said, leaning toward her slightly.

She removed her seat belt and set her purse on her lap. She shifted uncomfortably in her seat.

"Look, if you've got some big crime syndicate going on in there, you don't have to worry." He smiled. "I'll look the other way." He held up his hand mockingly. "Scout's honor. I'm just trying to find out what's happened to Bill."

It was the smile that did it. She didn't think he had smiled at her since they had met. It was her unfortunate luck that the smile took him from rugged to charming. Knowing that she would probably regret it later, Janelle threw open the truck door.

"Okay, have a look. Maybe you can find something."

A minute later she stepped over the threshold and lowered the zipper of her parka while Sam stood with his hands on his hips in the center of the doorway. Inside the cabin, he seemed even taller, maybe twice as large. It was almost like having a giant standing beside her. She took a step to her left. She could still feel the heat radiating off of him.

"So Connie said that Little Bill made up a story to get you out here to Mammoth," Sam began as he walked across the living room. He glanced around him at the furniture and then at the cowboy hats that hung along the wall. "Is that right?"

Janelle nodded as she shut the door behind him and took off her coat. She hung it on a hook near the door and tugged at the collar of her cashmere turtleneck. Was it just her, or had it gotten markedly hotter in here?

"Yes, that's what she told me, too," Janelle said as she walked toward the thermostat. She pressed the button to lower the temperature setting by about three degrees. She flapped her hands in front of her face, banishing the tiny beads of perspiration that were sprouting on her forehead.

"Why was he so fired up to get you out here?" Sam asked as he stepped into the kitchen. She watched in bewilderment as he started opening and closing drawers and cabinets. He ran a hand over the Formica countertop. He shifted back one of the bar stools.

"Pops thought he could . . . he thought that he could . . ."

Her words drifted off. It mortified her to admit something like this, particularly to Sam.

Sam turned back to face her. "Bill thought he could what?"

She stifled a sigh. So he wasn't going to let her off the hook.

"He thought he could keep me from getting engaged."

Sam's blue eyes widened.

"It's crazy, I know . . . and misguided." She shrugged. "He was coming from a good place, though," she hastily added.

Sam slowly walked out of the kitchen. "Why wouldn't he want you to get engaged?"

"I don't . . . I don't know," she lied.

Sam was accessing her openly now—no sideways glances.

She guessed he had gotten over her looking like his ex-wife. Either that, or this information was too intriguing to turn away.

"You don't know?"

He knew she was lying. She had always been a horrible liar.

"Well, I guess Pops . . . he doesn't like my boyfriend very much."

There. I said it.

Sam abruptly turned and headed down the hall. He pushed open the first door, revealing her grandfather's only bathroom. She rushed forward, hoping that she hadn't left anything embarrassing lying around—a bra on the tiled floor or her birth control pills sitting on the edge of the porcelain sink. She squeezed past him just as he swung open the medicine cabinet. She released a pent-up breath when she saw that the bathroom was relatively clean. No lacy bras or pills to be found.

Thank God.

"Why doesn't he like him?"

"Huh?" She tore her eyes away from the bathroom floor and looked up. They were almost chest-to-chest in the cramped bathroom.

"I asked why Bill doesn't like your boyfriend."

The warmth of his breath brushed her cheek. His gaze locked onto hers, and she felt restless again. She instantly wanted out of that room. She wouldn't have felt a more urgent desire to leave if she had seen flames and smelled smoke.

Janelle hopped back into the hall. "Are these questions supposed to help you find my grandfather, Chief?"

He smiled again. "I told you to call me Sam."

A second smile. He's on a roll today.

"Are these questions supposed to help you find my grandfather, *Sam?*"

"Maybe yes. Maybe no." He followed her back into the hall, his heavy footfalls echoing off the hardwood floor. "I figure it wouldn't hurt to ask."

"Well, if you can't say for sure whether they're relevant to your search, you won't mind me not answering them then," she said firmly then pushed the last door open in the hallway. "There's the bedroom if you want to check that next."

He cocked an eyebrow, looking taken aback.

Good, she thought. She had been stuttering and stumbling around him way too long. It was finally time to assert herself. She wasn't a woman who got easily flustered, and there was no reason to start now.

He walked into the bedroom and looked around, staring at the bed that she had already remade—the ancient comforter was back in place along with the two pillows whose cases she longed to wash if she knew where to find a washer and dryer around here. Sam dropped to his knees and checked the floor underneath the bed. She crossed her arms over her chest. All he would find under there was a pair of old work boots and dust bunnies.

"The boyfriend's a touchy topic with you, I'm guessin'," his muffled voice said from beneath the bed frame.

"He's not a touchy subject. I just don't understand how Mark is pertinent to—"

"Mark?" Sam raised his head and turned to look at her. The bright light coming through the bedroom window caught in his blonde locks, setting them aflame. He climbed back to his feet. "Mark is his name?"

"Yes, his name is . . . it's Mark Sullivan."

"Well," he said as he opened the night table drawer and peered inside of it, "Bill certainly didn't think this Mark Sullivan guy was up to snuff if he . . ." His words tapered off.

That's when Janelle noticed the open box of condoms in the night table drawer—the one she had found earlier. Sam had obviously noticed the box, too. The tips of her ears started to burn as a flush washed over her face.

"Those aren't mine!" she rushed out. "Th-they're Pops's! I-I found them."

Sam didn't comment. He simply pushed the box aside and looked at the address book underneath before shutting the drawer closed a few seconds later.

He probably doesn't believe me.

What nearly eighty-year-old man kept a box of Trojans in his night table drawer? Sam probably thought she had brought the box with her to South Dakota. Maybe she wanted to have some wild fling with a local guy because her relationship with her boyfriend wasn't stable, because Pops was right that she shouldn't get engaged.

"Look, there is nothing wrong with Mark. There is nothing wrong with *us*. We make sense! We're perfect for each other!" she argued to the back of Sam's head as Sam turned to walk across the bedroom. She remembered the previous times she had uttered those very words to Pops. And she remembered Pops's rebuttals.

He's a mama's boy.

He's all about flash and money.

He loves himself more than he loves you, baby girl.

That last one had particularly hurt.

"Pops is just . . . overly protective. He's never liked any of my boyfriends," she embellished, feeling guilty even as she said it. "He'll never be happy with any man I choose!"

Sam nodded. "I know what that's like," he said, making her pause.

"You do?"

"Yep." She watched as he walked around the bed and strolled toward the wooden dresser in the corner near Pops's tiny closet. He opened and closed drawers in succession after a quick scan. "Before he died, my father had nothing good to say about my wife, Gabby. 'She'll give you nothing but grief, boy.

That woman ain't meant for marriage, and she certainly ain't meant for you. You're a fool if you can't see that.' It burned me up to hear him talk about her like that. I couldn't understand why he said it. What the heck did he see that I didn't . . . that I *couldn't*? He told me he was just 'bein' honest.' I told him he was being one negative SOB, as usual. I told him if he couldn't accept Gabby, there wasn't any point of us being around him anymore. I didn't see or speak to my father for four years." Sam slammed shut the last drawer—making her flinch. He turned to face her again. "Sad part is . . . Dad was right."

She fell silent.

"Well," he said as he peered into the closet. He exhaled a long breath. "I can't find a damn thing and nothing looks out of the ordinary." He shut the closet door. "The cabin looks pretty much the way you found it, right?"

She nodded numbly, almost feeling whiplash from the rapid subject change.

"I'll head back into town, then."

Sam turned away from the closet and headed to the bedroom door. She followed him down the hall and into the living room. He was still talking—saying something about lunch and his meeting at City Hall—but she didn't catch the details. She barely paid attention. Her thoughts orbited in another solar system.

"'That woman ain't meant for marriage and she certainly ain't meant for you.' . . . Sad part is . . . Dad was right."

Was he insinuating that Pops might be right about Mark, too? Had that been the point of his story?

"You go on and take my number," Sam said, holding out a business card to her.

Janelle stared down at the card he extended to her as if he had just performed a magic trick and manifested it out of thin air. She took his card and shoved it into her jeans pocket. She was growing a small collection of these business cards.

"As soon as you hear from Bill, let me know. He's even starting to make me wonder where the heck he's gotten off to."

She dumbly nodded again, causing Sam to narrow his eyes at her.

"Are you all right?"

"Uh, yeah . . . yeah, I'm fine."

But she wasn't fine. She was lost. Mentally, she was back in her rental car driving in the dark forest, bumping along with no idea where she was going. She had come to Mammoth to find answers and find Pops, but nothing had been resolved, and now she had even more questions than before. She hadn't come here for this.

Sam placed a hand on her shoulder. The gesture caught her so off guard that she almost swatted his hand away. But she caught herself before she did.

"I'm sure Bill is fine. He'll come back, and he'll get used to the idea of you guys getting married. Heck, he'll have to, right?" He squeezed her shoulder. "You're already engaged."

She shook her head. "I'm not engaged. I-I didn't say yes. I would have said yes but I . . ." Her voice drifted off.

His hand lingered a bit longer. Her throat tightened as Sam opened his mouth as if to say something more, but then he clamped his mouth shut, dropped his hand, and turned back to the door.

"I'll head out, then."

A few seconds later, Janelle shut the door behind Sam. She surveyed the cabin and listened to the steady drip of the kitchen faucet and the tick of the clock over the fireplace. She pulled back the gingham curtains and gazed out the window. Neither a house nor an office building was visible from here. The storm clouds had long since disappeared. The sky was a clear blue, and the mountains stretched far into the distance. Many of the trees were still coated with a fine layer of ice, and the breeze created a light tinkling sound in the branches that reached her ears even in the confines of the cabin. The trees undulated like an ocean wave with each gust of wind.

It was strange to feel so much angst in such an awe-inspiring place.

I can't take this, Janelle thought indignantly. She couldn't take this doubt. Out here, the voices that she had managed to keep quiet for so many years were amplified. The foundation that she stood on seemed to quake and shudder. It was like she was hurled back in time to that little girl who needed reassurance, for someone to tell her that everything was going to be okay. She was back to being the deluded nine-year-old peering out her grandparents' living room window, searching for an approaching Lincoln Continental. She was back to listening at the door as her mother sobbed in her bedroom. She was back to watching in almost paralyzing horror as her father wrapped his hands around her mother's neck and wouldn't let go.

There was something about this place—the remoteness, the solitude, and the silence. She needed to escape it. She had to get back home, where things moved so quickly that you didn't have time to reflect or have doubts. She needed her Microsoft Outlook calendar that was full of meetings and to-do lists, the blaring horns from cabs, the steady stream of pedestrians, cars racing through traffic lights, and subway trains crowded with people. She needed her Pilates class and meeting up with the girls for drinks and tapas. She needed Mark by her side telling her "don't sweat the small stuff, baby," because unfortunately in Mammoth Falls, the "small stuff" didn't seem quite so diminutive.

Had that been the reason why Pops had wanted her to come here? Had he wanted to shake her up, to give her doubts?

"Thanks a lot, Pops," she muttered as she walked across the room and grabbed her iPad from the coffee table.

She'd follow up with Connie when she got back home. She'd try other ways to reach her grandfather. But she couldn't stay here any longer. She wouldn't be manipulated like this. She watched as the tablet's screen brightened with the press of a button. A few minutes later, she was searching frantically for the next flight to take her back to Virginia, back to safety.

CHAPTER 9

Hank finished the last of his bear claw. He then glanced around him in search of a leftover pale pink napkin from Joanna's Bakery. He couldn't find one, so he wiped his mouth on his sleeve instead. The flakes of pastry icing on his lips left a crusty streak on the black nylon of his jacket near the wrist, but he didn't care. He felt like a little boy forced to sit in detention while everyone else was whooping it up on the playground at recess.

So what, he thought petulantly. *I'll clean it off tomorrow.*

He then slouched back in the driver's seat and grumbled to himself as he drove.

Twenty minutes ago, the twenty-five-year-Mammoth Falls Police Department veteran had been just about to finish his shift for the day and head home to his wife, Barb. Tuesday was pot pie night. A cold beer awaited him on the second shelf in the fridge. He and Barb would sit in their padded leather recliners in front of the forty-inch plasma TV he had purchased last year at that Best Buy out in Rapid City. They would eat dinner on blue plastic trays perched on their laps while they watched their favorite TV shows: *NCIS* for Hank, for obvious reasons, and *The Voice* for Barb, because she loved singing competitions and had a schoolgirl crush on that Adam Levine fellow. They'd flip between the shows during commercial breaks while their Saint Bernard, Sadie, parked her big rear end on the carpet between them and dozed.

Hank had been looking forward to all of it—the cold beer in his hand, the cozy warmth of his home, the silent reassurance of Barb's company, and the sound of their pooch snoring at their feet. But twenty minutes ago, just as he was raising the partition between the front of the office and bullpen, the department's office manager/dispatcher, Rita, had called out for him to wait.

"Hold on, Hank! A call came in," Rita had said, lowering the dispatch desk phone back into its cradle. "Someone said there's something suspicious looking over near Eighty-five . . . off of Cedar Lane."

"What the hell is 'suspicious looking'?"

"Suspicious looking!" she had said again with widened eyes. "I'm just telling you what they said. They said they couldn't get a good look at it, but it looked like a car might have gone off the road, maybe it got waylaid in a ditch. Somebody might need some help, they said."

"Well, I'm heading home. Have one of the other guys do it," he had mumbled, shrugging on his coat.

"They can't do it! The chief has tonight off. Mitch is over at Toby's breaking up a fight between two drunken hotheads, and Brady is doing patrol at the festival. You're all we got right now. Besides, it's on your way home anyway."

"Bring in one of the part-timers."

"Hank—"

"If it's over by Cedar Lane, it's not even our jurisdiction. Call Lead and have one of their guys do it!"

"Hank—"

"I'm bone tired and I wanna go home, Rita."

"Hank Bachmann, you have done nothing all day but write two traffic tickets! You've kept your butt parked at that desk eating donuts and doing crossword puzzles! Just go check and see about the accident. Please!"

Behind his mustache, he had pouted. He had itched to tell Rita that since she had divorced her second husband she had turned into a real B-I-T-C-H, but he kept those thoughts to himself. Instead, he had stalked toward the door, shoved it open, and headed out of City Hall. A minute later he was in his truck and had it pointing it in the direction of I-85.

As Hank neared his destination, he continued to mumble to himself. He still didn't know why the Lead cops couldn't do it or one of those high and mighty deputies at the Lawrence County Sheriff's Office. Why did tasks like this always fall on folks like Hank?

It was the way of the world today, he guessed. With the exception of men like him, no one wanted to take responsibility for anything anymore. They all wanted a leg up and a leg over. They wanted subsidies and free health care and welfare. They were always crying about how someone was getting something that they should have gotten and how laws should be passed so they could get it, too. Meanwhile, God-fearing, hardworking men like himself were being left out in the cold.

It's a damn shame, he thought as he drove, slowing down to make a right turn onto Cedar Lane and listening to the chatter on his police radio.

He couldn't stand the lazy, no-good folks out there that made life hard for men like him—folks like the paper boy, Bobby Sawyer, who always, *always* threw Hank's copy of the *Mammoth Falls Gazette* and his *Pennysaver* on the far side of the fence, requiring Hank to walk an extra ten steps from his front door.

(He had counted!) Hank despised those good-for-nothings like his neighbor John, who borrowed his weed whacker last year, only to return it broken and claiming that the thing had never worked at all. And he inwardly loathed the entitled, like Police Chief Sam Adler, who had spent fewer years on the force than Hank, but had moved up the ranks faster simply because his daddy had happened to be police chief. Why wasn't Prince Sam the one out on the road, following up on "something suspicious" out on Cedar Lane? Hank bet Sam was probably home right now enjoying a cold beer, maybe a pot pie and *NCIS*, while Hank was still on duty.

It's a damn shame, he thought again.

The little injustices in life could pile up on a man. The cumulative weight of these indignities could break a fellow who was weaker than he was. But Hank was made of thicker stuff. He would persevere.

Hank slowed down to peer at the road, searching for the supposed accident Rita had told him about. He squinted his myopic eyes. He looked to his right then left and peered into the distance, but he still didn't see anything.

"Figures," he huffed.

He drove almost another half mile before slowly pulling to a stop near the shoulder, hearing the packed snow, now coated with ice, crunch under his Kevlar tires. He looked around again, still not seeing a sign that anything was amiss. He shook his head and started to do a U-turn. He would head back to 85. If he was lucky, he'd catch the last fifteen minutes of *NCIS* and watch Special Agent Gibbs do his magic. (Gibbs was a man who reminded Hank much of himself—hard-nosed, unflappable, and take-charge.) But just as Hank pulled into the lane heading northbound and reached for another bear claw in bottom of the bakery bag beside him, he caught sight of something from the corner of his eye. About twenty feet away he could see skid marks in the snow leading to a thicket of trampled shrubs and broken tree branches. With brows furrowed, he drove closer to get a better look. He slowed down when he saw the glint of shattered glass in his headlights.

Hank pulled over and threw open the truck door, grunting as he climbed out, and hopped down to the asphalt. He walked toward the splinters of glass before slowly lowering himself to one knee and grunting again. His eyes drifted back to the shrubs. Beyond those bare shrubs were the mountains. The mountain slope took a sharp dip that was hidden in a darkness that even his headlights couldn't reach. He rose to his feet—which warranted a third grunt—removed the flashlight that was strapped to his belt, flicked it on, and inched forward, careful not to slip and fall into the shadows below. He peered down the slope. He saw the slanted rear tire first, then the mangled rear end with its busted taillight and bent bumper. When he saw the two bumper stickers on the back—"Change We Can Believe in '08" and "If you can read this, you're riding too close"—he knew who the truck belonged to.

"Bill!" he yelled.

The driver's-side door to the F-150 was open and the truck's contents—a beat-up cooler, a magazine, and a heap of CDs—were splayed along the dark rock, looking as out of place as M&Ms sprinkled on a pile of manure. But Hank did not see the driver, and judging from how bad the truck looked, he'd imagine Bill was in the same shape as his truck—or worse.

"Shit, Bill!" Hank shouted, his breath catching in his throat. It came out in sharp bursts like he was running uphill instead of standing still on a roadway, staring at a car crash scene. "Hey, are . . . are you all right down there? Bill?"

No one answered.

Hank groped frantically for the radio on his shoulder and scrambled back toward his pickup truck, almost slipping in the snow. He dropped his flashlight, and it went sliding across the black asphalt before rumbling to a stop near a tree. He ran as fast as his 286-pound frame would allow as he called for assistance.

It looked like he wouldn't be catching the last fifteen minutes of *NCIS* after all.

CHAPTER 10

Sam stood at the foot of the cabin's front porch, took off his cap, and raked his fingers through his hair, which was now damp with sweat. It was a nervous gesture that had plagued him since he was a little boy.

"I can always tell when you've gotten yourself into trouble, Sammy," his mother would admonish with a winsome smile. "You start yanking away at that head of yours. Keep it up and you're gonna be as bald as grandpa! You won't have a lick of hair left!"

Of course, Sam's mother had been wrong. His hair was still lush and thick, though it was sprinkled with a lot more gray than when he started this bothersome habit thirty-eight years ago. Sam raked his fingers through his hair once more before donning his cap, taking a shaky breath, and steeling himself for the task ahead. He climbed the first step, then the second. The porch light to the left of the door flickered on. If the motion-detection light or his heavy footfalls hadn't woken Janelle Marshall, then his knocking certainly would.

He knocked on the front door then waited a beat. He knocked again.

"Mammoth Falls Police Department!" he shouted, gazing at the darkness beyond the living room curtains. "Miss Marshall?"

No one came to the door, though he knew she was home. Her rental car was still in the driveway.

"Shit," Sam muttered before knocking a third time. "I hate doing this."

It was, by far, the worst part of the job. Even his father, if he were still alive, would probably agree. (Though, frankly, they hadn't agreed on much of anything else.)

The old man had been on the force for almost forty years before he finally endured retirement by death, having a heart attack at his desk one morning and collapsing onto his desk calendar, knocking his bagel to the floor. Sam had been a police officer himself or worked in jobs related to law enforcement for almost half that time. Sam had heard at the family dinner table and seen in the course of his career just about everything small town crime had to offer, from bored teenagers who decided to hold up the local Stop 'n' Go with BB guns, to the town pastor and church secretary running away together with twenty thousand dollars' worth of parishioner donations, to a tough so violent and cranked up on meth that it had taken five officers and a Taser to finally get him down to the ground. But one story Sam never wanted to hear or share with others was that of the late-night visits to a victim's home to tell a family about their loved one.

There was nothing that gripped your heart with cold fingers quite like finding a police officer standing on your welcome mat at two o'clock in the morning, looking grave. And for a cop there was no worst agony than watching a mourning father as he sobbed uncontrollably or a mother fainting to a hallway floor. Sam hated it. He'd rather get bitten by a million fire ants. He'd rather get a kick squarely to the balls than to have to be the bearer of bad news, the grim reaper in a police uniform. But there was no getting around it tonight.

"A man's gotta buck up and do his job," as his dad would say.

Little Bill's car had been found a little more than two hours ago. Sam and a few of the other officers had already examined the scene and done accident reconstruction. They had a rough idea of what had happened before the crash but still didn't know what happened after. Of course, the number one question was "Where the hell is Bill?" With the exception of what looked like his boot prints in the snow not too far from the wrecked F-150, Bill had left no trace; not even a smattering of blood on the ground.

Sam had to tell Janelle all of this. He also had to ask her a few questions before the police department started contacting other agencies for assistance, though Sam still wasn't exactly sure what they would be assisting. Was this a missing person case? A kidnapping? A homicide? Hell, was it a *hoax?* That crazy coot wouldn't pretend to get in an accident and disappear just to keep his granddaughter from getting engaged, would he?

Sam had tried to explain as much to Mayor Pruitt during his drive to Bill's cabin. News had already traveled to Pruitt's ears via a leak in the police department. (Sam had no idea who it was, though he had money on either Sergeant Bachmann, who had discovered the deserted vehicle, or Sergeant Yates, who was a notorious gossip.)

"I don't care *why* Bill is missing. I just need you boys to find him ASAP, Sammy, do you hear me? *ASAP!*" Pruitt had said over the phone in a pompous tone he was notorious for. "We can't have something like this distracting from the festival. The town has put a lot of time and money into this, and we need those dividends. There's no reason why we can't compete with Rapid City or Deadwood when it comes to tourism. This is our chance, Sam. The festival *has* to be a success!"

Sam had wanted to tell Pruitt that he didn't give a damn about the festival, and whether it was a dud or a hit had nothing to do with Little Bill's disappearance, but he thought better of it. He kept those thoughts to himself.

"Of course, we'll put all our resources toward this, sir," he had said icily, deciding to leave it at that. "We'll try our best to find him."

"Well, keep me updated, Sam. You damn well keep me updated! You hear me?"

Finally, Sam saw a light turn on inside the cabin. A shadowy figure drifted past the window. A few seconds later, Janelle swung open the front door, and when he saw her, Sam got a kick to the gut. He had to blink to clear his vision. He could swear it was his ex-wife, Gabriela, standing in the doorway, wearing nothing but an oversized blue t-shirt and a parka with her long, golden legs glistening under the orange glow of the porch light.

It's not Gabby, damn it, he thought indignantly. *When are you going to get that through your thick head?*

Sam blinked again and, mercifully, Gabriela disappeared. Only Janelle stood in front of him, looking like she had just climbed out of bed.

"Sam?" She yawned, shoved her hair back over her shoulder, and wiped her eyes with the heels of her hands. "What are you doing here? What . . . what time is it?"

He didn't respond. Instead he cleared his throat. She gazed up at him quizzically. When she saw his dour expression and his hands clasped in front of him like a pallbearer at a funeral, her face changed. She knew this was not a social visit. The haze of sleep cleared her eyes.

"Something's wrong, isn't it?" she asked in a shaky voice.

Sam slowly nodded. "It's Bill, Janelle."

"Pops?" She took a step back. "W-what happened?"

"I'm sorry to tell you, but we found Bill's truck off of Highway 85 and—"

"Oh, God. Oh, God!" Her eyes went wide and bright. She

wobbled slightly, like someone had given her a hard shove. Her hand shot out and she reached for the door frame to steady herself.

Here it comes, Sam thought. His stomach tightened. He extended his arms to catch her before she fell to the cabin's hardwood floor.

The flailing and hysterics would come next. That's certainly what her doppelgänger, Gabriela, would do in this situation. Gabby didn't keep any of her feelings on the inside: not her highs and certainly not her lows. At her worst, she would sob, scream, and kick. Once, when he was late home to dinner, she actually threw a platter of churrasco at him before running into the bathroom and slamming the door shut. She had wept and refused to come out of their master bath for almost two hours.

"Latin women," a guy had joked back in Virginia when Gabby had had a full meltdown at one of their mutual friends' engagement parties. "They sure are fiery, huh?"

He had then elbowed Sam in the rib cage before guffawing like a jackass.

But Sam knew what the bigoted party guest did not. Gabby didn't make scenes and sob in the corner of their bedroom at night because she was Latina. The woman that Sam had loved and adored was "crazier than a shithouse rat," according to his dad. Or more accurately, she had bipolar-1 disorder, according to the doctors who had diagnosed her at Washington Hospital Medical Center, where she was admitted after several sleep-deprived nights and having an epic "episode" at the Brazilian embassy where she worked—slapping one of the receptionists who told her to calm down after she kept yelling about phantom children playing in the embassy's corridor. Gabriela had gone untreated for years.

When the doctor had uttered the words "bipolar disorder"— saying them slowly as he read from a file folder covered with multicolored tabs—Sam had accepted the diagnosis almost with relief.

So now the beast had a name, he had thought.

"Name it and claim it, son," his mother, the granddaughter of a bible-thumping Pentecostal minister, would often say to him while she was alive.

The doctors knew what was wrong with Gabriela and they could cure her, or at least help her manage the disease. They would give back Sam the old Gabby—or so he had thought. Looking back on that day at the hospital, he could only laugh at his naïveté.

Stupid Sam. Stupid, stupid Sam.

Sam now grabbed Janelle's shoulders to pull her upright. He watched with surprise as she shoved his hands away.

"No, I'm . . . I'm okay," she said, her voice still shaking slightly.

"Are you sure?"

"I'm fine." She closed her eyes and breathed in and out. She placed her hand on her stomach. Even her hand was trembling. "Just . . . just give me a minute."

Sam stepped back. *Remember . . . this isn't Gabby*, he told himself.

He got yet another reminder that this wasn't his ex-wife when Janelle stopped her Lamaze breathing and opened her eyes. Dark brown irises stared back at him—not the tortured hazel eyes Gabby would flash when she was in the midst of one of her manic episodes or when she was in the depths of a depression so low that the ocean floor seemed above her head.

He watched as Janelle pushed back her shoulders and looked up at him. Her demeanor was resigned yet stoic. At that moment, she seemed like a strong reed in a raging river—she might bend under the weight of the current, but she wouldn't break.

"Tell me what happened," Janelle said calmly. "Is Pops all

right? Is he . . . dead?" she asked, her voice cracking a little at the end.

"We don't know," Sam answered honestly.

"You don't know?" Her mouth twisted liked she tasted something sour. "What the hell . . . what do you mean you don't know?" She pushed herself away from the door frame, dropped her hands to her hips, and glared up at him. "What the hell kind of answer is that? Either my grandfather is alive or not! Just tell me!"

"I would if I could, but it's not that simple." Sam looked over her shoulder. "Look, can I come inside? I'll tell you everything we know so far, but I'd rather do it in there than out here."

"Why can't you just talk to me here?"

"Well, it's freezing, for one, and all you've got on are a coat and a t-shirt."

She glanced down at herself and looked chagrined, like she had just realized what she was wearing. She abruptly closed her parka, clutching the zipper in both hands.

"I left my robe back home," she muttered.

"And I have a few things I need to ask you. It won't take long."

Janelle paused. Her eyes followed the path of his gaze to the cabin's living room, then she turned back to him.

She was reluctant to let him inside, and he suspected it wasn't just because the news about her grandfather had knocked her off kilter. She had been reluctant to let him inside the cabin yesterday, too. When Sam thought about it, he realized she always seemed wary around him.

This was yet another difference between Janelle and Gabriela. When he first met Gabby at a crowded coffee shop in D.C., she had been overly friendly and talkative. She had practically flopped down at his bistro table, grabbed his newspaper, and started eating part of his multigrain muffin. Her accent had been so thick that he could barely make out what she was saying or the questions she was asking, but he was charmed by her. He didn't know what to make of the beautiful, foreign woman who would not shut up and acted as if they had known each other forever.

In stark contrast, Janelle was now staring at him guardedly and acting as if she wasn't sure if she should slam the door in his face and break out her rape whistle. And this was *after* Janelle had spoken to him several times.

"You can trust me," he said softly, hoping to alleviate any fears she might have. "I'm a cop."

She laughed. "Respectfully . . . that doesn't mean anything, Sam. There are cops out there that are scarier than guys without a badge."

He raised his brows, shocked into silence. "Well," he said, licking his lips, "you're right . . . I guess. But I'm not one of those cops."

"I know, but . . . but . . ." She hesitated again.

"I'm just here to help, Janelle."

Finally, she eased the door farther open with a slow creak and stepped aside, waving him over the threshold.

Sam followed her inside the cabin and shut the door behind him. Warmth swept over him like an incoming tide, snuffing out the chill from the outdoors. Sam took off his cap, lowered the zipper of his jacket, and began to remove his leather gloves.

He glanced around him and spotted a rolling leather suitcase sitting a few feet away from the door. Her Coach tote bag was perched on top of the suitcase. Neither had been sitting there the last time Sam had been in the cabin. Was she leaving?

"You can have a seat," Janelle murmured, gesturing to one of the lumpy plaid sofa cushions. "Would you give me a second to get dressed? I have a feeling that when I hear this, I want to be wearing pants."

He gave a half smile and nodded. "Sure. Take all the time you need."

She didn't return his smile. Instead she turned with head bowed and walked down the short hallway to the Little Bill's bedroom.

Twenty-five minutes later, Janelle sat in the armchair facing Sam with her knees together and her elbows perched on her thighs. She was in the same t-shirt from earlier, though it was now paired with silk pajama pants covered with little red hearts with arrows through them. Two cooling cups of French roast coffee sat untouched on the oak coffee table between her and Sam.

"So Pops is still missing," she whispered, staring at her clutched hands.

Sam had already told her about finding the badly damaged truck on the edge of a ravine off Cedar Lane. He had also told her about the boot prints in the snow leading away from the crash.

"We haven't found him, but the good news is that at least we know Bill survived the wreck. We know he was up and walking."

"Yeah, but its *freezing* out there! It was . . . what? . . . barely ten degrees last night. Even the healthiest person could die from hypothermia or blood loss, and Pops is an old man."

"He's old but he's *strong*, Janelle," Sam argued. "He's stronger than most."

"I mean . . . just look out there!" She gazed over her shoulder toward the dark night outside of the living room window as if she hadn't heard him. "Pops could be dead already."

Her voice choked and her eyes began to water. She looked away from the window and back at her interlocked fingers.

"Hey," Sam said, reaching out and holding her hands within his.

Her hands were warm and supple. When he touched them, he felt his stomach twist in knots again, but this time for a very different reason, one that unnerved him. Sam dropped her hands—like he had been zapped with a painful low-voltage charge. He cleared his throat and sat upright in his chair.

"We don't know that for sure," he said, taking on a more formal tone that seemed befitting a police chief. "Bill could still be alive. Don't you think the worst now."

Her jaw tightened. "No offense, Sam, but frankly it doesn't sound like you and your men know much of *anything*. You don't know where he is! You don't know what condition he's in! Why should I have any confidence at all in what you're saying? Why the hell shouldn't I think the worst?"

Anger. He had expected as much. Being angry was a normal reaction in a situation like this when one felt so powerless, but Sam couldn't help but find it frustrating that her anger was directed at him.

"Because until we know something, no one should jump to any conclusions, and that includes you. Until we find Bill's body, I'm going with the notion that he's still alive, and you should, too."

She stared at him for a long while before finally nodding. "You're right. You're right. I'm . . . I'm sorry."

"There's no need to apologize. You—"

"No, I was wrong. I should apologize. You're only trying to help. I know that. It's just . . . I thought Pops was okay. I came here believing he was lost in the mountains somewhere and needed my help, and then Connie told me he was fine, that this was Pops's stupid ploy to mess up my engagement. So I was pissed at him but relieved that he was all right. Now I'm being told that isn't true, either. He's back to being missing again and . . ." She swept a hand over her face, looking fatigued. "It's all just a lot to take in, you know?"

"I know. But I need you to hold it together, because we'll need your help if we're going to find Bill."

Her face lit up and she sat erect. "Sure! Of course. Anything you need!" She nodded eagerly. "Just tell me what you want me to do."

"Tell me when was the last time you talked to Bill. Tell me exactly what he said. And I'll need a physical description of him. Any birthmarks, tattoos, or details that would stand out and help anyone spot him. We could come up with a description ourselves, but you're his granddaughter, so . . ."

"No, I can do that." Janelle nodded again. "Absolutely!"

"We'll hand it out to the trackers and the other officers and deputies. Give me a few good pictures you have of Bill, too. Two or three of them would be best."

"I can do that. I can do that! Just let me . . . wait!" Janelle rose from the armchair. She started to pace around the living room, shifting aside random items like a stack of magazines and a dinner plate covered in crumbs. She scanned the space like she was searching for something. He watched her as she did it, his eyes locking onto the way the silk of her pajama pants swayed around her legs, outlining the shadowy imprint of her hips and thighs.

"It's around here somewhere," she mumbled under her breath, standing on the balls of her feet as she checked the top of the brick fireplace mantle.

Sam's focus raised by several inches. He noticed for the first time that Janelle wasn't wearing a bra beneath her t-shirt. Her breasts undulated with her jerky movements as she searched. Her nipples jutted proudly against the thin cotton fabric in a way that was so unwittingly provocative—like a lace thong peaking over the waistband of a pair of jeans or bra strap dangling off a shoulder—that he wanted to avert his eyes, but couldn't.

Janelle snapped her fingers, catching Sam by surprise. His gaze shifted away from her breasts guiltily.

"I know where it is! Jesus, where is my head lately?" she murmured before scampering across the room to her tote bag.

He watched as she dug into the bag's depths and then pulled out her iPad. "I don't have any photos in my wallet, but I have a few digital ones on here," she said as she typed her password onto the glass screen. "I could print them out or send you a file."

"That would help." He kept his focus on her face as he spoke, ordering himself not to drift any lower than that. "Send me whatever you've got. And I'm going to need you to stay in town for a little bit longer." He glanced meaningfully at her suitcase leaning against the wall near the door. "Can you stick around for a while just in case we have any other questions or need anything else from you?"

Janelle paused. She lowered her iPad to her side and gradually nodded. "Yes. Of . . . of course."

He frowned. "Is something wrong?"

"No," she said a little too loudly. She tapped the iPad restlessly against her thigh. "It's just . . . ."

"Just what?"

Her shoulders slumped. "I already called Mark and told him that I was taking a flight home tomorrow, so he made reservations at a restaurant and plans for something big . . . something important to him . . . I mean, to *us,*" she quickly added. She laughed softly.

He could tell from the mortified expression on her face that she knew how strange she sounded, comparing an elderly man lost in the woods to dinner reservations and "big plans." But she forged ahead anyway.

"It's just . . . I've disappointed him before. I feel like I'm disappointing him all over again."

Sam raised an eyebrow. Frankly, the more he heard about this Mark fellow, the more he wondered if Bill was right in not liking him.

"Well, I hope your boyfriend would tell you," Sam began in a measured voice, trying his best to hide his budding distaste for a man he had never met, "not to worry about any of that stuff and just do what you have to do to help find your grand-father. In fact, I hope he would be on the next flight out here to sit with you as we do our search. He should be by your side, holding your hand while you go through this."

"Of course, he will! That's . . . that's totally what he'll do! I'm just being silly." She fussily waved her hand. For a brief moment, the ghost of another expression darted across her face: appre-hension and maybe even a little fear. She blotted out both. "I'll tell Mark everything and he'll . . . he'll come."

"Good," Sam said before pulling a four-by-six-inch notebook from one of his jacket's interior pockets along with a ballpoint pen. He flipped it open to a blank page. "Now let's get started."

PART II

"Not until we are lost, do we begin to understand ourselves."

—Henry David Thoreau

CHAPTER 11

Tuesday, April 22
Somewhere

Little Bill woke up to the sensation of pain so bright and exquisite that he almost screamed as soon as he opened his eyes.
But he couldn't scream. All he could emit was a long, tortured
groan from his parched throat and lips. And he didn't open his
eyes, either, so much as feel his lids flutter slightly as sparse shafts
of light filtered through his lashes.

Besides the pain, he felt the light weight of sheets thrown
across his body and a pillow beneath his head—which was not
what he had expected. The last sensation he had had was cold
asphalt and melting snow beneath his cheek when he crumbled
to the ground from exhaustion after dragging his sorry ass out of
his truck and up that rocky hill. He could remember walking
then crawling a few yards or maybe twenty feet . . . or maybe
two miles, for all he knew. He also remembered that damn dog
with the big brown eyes, gazing down at him and panting stale
doggy breath into his face.

"Go . . . go get help," he had rasped to the dog, who had inclined its head and stared at him blankly.

A Lassie it was not.

"Well, if you ain't gonna get help, then don't just stand there looking stupid!" he had shouted before roughly shoving the dog's muzzle and then going limp.

Little Bill obviously wasn't on that roadway anymore. It was obvious, too, that he wasn't dead and in heaven, because he knew he could expect to find Mabel standing over him, yanking back the covers, and telling him, "Get up, Bill! The day is wasting, honey! We've got a lot of catching up to do."

So where am I, Mabel?

For once, she didn't answer him.

He willed his senses to focus, to climb above the pain, so that he could figure out this mystery.

In addition to the sheets and pillow, he felt heat—a warm, toasty heat. Was he in a hospital? He listened for the distinct sound of beeps from a monitor or the shuffling of rubber-soled shoes across linoleum tile but heard neither. Instead he heard the drone of a distant television, then a laugh track. He heard a dog barking. He heard a door opening, the ring of glasses knocking together, and a door slamming shut.

Little Bill sniffed the air like a hound locking onto a scent. It didn't smell like a hospital, either. He detected no bleached surfaces or penicillin or the stale odor of the sick and dying. Instead he smelled dirty carpet and a musky fragrance that belonged in the wilds of the Amazon or the back of a smoke-filled van where long-haired hippies lounged around singing "Kumbaya" or whatever the hell hippies usually did.

Reefer, Little Bill thought with shock. *Is that really what I smell?*

"*I do believe so, honey,*" his wife finally answered.

He could sense movement in his periphery. Something was coming toward him from his left. It got closer and closer, and then he felt a heavy weight plop onto the center of his chest, making him groan again in agony. He heard the purring next, then the soft flap of slippers rushing toward him.

Little Bill felt something soft and furry flick across his nose and cheek. Was it a tail? He tried futilely to raise his arms and swat the cat off his chest but the most he could achieve was a slight rocking from side to side, causing the bedsprings to emit a barely audible squeak underneath him.

"Mikey Gordon, you get off of that man!" a woman whispered shrilly.

Little Bill felt the cat being removed from his chest. It meowed loudly in protest.

"He's not feeling well. That's not how we take care of our patients," the woman admonished.

Patients? So he was at a hospital?

Little Bill gathered all the will he could muster to force his eyes open, at least for a few seconds. When he did, he was greeted by the sight of a skinny, middle-aged woman with long, strawlike blond hair adjusting a multicolored quilt at his feet. The cat—a fat gray Persian—sat on the floor, grooming itself and purring softly. The space was dimly lit but with what little Bill could see, he knew that the room was filthy. Two towering piles of dirty clothes sat in the corner opposite the cat. A bedsheet was held over the room's only window with masking tape. On the walls around Bill were several band posters with names like "The Grateful Dead" and "Phish." Another poster, old and water-stained at the edges, featured a glowing marijuana leaf.

When the woman finished adjusting the quilt, she glanced up at Bill. Her brown eyes damn near popped out of their sockets. She snapped upright when she realized he was staring at her.

"Holy shit!" she gasped before yelling over her shoulder. "Hey, doc! Doc! Come in here! He's awake!"

Little Bill heard the heavy thump of footsteps. He gazed over the woman's shoulder. Staggering into the room was a scrawny guy with wild gray hair, wearing sagging gray sweatpants and a stained t-shirt that barely covered his pot belly.

"Doc," the woman said, clapping her hands, "I think he's finally on the mend!"

Who the hell is he?

"I don't rightly know," Mabel answered back, seeming even more bemused than Bill.

This man didn't look like any damn doctor that Bill had ever met. He watched as the guy pushed smudged glasses up the bridge of his nose and leaned in close to Bill's face. When the man smiled, he revealed a gap between his front teeth as wide as a thimble.

"Far *out!*" Doc exclaimed just before Little Bill lost the battle to keep his eyes open and faded into blackness once again.

CHAPTER 12

SILVER ALERT
William Clancy Marshall
Missing: *4/20/16*
Age Disappeared: *78*
Sex: *Male*
Race: *Black*
Hair: *Bald*
Eyes: *Brown*
Height: *5'4"*
Weight: *140*
Missing From: *Mammoth Falls, S.D.*
County: *Lawrence County*
Narrative: *A South Dakota Silver Alert has been issued for William Clancy Marshall. He was last seen wearing a red, white, and blue Pabst cap, blue flannel shirt, denim jeans, and brown leather cowboy boots. He also responds to the nickname "Little Bill." He may be showing early signs of dementia.*

He was last seen April 20, 2016. His vehicle was later found at 8:30 p.m. April 22 in the area of Cedar Lane in

Mammoth Falls, S.D. The vehicle appeared to have been in an accident and was abandoned. Marshall has not been seen or heard from since this accident.

If you have any information regarding his whereabouts, please contact the Mammoth Falls Police Department at 605-555-5973 or 911.

"Can I help you, ma'am?" the plump woman behind the counter asked.

Janelle turned away from the corkboard where her grandfather's image stared back at her. Beside his Silver Alert notice was a flyer for a used cobalt blue Acura and a note handwritten in black marker, advertising a room available for rent in nearby Spearfish. Two stubs below the advertisement had already been pulled.

"I'm sorry . . . what? What did she say?" Janelle asked absently, blinking in confusion.

The woman gave her an indulgent smile. "I asked if I could help you."

"Oh, yes! Yes! Thank you." She placed her tote bag on the linoleum countertop and began to dig through it. She raised her gaze from her the bag's depths and grinned apologetically. "I'm sorry. It's . . . It's in here."

The woman nodded. Benevolent understanding painted her round, dimpled face. But Janelle wondered if the other people in the post office were quite as patient. An older guy with a graying buzz cut who stood behind Janelle loudly cleared his throat as he shifted a large stack of USPS priority mail boxes in his arms. A woman standing in line behind him handed her bored toddler a roll of shipping tape to play with. The little boy was now taping his arm to one of the metal bars of his stroller.

Truthfully, she was growing just as impatient with herself. It was like she was digging through someone else's tote bag. When had she accumulated so many receipts, tubes of lipstick, and so much loose change? How had her bag become littered with so much junk? Usually, she was much more organized, but that had fallen to the wayside the past couple of days.

"Here it is!" Janelle cried triumphantly, almost with relief. She tugged out a pink sheet of paper. "I saw this on the door yesterday. It said one of your carriers tried to deliver a certified letter to my grandfather's cabin but no one was there to sign for it. I was wondering if I could pick it up for him. Umm . . ." Janelle began to search through her tote bag again. She pulled out her wallet and flipped it open. "I can give you my ID if that—"

"That won't be necessary, honey," the woman behind the counter said.

Janelle looked up at her.

"You keep your ID. You don't need it to get a certified letter." The woman extended her hand across the counter and gently petted Janelle's arm, catching her by surprise. "Besides, we know who you are."

We?

Janelle slowly turned and found the older man behind her and the woman behind him staring at her. Unconcealed pity was in their eyes.

Janelle supposed she should be used to it by now. When she had arrived in Mammoth Falls four days ago, almost everyone she had met had stared at her warily, suspicious of the outsider. But now that news had spread about her grandfather's disappearance, she couldn't go anywhere around town without words of sympathy from random strangers or someone gazing at her sadly, like she was one of those poor, starving, doe-eyed kids on the Save the Children commercials.

Instead of making her feel accepted, it made her feel even more alone. Mark couldn't get here soon enough. She needed his presence for reassurance. Thank God his flight was supposed to arrive in Rapid City by 4:45 p.m. tomorrow.

"We're all praying for Little Bill," the woman behind the counter said. "We hope they find him out there."

"Thank you."

"My grandmother wandered off about two years ago," the woman with the toddler suddenly piped.

Her little boy had now shifted his attention from taping his arm to his stroller to wrapping his head like a bandaged mummy.

"She's got Alzheimer's, kind of like Little Bill," the woman continued, pushing her dark sunglasses to the crown of her head and adjusting her zebra-print diaper bag on her shoulder. "When the cops found her, she told them she thought it was 1968. She had hopped in the car and was headed to Montgomery Ward to pick up a new vacuum cleaner and a duster. I had to tell her that store had shut down almost fifteen years ago."

"It's a shame when old folks go soft in the head," the man with the buzz cut murmured behind his goatee.

The plump woman nodded and then made a sorrowful *tsk, tsk* sound.

Janelle's lips tightened.

Besides Pops's absence, the second hardest part of this whole ordeal was that everyone in town was now under the mistaken belief that Pops had Alzheimer's or had gone "soft in the head." And the mistaken belief was all because of one line in the Silver Alert that Janelle wished they would have never included: "He may be showing early signs of dementia."

"We'll keep it in there just as a precaution," Sam had assured her after she accidentally let it slip that Pops still talked to Nana, who was long dead, and sometimes he forgot things like where he put his keys and whether it was Wednesday or Thursday. "We'll say that Little Bill *may be* showing signs of dementia. That doesn't mean he has it. It doesn't mean he doesn't have it, either. We're just telling the people who are looking for him to be prepared."

But now Pops was transformed in the eyes of Mammoth Falls residents from the outgoing little guy with the big personality to a doddering old man who was wandering around in the forest, confused about where he was and who he was. It was something that would mortify her grandfather, who boasted about not wearing adult diapers or walking with a cane.

"I ain't as old as I look, baby girl," he would say with a grin.

"I'd . . . like that letter now," Janelle said as she pulled her arm from under the woman's hand. She then slid the notice toward her, ignoring the well-intentioned though thoughtless words of those around her.

The woman behind the counter nodded. "Of course, honey. I'll get it for you right away."

Five minutes later, Janelle was still trembling with indignation as she walked down the sidewalk, passing several festival tents on her way back to her car. Her cell phone began to chime, and she yanked it out her purse. She read the name on the screen and rolled her eyes.

"Hello, Lydia," she answered flatly.

"Hi, Janelle! Glad I caught you!" the assistant HR director said on the other end of the line. She sounded tense, but frankly the woman always seemed mildly high strung. "Uh, I was wondering if you got my email about those *really* important forms that need your signature. They were due *today* and—"

"Yes, I got your email. I had meant to turn in the forms early, but I didn't get a chance to do it before I left. I'd planned to download them here and sign them again, but I—"

Pop, pop, pop!

The sound of gunfire echoed around her. Janelle screamed and dropped her tote bag to the ground.

"Oh, my God, Janelle, is everything okay?" Lydia cried.

Janelle whipped around, clutching her chest in alarm, only to find three men aiming black plastic pistols at a red-and-white bulls-eyes twelve feet away. A woman was laughing and screaming gaily beside them, clapping her hands. A painted scene of the Great Plains was behind the targets, showing the rolling hills, bison, and wagon trains.

"Goddamnit!" Janelle yelled, reaching down and grabbing her tote bag from the sidewalk. Some of the festival goers looked at her uneasily, like *she* was the one toting a pistol. She took a deep breath. "Yes, I'm fine. Sorry. It's just . . . stuff going on here." She shook her head in exasperation. "I'm sorry. What was I saying?"

"You . . . umm . . . you said you had planned to sign the forms," Lydia repeated back to her.

"Yes! Yes, I had planned to sign them, but I didn't get to do it before I left. Do you think maybe you could send me a digital copy and I can sign it here and email it back?"

"Umm, well, I . . . I guess I can. I'm not really that familiar with that document system though. The last time I did it, the system crashed. Remember? Do you think you could just . . . I don't know . . . print the documents out and overnight them to me instead?"

"Lydia, the only printer and scanner around here that I can use is at the nearest Kinko's and that's almost thirty miles away . . . I think. I haven't had the chance to hunt it down yet." She shoved her hand into her frizzy curls. "I haven't had the chance to hunt down *anything*. I can't find any decent hair care products. I can't even find a Laundromat around here. I'm running out of clean underwear!"

Lydia paused. "I'm sorry, Janelle. I'm not following. What about clean underwear?"

"Who's the fastest gun in the West?" the man standing behind the counter ten feet away shouted. "Take your mark, gentlemen! Now . . . fire!"

Pop, pop, pop!

Janelle jumped again at the sound. "Goddamnit!"

Her trembling was getting worse. She could feel herself fraying at the edges. "Look, Lydia, let me call you back. This is a . . . bad time."

"Umm, okay," Lydia said in a squeaky voice, sounding panicked herself. "B-but can you tell me when you'll send the—"

Janelle hung up. She spotted her Jetta and fled toward it like it was the last helicopter leaving Saigon. She climbed inside her car and shut the door behind her.

"Breathe in, breathe out," she whispered. But the deep breathing exercises weren't working anymore. Maybe it was the altitude; the air was too thin up here.

She had to find her grandfather. She had to find him and get out of this godforsaken small town or she would go nuts.

I can do this, she told herself as she tugged the certified envelope out of her tote bag. *He's not lost and he's not "soft in the head." And I'll prove it.*

The instant she had seen the certified mail notice on Pops's cabin door yesterday afternoon, she had felt of rush of adrenaline.

It could be a clue, her hysterical mind had screamed. *Maybe it could tell us where Pops is or what happened to him!*

Maybe her grandfather had managed to get an encoded letter past his kidnappers that had directions to the secret location where he was hidden. Or maybe he had pre-mailed her a note before his disappearance.

"Dear baby girl," it would say, *"if this letter reaches you, then you are now in Mammoth Falls and the police think that I am*

missing. Just know that I am alive and well and I will be return-ing home very soon."

Janelle realized how ridiculous those scenarios sounded. She knew she was grasping at straws that were so flimsy they would break in two in her strong grip, but helplessness made her willing to grasp at anything that gave her a vague sense of hope. And this letter felt like a reason to hope and her first op-portunity to truly *do* something besides waiting and praying.

Though she had been prepared to stagger through snow and brush, she had been "strongly discouraged" (those were the exact words the cops had used) from participating in the search. Almost a dozen trackers with dogs, snowmobiles, and ATVs were now in mountains surrounding the town, sniffing every burrow and tree trunk searching for some sign of her grandfa-ther.

"If we get too many people—too many feet on the ground—it's going to hinder more than help," Sam had explained when she pleaded with him to let her look, too. "It's tracking 101, Janelle. If we've got one hundred kindhearted but clueless folks stomping around out there, trampling evidence, it's going to mess up the trail."

So she watched from afar as a myriad of SUVs and trucks from the Lawrence County Search and Rescue to the Deadwood Police Department paraded into Mammoth Falls, drawing more thunderstruck onlookers than if the Ringling Bros. Barnum & Bailey Circus had come to town. And during the day, Janelle could swear she could hear their engines revving and the dogs barking in the woods just an acre or so away from her grandfa-ther's cabin. She could hear the sound of the helicopters hov-ering overhead. She yearned to be out there rather than sitting by the phone, hoping that Pops would finally call her back or that he would step through the cabin door at any second.

Janelle set the certified envelope on the car horn and tugged off her leather gloves.

She suspected now that the real reason why Sam didn't want her out there wasn't because it would compromise the search but because the cops were no longer looking for Pops, but for his body. She had seen enough episodes of *Disappeared* to know that if a missing person wasn't found in the first forty-eight hours, the likelihood of their survival was almost zero. Pops could already be dead, and there would be nothing worse than his own granddaughter stumbling upon his decaying remains.

Still, it felt wrong, almost disrespectful, to sit around waiting. She owed Pops more than that.

Her eyes scanned the certified envelope's address label, making her frown. The letter was from MetLife Insurance. No encoded message. No dispatch sent from her grandfather's Caribbean hideaway. Her mind spun off in yet another wild direction, her thoughts scampering after another enticing trail of bread crumbs as she began to rip open the envelope.

Insurance . . . insurance money! That would enough motivation to make someone disappear, wouldn't it?

Maybe her grandfather had changed beneficiaries or added a new name. Maybe Pops had been coerced into doing it—plied with glasses of whiskey and a tale of woe. Then within days of signing on the dotted line his battered truck appeared on the side of a ravine . . . his *empty* battered truck. He'd be declared missing and then declared legally dead and someone in town would be six figures richer.

But who would he add as his beneficiary? Pops wouldn't do that with any random person, would he? No, he was impetuous but not stupid. Would he add his new wife?

Connie, you sneaky bitch, Janelle thought as her heart rate picked up its pace and she flipped the letter open with a one-two shake. *It makes perfect sense!*

She had suspected Connie might be behind this all along, hadn't she? From the moment she had walked into Toby's Bar & Grill and saw Connie sitting at the table with her low-cut top and "Buddy" tattoo, she had known Connie was nothing but trouble or, at least, not a woman to be trusted.

What could someone like Connie possibly see in an almost-eighty-year-old man anyway?

Nothing but dollar signs, Janelle thought with a contemptuous snort.

Connie had suckered Pops into thinking they had a real re-lationship, enticing him with a web of deceit and seduction, and then finally she had trapped him like a black widow spider in hip huggers. Maybe she had one of her trucker ex-boyfriends do her dirty work.

"Take care of the old man for me and I'll split the money with you fifty-fifty," Janelle could imagine the scene playing out like something straight out of a 1950s film noir.

Janelle paused.

But then again, Connie did seem distraught about Pops's ab-sence. Janelle had watched the normally outspoken woman grow quieter and more pensive with each passing day. She'd listlessly stare out of windows and would lunge for her cell phone, shouting "Bill?" only to slam down her phone when the person on the other end proved not to be him.

Connie wasn't that good of an actress, was she?

And when Sam had gone to Connie's shop with Janelle in tow to ask her more questions about the disappearance and the details of what had happened that night, making Connie retell her part of the story, it had been painful to watch Connie stut-ter and stumble her way through her answers.

"So Bill made you call Janelle?" Sam had asked her, inclin-ing his head and writing on a notepad as he spoke.

"Well . . . umm, yeah . . . I mean, no," Connie had said. Her eyes had gone unfocused again. She had gazed over Sam's shoulder at the Main Street sidewalk, peering at the faces of passersby.

He had squinted at her, seeming a lot less like a good ol' country boy and more like a hard-nosed cop at that moment. "Is that a yes or no, Connie?"

Connie had returned her focus back to Sam, ripping her gaze away from the store window. "I mean yes, he asked me to call her, but he dialed the number. I had never called her before."

"And then he gave you his phone?"

Connie had tiredly raised her hand to her brow and closed her dark eyes. The lids had been pink and threaded with blue capillaries. Her eyes had seemed to jitter beneath the lids. "Yes, Sam."

"And he told you exactly what to say before he did it?"

She had loudly groused and gripped the glass counter. "Yes," she had replied tightly, making Sam lower his notepad and stare at her.

"What's wrong, Connie?"

"There's nothing wrong. I just told you five hundred times what happened. He told me to lie to her to get her to come here! I don't understand why I have to tell you again!"

"You have to tell me because a man has gone missing. This is serious, Connie. We can't—"

"Don't you think I know that?" Connie had shouted. "Goddamnit, I know Bill is missing! I know it! I feel it!" She pressed a hand to her chest. "I feel it every time I take a . . . I take a breath!"

Sam had pursed his lips and lowered his notepad.

"You wanna know what he told me?"

She had abruptly walked behind the sales counter, bent down, opened a door, and pulled out her fringed leather purse.

She had plopped it on the glass top and a tube of lip balm fell out before rolling across the counter and landing on the floor.

"You wanna know what he told me to say?" She had pulled out a cocktail napkin and slapped it down on the counter like it was a hand in a game of poker. "Right there. That's what he told me to say."

Janelle had leaned forward and saw on the tattered cocktail napkin her grandfather's handwriting—the long skinny t's and the lopsided e's. She had read the words that Connie had said to her the night he disappeared.

"You can have it for your investigation," she had said to Sam, giving him the once-over. "But you better give it back when you're done. It's the last thing I have from Bill."

Janelle held her breath as she read the insurance letter's salutation.

Dear Mr. Marshall,

Thank you for being a valued customer of MetLife insurance.

We are writing to inform you of some of our coverage options changes that you will have effective Jan 1, 2017. We regret to inform you that we are discontinuing your current dental care insurance plan as of Dec. 31, 2016.

We have provided a detailed list of coverage options now available, but recommend a plan on the back of this letter. All options are available for your consideration. You can choose one of these plans at our website. The enrollment process is easy and you won't have to answer any health-related questions!

If you have any additional questions or concerns, please don't hesitate to contact us.

Janelle slowly lowered the sheet of paper. Her mind stopped spinning. The bread crumbs had led to a dead end.

She tore the paper into little pieces and tossed the pieces into the air like confetti, letting it flutter around her. She then dropped her head to the steering wheel and broke down into uncontrollable sobs.

CHAPTER 13

Sam watched as the double doors opened and a stream of men and women flooded out of the conference room. They were dressed in a rainbow of drab hues—tan, navy, gray, brown, green, and black—representing about a dozen police departments and search-and-rescue teams. On all of their faces was the look of sheer exhaustion, and it had been only two days since they started the search for Little Bill. Mind you, it was two days of ceaseless searching—scouring everything within an eight-mile radius of the crash site, all falling between the town limits and Pasque Lake—but still, a mere forty-eight hours. It was essentially the equivalent of a blink in a lifetime.

What if this damn thing drags on for three days . . . four days . . . hell, maybe even a week, Sam thought as his eyes scrutinized their furrowed brows, bowed heads, and austere-set mouths. *What if we never find Little Bill?*

Would their looks of exhaustion eventually give way to that of the downtrodden and broken?

Though his father had annoyed the hell out of him while he was alive with his need for perfection and his controlling ways, it was moments like this that made Sam wish he were more like his old man. If General Patton had been reincarnated, his battle-worn, cantankerous old soul surely would have been dropped into the body of Tom Adler. When he was alive, Sam's dad could inspire (and bully) even the laziest of specimens. He had even gotten Hank to put away the donuts and get a hop in his step while he had worked under him. He also would have kept Mayor Pruitt off his back. Pruitt wouldn't have dared called Tom Adler three times a day for updates on the search or with reminders of "Every day that black codger stays missing— stealing headlines—is another day he takes attention away from what we really need to focus on in this town, Sammy! I was watching KEVN last night and I swear they spent ten whole minutes on a story about Little Bill. How much time did they spend on the festival? A measly *three* minutes!"

Sam could only imagine what his father's response would have been to that observation.

And when that hiker had disappeared near Terry Peak two years ago and the Mammoth Falls Police department had taken the lead in the search, Sam's dad—then police chief— had been the perfect fit for the role of taskmaster and absolute leader. Thanks to Chief Adler they had found the hiker, short one arm but still alive.

But Sam was no Tom Adler—not by a long shot. His usual brand of leadership was the kind that you now found in the self-help book aisles—the type of hardbacks with titles like *Leading from the Back* and *Good Leaders Ask Questions*. The kind of books that would have made his father puke or chuck them onto a log fire.

"The only thing that sissy crap is good for is kindling," his dad would say.

Sam was a cheerleader, not a dictator. He was a consensus builder, not a bully. Even though he was trying his best, he knew he couldn't inspire that same sense of allegiance and determination as his father. He couldn't spur on these beleaguered officers and deputies, especially if his heart wasn't in it. Besides, he still wasn't sure if they were looking for a missing person or just a misguided man who didn't want to be found, who thought he could thwart his granddaughter's engagement by pulling some great disappearing act worthy of Houdini.

I've done my bit in trying to save someone who doesn't want to be saved, and I don't know if I'm up to doing it again.

Of course, Gabby had nothing to do with this, but Sam couldn't help but see the correlation. His ex-wife had wandered around in her own brand of wilderness for years—for *decades*—and when he thought they had finally discovered a way to get her out of those dark woods, she had given up. She had walked away from the rescue beacon with a shrug and waded back into the forest, absolutely infuriating him.

"You don't know what it's like," she had told him after he confronted her about the bottle of Lamictal that sat unopened in her medicine cabinet. "Those things make me . . . a . . . a *zumbi!* They make me dead. At least this way, I'm alive! I am human, Sam!"

As the last officer walked out of the room, Sam turned back around to face the conference room wall where an oversize map hung, showing the ground that they had already canvassed in the Black Hills. Multicolored thumbtacks on the map represented each search team.

Maybe Little Bill doesn't want to be found, Sam thought again as he absently fingered one of the tacks, *and I'm wasting my time all over again.*

"Hey, Chief!" Rita shouted from the doorway, making Sam whip around to face her. "Everyone's grabbing a quick bite to eat. Maybe stop by the festival to grab some pretzels and corn dogs. You want anything?"

Sam shook his head. "Nope, I'm good. Thanks, Rita. Hey, how are those tips coming along?"

In addition to being their office manager and dispatcher, Rita's new job was now fielding calls and gathering tips about

Bill Marshall that came into the police department. They would later be passed onto assisting detectives.

"Good," she said. "We're getting lots of them."

"Any of them sound promising to you?"

She wasn't a cop, but he trusted her opinion.

"Well, there was one that said Bill was being held in an RV in Spearfish by a group of commune hippies. There was another one that said all signs point to him probably being abducted by a UFO."

"Shit," Sam muttered.

"Yeah, pretty much."

"Ah, well, keep at it. I appreciate all your hard work. Enjoy a nice lunch and maybe some cotton candy—on me. You deserve it."

"Thanks, Chief."

He watched as she nodded but didn't budge. Her chipper smile stayed in place. She tucked a blond lock of hair behind her ear that had escaped her ponytail.

Behind her, he could hear the voices of the other officers and deputies filtering their way down the hall. He heard a door open and close and the sound of clanging keys.

"You coming, Rita?" someone called to her.

"Yeah," she said absently over her shoulder, keeping her green eyes focused on Sam, "I'll be right there."

For some reason, she lingered.

They stared at each other. Sam anxiously cleared his throat.

It wasn't often that he and Rita were alone in a room together. He knew he scrupulously avoided it, and he suspected she did, too. Any time they were alone, silences seemed to stretch wider and wider, and the distance between them seemed much shorter. He felt stifled by it.

All because of one mistake, he thought.

Though "the mistake" had happened two years ago, enough time still hadn't passed that he could unflinchingly look Rita in the eyes. That night had been a moment of weakness, the result of his final divorce decree that had arrived in the mail a week prior, and the downward spiral of disappointment, loneliness, and heartbreak he had experienced soon after. Nevertheless, "the mistake" definitely was not recommended in any of the leadership books he kept on his office desk.

To foster a sense of camaraderie, good leaders do not screw their assistants.

He knew he and Rita could never go back to what they had been before "the mistake," even though they both valiantly pretended that everything was normal. They still joked with each other. She still took his lunch order along with the other officers and made him a cup of coffee when he showed up in the mornings. He occasionally asked after Rita's new boyfriend—a car salesman based in Rapid City—and bought Rita one of those bouquets of chocolate-dipped strawberries, pineapples, and cantaloupes for her birthday with a card attached saying, "To the best damn dispatcher and office assistant on this side of the Missouri!" But it was all a façade and right now, it felt like a flimsy one.

"Are you all right, Chief?"

He nodded. "Sure. I'm fine. Why?"

She strolled into the room, and even though she was more than ten feet away, he automatically took a step back, almost bumping into a whiteboard.

"I just hope you aren't driving yourself too hard. You getting enough sleep? You've got to keep your strength up, you know!" She playfully wagged a finger at him. "Can't expect to keep going on a search like this if you're—"

"I'm sleeping fine, Rita," he said, cutting her off. If pretending to be just friends or police chief and dispatcher was trying, enduring her mothering was even worse. "Don't you worry about me."

She inclined her head and gazed at him from an unnervingly

long time, her green eyes a billboard of unspoken emotions. "It's hard not to worry about you," she said softly.

"Rita!" a voice shouted beyond the doorway. "We're hungry as heck! You still coming?"

"I better get going," she murmured before backing toward the door. "Catch you later, Chief. Huh?"

He nodded and watched as she turned and left.

Sam sat in his silent office with his feet propped up on the desk, staring at his phone, contemplating doing something that he hadn't done in almost two and half years. He chewed a stale onion bagel as he mulled over whether to make the call. The bagel was one of the few offerings left in the conference room from that morning's complimentary continental breakfast for the multi-jurisdictional meeting. It was either that or a half-eaten apple danish from Joanna's Bakery that was already starting to crust over. The danish's oozing, sugary filling seemed about as appetizing as feasting on a wad of snot.

Sam's stomach growled in protest as he chewed his bagel, but he ignored it. The bagel would have to do for now. He reached for the phone, paused, pulled his hand back, then reached for the phone again. He finally picked it up and began to dial the number from memory, wondering if it still worked, wondering if the person he remembered would be on the other end.

"Hello?" a male voice answered tentatively after three rings, making Sam grin.

"Hey, Kev," Sam said.

"Holy shit! *Sam?* Is that you! I saw the area code and thought it was a telemarketer! The Fraternal Order of Police or some shit. What's going on, man?"

Sam lowered his feet from his desk and leaned back in his chair. "Not much, Kev. Not much. How the heck you've been?"

He regretted not keeping up with Kevin. When he lived back east, he and Kevin used to be drinking and running buddies.

They were the guys who would exchange meaningful, exasperated looks over their wives' heads as the two women prattled on, ignoring their husbands during double date nights. In fact, they had met through their wives.

Gabby and Kevin's wife, Ingrid, had connected through the diplomatic circuit, when the Brazilian delegation attended one of the parties thrown by the Norwegian embassy. They had become fast friends and so had Sam and Kevin. When Sam spotted Kevin across the room with his side-part haircut and Dockers, drinking a Bud Light with a bemused expression on his face, he had known immediately that Kevin was a kindred spirit. A man cut from the same cloth. They were two Midwestern boys dropped in the dizzying world of foreign relations, politics, and a bunch of snooty folks who looked at them strangely whenever they revealed their humble backgrounds. Sam was a cop from a mountain town in South Dakota and Kevin was an engineer from a sleepy town in Missouri, both with populations less than any of the small enclaves that surrounded D.C. They might as well have announced that they grew up washing in a tin tub and playing the banjo from the reactions they got from people.

But his connection with Kevin was severed once he and Gabby separated. As with most divorces, husbands and wives split their assets, and not all are as tangible as the house, car, and furniture. One of the things Gabby got was their mutual friends, and that included Kevin. When the divorce was finalized, the two men stopped talking, like they had magically forgotten each others' phone numbers and email addresses. It hadn't hurt Sam's feelings. He knew how these things went.

"I'm good! So what's life like out there?" Kevin continued. He sounded almost giddy as he spoke, like a kid who had the chance to interview his favorite super hero. "I bet it's awesome! Nothing like the boring shit I have to deal with day to day."

Sam shrugged. "It's all right, I guess."

"*All right?* Just all right? Bullshit, man! That's cowboy country! I see the guys around here at the gym, playing racquetball and doing that pussy rock climbing and I think, 'I know guys who do stuff back home that you guys couldn't even dream of! Yeah, you can run a five-minute mile but I know guys who've literally wrestled steer!' But they don't get it, Sam. They just don't get it!"

Sam didn't comment. He hadn't planned for their conversation to veer in this direction. He had forgotten this part about Kevin: his ability to ramble and his weird idolization of the land out west, which in Kevin's mind was a place that was so rugged, rustic, and earnest that Sam doubted it had even existed a hundred years ago.

"Your nuts just shrivel up out here, man! It must be something in the air. Or maybe it's all the sitting around. God, I had to sit on this two-hour conference call yesterday that made me want to pull my teeth! And then that evening, I had to sit through kindergarten orientation with Ingrid at Siri's Montessori school. I mean it's kindergarten! How much orientation do you need? They draw with crayons and sing the alphabet. How complicated is that?"

"How is Ingrid?" Sam managed to wedge into Kevin's rant.

"Oh, she's fine, man. Bossy as ever!" He chuckled. "She wants to redo our garden so she's had me out there for the past two weeks. I'm up to my ass in potted soil and mulch. She's the world's best slave driver. She went to the farmer's market and got these—"

"Has she spoken to Gabby?"

There was a noticeable pause on the other end.

"I . . . I don't know, man. I guess," Kevin finally replied. The excitement had disappeared from his voice. He sounded cagey, like Sam was trying to trick him into revealing something.

"I just wondered, because I know they were close."

"They still are," Kevin mumbled.

"So she *has* spoken to her, then?" Sam could hear voices in the front office now. It looked like everyone was returning from their brief lunch break. He would have to meet with one of the lieutenants to get an update on the latest canvassing, but Sam didn't want to do it now. Not just yet. He rose from his chair and shut his office door before returning to his desk. "How is Gabby doing?"

Kevin loudly sighed. "I don't know, man. I guess she's . . . okay. She has her good days . . . and her bad days, from what I've heard. I'm a bad person to ask, though." He paused again. "Is that why you called . . . to talk about Gabriela?"

Sam briefly contemplated lying.

No, I called because I wanted to catch up, Kev. I haven't talked to you in two years and I was wondering if you were still alive. Sue me! he wanted reply. But he couldn't.

The truth was he couldn't stop thinking about Gabby, not since he had seen Janelle standing at the counter talking to Rita.

Gabby, what the hell are you doing here? he had thought when he saw her. His heart had nearly burst out of his chest. *Gabby wants to give it a second chance,* his frantic mind thought. She finally wanted, after all this time, to fight for her sanity and their marriage. But then Janelle had turned around, and he had felt a stab of pain when he realized it wasn't Gabby.

He had thought he had finally moved on, that he was at peace with what had happened. He had exorcised his ex-wife from his memory—sat her effigy on a boat, pushed it off onto a river, and set it aflame with the hope that eventually it would reach Valhalla. But he hadn't done anything quite that spectacular. Instead, he had only shuttered both the sad and the happy memories of Gabby in the back closet of his mind, allowing them to gather dust. Little Bill's disappearance and Janelle's subsequent appearance in town had flung that closet door open.

Now Sam was covered in dust bunnies, a deluge of memories, and unresolved feelings that kept him up at night.

"You should just call her yourself, Sam," Kevin said, making Sam shake his head. "She's . . . kind of hit a rough patch, I gather. She might like to hear from you."

"I doubt it."

She wouldn't want to talk to me.

He had walked out on her, hadn't he? When she needed him the most, he had thrown in the towel and told her he couldn't be married to her anymore. But he had had his reasons. He hadn't ended their marriage on a whim. Gabby's extreme highs and lows had not only exhausted him but left him questioning his own sanity some days. Then she told him she didn't want to undergo treatment anymore because she was tired of the unexpected side effects that came with each new drug, and the drugs weren't working anyway, and the doctors were suggesting electroconvulsive therapy as a last resort. Rather than putting her life in the hands of her doctors, she wanted to just "ride out the wave" and see where it took her.

"Then you're going to have to ride that wave without me," he had told her before packing his things and moving out. He filed for divorce soon after and accepted his dad's invitation to rejoin the police force back in Mammoth Falls.

"She doesn't blame you, man," Kevin continued quietly. "She . . . she understands."

Sam kept shaking his head, refusing to hear Kevin's words. He wouldn't accept any absolution for what he had done or the decisions he had made. Though he knew he had his reasons, he still felt guilt for walking out, for leaving her.

"Gabby knows how hard it was. She tells Ingrid that all the time. She won't even let Ingrid talk shit about you, and believe me . . . Ingrid wants to kick your ass. But Gabby sticks up for you. She knows you tried."

Sam finally stopped shaking his head and lowered his gaze.

He stared at a Bic pen that sat on the edge of his desk, his eyes tracing the plastic cylinder like it was the most important object in the world.

Gabby knew how hard he had tried to make it work. She understood. Of course she did. That was the reason why he had fallen in love with her, wasn't it? That woman couldn't stay mad at anyone for long. She had a seemingly endless capacity for compassion and forgiveness. She might even be willing to forgive him—the man who had deserted her—but could he ever forgive himself?

"Just call her, Sam," Kevin repeated. "I mean it."

"It was good talking to you, Kev," he said casually, like he hadn't heard his friend. "I've got to go, all right?"

"Oh, uh, yeah," Kevin stuttered. "S-sure, man. Look, I'll tell Ingrid you called."

"Thanks. Talk to you later. I'll give you a call back later this week," Sam said dazedly before lowering his phone back into its cradle. He sat silently for several minutes thereafter until he heard a knock at the door.

"You busy, Chief?" someone asked.

He shook his head. "No. Not anymore. You can come in."

Chapter 14

Lydia Roach <roach.l@bryantconsultinggroup.com>

April 24 at 3:34 p.m.
To: Janelle Marshall <jayjaymarsh@yahoo.com>
Subject: Just following up!

Hello Janelle,

I think we got cut off during our phone conversation earlier today. It sounded like there was a lot going on in the background, though. I realize you're dealing with a lot with your grandfather and everything, but I just wanted to double check with you to see if there is an ETA on those documents I mentioned to you. I hope you're sending them tomorrow! You are sending them tomorrow, right???

Sincerely,

Lydia Roach
Assistant Human Resources Director
Bryant Consulting Group Inc.

From Allison Bradbury
Text sent Thursday 6:32 pm
Hey Jay! I'm at the restaurant. Can't believe I beat U here! I'm at one of the tables in the back. I ordered sangria.

From Allison Bradbury
Text sent Thursday 6:51 pm
Where R U? We were supposed to meet at 6:30 for the baby shower stuff, right? Having trouble finding parking?

From Allison Bradbury
Text sent Thursday 7:23 pm
OK this isn't like you at all. REALLY starting to worry. Seriously WHERE R U???? Why haven't U texted me back?

From Allison Bradbury
Text sent Thursday 7:47 pm
Finished sangria, guac, and nachos and now more than a lil pissed U stood me up and didn't call. Please don't tell me U had an accident!

From Allison Bradbury
Text sent Thursday 8:19 pm
Leaving restaurant and heading to your place to see if U R still alive!!! :P

Regina Marshall <Lovelylady1957@hotmail.com>

April 25 at 5:51 a.m.
To: Janelle Marshall <jayjaymarsh@yahoo.com>
Subject: Any updates?

Hey, sweetheart!

Haven't heard from you in a couple of days. I know you said that I didn't have to book that flight back home, that you had it all covered, but now I'm feeling like I should've!

Malta was nice—lots of history and pretty beaches. The tour guide took us to this big rock temple with a name I still can't pronounce and we went to St. Paul's Cathedral. (I took a few pictures. I'll send them to you when I get the chance.) But I'll be honest with you, honey, I found it hard to concentrate because I kept worrying about Daddy. I'm still worried about him. But I told myself, "Reggie, it's no point in worrying. You're stuck on this ship for the next two days." (We're sitting off the coast of one of the Greek islands.) So even if I wanted to take a flight back home, I'd have to wait.

Happy to hear that Mark is on his way. At least you won't be alone up there anymore though your mama wishes she was there with you, honey! I know this can't be easy.

I meant to ask you, are those hillbilly cops working with the FBI? A man I met on the ship (He's nice. He's a widow and he's my age but doesn't look it. He doesn't have a bit of gray and still has a full head of hair) used to be an

ATF agent, which is kind of like the FBI. He said they handle missing person cases all the time. So are they talking
to the FBI??? Or maybe we can hire a private detective.
I've been researching it on the Internet. There's a PI in
Montana who will give you a discount if you sign a con-
tract with him before the month of June. (I guess a lot of
people go missing in June with the summer weather
and all.)

Anyway—I plan to be on a flight to the U.S. in a few days.
Stay strong and hold tight, baby. Mama's on her way!

Luv you!
XXXX

Janelle had lain awake in bed for hours, listening to the buzz
of her cell phone on Pops's night table with each new text message and email. She lay unmoving, yet unable to sleep or quiet
her chaotic thoughts. She watched the sky through a crack in
the bedroom blinds as the horizon turned from pitch black to
dark blue then purple. By the time it was a pale blue with
brushstrokes of marigold, yellow, and orange at its fringes, she
managed to drag herself out of bed. She tiredly climbed into
the shower, feeling the hot blast of water on her back and
shoulders. When she stepped onto the bath mat ten minutes
later and gazed at the bathroom mirror, she could feel the
bleak mood descending over her again. She told herself to
shake it off. She didn't have time to be depressed. She had to
prepare for Mark's arrival in Mammoth Falls later that day.

Keep going. Keep moving.

She dressed and began to tidy up the cabin, though it was already spotless from the endless hours she had scrubbed,
dusted, and swept. She used a scouring pad on the kitchen
sink, a magic eraser on phantom spots and streaks on the cabin

walls, and she swept the hardwood floors with a determined ferocity that scared even her. She did it to keep occupied. She didn't want to think about . . .

Keep moving, she told herself when her thoughts drifted to visions of Pops wandering alone in the woods or him facedown in a pile of melting snow, his skin darkening with gangrene and covered with a fine layer of frost that made him look like a macabre Snow Miser.

She dropped her dustpan and broom, letting them clatter to the floor. She strode across the cabin's living room, grabbed her car keys, donned her parka that had finally lost its musky smell, and headed back out the door to run some errands, to keep busy.

Keep going.

She drove past the Victorian and Craftsman-style houses that took her through the major artery leading to the heart of Mammoth Falls. She was finally headed to Kinko's to print out those documents she still owed Lydia but got stuck behind the world's oldest traffic jam: a series of stagecoaches and horses headed to the festival. One had broken its wagon wheel and was holding up all the cars and trailers behind it. After waiting for nearly twenty minutes, Janelle decided make a U-turn and head down a side street. She couldn't go back home, not back to the silence of Pops's cabin, so she parked her car instead.

"I'll buy more food," she murmured flatly, sounding almost robotic as she opened the door to her Jetta, conveniently forgetting that every shelf in the refrigerator and kitchen cabinets was already packed with goods, thanks to her trip to Mason's Grocery yesterday morning.

"Gotta pick up dinner for Mark," she muttered.

Keep going. Keep moving.

Yesterday had been a mistake. She should have never hung all her hopes on one letter. It seemed so ridiculous now, believing that she could find out where her grandfather had disappeared by deciphering some secret message in the mail. Who did she think she was? Sherlock Holmes? Inspector Clouseau? This wasn't a game of Clue. She couldn't shout that the butler did it in the library with the candlestick.

See, Sam! Solving cases isn't that hard, she now thought flippantly, ridiculing her own naïveté.

If you needed an HR form, she'd have it ready for you with a pen attached and a Post-It labeling where it had to be signed. If you needed to schedule a meeting, she'd plug it into her Outlook calendar, send an email to all the necessary parties, and have a basket of muffins and complimentary orange juice waiting for everyone in the conference room by the time the meeting started. But crime solving was obviously not her area of expertise. This was a problem she could not solve, and that realization for someone like her was almost crippling. She would have to leave the detective work to the professionals; let the cops and trackers do their jobs.

Meanwhile, she would keep moving.

As Janelle climbed out of her car, she tugged her hood over her head only to lower it when she didn't feel the customary blistering blast of wind that usually greeted her as soon as she stepped out of the cabin's front door or her car. She looked around her in bewilderment. The air had lost its chill entirely. Why hadn't she noticed this before? Colorful puddles mixed with mud, brine, and car exhaust were starting to fill the town streets. She raised her eyes. Along with the silhouette of two search helicopters, she saw birds perched on awnings and the old-fashioned street lamps dotting Main Street.

She realized that several festival goers a few blocks down weren't even wearing coats. They had increased in number also from a trickle to a steady stream of people. They created a wall of sound—screams, laughs, shouts, ringing, popping, and clapping—rivaling the country music that seemed to be playing on the stage speakers night and day, regardless of whether an actual band was performing.

Janelle quickly dug into her tote bag and pulled out her phone, calling up her weather app.

"High of forty-five degrees with current temperature thirty-nine degrees," she read aloud.

It was practically balmy compared to the frigid cold she had endured for most of the week. It looked like spring had finally arrived in Mammoth Falls.

She dropped her cell back into her bag, lowered the zipper of her parka, and continued down the sidewalk toward Mason's Grocery. A Pepsi machine sat near the entrance, and the shop's display window was decorated in honor of the Wild West festival with cowboy hats, tomahawks, lassos, and a few fake tumbleweeds. Several leaflets of every neon color imaginable were taped to the glass advertising a new knitting circle, a party at the American Legion next month, and a Girl Scout fund-raiser. Her eyes intentionally skipped over the smiling image of her grandfather in his Silver Alert notice that was also taped to the window.

Keep going. Keep moving.

Janelle pushed open the shop door, and a bell jingled overhead, signaling her arrival.

The store was larger on the inside than it looked from the sidewalk. It was filled wall-to-wall with metal shelves and a flank of freezers at the back. It didn't have the grocery store or warehouse fluorescent lights Janelle was used to back home or the Muzak playing in the background. Instead metal track lights hung over each aisle and an ancient Casio boom box sat on the counter, playing old country tunes. The shopkeeper looked up when she entered.

"Miss Marshall?" the old woman said, lowering the copy of the *Mammoth Falls Gazette* she had been reading. Janelle's eyes shifted again when she caught sight of the headline on the cover of the newspaper, above the fold: "Area Resident Missing, Police Search Continues."

The old woman stared at Janelle quizzically. "Back already?"

Janelle nodded and grabbed one of the plastic baskets near the doormat. "Yeah," she said quickly, not wanting to get dragged into a conversation, "just wanted to pick up a few more things."

Keep going. Keep moving.

"And here I was thinking you bought everything but the kitchen sink yesterday," the shopkeeper said with a chuckle that sounded more like a cough. "Let me know if you need any help."

Janelle made her way toward the back of the store. As she did, she calmed a little. There was something delightfully mind-numbing about grocery shopping. The worries of the world seemed far away when you considered whether to get string beans or broccoli or whether to purchase two jars of mayonnaise because if you bought one the other was half price. She zipped down the dairy aisle and pinged past the dry goods.

Keep going. Keep moving.

She breezed past a display of marked-down oranges and finally reached the meat section. Janelle gazed at the selection, considering the tenderloin versus hamburger meat. She had planned to serve Mark a rosemary-and-lemon-flavored chicken breast with mashed potatoes as his welcome dinner but perhaps she could make a marinated beef instead.

Or maybe I can . . .

Suddenly, her phone began to ring. She withdrew it from her tote bag again and winced when she saw the name on the screen.

"Ally!" she shouted after clicking the button to answer and slapping her forehead. "I'm so . . . *so* sorry! I meant to call you back. I know we were supposed to have dinner yesterday!"

"Uh, yeah," Allison answered sullenly. "We were supposed to meet at six thirty and you were a no-show."

"I know. I'm sorry."

"I called you and texted you like four times, Jay!"

She had seen the texts and deleted them and all the voice mails without listening or reading either. But after the certified letter fiasco, she had been in no state to talk to anyone.

"See the thing is, Ally," she began as she reached for the beef tenderloin, "I'm not even in town. I flew out to South Dakota to—"

"Yeah, I know. Mark told me everything."

Janelle lowered the cellophane-wrapped tenderloin into her basket. She paused. "He did?"

"When you didn't answer my calls, I went to your house to see what the hell happened. I mean it's not like you to just *not* show up or return phone messages. You're usually so punctual. I thought you had been murdered or kidnapped or something."

"I know. I know. Again, I'm sorry, Ally!"

"Well, anyway, I went to your house and that snobby woman opened the door."

Janelle rolled her eyes as she made her way back to the vegetable aisle to grab a few cloves of garlic for the marinade. *Brenda,* Janelle thought with exasperation.

"She said you weren't there," Allison continued, "and was about to close the door in my face. I thought something was seriously wrong, and then Mark walked up and explained everything. He told me you went to go see your grandfather . . . a family emergency or something. He said you left days ago."

"Well, I'm glad Mark explained what happened and I am truly, deeply sorry if Mark's mom was rude to you. I guess she didn't—"

"His mother wasn't there. Or at least, I didn't see her."

"Huh? But I thought you said a snobby woman answered."

"Uh, yuh-ah!" Allison answered in her usual way that could be both amusing and infuriating. "But she wasn't his mother. She was way too young. I think I ran into her at your house-warming party. Her name was Shana or something or other."

Janelle halted in the center of the produce aisle.

Keep going. Keep moving. Keep going. Keep moving, the mantra kept repeating in her head like a record that was skipping in the same place. But she couldn't move. Her feet seemed affixed to the store's linoleum floors.

"Shana answered the door? Are you sure?"

"Yeah, I think that's who it was."

Janelle sat the basket on the floor, urging her mind not to race to any irrational conclusions, which it often did nowadays. But she couldn't stop the wheels from spinning. Why was Shana there? Why was she answering the door? And why was she alone with Mark?

Then Janelle remembered watching from the opposite side of her living room during her housewarming as Shana stood at Mark's side during a conversation he was having with a few of his colleagues. Shana had stood so close that they were almost touching. She had been laughing as she gazed up at Mark, and Janelle could have sworn she saw adoration in the young woman's eyes. Any casual onlooker could have easily mistaken Mark and Shana for the couple holding their housewarming. They could have sauntered up to Shana to tell her that the chaise longue in the sunroom was gorgeous only to have Shana bashfully admit that it wasn't her chaise longue. It wasn't even her home or her boyfriend.

"I didn't start anything, did I?" Allison asked anxiously, seeming to be unnerved by Janelle's protracted silence. "I wasn't trying to cause any drama by telling you this. It seemed perfectly innocent, Jay. It's not like I caught them in bed together. I mean—"

"No, no! Not any drama at all." Janelle forced a smile. "She's a family friend. She's at the house all the time. I just . . . I just didn't know she had stopped by."

"Well, anyway, Mark explained everything . . . like I said."

Janelle nodded blankly.

"We'll just reschedule when you get back. Crystal's baby isn't due until late July, so we have some time."

Janelle continued to nod, her mind now a thousand miles away.

Don't worry. Mark is on a plane. He's coming to you. You're the one that he loves, she told herself.

"Sure," she muttered.

Janelle arrived back at her grandfather's cabin with four grocery bags in hand. She opened the fridge and realized that it would require some extreme maneuvering to fit what she had just purchased. She decided instead to leave them on the kitchen counter and sort them later.

"Marinade," she muttered, pulling out the garlic cloves from one of the bags and opening cabinets. She found the bottles of balsamic vinegar and olive oil. She dug through another cabinet and found the pepper. In yet another, she found a saucepan that was slightly rusted at the bottom but it would have to do. She began to cook, feeling the old self-assured and orderly Janelle begin to reassert herself. She pushed her worries aside like clamoring children begging for her attention.

Not today, kids. Mama's busy.

Just as she sat the saucepan on the open flame, her cell phone began to chime with that incessant singsong ringtone that she wished she had changed. The jingle-jangle bouncy tune had seemed funny a month ago when she selected it, but in her current mood it almost ridiculed her with its perkiness.

The phone now sat precariously on the kitchen counter, hovering over the edge of the newly scrubbed sink. She grabbed it and stared at the screen. When she saw that Mark was calling her, her hand started to shake.

"Please don't tell me your flight was canceled!" she cried in one exhalation before he even had the chance to say hello.

"Uh, no."

"Oh, thank God!" She dropped her hand to her chest and grinned. "You scared me for a second there."

Janelle paused and glanced at the clock on the fireplace mantle. Her smile disappeared. She let the phone rest between her chin and the crook of her shoulder as she reached for the garlic she had finished chopping seconds earlier. She swept it from the chopping board, into her palm, and tossed it into the pan. It sizzled and popped, and she jumped back to keep from getting scalded by the oil.

"So was your flight delayed? Are you stuck at the airport then?" she asked as she turned down the flame a bit and grabbed a spatula. "I saw on the news yesterday that there's a bad storm front coming through—"

"I'm not at the airport or on the plane, baby. Look, I won't be able to make it out there. Not today, anyway."

She blinked furiously, trying desperately to comprehend what he was saying. She had to be misunderstanding him. *"What?* What do you mean you aren't coming?"

"I can't fly to South Dakota. I want to be out there with you. I really do. But it's . . . it's a bad time. There's a lot going on back here, and I can't get away right now. I'm really sorry."

"B-but I told my mom she didn't have to come because you were on your way. She was going to take the first flight—"

"I know. I know. Like I said, I'm really sorry, baby." His voice sounded muffled. "Yes, tell them I'll be there in about five minutes. I'm on a call right now. Yes . . . yes, thanks, Jocelyn."

Jocelyn was the quirky intern at PCA Financial Services, where Mark worked. She had become his de facto personal assistant. She wore Buddy Holly glasses, liked to cosplay, and kept a Wolverine bobble-head doll on her desk that she had gotten from the comic book store.

"Will do, Mr. Sullivan," Janelle heard Jocelyn say in the background.

Janelle angrily tossed the spatula into the sink. "You're at the office?"

"Huh?" he answered distractedly. She could hear the shuffling of papers.

"You're at work! You're still at the office! Did you even pack? Did you even plan on coming here?" she shouted.

"Of course I did! Of course, I packed. What kind of question is that? That's all I did last night! But then Bob called this morning to remind me that we have an important meeting with one of our big clients. I'm in charge of the account. Baby, this could make or break my promotion. They've got a huge portfolio and—"

"No, it wasn't."

"What?"

Janelle's jaw tightened. "No, packing wasn't all you did last night. Allison told me she stopped by yesterday. She said a woman was with you. The woman wasn't your mother."

The phone went silent.

"Was it Shana?"

He laughed uncomfortably.

"It was her, wasn't it?"

"What does this have to do with anything? Where are you going with this, baby?"

"Just answer the question!" she barked, feeling the tendons stand up along her neck. The garlic, oil, and vinegar continued to sizzle and crackle behind her.

"Yes, it was Shana," he answered evenly. "She was dropping something off for Mom. I asked her if she was hungry, and she stayed for dinner."

Janelle raised her hand to her forehead. The cloves started to blacken and curl in the sizzling heat behind her.

"I didn't think it was a big deal. She's been over plenty of times before. All we did was order Chinese takeout and watch cable."

"Oh, did you? Did you order the shrimp tempura?" She began to laugh shrilly like a hyena. She sounded crazy to her own ears. "Or did you get the crab rangoon?"

"Jay, are you all right?"

"I'm fine! Just fine! I'm only curious as to what you've been up to. I bet you're just living it up back there now that your allergy-riddled girlfriend isn't in town! Seafood morning, noon, and night! I bet you're just . . ."

Janelle couldn't finish. Instead, she closed her eyes, feeling the lashes dampen with tears. Thin tendrils of smoke began to rise from the saucepan.

"Jay, I know you're under a lot of stress with your grandfather," he began slowly, "so I'll chalk this outburst up to that."

"Is it because I didn't say yes?" she blurted out. "Is it because I didn't say yes when you asked me to marry you at the party? Ever . . . ever since then, you've been acting strange like . . . like I've been choosing sides, like I chose Pops over you. But that's not what happened. That's not what happened at all! I just can't—"

"That has nothing to do with this, Jay. You're mixing apples with oranges." There were more muttering voices. He made a sharp impatient sound. "Look, I've *really* got to go, baby."

How could he be so calm? She felt like their relationship was hanging in the balance and he was acting as if this was a minor disagreement, one that was so trivial that it wasn't even worth staying on the phone to finish.

"The meeting with the client has already started, and Bob is stalling for me. I'll reschedule my flight. Okay? I'll get there . . . just not today."

"Then when?" she asked, wiping away an errant tear that slid down her cheek. "When will you get here?"

"Soon," Mark answered.

No, don't say that. Please don't say that!

"Daddy will see you soon, sweetheart," her father would promise over the phone, and she would wind up sitting on the window ledge, staring at the roadway, waiting for the white Cadillac with the rusted doors to appear, and knowing in her heart that the car would never come.

"I'll be there soon," Mark assured again.

Janelle hung up after that, not bothering to say good-bye to Mark. She numbly sat the phone back on the counter. She stared at her phone until it was nothing but a black blur on off-white linoleum. Suddenly, a sharp beep filled the kitchen. It pierced the silence that had fallen in the wake of Mark's phone call. Janelle looked up and saw the smoke alarm overhead, flashing. She turned back around to find the saucepan in flames. She screamed, hastily groped for the handle, and tossed the pan into the sink before turning on the water. A black haze of smoke billowed toward the ceiling and spread like a heavy fog. She dashed across the room and flung open the living room window, then the door. She then ran into the open air hacking and coughing, searching for relief.

CHAPTER 15

"Connie," a voice shouted from the other side of the polka-dot-print dressing room curtain. The sound of rustling crinoline and clanging hangers soon followed. "Coooonniiiie!"

Connie paused from assembling jewelry in the display case, a task that she had hoped would keep her busy and help her block out the reverberation of helicopters flying nearby. But she couldn't keep from hearing the distant *whomp, whomp, whomp*—even when she turned up the volume of her iPod dock and the song, "Somethin' Bad," filled the shop.

No one else seemed to hear the noise, not over the sound of the country music and the festival shouts two blocks down.

"I think it's all in your head, honey," one of her frequent customers had said yesterday, gazing at her with an uneasiness that made Connie briefly question if she was, indeed, slowly going crazy.

But it's not in my head, she thought hours later. She could hear the helicopters, and she couldn't ignore them. Nor could she help wondering and worrying no matter how hard she tried.

Are they looking for Bill? Is that what I'm hearing? Have they found him yet?

She sat aside the turquoise bracelet she was holding and glanced over her shoulder. "What is it, Peg?"

"I don't know what's wrong. Maybe it's the cut or the fabric, but this gown won't fit me!"

"We can try another one," Connie called back as she walked across the store toward the clothing racks several feet away. She rifled through a series of hangers filled with dresses she planned to show at the festival fashion show, pausing to examine the tags.

Is he still alive? Dear God, is he wandering around all alone out there?

"Maybe this one will work," she muttered, removing one dress from the rack—a purple lace number with an elastic waist. She walked back toward the dressing room and eased the curtain aside. She held the dress aloft for Peg to examine.

"All right, I'll try it," Peg muttered with a resigned sigh. "I just wanna look nice, you know? If I'm going to be up there on that stage modeling in front of the whole town, I don't want to look silly."

"Uh-huh." Connie walked back to the jewelry counter.

Bill's not senile and lost. I don't care what the cops say, Connie thought as she adjusted a gold pendant on a faux-velvet neck stand. *Just because he talks to a dead woman doesn't mean he's crazy. Something bad happened to him out there. I can feel it!*

"Did I tell you that I did pageants when I was a little girl?" Peg piped from the other side of the curtain. "I even won a few crowns. I was Little Miss Sparkle 1984. It's been years since I've done anything like this, though."

"Uh-huh," Connie murmured again, barely paying attention as Peg rambled.

Whomp, whomp, whomp, whomp.

The sound was getting louder now. Connie gazed out of the

shop window. Were the helicopters closer, or was it her imagination? Connie swore she could felt the shockwave of the helicopter blades vibrate in the shop's hardwood floor and in every bone in her body.

Damn, I miss you, Bill, she thought.

She missed his smell—a mix of leather, Old Spice, and his favorite dark roast coffee. She missed his hoarse laugh and the way he would thump the heel of his cowboy boot on the floor and slap his knee for a good joke. She missed the feel of his arms wrapped around her. She clung to her memories of Bill like they were a lone life raft in a vast ocean. She feared that it was all she would have left of him. And it was easier to cling to those memories than to consider what might have been.

I could've been more than his "special friend," Connie thought as she ran her hands along the glass display case. Her gaze settled on a series of cubic zirconium rings. She picked up one—a modest solitaire with a fake gold band—and fingered it. If it were up to Bill, she would be wearing a ring similar to this one.

Dakota. The weather had been scorching all day. T-shirts stuck to skin, dragonflies seemed to drop out of midair from heat exhaustion, and even the ducks on Pasque Lake were fanning themselves. Connie had hated it and wanted to stay indoors with the AC cranked to the highest setting, but Bill, a long-time southerner who had dealt with worse summers, had called her a wimp and talked her into going on a stroll with him on one of the mountain trails.

"If my old ass can take it, you sure as heck can," he chided.

As he admired the fireflies and the forest and she swatted at mosquitoes and whined they were *both* too old to be gazing at nature while they sweated like whores in church, he fell to one knee on the packed dirt. She reached out to him and grabbed his shoulders, terrified that despite all his bravado, the heat had finally gotten to him and he was about to faint.

"Jesus! You okay, Bill?" she gasped.

But in the twilight, she saw him shove his hand into his jeans pocket. He pushed back the bill of his trucker hat and pulled out a diamond ring.

"I'm fine, honey. I was just gonna ask you to marry me."

She was struck speechless.

"Well?" He inclined his head. "You gonna leave me down here or say yes?"

"Yes! Hell, yes!" she said before leaning down to kiss him.

She wished she could have held on to that feeling: the delight of the unexpected. A man—a *good* man—had fallen in love with her and wanted to marry her, despite her faults, despite her dark past. No more sorry sons-of-bitches who would cheat on her, beat her up, and leave her with a black eye and a broken heart. Those days were over. She was fifty-one and she was finally going to get the life she always wanted. It had certainly taken her long enough, but better late than never, right?

Of course, that feeling didn't stay. The uncertainty crept in like a bad smell that makes you wrinkle your nose.

You make bad decisions, Connie Black Bear, the little annoying voice said in her head that night as she and Bill slept in bed together. *Why should this be any different?*

She wondered whether it was smart to marry a man who was almost thirty years older than she was. Bill had always seemed younger than his age, but he was in his seventies. How many years could they realistically have together?

She questioned whether his family would accept her. She and Bill had kept their relationship a secret from his daughter and his granddaughter for so long. And why had he kept it a secret, anyway? Maybe Bill was really ashamed of her but had never admitted it.

She wondered if she should marry a man who was still so in love with his deceased wife. Bill didn't know she could hear him talking to Mabel late at night when he thought Connie was asleep. Some of those earnest words of love and longing he had whispered to Mabel in the dark had made Connie's heart ache.

How could she take such a chance? *Why should I*, she had wondered as she lay awake in bed staring at the ceiling.

Now she had her answer: because you may never get the chance again.

"Darn it! This dress doesn't fit either, Connie!" Peg shouted. "You got anything else? Maybe something in red. I saw this ruby red gown that Jennifer Lawrence wore in *InStyle* magazine and I thought 'Hot damn, I'd look good in that!'"

"Umm." Connie sniffed and wiped at the lone tear that had fallen onto her cheek. She sat the ring back in the display case and shut the glass door. "Let me see," she said, sniffing again as she headed back across the shop and dug through the rack.

She searched for another dress, trying her best to ignore the maudlin thoughts that kept making their way past the wall she had erected inside her head—the wall she hoped would keep her sane.

"How about this one? I've got a red satin A-line in a size fourteen. It'll give you a—"

"A size fourteen?" Peg yelped.

The dressing room curtain flew open. Peg gaped. The dress dangled around her arm and her neck like a purple lace toga. The three-way mirror behind her gave Connie a full view of Peg's mismatched bra and daisy granny panties as well as her dimpled thighs and doughy middle.

"Are you serious? I can't wear a size fourteen! I've been a size twelve since I was eighteen years old. If I had to wear a size fourteen, I would just . . . just *die!*"

Connie resisted the urge to roll her eyes. Yes, because there was no worse fate than wearing a dress size that the average woman in America wore. Connie couldn't think of anything in the world that would be more torturous or horrendous—except maybe being a man stranded alone on the side of a mountain or knowing that you had tossed away the one chance to marry someone you loved dearly and may never see again.

Connie could still hear the helicopters. She could still feel the agony building within her even though she tried her best to keep it at bay, and here she was listening to a tirade about a dress size.

"You won't die, Peg," Connie argued, walking toward the dressing room stall and holding the dress out to her. "No one in the crowd will know the difference. They won't know what size you're wearing. I promise."

"But *I* will!" Peg exclaimed, angrily shoving the dress away. "I'm the one that'll feel like a hog in that . . . that *thing!*"

Connie dropped a hand to her hip, her patience with Peg— one of her best but most demanding customers—now wilted. "Do you wanna feel like a hog or *look* like a hog? It's up to you!"

Peg's eyes went wide. They started to glisten with tears, and her chin began to tremble. "How . . . how dare you tell me I look like a hog! That was a hateful, mean thing to say, and it wasn't Christian of you . . . not Christian at all!"

"Yeah, well, I'm not feeling very Christian-like today, Peg," Connie muttered as she tossed the dress onto a nearby hook that was already covered with several ensembles that Peg had rejected.

"If you're going to act this way, then I don't want to be in your fashion show!"

"Fine with me," Connie answered drily.

"Oh, is it now?" Peg snapped as she yanked off the purple dress, hurled it to the floor, and reached for her clothes. She shimmied back into her skirt and tugged her sweater over her head. "You can't abuse people just because your man wandered off somewhere. Maybe you should have told that old black bastard to stay put!"

Connie's back went rigid.

"After you get dressed, make sure you don't leave anything behind," she said in a low, menacing voice, "because you are no longer welcome in this store. You hear me?"

"That's fine with me!" Peg grabbed her coat and her purse. She shoved her arms into one of the coat sleeves, even though some of the buttons on her sweater were still open and her skirt zipper was undone. She marched toward the shop's entrance with her wool scarf trailing behind her like a wedding train. "I guess you won't mind if I tell everyone in town this is how you treat your customers now. And I mean *everybody!* You'll regret talking to me like this, Connie Black Bear!"

Not really, Connie thought, crossing her arms over her chest. On the long list of regrets Connie had, pissing off Peg Whitcomb wouldn't be one of them. She laughed softly as she watched Peg storm off.

"Don't let the door hit you in the ass on the way out!" Connie shouted just as Peg yanked open the shop door, making the bell overhead jingle.

Peg shoved her way past Janelle, who was already standing in the doorway. She did not bother to excuse herself.

Janelle stared after Peg as the angry woman made her way down the sidewalk. When Peg disappeared past the shop window, still muttering to herself, Janelle turned around to face Connie with her brows raised. "What was that about?"

"Nothing. Just some..." Connie made a shooing motion, feeling more tired now than she had been twenty minutes earlier. "It was nothing."

She watched as Janelle stepped inside the shop, closed the door behind her, and wiped her booted feet on the doormat. The bell jingled again as the door softly shut.

"So what are you doing here?" Connie paused. "Heard any news about—"

"Pops?" Janelle lowered the zipper of her coat and shook her head. "No, I haven't. *You?*"

Connie also shook her head. She leaned against the cashier's counter. "I can't believe they haven't found him yet. It's been three days since they found his truck . . . *five* days since anyone's last seen him! How does a person disappear into thin air like that?"

"I've asked myself the same question every day since I found out Pops went missing."

"Dammit, I hate this!" Connie pushed herself away from the counter. "I hate it! I feel like my hands are tied behind my back, like a chain is around my leg. I wish they'd let us help with the search."

"I do, too, but Sam said that it can mess up the trail the trackers are using if too many people are out there."

"Bullshit!" Connie snapped. She started to pace in front of the clothing racks. She stuck one of her painted nails into her mouth and began to gnaw at it even though the polish tasted horrible. "You know I tried looking for Bill myself anyway?"

"Me too," Janelle whispered, lowering her eyes.

"Went driving up and down Highway 85," she continued, barely listening, "then I stopped and walked about two miles into the woods. Scared the hell out of a family of deer, but that's about it."

Janelle pursed her lips and shoved her hands into her pockets. "I appreciate you doing that—even if the deer didn't."

"Yeah, well, it still didn't do a damn bit of good. I didn't find him." Connie stopped pacing. "You never told me why you stopped by."

Janelle shrugged. "I just wanted to get out of the house. I *needed* to get out of the house. I tried reviewing résumés, writing emails. It was pointless. I can't form one comprehensible sentence anymore. I was going stir crazy in there. I even went to the festival and walked around for a while to try to distract myself." She gazed out the store window. "It wasn't really my thing."

"Yeah, well," Connie said again, turning back to the counter, "you'll have plenty to occupy your time soon enough. You're picking up your man today, right?" She glanced at the wall clock. "Shouldn't you be heading out to the airport? That stagecoach dust-up isn't blocking your way out of town, is it?"

"No, they cleared it—finally." Janelle tore her eyes away from the window and looked at Connie. "But it doesn't matter. I don't need to get to the airport anyway. There's been a change of plans," she said softly.

"Huh?"

"He's . . . he's not coming. Not today. There's a lot going on back home, and Mark can't . . . he can't get away right now."

Connie gazed at Janelle more closely. The young woman's eyes were pink and the lids were puffy, like she had been crying. Connie's brows knitted together with fury. "That son of a bitch," she mumbled.

Janelle held up her hand. "Connie, please—"

"What the hell is so goddamn important that man can't be with you at a moment like this?"

"I don't want to talk about it," she answered firmly. "Please just . . . just drop it, okay?"

Why can't you let things go, Mama? she could hear Yvette say at that moment. *Why don't you just know when to leave well enough alone?*

"Okay, we don't have to talk about it. I just hate to see you sad like this. You aren't my granddaughter, but you're Bill's, so I kind of feel like . . . like I should be looking out for you. He would have wanted me to."

Janelle gave a small smile. "I appreciate that."

The two women fell into an awkward silence. Connie glanced at the dressing room that was still in disarray.

"Look at this mess," Connie muttered, sucking her teeth as she walked across the shop. She dropped to her knees and angrily snatched the purple lace dress from the hardwood floor. "Damn you, Peggy."

"Look, Connie, I . . . I owe you an apology," Janelle said as Connie rose back to her feet and reached for one of the hangers in the dressing room.

"An apology for what?" Connie asked distractedly from over her shoulder.

Now thanks to Peggy, she had not only several dresses to place back on the rack, but she also was short one model for her fashion show with less than four days to replace her.

Like I need another worry, she thought. It was yet another concern to add to her growing list, but at least it was low in the rankings.

"I know we didn't start things off in the best way," Janelle continued. "I could've been nicer to you. I apologize for being so short . . . maybe even a little rude."

"I lied to you to get you here. I understand why you were pissy with me." Connie paused to hang the purple dress on a nearby hook, wiping away the wrinkles with a few quick swipes. "Anybody would be—"

"But I judged you unfairly—very unfairly. More than you realize. I shouldn't have done that. You didn't deserve it."

Connie shook her head. "It's no problem, honey. I'm not holding any grudges."

"You don't seem like you would." Janelle lowered her eyes. "All the same, if I could make it up to you for how I behaved, I would. Believe me."

At those words, Connie paused midmotion. She slowly turned. "What size are you?"

Janelle's brow crinkled in confusion. "Huh?"

"A size eight, right?" Connie grabbed one of the fashion show dresses from the hook in front of her and glanced at the label. She paused to scan Janelle openly as if seeing her for the first time—her long legs, her full breasts, and round hips.

"Most of the time I'm an eight," Janelle said distantly. "Sometimes a ten, if I've had one raspberry cheesecake too many. Why?"

"You really want to make it up to me? Be in my fashion show next week!"

Janelle's mouth fell open. She pointed at her chest. "You want me to be in your fashion show? *Me?*"

"Sure! Why not? I'm short one model now thanks to Peggy. I need a quick replacement. You'd be perfect. And I've got the perfect dress for you!" Connie brandished a short suede dress with a sweetheart neckline and silver stud embellishment along the hem.

Janelle stared at the dress. She shrank back and cringed, like the garment was covered in feces.

Connie's shoulders slumped. "Well, if you don't like this one, we can always pick another one. Whatever you want to wear . . . it doesn't matter to me!"

Janelle shook her head again. "Connie, I really, *really* don't think I'm the best candidate for this. I've never modeled before. I don't even know if I'd be good at it!"

"That's okay. It's pretty easy. You just walk up and down the stage. Smile at the crowd. Try not to trip. It's not that complicated."

"But wouldn't you rather I help instead? Maybe with getting the models dressed and ready and . . . and stuff."

"You can do that, too! You can just walk at the end of the show if you're really nervous about modeling in front of a crowd and spend most of the time backstage helping me."

Janelle stared at the dress again.

"What do you say?"

She watched as Janelle took a deep, long breath. "Okay, I'll . . . I'll do it."

"Great! Why don't you try this dress on and see how it—"

"I'll do it . . . on a *few* conditions," Janelle clarified, making Connie squint and lower the dress.

"What conditions?"

"Well, more like an exchange or a . . . a trade."

Connie frowned. "My people don't have many good experiences with trading, honey. I don't know if I like the sound of this."

"I'm not asking for much . . . just clean underwear."

"Huh?"

"Clean underwear. I haven't been able to find a Laundromat around here, and Pops doesn't have a washer and dryer. I wasn't sure if I was going to have to revert to scrubbing my bra and panties in the bathroom sink. I need a place to wash and dry my clothes."

Connie laughed. "All right. You can use mine."

"I also need the use of a printer for a few hours and a scanner to send some stuff back home. Could I—"

"All you had to do was ask. Of course, you can use it. The printer and scanner are in my office." Connie raised her brows expectantly. "Is that it?"

Janelle nodded. "Yeah, that's it."

"Good. You've got a deal. Now try this on." She held the dress toward her again. "Even if you don't like it, it'll give me an idea of what looks good on you."

Janelle took off her parka and hung it on a nearby hook. She then took the hanger that Connie offered her and walked toward the dressing room.

Too bad you aren't here to see this, Bill, Connie thought. Janelle and Connie working side by side . . . It's something Bill would have wanted, something he would have loved.

"Evie, won't mind, will she?" Janelle asked, pulling shut the dressing room's polka-dot curtain.

"Huh? Won't mind what?"

"I mean will Evie mind me helping you with the fashion show?" Janelle shouted over the top of the curtain as she began to remove her clothes. Connie could hear the clanging of hangers again. "I don't want to step on anyone's toes."

Connie rolled her eyes. "She'd have to actually show up for you to step on her toes. She barely even comes here to help me at the shop. You don't see her standing around here, do you? She's probably off with that damn Tyler Macy again."

Janelle paused. Her jeans were pooled at her ankles, and Connie could see her brown calves beneath the bottom of the curtain.

Nice, strong calves, Connie thought. *Her legs are going to look nice in one of the short dresses or maybe one with a high split.*

"Tyler's the guy you don't like, right?"

"No," Connie said icily, "he's the guy that I *hate.*"

Whenever she saw Tyler Macy and that hog of his, she was reminded of her ex—Yvette's father. The two men had the same wide-legged strut, like they had cocks too big to fit in their pants. They had the same dewy green eyes that made them look dreamy at first but then like complete simpletons after you had to gaze into those eyes while they made the umpteenth excuse for why they were late, drunk, or in the county jail. And both men had the same penchant for trouble. Tyler had a rap sheet as long as his arm. For now, he seemed happy with petty crimes and misdemeanors—shoplifting, disorderly conduct, and possession of drug paraphernalia—but Connie wouldn't put it past him to eventually move up to the bigger offenses. He was one stolen car away from a high-speed chase and police shoot-out, in her humble opinion. He was one bar fight away from an attempted murder charge. Even Little Bill had thought Tyler was nothing but bad news.

"Evie better watch out," Bill had said a month ago as he drank a cup of coffee and peered out Connie's kitchen window, watching as Yvette bounded down the porch steps to hop on the back of Tyler's Harley Davidson. "Mark my words . . . you're gonna find that boy on the front page of the *Mammoth Falls Gazette* one day, and it ain't gonna be because he's running for town mayor."

And Tyler had sensed how Bill had felt about him. The two men used to glower at each other whenever they were in the same room, like two cowboys holding a shoot-out at high noon.

Connie paused. *Bill . . . Tyler.*

Bill's truck had gone off the road on Cedar Lane. Cedar Lane was not too far from the Macy family's piece-of-shit trailer where a rusted-out Ford truck sat in front on cinderblocks and a Rottweiler barked day and night.

The cops hadn't found Bill, just boot prints in the snow that abruptly stopped not too far from the crash site.

Like someone picked him up, Connie thought, feeling lightheaded, *like he hopped in someone's car or . . . on the back of a motorcycle. That's why we haven't found him! Someone took him away.*

"All right. What you think?" Janelle said, pulling back the curtain. She gazed down at herself before tugging up the top of the sweetheart neckline. "I don't know. It seems a bit revealing to me." She pointed at her breasts that were almost spilling over the top of the dress.

Connie stared at Janelle, startled out of her daze. For a minute, she had forgotten the younger woman was in the shop with her. Connie slowly nodded and forced a smile. "It is a bit more sassy than classy. We can try another dress."

Janelle dropped her hands to her sides and squinted at Connie. "Are you okay?"

She didn't want to alarm Bill's granddaughter with her secret worries, because if they were valid then Bill was a lot worse off than she had feared.

"Oh, yeah! Right as rain, honey! Just . . . uh . . . let me look for that other dress. I'll be right back."

Connie then turned away, feeling her arms and her legs tremble as she walked.

CHAPTER 16

Sam climbed out of the sedan and paused in front of the Mammoth Falls Police Department emblem on the driver's side door before slamming the door shut. He stifled a yawn.

It had been a long day in an ongoing march of long days, and he was tired and verging on exhausted, but this would be his last stop. Then he would return home to his quiet house, his golden Labrador retriever, Quincy, and the beer that awaited him in the fridge. He'd sleep for a few hours and wake up before dawn to start the cycle all over again.

He glanced up at the dark sky with its canopy of twinkling stars and half moon, and felt the light breeze on his face. He strolled toward the cabin stairs, listening to the gravel crunch underfoot.

There were days Sam liked being a small town police chief; the people were nice, crime was minimal, and every person he encountered he had either met or knew by reputation. Unfortunately, today wasn't one of those days. Being responsible for maintaining the law, order, and welfare of the 2,687 citizens of Mammoth Falls was one thing. Being responsible for maintaining the law, order, and welfare of those 2,687 citizens who knew you back when you were in diapers, who had been in the same bowling league as your father or in the same scrapbooking club as your mother—that could be challenging. Almost everyone approached him with a familiarity that could be annoying in the best of times and downright galling when they caught him at a bad moment.

"See here, Sammy," one old-timer had said to him as he walked into Cuppa Cup of Joe that morning to grab a quick cup of coffee.

The old man had clapped Sam on the back so hard that he almost had made him spill his French roast over the rim of his paper cup. He had leaned toward Sam's shoulder, sending flecks of spittle into Sam's ear.

"Make sure that the fellas you've got out there are working with the right tracking dogs. Some of them will let just any ol' mutts on a trail. I prefer purebred hounds myself."

"Now I'm not trying to tell you how to do your job, Sam," Agnes at Mason's Grocery had told him during his lunch break as she pushed the sleeves of her sweatshirt up her spindly forearms and rested them on the counter, "but are you lookin' into the criminal element in town? You know . . . in regard to Little Bill's disappearance?"

Sam had squinted at her as he set a pack of granola and antiperspirant near the cash register. "What criminal element?"

"Like did you think that maybe the Hell's Angels did it or a Mexican drug cartel?" she had asked in a whisper with an expression so grim and grave that he almost burst into laughter.

Then that afternoon, Connie Black Bear had cornered him in his office.

"Tyler Macy is behind this, Sam!" she had shouted as she shoved open his office door and stood in front of his desk. "I'd swear on the Bible that he is!"

"I'm sorry," Rita had said, standing behind Connie in the doorway, looking perturbed. "I told her you were busy. She barged in here anyway."

"And I told *you*, Rita, that I don't care that he's busy! This is important!"

Sam had been in a middle of a meeting with Mayor Pruitt, and under normal circumstances would have dropped to his knees in thanks for the interruption. Pruitt had been boring him into a coma with a story about his recent fishing trip in the Caribbean when Connie had stomped into the room. Sam could use a distraction. He just didn't think this type of distraction was the best one.

"Look, Connie," Sam said, rising from his desk chair, "if you'd like to come back tomorrow morning, I'd be happy to—"

"No, I'm not waiting another damn day! Arrest him now!"

"Arrest who?"

Pruitt had linked his thick fingers over his portly chest, looking between Connie and Sam with keen interest.

"I told you! Tyler Macy!"

"*Tyler Ma*—. You mean Evie's boyfriend?"

She had nodded, and Sam had loudly groused in response. "Look, Connie, I know you aren't fond of Ty. Frankly, few in town are, but that doesn't mean he—"

"This has nothing to do with me 'not being fond of him!' He never liked Bill, and Bill never liked him, either. He hated his guts! I bet Ty had something to do with this. I'd have your men check his trailer for evidence if you haven't already."

"Connie, we can't just charge into the Macys' trailer without probable cause. That's not how this works. There is nothing linking that man to—"

"Then find the link, dammit!" she had barked. "That's what you guys are supposed to do, isn't it? Do your jobs!"

He had then watched in shock as she stormed out of his office, catching even Rita by surprise.

"Sorry, Sam," Rita had mumbled seconds later. She then had shut his office door.

Sam had turned back to Mayor Pruitt. The middle-aged man was actually smiling up at him.

Pruitt didn't have a nice smile, even though he had the pearly white teeth that you saw on display in dentists' offices, the ones that hygienists said you should aspire to. But Pruitt's grin made Sam's blood run cold. It was the type of grin Sam was sure the devil gave right after you traded your soul for a bag of silver.

"She's got a point, you know," Pruitt had said in his heavy baritone.

Sam had frowned in response. "A point about what?"

"Tyler Macy." Pruitt had leaned back in the chair. He did it like it was *his* chair and *his* office. "That boy's got a bad reputation—to put it mildly. He could be the culprit. Searching his trailer might help you boys find Little Bill."

Didn't Pruitt hear him mention probable cause? "I can't do that, Dick. This isn't communist China. There are laws, you know."

"Oh, come on, Sammy!" Pruitt had pushed himself to his feet. He wasn't a tall man—certainly not as tall as Sam—but he had a huge presence that he used to his advantage. "Not everything has to be by the book! This search has dragged on long enough. End it before even *more* press comes to town. Hell, maybe even the goddamn NAACP will get involved if this thing keeps going. They show up for everything else! If you just made an arrest and put Tyler Macy in jail, maybe people could move on. They could start talking about other things."

"You mean the festival?" Sam had asked with disbelief, raising his brows. "You really want me to put a possibly innocent man behind bars so that tourists can watch wagon train reenactments and eat funnel cake?"

Pruitt had angrily narrowed his eyes in response.

Sam knew he was pushing his luck. Pruitt was a jackass but he was still Sam's boss and could fire him on the spot if he wanted, though it might be dicey for Pruitt politically to get rid of a popular police chief. But even if Pruitt didn't go after Sam directly, he had other ways to get to him. Budget line items for new weapons for the officers, equipment for their vehicles, or even the damned microwave in the break room all had to go before the mayor and the town council for approval. And those requests could easily be denied for any number of feeble reasons. Pruitt could make life very hard for Sam in Mammoth Falls, and Sam knew Pruitt wasn't above doing it.

They had both reigned as golden boys in their small town in their day. But while Sam had accepted his role reluctantly, Pruitt had basked in all the adoration and attention, oozing authority and superiority from his varsity jacket to his gelled mullet. Inside, even after all these years, Pruitt was that same guy—just with a receding hairline and a paunch.

"The town needs closure, Sammy," Pruitt had said in a low voice. "We've lost one of our own, and we need time to heal and feel good again. All you would be doing is making an arrest. It's up to a judge and jury to decide whether Tyler is guilty or not." He had cocked an eyebrow. "That is the law, isn't it?"

"So you want me to wrap this up with a neat little bow? You want me to make Ty the sacrificial lamb?"

Pruitt had laughed. "*Sacrificial lamb?* Oh, you college boys and your twenty-dollar words!" The alarming smile had returned. "Call it whatever you want, Sammy. Just make sure this search comes to some kind of a close—either with a body, an arrest, or both." He had slapped Sam on the shoulder and opened the door. "Keep me updated."

He had then walked out, shouting good-bye to Rita, leaving a nasty taste in Sam's mouth.

The worst part of all this was that Sam still wasn't convinced Little Bill was missing. Even though the searchers were sure that the rising temperatures and thaw might uncover more evidence or even a body, Sam still suspected that Bill was hiding out somewhere. The old man was operating under the flawed reasoning that his absence was helping his cause, which was to keep his granddaughter from getting engaged. But it really was only succeeding in creating a vortex of unrest that Sam could feel expanding wider and wider in town each day. People were sharing their own outrageous theories on what had *really* happened to Bill at barber shops, over gas pumps at the Stop 'n' Go, and at tables at Toby's Bar & Grill, and those theories were gaining more credibility the longer Bill stayed gone. Rumors were spreading faster than VD at the Playboy mansion, and in a small town rumors could turn from a nuisance to something dangerous. Sam hoped this wouldn't get out of hand.

All this collective anxiety probably was for naught—a massive waste of time and energy. But Sam would continue to tell everyone to keep a level head. He'd perform duties as police chief without complaint. That was the reason he was at Little Bill's cabin tonight: to give Janelle Marshall an update on the search. Well, it was one of the reasons he was here.

The truth was he *wanted* to see Janelle again, though that realization was somewhat unsettling. He barely knew this woman, yet he had already remembered the exact way she wrinkled her nose when she heard something she didn't like, and how her voice was low and throaty, like one you would expect to be waiting for you on the other end of a sex hotline. He remembered the prim tone she would take when she was cornered or how she'd gnaw her bottom lip when she was anxious. He wanted to catalog more of these tics and details about her and find out what lay beneath them. Who was this woman, really? Janelle Marshall intrigued him.

Talk about wasting your time. The woman's already in a relationship, a voice in his head reminded him as he climbed the cabin steps. *They're practically engaged.*

It was the logical voice that told him when he needed to go to sleep or when he had one beer too many. He sometimes loathed that voice, but he often listened to it.

But they aren't engaged, and even her own grandfather didn't think he was good enough for her, Sam countered as he knocked.

But she *thinks he's good enough,* the voice argued. *And in the end, that's all that matters.*

The cabin door slowly opened, and the smell of something warm and hearty cooking on the stove wafted toward him along with the sound of jazz music, a dueling melody of saxophone and piano keys. Sam found her standing in the doorway, wiping her hands on a dish towel. She had on jeans and a t-shirt knotted at the waist. Her curly hair was pulled atop her head in a haphazard ponytail. She looked him up and down, assessing him with her dark eyes.

"Every time I see your police car pulling into the driveway, I'm always torn between not answering the door and opening before you knock. I never know if you're about to tell me good news or bad news."

"Sorry to say that it's usually no news at all. But thanks for answering my knock either way."

She leaned against the door jam. "So they still haven't found Pops, then?"

He shook his head.

"No trace at all?"

"I'm afraid not. Not so far, anyway," he murmured, watching her blow a curly tendril that had fallen into her face.

"Those cop shows on TV are definitely false advertising. They give the impression that every missing person can be found in a couple days, or at least by the end of the episode."

"I wish it were that simple, but no matter what, we'll keep trying."

"Yeah, I know. I know." She lowered her eyes and nodded, then suddenly lifted her head. Her eyes widened to the size of saucers. "Oh, no! No, no, no, no! Not again!" She then turned and ran toward the kitchen.

He lingered near the doorway, unsure of what to do next. He had given her the update. He could leave now.

He should have called a good-bye to her as he watched her rush toward her stove, grab a pan, and remove it from the flame. But he didn't. Instead, he took a tentative step inside the cabin, then another. He removed his cap.

"Everything all right?" he asked as he stood on the welcome mat.

She waved her hands furiously over the pan and set it on an empty burner. "Oh, it's fine!" she called over her shoulder. "I just thought I had burned dinner again. I scorched a marinade I was working on this afternoon. I was talking to my boyfriend and got . . . well, distracted." She turned to him. "I was trying to avoid a repeat."

An unreadable expression crossed her face when she mentioned her boyfriend.

"Is he headed out here, then?" Sam asked, taking another step forward, watching her face more closely.

She shook her head, and he finally recognized the emotion that marred her features: disappointment.

"There's just a lot of stuff going on back home, even more than what's going on here. He's a financial consultant with big clients. He's been trying for a while to get a promotion and . . . and . . ."

Her words faded. She turned her back to him and gripped the edge of the kitchen counter.

"Are you all right?"

She didn't answer him but instead continued to hold on to the countertop, like she needed it to stay upright.

He quickly crossed the living room and walked into her kitchen. He placed a hand on her shoulder and felt her back go rigid at his touch. He dropped his hand instantly. "I'm sorry. I just wanted to make sure you were okay. That you weren't gonna faint on me."

She turned to face him. Her eyes were red and brimming with tears. "No, no fainting."

"I know it's hard."

"'Hard' is putting it lightly. I'm a fucking emotional wreck!" She laughed bitterly and sniffed.

"I think anybody would be a wreck considering what you're going through."

"Not me, though. I'm never like this!" She sniffed again. "I actually thought I was holding it together pretty well until the past couple of days. I was sad but . . . I completely fell apart when Mark told me he wasn't going to make his flight." She dabbed at the corner of her eye with the dish towel. "It may sound selfish, but I thought, 'Work and obligations be damned, I want him to be here.' I *needed* him here."

And the bastard should be here, he thought vehemently. *What man would leave a woman alone to deal with something like this when he's supposed to be in love with her?*

You mean like how you left Gabby? the voice in his head asked. He ignored it.

"I'm . . . I'm losing my footing, Sam." He could see her reluctance to confess this. "Everything feels so shaky now. Do you get what I mean by that? Am I making any sense?"

"I get it. I've been there before. Not in the same situation, but I've been there."

"And how'd you get through it?"

"You handle it day by day." He shrugged. "Some days are better than others."

And some days will slap you right back where you started, he thought, but didn't say it aloud.

She nodded thoughtfully, then turned back to the stove.

"Well, I didn't burn dinner this time. That's an improvement, at least." She looked up at him and smiled, and something surged in his chest—an old feeling he had long forgotten. She seemed to consider him for a bit. "Are you still on duty? Have you eaten dinner yet?" She pointed to the pan. "I have extra food if you'd like some."

He nervously raised his hand to shove his fingers through his hair. "Uh, no . . . that's kind of you, but you don't have to do that. I was just heading home to—"

"I know I don't have to, I *want* to."

Janelle then turned to open an overhead cabinet. She reached up and grabbed two mismatched plates and glasses, making her t-shirt rise, revealing a long torso, and rounded hips over the tops of her faded, wrinkled jeans. His eyes dropped lower, and his gaze was almost magnetically drawn to her ass. Sam experienced another feeling that he also thought had long been dormant.

"Mark was supposed to arrive today." She sat the plates on the counter and the glasses beside them. "I overcompensated and bought enough food to feed a small army, but it's just me now, and I can't possibly eat all of this by myself. So . . ." She clapped him on the shoulder, startling him, making him focus on her face again. "Let me thank you for all the hard work you've been doing . . . for trying to find Pops. Let me cook you dinner."

He opened his mouth again to politely beg off. He was intrigued by her, but he wasn't completely stupid. It was one thing to think about her at odd times of the day and secretly ogle her when she wasn't looking. But it was another thing to have dinner with a woman who was weighed down with grief over her missing grandfather and dismayed at her boyfriend for deserting her in her hour of need. She'd probably down that bottle of Woodbridge Pinot Grigio he saw sitting near the fridge, have a good cry, and wake up in the morning refreshed and ready to deal with the world again. She'd call back home and make up with this Mark fellow, even though he probably didn't deserve it.

Yeah, that's probably how it'll all play out, he thought grudgingly.

Sam began to make another excuse when her cell phone began to ring. He watched as she grabbed her phone, which sat on the counter near the sink. "I'm sorry," she mumbled, before reading the name "MARK" on the glass screen.

Speak of the devil, Sam thought as he began to ease back toward her opened door, prepared to make his exit.

"Wait!" she called, setting down the phone. It was still ringing.

"Go on and take your phone call." He waved his hand.

She smiled and shook her head. "No, it can wait! It's not important. I can call them back later. Please stay. Have dinner with me."

Sam stopped in his tracks. *Not important?*

He wasn't completely stupid, but he was certainly a glutton for punishment. "Well, I *am* hungry," Sam said.

It would be the first home-cooked meal he had had in almost a week. So far he had been subsisting on granola, coffee, and bagels.

"So it's settled, then." She gestured to one of the bar stools facing the counter. "Pull up a chair."

"So I still can't believe the searchers haven't found a trace of Pops. Not a hat? Not even a *glove?*" she asked while slicing into her chicken breast.

"The snow and forest can cover a lot of evidence," Sam explained as he chewed and a bluesy tune clicked on to her iPad that sat on the kitchen counter. "It's a lot harder than you think to find a person, let alone a clue, out there."

So far she had spent most of the meal querying him about the search and how it was progressing, but he didn't mind talking shop with her. He liked talking to her.

They sat on the two bar stools at the kitchen counter, almost knee to knee. Whenever she shifted, her thigh or elbow would brush his arm or leg, and he would get that old tingle again.

You're a man—a living, breathing man—and you aren't dead below the waist, the tingle said.

He had been embarrassed by it at first, like it was a burp or a fart he had unwittingly released. But now that he was on his second glass of wine, he welcomed the tingle. He damn near relished it.

The fatigue Sam had felt earlier had disappeared, too. He now felt invigorated, like he had swilled back three cups of coffee. He'd forgotten what this was like—to eat dinner and have a conversation with a woman he was attracted to. He wondered why he had buried this part of himself for so long. This wasn't a date, far from it. But it was the closest he had come to one in quite a while, which was sad, he realized. It was damn near pitiful.

"But they've been at it for three days now, Sam! I mean . . . are they going to bring in more people? Maybe the FBI?"

"The FBI?"

"That's what my mom suggested."

"Look, I've got nothing against the feds, Janelle, but respectfully, we don't need some suit from Minneapolis or Omaha telling us how to conduct this search. Our boys know what they're doing."

"But maybe they can—"

"Trust me. They're good at what they do. They know the terrain like the backs of their hands. If Bill is out there, they'll find him."

"*If* he's out there? What do you mean 'if'? You don't think Pops is in those woods?"

"I'm not ruling anything out. That's why we have the trackers in the forest, patrols on the roads, and officers and deputies from four different departments going door to door."

She pursed her lips. "You do sound like you're covering all your bases."

He nodded before taking a sip from his glass, momentarily letting the white wine pool on his tongue, before returning his attention to his plate. "We are . . . at least until we find any evidence that can lead us in one direction. Then we'll put all our resources toward that."

She released a deep breath and slumped forward. "So you really trust these guys?"

He laughed. "Yes! I've worked with them before on other searches, and I've known some of them for years. Hell, I went to high school with a few of them. They're good guys."

"Oh, yeah! That's right. Connie told me you grew up here in Mammoth . . . that your dad used to be police chief."

"Yep, for almost twenty years," he said, spearing his broccoli with his fork.

"So, if you don't mind me asking . . . how does a guy from Mammoth Falls end up in Vienna, Virginia?" she asked between chews, resting one elbow on the counter and her chin in the cup of her hand. "I've been wondering about that since you told me you used to live there."

Her knee brushed his thigh and he had to focus on what she was saying, what she was asking him. The conversation had shifted. They were no longer talking shop but veering into the personal but, with this woman, he didn't mind. Maybe he could find out more about her, too.

"*Wasting your time,*" the voice in his head chided yet again. And again he ignored it.

"I went to D.C. for a police conference about nine years ago . . . some summit. I can't even remember the name. Dad was supposed to go but he had foot surgery coming up. It was a last-minute thing and had already cost the town money to send him. He didn't want to back out, so he asked me to go in his stead." He paused to take another drink. "So I went and decided to stay."

"You stayed? Just like that?"

"Well," he said, inclining his head, "the plan was to stay an extra few days, then maybe a week. It was the first time I had ever been to the East Coast . . . to D.C., so I wanted to explore and enjoy myself."

"Check out the tourist sites?"

"Yeah . . . you could say that."

Sites, my ass. Unless those sites were from a Victoria's Secret catalog, he thought with an inward laugh.

He recalled the young man he had been back then, full of vigor and full of himself. Though his cowboy hat and small-town charm had drawn contempt from some, there were plenty of women back east who had found it exciting, even sexy. He was the new pair of designer shoes that season that all the girls wanted and he had taken full advantage of it. If what happens in Vegas stays in Vegas, then what happened that April week at the Days Inn on Connecticut Avenue in D.C. would also stay within those four walls.

"So how did a week turn into . . . how long was it?" she asked, toying with the gold pendant at her throat.

"Almost six years," he said, lowering his fork.

"Six years? How in the world did that happen?"

He contemplated making up a lie to answer her question. The admission sounded so cheesy when he said it aloud, like "I love puppy dogs," or "My favorite movie is *Sleepless in Seattle.*" It would seem like a sappy pickup line orchestrated to win her over, but it was the truth.

"I met my wife, Gabriela, the day before I was supposed to head back home," he said, staring down at his half-eaten plate.

Janelle dropped her hand from her face. "So you stayed for *her?* You gave up everything back here to be with her?"

"Well, it wasn't like I had much to give up."

"Of course you did! You had your . . . your friends, your family, and your career." Her affable smile disappeared. She went very serious. "That's a lot in my book."

"I didn't set out to give it up. I just stayed because I wanted to get to know her better. Then after a while life in the city, life with her turned into a reason to try something new, to stay for the long haul."

"Oh, my God." She stared at him slack jawed, as if seeing him for the first time. "That is the most romantic thing I've ever heard."

He rolled his eyes, reached for the wine bottle sitting between them, and refilled his glass, then noticed hers was also empty and refilled hers, too.

"So what happened?"

He dug back into his mashed potatoes and looked up at her in confusion. "What do you mean, what happened?"

"The great love story! Why didn't you two ride off into the sunset together? Why aren't you still married to her?" she asked breathlessly, her dinner seemingly forgotten.

He grimaced, and she blinked as if suddenly realizing what she had asked him. She placed a hand on his forearm. "I'm sorry, Sam. That was unbelievably nosy of me. I shouldn't—"

"It's all right," he muttered. "It's a natural question anybody would wonder about." He took a deep breath. "Gabby has been . . . sick for a long time. Not *sick* sick. She's not dying of cancer or anything, but she has a mental illness. She's bipolar." He paused to take a drink. "When she was off her meds, she'd act strange. She could . . . start to hallucinate. Sometimes, she'd even be suicidal. She was a little better when she was on her medication, but she hated the way it made her feel. She could-n't take it anymore. Then *I* couldn't take it anymore. Then, well . . ." His words drifted off. He swallowed the lump that had formed in his throat, knowing that it wasn't the mashed potatoes.

Janelle nodded. "I understand," she whispered, rubbing his arm gently, causing the tingle to come back. "Here I was think-ing you had walked straight out of a western. You're a lot more complicated than I thought."

"Thanks . . . I guess." He laughed, making her laugh, too. "So tell me your love story. Tell me more about this Mark fella."

She abruptly withdrew her hand and sat ramrod straight on her stool. "There isn't much to tell." She then picked up her fork and began to eat again. "Mark and I are pretty unexcep-tional. I'd bore you with the details."

"Every couple has a story, no matter how boring it is. How'd you two meet?"

She started to look uncomfortable again, and something told him to stop prying, to bring the conversation back to Little Bill and the search, which is what they probably should be talking about. But Sam couldn't stop himself. He *had* to know more.

She fidgeted on her stool as he began to eat again. "Well, we met at a dinner party a friend of a friend was having. I didn't want to be there, but my girlfriend talked me into going. I re-member she even had to dig through my closet and find an outfit for me. I told her I didn't have anything to wear, so she pulled out this red dress that I hated! I ended up finding an-other outfit just to get her off my back."

"Why didn't you want to go to the party?"

"I was in a funk." She returned her attention to her meal and sliced into her chicken breast again. A lock of hair drifted near her eye once more, and he longed to reach out and tuck it behind her ear. "I had just broken up with someone—a guy in a long list of guys who were complete disasters. He was a *National*

Geographic photographer who traveled the world and seemed so cosmopolitan and sophisticated." She sighed and chewed. "I thought he was perfect for me, but it turns out that he was the same as all the others, just well-traveled and with a better vocabulary. I'd been trying so hard to find a guy who wasn't like my dad, but I kept running into some incarnation of him. So I went to the party and I spotted Mark that night with his wire-framed glasses and his bow tie and his navy blue sports jacket. Oh, my God, he looked so clean-cut, so *uptight!*" She laughed, reminiscing. "He wasn't the sexiest man in the world, but I knew that he was . . . that Mark was different than the rest."

"Was?" he asked, raising a brow.

"Is!" she quickly clarified. "I mean he *is* different."

"How's that?" he asked, feeling the urge to pry again. "What makes him different?"

"Well, he's . . . safe . . . predictable . . . dependable."

He smirked. "Sounds boring."

"It's not boring! Besides, excitement is overrated. I've had excitement, and all it gets you is lots of tears and heartbreak. I like that I usually know what to expect from Mark. He doesn't disappoint."

"Usually?"

"Well, people surprise you . . . every now and then," she said cryptically before drinking from her glass.

"I'm guessin' your father wasn't predictable or dependable—if you don't mind me asking?"

"He was a drunk and a junkie who cheated on my mom and ignored me completely." She clapped her hand over her mouth. "God, I can't believe I just blurted that out!" She eyed the glass she was holding and set it near her plate like it was spiked with some drug. "I think I better slow down with the wine."

"I'm sorry your father was like that."

She shrugged, putting on a mask of indifference. "No father's perfect."

"Mine wasn't," he confided between chews, wondering if the wine was starting to get to him, too. "Oh, my dad was noble! Everyone in town admired Tommy Adler and respected him. I did, too, I guess. But he wasn't . . . warm. He certainly wasn't the hugging type. I don't think I even remember him hugging Mama! And he expected a lot outta you. He was always ridin' me. I never felt like I could . . . I could please him. I never felt like I was ever good enough."

"I don't think my father cared one way or the other. My mom told me, 'He doesn't want anything to do with us, Janelle, so why should we want anything to do with him?' But I still wanted his attention, you know? I wanted something to show that he cared . . . a little. So to get a reaction out of him when I was eighteen, I changed my last name from Jones to Marshall—my mom's maiden name. I called him up to tell him—to wave it in his face like a, 'Nah-nah-nah-nah-naaaa! Look what I did! Did it piss you off?' He didn't even answer the phone."

The kitchen fell into an uncomfortable silence. He drank more of his wine while she chewed.

"Well, at least your boyfriend's nothing like your dad," Sam finally ventured.

"No . . . which is what I liked about him."

Liked . . . She was using past tense again.

"Mark represents everything I've ever wanted . . . all the things I never had when I was a girl. He represents stability."

"And you like that because you won't lose your footing," he said, repeating her words back to her. He looked down and noticed his plate was now empty.

She paused and inclined her head. "In a manner of speaking—yes."

He leaned toward her and dropped his voice to a whisper. "You know what they say about putting folks up on pedestals . . . you're bound for disappointment. My father used to say it's even worse when you make them the pedestal you stand on. 'They're bound to crumble on you.'"

Her mouth fell open, and her brows knitted together, like she was about to argue with him, but he pushed back his stool and rose to his feet. "I should be heading out. I bet I've probably got one pissed-off dog waiting for me back at my place. It's well past his mealtime."

He grabbed his hat off the counter, along with his holster and phone, which he had purposely kept nearby.

"Thank you for the dinner." He tugged his cap onto to his head. "I haven't had a meal that good in quite a while. I'll let you get to your—"

"Wait!" she shouted angrily, hopping off her stool and marching after him. "You can't . . . you can't just . . . just leave! What the hell was that?"

He raised his brows, stopping midway across her living room. "Pardon?"

"Pardon?" she repeated, mimicking him comically before her face clouded with anger again. "What . . . was . . . *that?* You tell me your story and I say it's the most romantic thing I've ever heard, and I tell you my story and you say that I shouldn't depend on Mark because he'll crumble on me! Who does that?"

He held back a smile, more amused than incensed by her outrage. "I'm sorry if I spoke too plainly. I wasn't trying to offend you."

" 'I wasn't trying to offend you' is a non-apology apology. You lobbed a verbal hand grenade at me about my relationship. Of course, I would be offended! Mark isn't perfect, and our relationship isn't perfect but . . . but . . ." She sputtered helplessly.

He took a step toward her and gazed into her eyes. "I am sorry I said that . . . with no qualifications."

"Thank you," she whispered, staring up at him. Her furrowed brow softened.

That's when he couldn't resist it anymore. He reached up and tucked the lock of hair that had fallen into her face and pushed it behind her ear—a gesture so tender that it bordered on inappropriate.

He waited for her response. She gazed at him with a look of amazement.

"I better get going," he said again before turning around.

He reached her front door and opened it.

"Wait! Wait, Sam!" she shouted, making him pause in the doorway. He faced her.

"Th-thank you for having dinner with me."

"No, I should be the one thanking you."

"But it helped me. Today was a rough day, but now I feel . . . better. Much better. I'm glad I invited you to . . . to stay."

"Well, you know what they say . . ."

She frowned. "No, what do they say?"

"When you arrive in a new town, make friendly with a cop and a bartender. You're probably going to need one or the other at some point."

She laughed. "I'll remember that."

He turned back toward the porch.

"You know, I still have plenty of food left," she said, halting him in his steps again. "I'm making a big meal again tomorrow if you'd . . . like to come back."

This time he was the one who was surprised.

"I mean if you have the time," she continued tentatively. "You could . . . uh, tell me more about the search. I won't have to keep calling you for updates."

He stared at her blankly and she lowered her gaze.

"But please don't feel obligated. I know how busy you are, so I completely understand if—"

"I'll be here," he said, knowing full well what he was agreeing to but wondering if she realized exactly what she was asking.

Another dinner alone with a man who wasn't her boyfriend. This time it did seem eerily like a date. "I probably won't be able to come until 8:30 or nine o'clock, though. I'm pulling long days now."

"That's fine. I'm in no hurry." She beamed. "I'll see you then."

"See you then," he replied as closed the door behind him.

CHAPTER 17

Yvette Black Bear hopped off the back of the Harley, tugging down her denim skirt as she did it. Why couldn't she have fallen in love with a guy who drove a pickup or better yet, a Hummer with wide, comfy, heated leather seats and plenty of leg room? No, instead she had fallen for a guy who drove a motorcycle that left her with gnats in her teeth, helmet hair, and a wind-chapped ass.

She yanked off her helmet and fluffed the lime green curls that had become matted to her head. As usual, it drew curious stares from several onlookers, including a little kid walking by who was sampling an ice cream cone. He gaped so openly that his mother had to yank him out of his stupor and drag him toward the festival gate entrance that was manned by two burly security guards.

"Casey Jason Montgomery, what did I tell you about staring at people?" the woman asked in a harsh whisper, making the boy whine in reply.

Yvette tossed her helmet to Tyler, who whipped off his aviator sunglasses and tucked the helmet in the crook of his arm.

"Catch you later, huh? I'll call you tonight," she said before leaning toward him to give him a warm, sloppy kiss good-bye.

Her tongue glided enticingly across his lips but those pouty puckers stayed firmly closed.

"What was that?" she shouted, shoving at his chest. "I've gotten hotter kisses from my grandma!"

"Sorry, babe," he muttered, looking uncomfortable.

"What? What's wrong?"

He shook his head and shifted on his seat. "Nothin'."

But it wasn't "nothin'"; she could tell. For a fleeting moment, she wondered if the reason he didn't want to kiss her was because he didn't want her anymore. She was used to that: men tossing her aside for someone cuter, someone hotter. Maybe he had eyes for Becky Rucker, the blond waitress with the big tits at the bar they liked to go to in Lead—Kurt's Hogs, Dogs, and Brews, the one with the wraparound porch and the vintage hubcaps hanging over the door.

Becky had a thing for hot guys with motorcycles. She'd be the first to greet the grizzled, dusty bikers who stepped into the bar on their way to the Sturgis motorcycle rally every year and she'd also be the first sitting on their laps before they finished their first beer. But when the rally wasn't in town, Becky kept her attention local.

Yvette had caught her flirting with Ty a few times, more than what was necessary to earn a big tip. Yvette had warned her off by telling her she'd punch her Chiclet teeth clear out of her mouth if she caught her talking to her man again, but Yvette knew her biggest worry wasn't Becky, but Ty. He had a soft spot for nice tits. Unfortunately her perky B cups were no match for Becky's double Ds. She knew that from her strip-club days. The girls with the big tits were always the highest earners, even if they had cellulite dimples, stretch marks, and the face of a mastiff. Had Becky tempted Tyler away when Yvette wasn't looking?

"What is it?" she asked, feeling her anxiety turn up like a radio dial as he stared at her. "Just spit it out!"

He leaned forward, grabbed his crotch, and cringed. "I gotta take a piss, all right?" he whispered.

Yvette felt a wave of relief. She slapped his leather-clad back. "Why didn't you just say so? Come on!"

She then turned in the direction of her mom's shop. She started to walk toward it with hips swaying. "You can use the bathroom in the back. Just . . ." She paused when she turned back around and realized that Tyler wasn't following her. Instead, he stayed perched on his Harley. He shook his head and formed his mouth into a thin line.

"That's all right. I'll just head to Toby's or use one of the port-a-johns," he said, clenching his sunglasses in his sweaty fist.

"Why the hell would you do that when a bathroom is right here?" She pointed to the shop door. "Besides, have you seen the lines heading to the port-a-johns?"

He exhaled heavily, and his shoulders sagged. His green eyes scanned the glittered sign overhead. "Evie, your mom hates my guts. She ain't gonna let me in there."

"You're just taking a piss, Ty! If she bitches about it, I'll tell her she's lucky you did it in the bathroom and not in the middle of the shop floor." She giggled and waved him forward.

Reluctantly, he cut the engine and dropped the Harley's kickstand, letting his motorcycle rest near the sidewalk. The chrome glistened in the midday sunshine. He set their helmets on his seat, lowered his jacket zipper, and walked toward her. They strolled to Hot Threads & Things. She playfully looped an arm around his neck to reassure him, ruffled his greasy hair, and licked the side of his bearded face. He smiled, revealing the tooth he had chipped when he got into a fight with another guy at a bar last year. The fight had landed him not only the dental flaw but also a night in Lawrence County jail.

Yvette unwound herself from around Tyler and reached out to open the shop's glass door but paused when she saw who was standing behind the counter. Instead of seeing her mother, she spotted Janelle Marshall digging through the jewelry display case, the key dangling from her wrist by a plastic chain. She was removing necklaces and earrings from the glass shelves and setting them on top of the case, like she worked there, like she *owned* the place.

Yvette's confident stride faltered. Her hand lingered on the doorknob a beat too long. *What the hell*, she thought, at first confused. Then she felt a rush of adrenaline and an inexplicable pang of anger. She yanked open the door, and the bell overhead swung wildly as it jingled.

"What are you doing?" she yelled, making Janelle drop the gold-and-cubic-zirconium necklace she was holding and turn to look at her.

Janelle stared at her mutely.

"Just what the hell do you think you're doing?" Yvette asked again, taking another step toward the counter.

Janelle held up her hands and backed away, like she was being held at gunpoint. "I was . . . I was just—"

"Where's Mama?" She looked around the shop. Her mother was nowhere to be found. "Does she know what you're doing?"

Yvette heard her mother's rushed footsteps. The older woman emerged from the stockroom with dark brows lowered, holding a cardboard box filled with sunglasses. "Evie, what are you yelling about?"

"Why is she standing behind the counter, digging through stuff like she works here?" Yvette asked, jabbing her finger at Janelle.

Connie rested the box on a nearby display table filled with spring merchandise. "She's helping me with the fashion show. I told her to pull some jewelry for the models."

"What do you mean she's helping you with the fashion show? I thought I was helping you!"

"I thought you were, too. But you haven't shown up here in three days! I couldn't wait around forever."

Yvette crossed her arms over her chest, her anger multiplying tenfold. "So you just gave my job away without telling me?"

"I didn't give it away! She agreed to do it yesterday when you weren't here . . . because you're *never* here, Evie, so don't act mad. I told you that I needed help with the show."

Yvette dropped her arms from in front of her chest. Her face fell.

Connie took a step toward her daughter and sighed. "Look, honey, I wasn't trying to . . ." Her words faded when Tyler stepped into the doorway, and her facial expression abruptly changed. It settled into a stony scowl.

"What's he doing here?" Connie asked in a voice so low and menacing that it caught even Yvette by surprise.

"He had to use the bathroom." She glanced over her shoulder at Tyler, who looked on edge, either because he still had to take a piss or because he could feel the thick tension between mother and daughter. "I told him he could—"

"You get the hell out of my store!" Connie exploded at Tyler, marching toward the doorway, baring her teeth like a guard dog ready to pounce. "And if I catch you anywhere near here again, I will call the—"

"Don't talk to him that way!"

"Babe, it's fine," Tyler said, backing away from the entrance. "I'll just head to Toby's." He turned on his muddy boot treads and walked down the sidewalk in the direction of Toby's Bar & Grill with his head ducked down and his hands shoved into his jacket pockets.

"No, don't . . . don't go, Ty!" she sputtered before whipping around heatedly to face her mother. "What is your problem?" she shouted.

"Don't you ever bring that man to my place of business again. Do you hear me, Evie? Not ever."

Connie gave the order in a voice so firm, flat, and cold that it no longer sounded like herself. Her face had gone harder than the visage of George Washington carved in granite thirty miles away.

"Mama, I don't know what crawled up your ass and died, but I can bring whoever the hell I like around here. It's a free country! Besides, if Ty can't come around, then *I* won't come around, either."

Connie gazed at her a long time then finally nodded. "So be it."

So be it?

Yvette flinched as if her mother had struck her across the face. She stared at Connie like the older woman had morphed into someone else—the counselor at the twenty-eight-day rehab facility who rolled her eyes when Yvette told her she didn't have a coke problem but a life problem, or the cop who took one look at her green hair, low-cut top, and miniskirt and put her in handcuffs because any girl who looked the way she did was either in trouble or would soon cause trouble. Her mother didn't bear any resemblance to the woman she had known for the past twenty-six years.

She glanced at Janelle, who sheepishly shifted her gaze to the jewelry assembled on the display counter, like she wasn't eavesdropping.

"So that's it, huh? You're through with me now," Yvette said. She could still feel the sting of her mother's words. She felt it more vividly than if Connie had really slapped her. "Is she your new daughter? You're gonna confuse a lot of folks. She doesn't look a thing like you."

She had said it with a laugh in her usual smartass way, but the tone was a mask over her true feelings of hurt and betrayal, a mask Yvette had worn for a very long time.

"What are you talking about?"

"She's doing the fashion show with you. You're kicking me out . . . you've found a good replacement, right? A classy one who wears cashmere sweaters and doesn't have a criminal record or a boyfriend covered in tattoos. That's what you wanted, isn't it?"

Connie tiredly closed her eyes. "Evie, don't start."

"Don't start? *Don't start?*" she shouted before backing toward the door. "You know what, Mama, unlike everybody else in this town, I see right through you. Right through!" She jabbed her finger at her. "I hope she's all you ever wanted, but I'll warn you, Janelle,"—she stopped to give the other woman a cryptic smile—"Mama's not all she pretends to be."

She then turned and left, slamming the door behind her. She walked back to Tyler's Harley, all the while feeling tears stream down her reddened face. Her mother was one of the few people who could bring her to tears.

"Fuckin' bitch," she muttered, wiping her runny nose and her eyes on the sleeve of her coat, seeing smears of blue metallic eye shadow and mascara on the bright wool fabric. She stopped in front of the Harley, feeling her heart pounding furiously in her chest. She leaned against the motorcycle with her eyes downcast and waited for Tyler to return. The laughter, shouts, and gaiety of the festival music seemed to mock her dark mood.

It was moments like this that she missed the woman her mother used to be. Not that she particularly liked when her mom would stroll through the front door loud, drunk, and clinging to the arm of some random man, or when she sat sullenly at the kitchen table, bitching that the electric bill or water bill was so high because Yvette never turned off any of the damn lights around the house and took twenty-minute showers. But at least back then, Yvette had known what to expect from her.

Connie Black Bear was a terrain she had traveled many times before. Turn left and you'll see Connie pulling a pack of frozen peas out of the fridge to put on the shiner one of her boyfriends had given her. Turn right at the fork and you'll see Connie complaining about the dishwasher never being emptied or that the laundry needed to be folded and "Could you just help me out for once, Evie?"

But Yvette didn't know her mother anymore. That was plainly obvious from the way her mother had behaved today. The terra had twisted and shifted like sand dunes slowly making their way across the Sahara Desert, pushed forward and backward by heavy winds and time. Ever since her mother had hooked up with Little Bill and started her boutique at his urging, she had begun changing in ways that Yvette knew many around Mammoth Falls would view as for the better. She wasn't as quick to anger. She'd have a drink every now and then, but stopped long before she was fall-down drunk. She didn't have a man stumbling through the front door every night and out the door before the cock crowed. Even Yvette had been fooled for a while. She had thought her mother had turned into the "new and improved Connie"—but that wasn't true.

Her mother had just gotten sneakier, and worse, she had become a liar.

"What happened?" Tyler called out as he walked toward Yvette while chomping into a Snickers bar.

"Nothin'," she muttered, wrapping her arms tightly around herself to ward off the chill inside and out. "Let's just go."

He stood in front of her, chewing slowly and examining her with a wary eye. "What's wrong?"

"I said it's nothing!" She slapped the driver's seat with her open palm. "Just drive."

He finished the last of his candy bar and tossed the brown wrapper to the ground. "Okay. Where do you wanna go?" He sucked at the peanuts and nougat stuck in his teeth.

"I don't care. Let's just get out of here."

He stared at her worriedly for several more seconds before shrugging, putting on his sunglasses, and throwing his leg over his Harley. He pointed it away from the festival gates, away from the singing, dancing, and shouts. She hopped on the bitch seat and tugged on her helmet. They pulled off a minute later with a rumble and then a guttural roar.

Yvette lowered her head into the crook of Tyler's shoulder, inhaling the smell of leather mixed with the scent of gasoline and cigarette smoke that clung to the jacket's surface. She kept her eyes focused forward, staring at nothing and everything. She cried, but her tears were whisked away by wind whipping across her face.

As they drove, she closed her eyes and thought back to a similar ride one night nearly a year ago on a muggy day in late July.

Tyler had driven her home that night. They had partied hard and drank even harder and Yvette was happy the cops hadn't pulled them over. She had intended to spend the night with him but wanted to stop home to grab the leather teddy she had bought the week before and unwittingly left in her bedroom. When Tyler drove up to her front porch, she cackled after hopping off the back of his motorcycle and almost tumbling face-first into a thorn bush. Across the street, the neighbors were loudly blasting Lee Greenwood's "God Bless the U.S.A." in honor their grandson's deployment to Qatar. Several cars were parked along the shoulder and driveways, leaving only a narrow pathway for cars to pass.

"I'm prooooud to be an American, 'cuz at least I know I'm freeeeee!" Yvette belted at the top of her lungs.

"You are so fuckin' drunk," Tyler said with a grin. "You need help getting in?"

Yvette laughed again and blew him a kiss before stumbling toward the wooden stairs. She gripped the handrail to steady her wobbly feet and pushed the screen door open. It closed behind her with a *thwack*. She swerved into the kitchen with its tulip wallpaper and pale green tile that Yvette often joked was a shade somewhere between pea soup and puke. She yanked open the fridge door, pushing aside a jar of mayo and a metal tin filled with leftover apple pie in search of the Red Bull she had opened that morning. That's when she heard it—the moan. Though she couldn't tell for sure thanks to ol' Greenwood next door, it sounded a lot like her mother's voice.

Oh, hell, Yvette thought as she tipped the Red Bull to her lips and took a sip. She shut the refrigerator door and raised her eyes to the water-stained ceiling. Her mother's moan was followed by a thump, a muffled male voice, then a rhythmic squeak that sounded like bed springs.

It looked like Little Bill was spending the night. He had been staying over at their house off and on since he and Connie had started dating, though he would barely make his presence known. (The exception being the toilet seat he left up in the bathroom she shared with her mother.) But it seemed that tonight Little Bill couldn't be ignored. Yvette would be forced to listen to the sounds of the newly engaged couple's geriatric lovemaking.

"Oh, goodie," she slurred sarcastically before walking through the kitchen to the stairs leading to the second floor. She tiptoed up each riser, careful not to make too much noise, though the old wood squeaked with each step she took despite her best drunken efforts, making her cringe. She finally reached the upstairs landing and started to scurry past her mother's bedroom door, which was ajar. She was halfway down the dimly lit hall when she made the mistake of glancing over her shoulder into the open doorway. What she saw stopped her in her tracks.

A wide, hairy back slick with sweat and a pale pimpled ass hovered over her mother, who lay naked on the bed with her legs spread wide. The man grunted as he stood on the edge of the bed with his jeans pooled around his ankles as he humped for dear life. His belt buckle jingled on the floor against his work boots.

Gradually, the image in front of her and the realization of

what she was seeing fell into place in Yvette's liquor-addled brain, clicking together like tumblers in a lock.

That's not Bill, Yvette thought, swaying on her feet. *That's not Bill in there.*

She watched the couple for a minute longer before slowly shaking her head and sadly laughing to herself.

Old habits die hard, huh, Mama, she thought, feeling a mix of resignation and disgust. She then continued on her way down the hall.

In her room, she turned on the overhead light and set her now forgotten Red Bull on a dresser that was already littered with smashed cans, magazines, and crumpled fast food bags. She quickly opened one of dresser drawers and yanked out her teddy before heading back into the hall then to the staircase. She didn't rush down the stairs as she made her way out of her house. She didn't walk quietly, either. Her footfalls sounded like clomping horse hooves on ceramic tile. She wanted her mother to hear her and know that she was there.

I know who you are, Mama. I know what you are, you fucking hypocrite.

But Connie's moans, the guy's grunts, and Lee Greenwood's ode to patriotism continued unheeded.

Yvette made her way across the kitchen, then lunged for the screen door, letting it slam shut behind her.

The Harley was ripping through town now. The couple blazed down Main Street, dodging trucks and cars, and barely making it through yellow lights before they turned red. All the buildings passed in a hazy blur—Joanna's Bakery, Mason's Grocery, Cuppa Cup of Joe, the post office, and City Hall. As they drove, several faces and eyes turned in their direction. An old man hobbling with a cane paused to look up at them. A blond woman holding several grocery bags glanced at them over her shoulder. All bestowed them with looks of disdain or outright disgust.

Fuck all of you, Yvette thought as she wrapped her arms tighter around Tyler.

Who were they to judge them? Who knew what secret indiscretions that woman committed behind closed doors? Who knew what lies that old man had told in his decades of living?

We never really know anyone, do we?

"Faster, Ty," she whispered in his ear. She wanted to get away—far away from this place, leaving all her disappointments behind.

CHAPTER 18

"So what's the next step?" Janelle asked as she and Sam sat on the plaid couch in her grandfather's living room. They were finishing off the rest of a bottle of Merlot in front of the fireplace where a few logs burned, filling the living room with light popping sounds and the smell of burning embers.

Sam had agreed to have dinner with her again under the guise of giving her more details about the ongoing search for Bill. Over beef tenderloin and Caesar salad, he had talked about terrain, what leads seemed the most promising so far, and search-and-rescue patterns. But the truth was he was really here because he wanted to see her. Knowing that he would spend a few hours talking and laughing with Janelle had been the one thing he could look forward to at the end of an arduous day.

"What do you mean, what's the next step?" he asked as he drank from his wineglass.

"I mean . . . we're approaching day four of the search. You guys have already covered the terrain twice. The door-to-door canvassing hasn't turned up anything . . ." She let her words trail off.

"We keep looking. We keep trying. That's all we can do."

"But you can't keep looking forever, right? You're going to stop at some point."

She was right. If this dragged on for too long, eventually the men would have to return to their regular duties. Some were doing it already. Eventually, the disappearance of William "Little Bill" Marshall would become a cold case file that would wait for some industrious detective in the future to solve, or it would sit abandoned and forgotten.

But he wasn't sure Janelle was ready to hear all this quite yet, so he decided to keep it to himself.

"Yes, the *official* search will stop one day," he said, willing to give her a sliver of the truth. "But *I* won't give up until I can give you some answers. I can promise you that."

"Thank you, Sam. I appreciate it."

He nodded.

"You know, sometimes . . ." She rubbed her thumb along the rim of the glass, gazing into the dark red pool inside of it like she was reading tea leaves and deciphering the future. "Sometimes I feel so guilty because I'm starting to lose hope. I *want* to believe that you'll find Pops, but some days I wake up in the middle of the night and I think, 'Oh, God, I'm never going to see him again. Am I?' I mean, I knew he wasn't going to live forever. Pops is spry, but he's old. I knew that. But I never thought I'd lose him like this. And there are so many things I wish I had said to him, Sam. So many things . . ."

Her words drifted off again.

Utter desolation . . . that's what he saw on her face. Sam recognized that feeling. He longed to touch her, to make her feel better, but he didn't. Instead, he shook his head.

"Don't feel guilty. A thing like this is bound to make a person sway between hope and misery. I wouldn't beat myself up for feeling either way."

She closed her eyes and nodded.

"But don't sink too far under, either. Try your best to distract yourself, if you can. Connie's fashion show is a good outlet for that."

She opened her eyes and stared at him. A faint smile finally crossed her lips. "How in the world did you find out I was going to be in the fashion show? I just told her yes yesterday!"

"I guess she told somebody, somebody told somebody else, and they told me. I don't remember who." He chuckled. "Don't underestimate small towns. Word gets around fast in Mammoth."

"Oh, *greaaaaaat!*" She lowered her wineglass to the coffee table and dropped her head into her hands. "Now I'm imagining a hundred pairs of eyes staring up at the stage, waiting for the black city girl to make a fool of herself. Like I'm not anxious enough!"

"Oh, chin up! It won't be that bad."

"Won't be that bad?" She barked out a laugh.

He liked listening to her laugh and watching her do it. He liked how she threw her head back and closed her eyes, how her mouth went wide. He wondered if that was the same face she made in bed.

"You should have seen one of the dresses she wanted me to wear. It was awful! Just awful! Rhinestones with fringe along the hem . . ." She shuddered, making him laugh again.

"Well, it *is* a rodeo queen–themed fashion show, isn't it?"

She stubbornly shook her head. "I'll wear a cowboy hat. I'll even wear cowboy boots, but I'm drawing the line when it comes to fringe!"

He shrugged and took a drink from his wineglass. "We'll see. Connie can be pretty convincing when she wants to be."

"Oh, believe me. I know!" she said ruefully with widened eyes. She then adjusted her top. Janelle was wearing one of those sweatshirts that hung off one shoulder, like that gal from the movie *Flashdance.* He fought the urge to lean over and place a warm kiss on her collarbone.

"I thought I was getting a good deal out of this since she was letting me use her washer and dryer and her scanner, but now I'm starting to question my decision."

"You'll be fine."

She grumbled in reply.

"And hey, if I can break away for a bit, I'll come by for moral support—if you want me to."

"*Really*? Would you have the time to do that?"

Honestly? No, he wouldn't. In his mind, he assembled a list of things—professionally and personally—that he had to do that took precedence over stopping by a fashion show, but then she eagerly reached out and placed her hand on top of his forearm. She gave it a squeeze that made him forget the list, that made the hair on his arm stand on end, and made his pulse race. It was like being a teenage boy all over again.

"I know I sound like a baby, but it would be nice to have a friendly face in the crowd. I'd appreciate it."

He glanced down at her hand and then up at her again. The room fell silent with the exception of the crumbling logs in the fireplace.

And this is when the night diverged into three different realities. He could feel the split happening, like his body and the world around him divided evenly into what he thought he should do, what he *really* wanted to do, and what he ultimately ended up doing.

In the first reality, he nodded and rose from the sofa before telling her he should head home. She walked him to the door and thanked him again for having dinner with her. He insisted he should be the one thanking her. He then waved good-bye and told her he'd see her tomorrow.

"It's a date," she said before shutting the cabin door behind him.

In the second, Sam picked up the hand she had rested on his forearm. He ran his thumb over the knuckles, making her dark eyes flicker toward his. He held her gaze for several seconds before leaning forward and pressing his lips lightly against her own. Her lips were full and soft—just like he had imagined.

He waited for her to pull away or to push him off of her, but she didn't. Instead she kept her lips firmly against his, taking shallow breaths that sent hot blasts of air through her nose onto his cheek. He ran his tongue along her lips, urging them to part. When they finally did, he delved his tongue inside her mouth, licking along the rim. She tasted like Merlot. She wrapped her arms around his neck as the kiss deepened and he slid his hand up the back of her sweatshirt, feeling the warm skin on his fingertips. She moaned softly and the kiss increased in fervor. Then grudgingly, he pulled away, still feeling the sensation of her lips on his even as he stood to leave.

"I should probably go," he said, and she nodded dully, watching him as he walked alone across the cabin's living room to the front door.

He then opened the door and shut it behind him, knowing that he would be back tomorrow night and anticipating the possibility that the next kiss would turn into something more.

In the third scenario—*true* reality—he picked up the hand she had rested on his forearm. He ran his thumb over the knuckles, making her eyes flicker toward his. The moment stretched on longer than it should have as he waffled over what to do next. Finally, he raised the knuckles to his lips and kissed her hand. He then lowered the hand back to her lap and bid her good night.

"I should be heading out now," he murmured as he rose to his feet. "It's getting late. I'll let you get your beauty sleep."

"Oh? Uh . . . yes. It is . . . it is getting late." She loudly cleared her throat. "I'll . . . I'll walk you to the door."

The next morning Sam stumbled out of bed at five a.m., still exhausted and feeling like he had slept two hours, not six. He peered into his hallway, only to find his dog, Quincy, waiting patiently near the front door with his leash in his mouth and his tail thumping on the floor so hard it could have beaten a hole through the warped hardwood.

"All right, boy," Sam called out as he wiped the sleep from his eyes. "Hold your horses! I'm coming."

He hastily washed, dressed, and ran out the door with Quincy at his side just as the first pinpricks of dawn were on the horizon. They thumped down the stairs to his front yard.

The duo traversed more than a mile, zigzagging over trails partially hidden by brush and thawing snow, going deeper and deeper into the woods. Sam would pause every now and then to throw a tennis ball and let Quincy fetch it.

"Go get it, boy," Sam said as he stopped again to toss the yellow ball into the distance.

He watched as it bounced once, twice, then rolled down the hill and disappeared into the shadows beneath low tree branches and a thicket of shrubs.

Though Sam had lost sight of the ball, Quincy's eyes were considerably better than his master's. The golden Lab went chasing gleefully after it—sending up a spray of white snow and fallen pine needles. Sam reluctantly followed.

He wasn't enjoying this quite as much as Quincy. Sam was now wading ankle-deep in thawing snow, feeling the hem of his jeans become soaking wet. The tree canopy overhead was also dripping water onto his head. All the while, Sam kept glancing down at his watch, feeling the minutes ticking by, knowing he'd have to report to City Hall in a half an hour.

But he didn't call Quincy back. He knew he owed the dog this. He had returned home late several nights in a row and hadn't given poor Quincy a decent walk in almost a week. He wasn't even giving Quincy his full attention now. His mind instead kept drifting back to Janelle.

As Janelle had walked Sam to her front door last night, she

had looked disconcerted by what had transpired, and he'd felt a pang of guilt for kissing her hand, but it quickly passed.

It was *her hand*, not her mouth—or any of the many other extremities he had fantasized about kissing when he was with her.

Sam knew what he was doing: pushing the boundaries between appropriate and inappropriate just far enough that neither could feel guilty. They could pretend he was the well-meaning police chief, having dinner with her to bring her solace. She could pretend that she was still in love with her boyfriend. But the subtext was there; he wanted her, and he suspected she was starting to feel something for him, too. He just had to wait for the moment when she would finally acknowledge those truths.

Quincy bounded back to Sam with the tennis ball in his mouth. The dog's fur was damp and covered with dirt and slush along his belly and paws. He opened his jaw and dropped the ball at his master's feet, making it sink into the snow. He then looked up eagerly at Sam.

Throw it again, boss, the look said.

Sam chuckled, picked up the soggy tennis ball, and tossed it again—farther this time with the ferocity of a pitcher aiming for home plate. Again, Quincy went chasing after it. Sam watched the dog disappear behind a line of trees. He stood in the snow with his hands in his jacket pockets, waiting patiently for Quincy to return. A minute passed and then another and Quincy still hadn't come back with the ball.

"Quincy!" Sam yelled, cupping his hands around his mouth like a megaphone. "Hey, Quincy!"

Had he thrown it too hard?

He squinted into the distance, listening for Quincy's bark or the sound of the Lab trampling through the brush. He heard neither.

"Quincy!" he called again.

Suddenly, his cell phone began to ring, a piercing chirp in the aching silence of the forest. Sam tore his gaze away from the brush long enough to reach into his pocket and pull out his cell. He squinted at the name and number on the screen. When he saw who it was, his heartbeat instantly picked up its pace. His hands shook.

"What've you got?" he barked, not even bothering to say "hi."

As he listened to the voice on the other end of the line, Sam heard the sound of breaking twigs and rustling leaves. Quincy galloped toward him, holding not the tennis ball Sam had thrown, but a baby doll in his mouth. One of its blue glass eyes was missing, along with one of its plastic legs. Quincy proudly dropped it at Sam's feet and panted.

Sam gazed down at the doll that had sunk face-first in the snow. According to the lieutenant now on the phone, it seemed that Quincy wasn't the only one who had made a discovery in the woods.

"All right. . . . All right. I'm heading into City Hall. Catch me up on the details when I get there," Sam said before ending the call, not knowing whether to be relieved or sick to his stomach.

CHAPTER 19

The rumor began as a whisper a little after dawn, but by noon it had turned into a roar. Rumors spread quickly in small towns and this one had the momentum of a mudslide after a heavy rain; there was no stopping it once it started.

"Hey, did you hear about what the trackers found last night?" a customer shouted over the sound of the espresso machine to the girl behind the counter at Cuppa Cup of Joe as she toasted his wheat bagel.

"I hope it isn't true," the older woman whispered to her companion as she held a stack of envelopes against her saggy bosom. They lingered in front of the glass door of the Mammoth Falls Post Office and stepped aside for another woman pushing a stroller. "If it is true, it would be awful. Just awful!"

The crime reporter at the *Mammoth Falls Gazette*—a transplant from Cleveland who had always had dreams of working at the *New York Times*—nearly choked on his hash browns when his editor tossed the tip onto his desk. He quickly dialed the direct number to the police department to get confirmation.

He could see the story now in his head, from the lede to the closing sentence. It would be the article that would propel him to the big leagues! Mentally, he was already rehearsing his Pulitzer Prize acceptance speech.

"Come on! Pick up!" he shouted, though his call was kicked to the automated messaging system.

The lines had been flooded since eight a.m. with similar calls from residents who all wanted to know if the rumor was true.

Did the search teams really find a body in the woods late last night? And was it a man or woman? Young or old?

Was it Bill?

No one knew for sure. It depended on what version of the rumor you had heard. Some said it was a young man who showed signs of a stabbing. Others said it was an old woman who had been shot three times—once in the head, twice in the chest. And some said the body was so gruesomely charred that only dental records could reveal the person's true identity.

But they all agreed on one thing: the cops had finally found something.

When word reached Connie's ears, she saw little pinpricks of bright light in her vision just before everything dimmed, like someone had flicked a switch from on to off. She almost crumpled to her knees on the tiled floor, but she gripped her kitchen counter to catch herself. She managed to stay upright long enough to ease into a chair at her dinette table.

"Connie?" the voice called out from the phone. It was Linda, one of her girlfriends whom she played poker with on weekends, whom she had partied with in the old days. "Connie, you still there?"

Connie couldn't answer. Words eluded her. She couldn't stop trembling. She felt like she was going to explode—go supernova right there in her kitchen and burst into a billion pieces.

She sat the cordless phone on the table and dropped her head between her knees. That's what you were supposed to do when you were hyperventilating, right? Her legs had gotten pale during these past winter months. She barely recognized them.

"I'm so sorry, honey," the tiny voice said above her from the handset on the table as she sat unmoving. "Maybe it isn't Bill. Maybe it's somebody else."

Connie closed her eyes. Her throat became even tighter, as if someone had wrapped a rope around it and was pulling for dear life.

"Mama, what the hell are you doing?" Connie expected Yvette to say when she walked into the kitchen and found her mother silently sobbing with her head between her knees. But then Connie reminded herself that Yvette wasn't home. Yvette hadn't been home in two days.

She's probably with him, Connie thought, finally sitting upright. Her head lolled to the side drunkenly. *She's probably with the son of a bitch who killed my Bill.*

He's never coming back, Connie thought, letting the finality of that knowledge settle into her hours later as she stared blankly out her shop window at Main Street. She watched the festival goers as they lollygagged along, toting balloons and stuffed animals. Two blocks down they were holding a fake calf roping contest, where four competitors hopped on inflatable plastic horses and lassoed a straw "calf" before hopping back down the street. The crowd roared with laughter. Some took pictures of the contest with their camera phones.

How could people go about their business, like the entire world hadn't ended?

It didn't matter to her that Sam had called the shop to tell her not to lose hope.

"We're letting the medical examiner look it over," he had said in that annoyingly calm voice of his. "We haven't confirmed the identity yet. It's so disfigured that we'll probably have to use dental records."

"What the hell do you mean 'disfigured'?" Connie had yelled into the phone.

"I can't go into more detail right now, Connie. When I get a chance, I'll sit down with you and Janelle. I'll explain everything, but things are a little crazy over here right now."

He hadn't sounded like things were crazy. He had sounded like he had his feet up on his desk and he was flipping through the latest issue of *People* magazine. Meanwhile, Bill was dead, and the people who had killed him were going unpunished.

"Let's just wait to see what the analysis says," Sam had continued. "I don't want anyone jumping to any conclusions."

"Well, while we wait, are you following up on that thing I told you about? About Tyler Macy?" she had asked. "What are you gonna do about that, Sam?"

He had paused for a long time. "I'm sorry, Connie, but . . . there's nothing to do. There's still nothing connecting Tyler to this. Look, I know you want someone to take responsibility for what's happened to Bill, *whatever* has happened to him," he said, when she loudly started to grumble. "But we can't just blame people at random. I can't—"

"Yeah, well, thanks for the update, Sam. Or should I say, thanks for nothing?" she had spat before hanging up on him, feeling hot tears of fury slide down her cheeks.

Blaming people at random . . .

Don't jump to conclusions . . .

She knew the truth in her heart. She knew Bill was dead and Tyler was behind it. Sam could believe what he wanted.

She was tired of hoping and praying. She just wanted the worry to end, and with news of a body discovered in the woods, Connie finally had her ending. And with that came an anesthetizing acceptance. She would never get to make amends, to make up for what she had done to Bill last July.

When she had gone out to the bar with Linda for a girls' night out—the first since her engagement—she hadn't intended to meet anyone, let alone bring a man home. But that's what she ended up doing, and it was doubt, not the five shots of tequila, that made her do it.

Am I making the right decision to marry Bill? Will I mess this up like I always do? Am I good enough for a man like him?

The constant questioning made her so nervous that she had started to break out in hives.

"Something irritating your skin, honey?" Bill had asked as he ran his fingers over the red bumps and welts on her back and shoulders while they sat in bed the night before.

"No," she had answered irritably, shoving his hands away. "It's nothin'."

She wanted to escape, to leave her worries behind, and she did it that night, laughing with Linda, flirting and dancing with strangers, and ultimately, kissing a burly guy with sideburns who looked like an overweight Burt Reynolds.

She and Linda downed so many shots that they were way past tipsy and couldn't drive themselves home. The guy Connie had kissed at the bar—she still couldn't remember his name (Kurt? Kenny? Something with a K)—had offered to give them a ride. He had dropped off Linda first because her house was closest to the bar.

"Get her home safe, you hear me?" Linda slurred before stumbling out of the pickup to her porch steps.

When he reached Connie's house, she threw open the truck's door and paused as the truck sat idle a few feet from her driveway. She slowly turned to him.

"You wanna come in?" she asked, blurting out the words before she had a chance to take them back.

He eagerly nodded, like he had been waiting the entire drive for her to ask. She noticed then that two of his teeth were missing—one of his canines and a molar on the other side. In the truck compartment's overhead light, she noticed that his gray hair was a little greasy and dotted with flakes of dandruff. She shifted her gaze and saw that he had sweat stains underneath the armpits of his gray t-shirt. An acrid mix of alcohol, perspiration, and dirt rose off of his skin.

Connie smiled in return.

Yes, this was definitely a man she was good enough for. This was a man she wouldn't disappoint.

She inclined her head and hooked her finger, beckoning him to follow her. Within twenty minutes, they were in bed together.

The next morning, Connie made her tear-filled confession to Bill. She hadn't meant to hurt him, she explained. She hadn't wanted to disappoint herself by being everything that she suspected she always was: a middle-aged, low-class, drunken whore. But he had forgiven her. She didn't know why. Maybe it was the tears or her begging, or maybe it was because he had loved her that much, but he forgave her. He just didn't forget.

She realized this when he never again brought up them getting married and when he started wearing condoms—something he hadn't done the entire time they had dated.

"They say everyone should wear them . . . no matter what the age," he had whispered before ripping open the foil packet with his teeth.

She saw it in the lingering looks he gave her and heard it in his loaded questions. "What did you and the girls get up to last night?" or "You know Danny well, do you?"

From that point on, Connie had decided that her goal for the rest of her life or his, with him being so much older than she was, was to help Bill eventually move on and forget what she had done. She'd be the perfect girlfriend—sweet and accommodating. She'd be the ideal mother to Yvette. Stepford wives would have nothing on her! But now she would never have that chance. Now he was gone.

Connie finally turned away from the store window and the last boxes she would load in her truck for the fashion show tomorrow, though, honestly, her heart wasn't in it anymore.

What did she care about coordinating cowboy hats with dresses and preparing the right accessories when the man she loved was dead?

She slowly walked across the shop toward the stockroom. When she entered, a thin shaft of light illuminated the space. It came from her office, a glorified walk-in closet adjacent to the stockroom that contained a small metal desk, rolling chair, computer, inkjet printer, and water cooler. Janelle had taken over Connie's tiny office for the past three hours and had been printing and scanning documents. Connie could hear the printer's metallic hiccupping even on the shop floor.

Connie didn't understand how the young woman could think let alone work after hearing the news they had heard today, but she suspected it was Janelle's coping mechanism. She buried herself under work and to-do lists—like Connie had buried herself under alcohol and men in the old days. But it was time that they both took a break and ate something, in Connie's opinion. She had two spare microwave dinners in the fridge with their names on them.

She raised her hand to knock on the cracked open door but paused when she heard Janelle's voice.

"Yes, I'm okay," Janelle murmured with a heavy sigh. She sat in Connie's chair with her head in one hand and the other holding her cell against her ear. The desktop screensaver flickered behind her. "Really, I am. Thank you for calling again and checking up on me." Her voice grew warmer. "I know how busy you are now."

Connie cocked an eyebrow. So Janelle had made up with her boyfriend? He had broken out of his busy schedule to give her a call?

He's lucky she's willing to forgive him, Connie thought. But she figured she wasn't one to talk about forgiveness.

"On one hand, I'm glad the trackers finally found something, but on the other hand I'm still hoping it isn't Pops," Janelle continued.

Poor girl. She's so in denial. Connie shook her head.

"Yes, I know . . . I know . . . I'll hope for the best . . . Yes, that's all I can do." She raised her head. "Oh, please! You don't have to apologize for not being able to come over. I told you. I know you're busy." She laughed softly. "Yes, I'll give you a rain check. The chicken cutlets will be waiting in the fridge. They aren't going anywhere."

Connie frowned. *Chicken cutlets?*

"Of course . . . Of course," Janelle said again. "Don't worry about it . . . Just keep me updated . . . Okay, talk to you later. Bye, Sam."

She then lowered the phone from her ear and set it on the office desk.

Sam? She was talking to Sam?

Connie shoved the door open, and Janelle looked up at her.

"Oh, hey, Connie!" The young woman glanced at the pile of papers on the desk. "I'm almost done here. I'll be out of your way in ten minutes or so. I just need to send this—"

"What's going on between you and Sam?" Connie asked, cutting straight to the point with a razor sharpness that surprised even her.

"Huh?"

"What is going on between you and Sam Adler?" she repeated more slowly, feeling her annoyance morph into anger.

Connie didn't know why she was angry. Less than a week ago, she and Yvette had practically been trying to marry Janelle off to Sam. But, of course, that was before she knew the type of man Sam really was.

A disappointment.

A coward.

"What do you mean, what's going on between me and Sam?"

She laughed anxiously. "Nothing is going on between us! I don't know what you're talking about."

"You're a bad liar. I heard you talking to him on the phone." She pointed at Janelle's cell. "It didn't sound like nothing to me."

Janelle's jaw tightened. "You were eavesdropping?"

"I wasn't 'eavesdropping.' I was coming back here to—"

"Yes, you were!" She shot to her feet. "You were standing behind the door, listening to my phone conversation, which is . . . is *completely* inappropriate! Do you realize that? You know, if I knew you would do something like that, I wouldn't have taken a call here. I wouldn't have *used* your office at all!"

Connie narrowed her eyes at her, taking in Janelle's defensive stance, her blustering, and her outrage. Yeah, something was going on between her and Sam. A cheater knew another cheater, and Janelle had guilt written all over her.

"Have you told your boyfriend?" Connie persisted.

"Told him about what?"

"About Sam."

"No!" Janelle said indignantly. "And I don't need to. I told you, there's nothing to tell! We're just . . . just friends!"

"Friends?"

"Yes, friends. I mean . . . I've . . . I've had him over for dinner, and we've talked a few times."

Connie's brows rose almost to her hairline. "You had him over for dinner?"

"Yes." Janelle dropped her hands from her hips. "Maybe once or twice, but who cares! I'm an adult. I'm capable of having dinner with a man without doing anything, Connie."

"That's what they all say. It always starts out like that, and then it turns into something more. You'll end up doing something you'll regret later," Connie warned, trying her best to blot out the memory of her own transgressions. But she couldn't let go of the vision of Kurt/Kenny looming over her, leering down at her. "It's best to be up front about these things. If you're starting to have doubts about what you and Mark have going on . . ."

Janelle opened her mouth to argue again, but Connie quickly held up a hand.

"I'm not saying that you *are!* I'm just saying if. *If* you have doubts, just be honest with him. I don't know your boyfriend, but any man or woman deserves that . . . for someone to be honest. That's the least they deserve."

Janelle fell silent. She gradually lowered herself back into her chair. "You sound like you're speaking from experience."

Connie leaned against the door frame. "I told you before, I don't always make the best decisions."

"No, you said you didn't make good decisions before you got with Pops."

"Before—and after," she clarified in a barely audible voice.

Janelle opened her mouth, then closed it. She shook her head. "Never mind."

"No, go ahead. Say whatever you've gotta say."

"Why . . . why didn't you and Pops get married?"

Connie stared at the younger woman in surprise. "Who told you we got engaged?"

"No one. I saw the marriage license in Pops's bedroom. I saw that it wasn't signed."

Connie sucked her teeth and pushed herself away from the door frame. "Why the hell did he hang on to that?"

"Maybe he was hoping that one day you guys would finally get married."

"I wouldn't count on it."

"Why?"

"Because your grandfather forgave me, but he will never forget what I did. I know he won't."

"Did you cheat on him?" Janelle blurted out, then immediately looked like she wanted to suck the words back in.

Connie's face remained impassive. "I'd rather not go into the dirty details, if you don't mind. It's not exactly something that I'm proud of."

Janelle grimaced. "Yes, I'm sorry. I didn't mean to—"

"I disappointed your grandfather. I told him what I'd done, and it broke his heart. And I will live with that for the rest of my life." She took a deep breath, making her shoulders rise, then fall. "You're a smart girl. Learn from my mistakes. Don't do the same thing I did."

"I told you. Nothing is going on, Connie. Sam and I are just friends. Just . . . *friends*. Okay?"

You're lying to yourself, honey, Connie thought. But she could see that any further argument was a waste of time and effort. She could see from the look in the younger woman's eyes and the firm set of her jaw that she wasn't going to listen to any warnings Connie offered.

I wouldn't listen to me, either, she thought forlornly before turning back toward the stockroom.

"Come on," she muttered. "Let's eat."

PART III

"What can everyone do? Praise and blame. This is a human virtue, this is a human madness."

—Friedrich Nietzsche

CHAPTER 20

It was a tense allegiance between Little Bill and The Mutt. Little Bill still didn't have much affinity for dogs, especially this dog—the one lying at the foot of the bed with his paw draped over Bill's ankle. After all, the dog had almost killed him by aimlessly wandering in front of his truck on a dark road. He never would have had that accident if he hadn't swung his wheel to avoid hitting the dog. But it wasn't The Mutt's fault that he was a stray who hadn't been taught to run when he saw headlights coming toward him.

The Mutt, which is the title Bill had given the dog since he couldn't think of another name that was more appropriate, seemed to like Bill, too. Bill didn't coo to The Mutt and rub his back and tummy like the blond woman, Snow, did, but he'd sneak The Mutt yummy human food when she wasn't looking. She kept trying to get The Mutt to eat some vegan dog food that tasted like tree bark. It made The Mutt suspicious of her. No sane human would think a dog wanted to eat that crap.

Bill and The Mutt also were united in their joint hatred of

the fat Persian cat, Mikey. The Mutt hated Mikey because . . . well, because Mikey was a cat, and that's how dogs usually felt about cats. Bill hated Mikey because the cat seemed to act like a prison guard, keeping stern watch over his captives from where he sat in front of the bedroom door. Every time Bill shifted or rose from the dirty mattress in the bedroom at the back of the trailer, the cat would climb to its feet and arch its back. Mikey's tail would stick straight up it the air like a gray feather duster and he would let out this horrible yawl and hiss that sounded like bacon on a skillet. When Bill lay back down, the cat would lower its haunches, purr, and fall back to the floor in a great furry heap.

If Bill could find a way to get around the cat, he was sure he was halfway to freedom.

"Sic him, boy," Little Bill whispered fiercely to The Mutt. "Bite that kitty."

But The Mutt only glanced at him indifferently, then continued to stare at the wall in front of him.

"And how is the patient doing today?" Snow asked while walking into the bedroom, holding a tray covered with crackers, a glass pot filled with herbal tea, and a chipped coffee cup. She set the tray on the stack of newspapers beside the bed and smiled as she pushed up the billowing sleeves of her teal kimono, which looked frayed and old.

"I'd be fine if y'all would just let me go home," Bill muttered as she poured tea into a mug.

She paused midway in handing it to him. "You're free to go home any time you like, Bill—as soon as you're well enough to do it."

"That's what she always says," Mabel mumbled petulantly in his head. *"But why do they get to decide what's 'well enough'?"*

He wondered that, too. They acted like he was a guest, but he felt like a prisoner.

Bill yanked the mug out of her hands and took a sip. He had

refused to drink the tea the first few days she offered it to him, worried that it was laced with some drug that would make him enervated. He finally broke down and realized it was plain old green tea. Though he still preferred coffee, he was starting to acquire a taste for the stuff.

"Who died and made you Nurse Ratched?" he snapped.

She stood ramrod straight. Her skinny body went rigid, and her smile disappeared as she glared at him. "I am *not* Nurse Ratched. That woman was horrible! She was definitely out of tune with her *chi*. She could have benefited from meditation and deep cleansing. I'm a kind and giving spirit, Bill. I'm only trying to help!"

He rolled his eyes and grumbled. Bill reluctantly had to give her and Doc their due. Whatever holistic mumbo jumbo they had performed on him, it had worked. His back no longer felt like someone had taken Thor's hammer to it, and he was slowly regaining his strength thanks to the short walks he took in the front yard while leaning against Doc's side. But now that he was walking and relatively healed, he didn't understand why they couldn't just give him a ride back to his cabin. Why was he still here?

"When you do something bad, you have to make amends," she continued, setting the plate of crackers on the stack of newspapers. "That's how the universe works. You get back what you give and—"

"What do you mean, 'when you do something bad'? What did you do?"

She paused and swallowed loudly. "Well, I . . . I didn't do it. Doc did it, b-but he and I are soul mates, and the path he takes, I take with him."

Bill wrinkled his nose. "What?"

"He didn't mean to hit you!" she burst out. She started toying with her kimono belt. "It was an accident. We were driving on the road to meet a . . . umm . . . a very important friend."

Bill wondered if it was one of the many "friends" that came to the couples' trailer. The line of folks Bill had seen walk past his small bedroom window and leave a few minutes later clutching baggies or making furtive glances around them included all types: grizzled bikers covered in tattoos, pimpled teenagers wearing glasses, and even a housewife type who had worn big, dark sunglasses, a silk scarf on her head, and a trench coat that made her look like Jackie O back from the dead.

"Doc was tired, and I should've taken the wheel, but I didn't," Snow continued. "I get so nervous driving at night." She started wringing her hands. "And then we turned a bend and we must not have realized he had hit you, because there you were lying in the road. He saw you before I did. He saw you in the rearview mirror and he slammed on the brakes." She closed her eyes and took a shaky breath. "He felt awful, Bill. Just awful!" She opened her eyes and gazed at him. Tears were on her ruddy cheeks. "Doc really hopes that you can forgive him."

They hit me?

Why didn't he remember any of this happening? His last memory had been his own car accident and lying in the middle of the road. Had they hit him after that? Had they even hit him at all?

"So until you're in tiptop shape," she said, stepping back with the tray in her hands, "until Doc feels that he's brought your body and your state of being to what it was before we hit you, you can stay here. We saw on the news that those folks are looking for you, but you're in good hands, Bill. They don't have to worry, and you can tell them where you were when you get back."

"*What?* People are looking for me?"

Her mouth clamped shut. She looked as if she had said too much. "Is there anything else I can get for you, Bill?" she asked, her voice brightening.

"Who's looking for me?" he persisted.

She didn't answer him. Instead, she rushed back to the bedroom door, climbing over Mikey, who was stretched across the doorway again.

"Who's—"

The door slammed shut before he could repeat his question.

"What did you get yourself into, Bill?" Mabel asked a few seconds later after the bedroom fell silent.

"A whole heap of trouble," he whispered as he watched Mikey stretch yet again and roll onto his back.

CHAPTER 21

"Oh, honey, you poor thing!" Nancy Wannamaker cried as Connie walked into the festival backstage area—a ten-by-twenty-foot section cordoned off by steel poles, black curtains, and a well-worn gray carpet that revealed the asphalt roadway beneath in some spots.

Connie barely had time to drop the cardboard box she was holding before Nancy reached out and pulled her into a tight embrace. Connie blinked and kept her arms hanging limply at her sides, letting the smell of Nancy's overpowering perfume fill her nostrils, feeling herself crushed against Nancy's bountiful chest.

"You poor, poor girl," Nancy repeated, patting Connie's back like a crying babe. "I'm so sorry to hear about Bill!"

The fashion show would start in less than an hour, and Connie had about three hours' worth of things that needed to be done. Her truck still contained the last of the boxes and garment bags filled with dresses and shapewear, boots and high heels that needed to be sorted or steamed. A quick glance around her showed that she was still short about a half dozen models whom she would have to track down to find out if they were on their way and would arrive in enough time for the show. She had about five million tasks on her to-do list and wanted to get to them all, but she kept being stopped by random townsfolk, offering their condolences, telling her how Bill was in their prayers. And they would all ask her the same question, "How are you doing?"—like they really wanted to know the answer.

I'm on an emotional high wire and could go plummeting to the earth at any moment where I would go splat, she wanted to tell them. *I've lost Bill. My daughter isn't speaking to me. I feel hopelessly alone.*

But instead, she'd paste on a kind smile and quietly accept their words of sorrow before murmuring, "I'm getting through."

They'd then nod their heads sadly, move along, and leave her to do her work.

She'd have to do the same thing now, whenever Nancy finally released her from her death grip.

After a minute or two, Nancy took a step back. She gazed at Connie and frowned. "Oh, honey, you look horrible!"

"Thanks," Connie answered flatly.

Nancy sniffed. "Well, I mean you don't look very . . . rested. But I wouldn't expect you to be, considering . . . well . . . everything!"

It was true that she wasn't very rested; she had had only two hours of sleep last night, but Nancy's version of "you look awful" didn't just include the bags Connie was carrying under her eyes. Connie also had foregone wearing makeup today— something Nancy would never do and frankly, something Connie hadn't done in quite a long while. It was the first time she hadn't worn makeup since she was thirteen years old and had stolen her foster mother's frosted pink lipstick and coated her mouth with so much of it that she looked like she was wearing a vat of Vaseline on her lips. But she didn't want to wear makeup today. She wanted to be clean.

That morning, she had stood in the scalding hot water, scrubbing her face so much that the skin started to burn. She had been sobbing as she did it. She had cried to the point that she had vomited on the shower's tiled floor, choking on her own sobs. When she had emerged from the shower stall, a fine coat of steam was on her bathroom mirror and walls. She stood naked on her powder blue bath mat, feeling the heat from the shower rise off of her skin and the blood drain from her head.

When she was a little girl, her grandmother had told her stories about the *inipi* ceremony—what the Lakota would do to purify themselves. White people called it a sweat lodge. Connie had felt almost purified standing naked in her bathroom with her body cooling in the draft coming through a crack in the room's only window. She had stared at herself in her bathroom mirror for a good twenty minutes, examining her crow's feet, her frown lines, and every blemish she had accumulated in the last fifty-two years. She ran her hand over her body. Her breasts were losing their buoyancy. The gray strands on her head and in the thick patch of hair over her vagina were growing in number. Her hips had widened and so had her thighs, which had once been so thin that she could see between them.

Why had she been hiding this for so long under lipstick and mascara, balconette bras and skinny jeans? This was who she was. This was the *real* Connie Black Bear, the woman whom Bill had loved, for whatever reason.

This is what I want the world to see when I talk about my Bill, she had thought while gazing into her mirror.

She had decided that she would dedicate the fashion show to him. Instead of talking about designs and fifty percent discounts, she was going to do a speech about Bill, since she would probably never get the chance to do a proper eulogy in his honor.

It felt good to do it. It felt right.

"I've got something you can put under those eyes that'll help," Nancy said, scurrying to one of the tables in search of her makeup bag and a concealer.

Connie ignored her and started to walk into the crowd, looking for Janelle. She found her standing in a bathrobe, pulling rollers out of her hair as she nodded and smiled at two women: Mary Elizabeth Barnes and Bernice Faber, collectively known around town as "the church ladies."

The church ladies weren't in the Hot Threads & Things fashion show. In fact, they probably believed they would burst into flame being in proximity to clothes that were so indecent.

Bernice was the widow of the long-deceased reverend of Christ Church, and Mary Elizabeth was her gal pal. The two women had been virtually connected at the hip since 1997. They dressed in the same ankle-length dresses and baggy sweaters that made them look like they were wearing burlap sacks, finished each other's sentences, and seemed to consider it their vocations to separate the wheat from the chaff among God's flock.

Connie knew from the looks they gave her whenever she ran into them in town what category they thought she fell into.

She couldn't hear what Bernice and Mary Elizabeth were saying to Janelle, but she could tell from Janelle's eyes and the look on her face as she approached that she wanted out of whatever conversation the three were having.

Save me! Janelle silently pled as she turned to her.

"Bernice . . . Mary Elizabeth," Connie said, "how are you doing today? Can I help you with anything?"

The two women turned in unison to stare at Connie like those creepy little twin girls in the movie *The Shining*. Their polite smiles disappeared. Pure contempt was on their wrinkled faces.

"No, Connie, no assistance necessary," Bernice said primly. "We were—"

"—just telling Janelle here that we were performing today and planned to dedicate a song in our performance to her grandfather," Mary Elizabeth finished for her.

"Oh? Well, that's nice of you," Connie said.

"Janelle," Bernice said, turning back toward the younger woman, "you are new to our fair town, but know that your grandfather was a man who was well liked . . . dare I say, *loved* by many in Mammoth Falls—myself included."

At that, Connie almost snorted.

Bill had told her that he had tried to shake Bernice's hand once at some town event, and she had given him a look like he had lowered his zipper and taken a piss on her shoes.

"We would like to venerate him as a soldier of the Lord, a servant of God," Mary Elizabeth explained, "to—"

"—to honor him, and bring some healing to our little hamlet with the good word," Bernice finished for her with a big smile.

Connie took a tiny pleasure in seeing Bernice had a smear of pink lipstick on her teeth.

"I agree," Connie said, speaking up again. "I'm dedicating the fashion show to Bill, too. It's about damn time everybody stops talking about him like he's some crazy old coot. I'm gonna set the record straight and let everyone know what a great man Bill is."

The duo stared at Connie.

"The fashion show?" Bernice asked. "You mean—"

"—a show where women wear low-cut dresses with their bosoms hanging out?" Mary Elizabeth said the word "bosom" in a breathy, scandalized whisper that made Connie frown.

Bernice scrunched her pug nose. "Where they're wearing more makeup than dime store floozies?" She blinked her watery blue eyes rapidly. "You *really* think that honors Bill's memory with such a . . . a crass presentation?"

Connie lowered her brows. Her lips tightened. She opened her mouth to respond, but Janelle cut her off.

"Well, thank you so much for letting me know, ladies! I'll be sure to keep an ear out for the song."

"God bless you, dear," Bernice said before reaching out to squeeze Janelle's hand.

"Bless you," Mary Elizabeth echoed like a parrot.

They then turned away, not bothering to say good-bye to Connie.

"Those self-righteous old bitches," Connie muttered, shaking her head.

"Just ignore them," Janelle urged. "Let's focus on the fashion show, okay?" She glanced at a nearby rack filled with clothes. "All the dresses look great, by the way! I'm sure it'll all turn out fantastic! You should be really proud."

Connie didn't respond. Instead, she stomped back toward the black curtain, simmering with anger.

CHAPTER 22

Regina Marshall <Lovelylady1957@hotmail.com>

April 28 at 1:58 p.m.
To: Janelle Marshall <jayjaymarsh@yahoo.com>
Subject: What do you mean Mark isn't there???

Hi Sweetheart!

How is Mark not there with you? Did he say why he couldn't come? Did his mama die?

There's a hurricane in the Atlantic. Can you believe it??? It's not even hurricane season yet! They aren't sure if it's going to touch down in N.C. or N.Y. so, needless to say, my flight home got canceled. (I KNEW I should have booked that first flight back home when I had the chance!)

Are those hillbilly cops still trying to identify that body they found? I've made many promises to God, telling him I'll do anything he wants as long as it isn't Daddy who they dug up!

Again, wish I could be there with you, honey. I'll try to book the next flight as soon as I can. My heart is with you (even If I can't be.)

Luv you!

XXXX

Lydia Roach <roach.l@bryantconsultinggroup.com>

April 28 at 2:04 p.m.
To: Janelle Marshall <jayjaymarsh@yahoo.com>
Subject: How are you?

Hello Janelle!

Thank you for sending those documents. They were a bit late, but you do what you can, right?

I wanted to check in with you again to see how things are going. Please let me know how you are doing! We are all thinking of you and several of your colleagues have asked me for an update. I told them that unfortunately, I haven't spoken to you in several days but that's understandable considering the circumstances.

Also, when you get the chance, if you could give me an estimate for when you plan to return to work. That would be lovely! There's no rush (please don't rush!) but I really need to know. We have that important training seminar coming up next week so I may have to bring in assistance if you won't be here.

Sincerely,

Lydia Roach
Assistant Human Resources Director
Bryant Consulting Group Inc.

Mark Sullivan Jr. <Sullivan.MarkJr_113@gmail.com>

April 28 at 2:23 p.m.
To: Janelle Marshall <jayjaymarsh@yahoo.com>
Subject: ARE WE REALLY DOING THIS?

I've called you and texted you and emailed you for almost THREE DAYS now. WHY AREN'T YOU RESPONDING?

I said I was sorry I couldn't fly out there, Jay. Again, I know you're going through a lot but let's not be childish about this. If I could get away, I would, but unfortunately I don't have a job with the same flexibility as yours. I've checked my schedule and I should be able to catch a flight tomorrow, though I would have to take the next flight back Thursday night. (Another important meeting Friday.) But frankly, I'm not sure if I should buy a ticket. DO YOU STILL WANT ME TO COME???

—M

BTW, I didn't say it at the time but I resent you insinuating I have something going on with Shana. And we had teriyaki beef and wonton soup that night, if you really want to know!

* * *

It was ten minutes to showtime, and Janelle was adrift in a sea of barely contained pandemonium. Between the shouts for lipstick, blush, eyeliner, curlers, hairspray, and double-sided tape (there were several calls for that one), and the pitchy singing from the gospel duo currently on stage, Janelle could barely hear herself think, let alone hear the chime of her cell phone. But she caught the trill, even as the woman in front of her started to whine that her boots were too tight and the woman behind her screamed that she needed a safety pin.

Her phone chimed yet again, letting her know that she had another email—one of several today that sat unread. But she'd have to ignore it. There was too much going on around her and way too much she had to do to answer her phone right now.

"Are you Connie's assistant?" a bottle-blonde with curls made big and wide by styling spritz and a teasing comb asked Janelle.

Janelle numbly nodded.

"Can you get this for me? I can't reach that far back," the woman said, wrapping her arm around her shoulder and clawing futilely at the dangling zipper of the denim dress she was wearing.

Janelle stepped forward. She furrowed her brow at the puckers of pale back fat bubbling over the top of the dress. She gritted her teeth and slowly pulled up the zipper, feeling it tense against her fingertips with each inch. When she finished, both she and the woman let out a loud breath of relief.

"Thanks," the woman said before adjusting her silver belt buckle around her corseted waist and reaching for her white bolero on a nearby table. She then turned back to Janelle. "Hey, you're Little Bill's granddaughter, right?"

Janelle paused, slightly surprised that the woman already knew who she was, but then she reminded herself, *This* is *Mammoth Falls.*

"Yes, I'm Janelle Marshall," she said with a smile and extended her hand.

"Norma," the woman said, shaking the hand Janelle offered. "And I'm real sorry about your grandpa."

"I am, too," Janelle admitted, though she was ashamed to also admit that she had hoped for a few blissful hours that she could push her missing grandfather to the recesses of her mind and instead focus on the fashion show. But she couldn't. No one would let her.

"Everybody's torn up about it," Norma continued. She reached out and squeezed Janelle's shoulder. "You have my condolences, honey," she whispered, making Janelle frown.

"Condolences? Why?"

Norma's drawn-on eyebrows rose comically. For a second, she looked like an emoticon wearing too much rouge. "Well, for your grandpa, of course!" Norma lowered her hand. "It's a shame that he died out there, but at least now you're no longer wondering what happened to him. You can give him a proper burial and, I promise you, we'll all be there! Mammoth Falls turns out for its own."

Proper burial?

"And if someone is really behind what happened to Bill, I hope they find that son of a bitch," Norma said, dropping her voice and leaning toward Janelle's ear. "I hope they throw the bastard in jail and he gets his balls ripped off! I'd do it myself if I could."

"Everybody line up! We've gotta be on stage in two minutes!" Connie barked from the stage stairs.

Norma grabbed a white Stetson and gingerly placed it on her head. "That's our cue! Guess we better get ready."

Norma then darted to the rudimentary line near the stairs that was more like a huddle of big-haired women before scrimmage.

Janelle stared after her, dumbfounded. She watched as Norma whispered something to the woman standing beside her—a plump redhead wearing turquoise suede chaps with rhinestone accents. The woman nodded, turned, and glanced at Janelle. Pity was in her big hazel eyes.

So they all think he's dead.

Janelle felt that realization tumble onto her like a boulder.

The entire town of Mammoth Falls was ready to dig her grandfather a six-foot-deep plot and carve a headstone in his honor.

Here lies Little Bill—a doddering old man who went soft in the head and froze to death in the woods.

How could they all give up on him when Janelle—his own granddaughter—refused to allow herself to do the same? What gave them the right?

"Janelle?" Connie shouted. "Janelle!"

Janelle snapped out of her malaise and turned to find the older woman striding toward her. Connie didn't look good. Her clothes were disheveled. She looked tired and haggard. She seemed moody and short-tempered—more so than usual. Janelle was really starting to worry about her.

"There you are," Connie said. "I've been looking all over for you!"

Connie then began to talk and point over her shoulder, but Janelle wasn't listening. Her thoughts drowned out whatever Connie was saying.

Does she think Pops is dead, too? Like everyone else?

She wanted to ask Connie that question, but couldn't work up the nerve to do so. She wasn't sure if she wanted to know the answer. Just like she wasn't sure she wanted to know the answer to another question that had been plaguing her since yesterday, since their confrontation in the stockroom.

Why did she accuse me of cheating?

Over and over again, Janelle replayed in her head her phone conversation with Sam, trying to remember if she had said something improper, some twist of phrase that sounded like a double entendre. She could think of nothing.

She heard it in your tone, the annoying voice in her head chided. *She heard it in the way you were talking to him. You were practically* caressing *him.*

No, I wasn't. That's ridiculous!

She was just being kind, treating Sam with the warmth that he had treated her with for the past few days.

But Connie's right. You should end it. No more late-night dinners. No more convos on the couch over wine—so nothing can be misconstrued, the voice insisted.

Janelle had contemplated this already.

That night, after Sam had kissed her hand, she had considered making up an excuse so he wouldn't come back for dinner. She'd tell him that she had a sudden onset of a cold or the cabin had a rat infestation or she was going through the world's worst menstrual cramps. She'd tell him anything so that they would never be alone in that cabin again. But, as she lay in bed, rubbing her hand so much that the flesh started to burn and ache, she had changed her mind. She replayed the moment of him kissing her knuckle—those cool, dry lips on her soft, warm skin, and a delicious thrill went through her at the memory.

Yes, it was a thrill. She could admit that now.

How had a gesture so simple ignited a flame so big?

When Janelle finally closed her eyes that night, she had decided that she wanted Sam to come back. She knew she was being hypocritical, making plans to have dinner with a man three nights in a row while she had chastised Mark for doing the same with another woman. She knew if she steered too blindly, her relationship with Sam could head in a direction that might have serious repercussions for her in the future. But she no longer cared. Sam had shown her more compassion and patience during this whole ordeal that anyone else had—including Mark.

All the questions, longing, and sadness she had endured were pounding at her like a persistent wave breaking along a seashore. And her resistance to anything that might give her some respite had gone from a stone moat to a crudely made sand castle.

I like Sam, Janelle had thought stubbornly. She liked the way he made her feel. *Why shouldn't I be friends with him? Why shouldn't I eat dinner with him again?*

"Janelle, are you listening?" Connie barked, and Janelle swiftly nodded, though she had no idea what Connie was talking about. She had been lost in her own thoughts.

"I'm gonna need you to stand at the bottom of the stairs, checking all the models to make sure everything is okay before they come on stage. You come out second to last. Check all the accessories and make sure every zipper is up and every button is buttoned. And make sure they go out *one at a time.* Okay?"

"Of course!" Janelle said, nodding again. Her neck was starting to hurt from nodding so much.

"I'm gonna be on stage. I'm going to give my speech about Bill as an intro, then talk about the fashions as the girls come out."

"Gotcha," Janelle said, then frowned, looking at Connie more closely.

Connie was bouncing on the balls of her feet, clenching and opening her hands, and looking cagily around her. Janelle wanted to dismiss the other woman's jitters as nerves about the impending fashion show, but they seemed worse than that. Connie had the same twitches that a junkie would have right before she met up with her dealer.

Janelle's stare must have been more conspicuous than she thought because Connie glared back at her.

"What?" Connie asked tersely.

"Are you . . . okay?"

Connie sucked her teeth. "Why the heck does everyone keep asking me that? I swear you people are like a broken record."

Janelle opened her mouth to answer, but stopped when Connie glared at her wristwatch.

"Dammit, they're going over their time! Those yodeling bitches are doing this on purpose! I know they are! Fucking *Wasi'chu,*" Connie muttered before marching toward the stage stairs.

Janelle let out a long breath as she watched Connie stomp up each step before disappearing behind a fold of velvet curtains. She turned back to one of the tables and leaned down to examine her reflection in a small oval vanity mirror that most of the models had been using and was therefore covered with a fine sheen from face powder and tanning spray. She adjusted her Pepto-Bismol pink cowboy hat and pushed her curls back over her shoulder. She ran her finger over one of her false eyelashes. They were both starting to droop into her eyes.

Janelle looked like a Little Miss beauty queen on steroids. She looked ridiculous. She *felt* ridiculous. But when was the last time in the past week that she had felt remotely normal?

She startled and whipped around from the mirror when she heard the crash behind her. Then she heard the feedback through the stage speakers that made her wince and clap her hands over her ears.

"Let go! Let go, you harlot!" a shrill voice shouted from the stage.

"Call me that again, and I'll punch you in the nose! Give it to me!"

Janelle recognized the second voice. It was Connie's. She rushed across the space, tripping in her cowboy boots over the hem of her dress, shoving her way through the models.

The women were all gawking and pointing at the ruckus now on stage.

As Janelle neared the foot of the stairs, she caught sight of Connie wrestling over the microphone with one of the performers, one of the weird women who had introduced themselves earlier to Janelle. The two looked like they were engaged in a serious battle, like they were close to coming to blows.

"Connie!" Janelle shouted.

CHAPTER 23

"Oh, come on, Phil! What do you mean you're pulling your men, too?" Sam lamented. "We're still—"

"I'm sorry, Sam, but we need our guys back here on duty. We've still got cases to solve . . . patrols to do. We had that big drug bust just last week. You know how it goes," the lieutenant answered.

Sam sighed and slumped back into his chair, barely listening to the voice that droned on the other end of the phone line. He had heard this so many times from other agencies in the past few days that he could spout the halfhearted apologies and excuses verbatim.

Resources for the search for Little Bill were slipping away faster than salt through a sieve. The county already had withdrawn its helicopters two days ago for another emergency fifteen miles away. More than half of the other police department officers and the sheriff's office deputies had already returned to their regular duties. And the rescue teams—who had searched the same terrain twice and found squat—were starting to lose hope. When that body was found, everyone seemed to use it as an excuse to throw in the towel or take time to regroup.

Sam glanced at his desk. A strewn pile of photos showed the corpse they had unearthed.

It had been in horrific condition when the trackers found it: rotted by melting snow and torn and mangled by wild animals. What little clothing the person had worn was almost entirely gone now. The medical examiner said, confidentially, that the body was so decomposed that it had to have been out there a lot longer than a week or two. It probably wasn't Little Bill, but he couldn't say for sure without doing a complete autopsy and running a few tests. Until then, they would have to wait a few weeks before they could make a positive ID, if at all.

"Look," the lieutenant continued on the phone line, "if you've got any new developments. If anything pops up—"

"Yeah, I understand," Sam mumbled. "Thanks, Phil."

He then slammed down his phone and glanced at his office wall clock.

2:38 . . .

The fashion show had started almost ten minutes ago, and he had told Janelle he would attend. Sam scanned the stack of papers on his desk and the multiple open windows on his desktop monitor. He had plenty of work to do, but if he still couldn't give Janelle a definitive answer for what had happened to her grandfather, the least he could do was show her some moral support. Seeing the fashion show would just take fifteen minutes of his time.

Sam reached over, turned off his computer, pushed himself out of his chair, and grabbed his cap, which sat on the edge of his desk. He placed it on his head and started to walk toward his office door, when his phone rang. He turned and glanced over his shoulder, checking the number on the caller ID. When he saw the area code then the name beneath it, he picked up the phone.

"Hey, Kevin!" he said with a grin. "I meant to call you back last week. Things have been crazy around here, I hadn't had the chance to."

"That's . . . that's okay," Kevin answered softly.

Sam glanced at his wall clock again.

"Sorry for being a dick and putting you off again, but I was just . . . uh, heading out on police business," he lied. "Can I call you back? I swear I'll do it this time."

Kevin didn't reply. Instead, Sam heard silence on the other end. His smile faded.

"Kev, you still there?"

"She's dead, Sam."

"What? Who's—"

"Gabby. She's . . . Gabby's dead. She killed herself last night . . . I mean, early this morning, I guess. Sometime around two o'clock. She jumped from . . ." Kevin paused to clear his throat, filling the phone line with a phlegmy, ripping sound. "She jumped from her apartment balcony. I thought you . . . I thought you should know."

The air was sucked out of Sam's lungs. He felt like he had been shoved to the bottom of the ocean at a hundred miles an hour and the pressure would pulverize him if he didn't black out first.

"Gabby's dead?" he repeated dumbly.

"Yes, Sam. Her rough patch was worse than everyone thought. I'm . . . I'm sorry."

She had hit a rough patch, and he hadn't been there to help her out of it.

Sam turned and caught his reflection in the black screen of his computer monitor. His face was blank. The emotions he felt were too overwhelming to find any form of expression— sadness, anger, or regret. He didn't know it was possible, but much like a computer, he had reached a system failure. Everything had halted.

"Thank you for telling me, Kev," he finally said in a voice so calm he no longer sounded like himself. "I . . . I appreciate it."

"Are you okay, Sam?"

"I'm fine. I just . . . I have to call you back."

He let the handset fall back into its cradle and turned away from his desk. He walked dazedly into the short hall leading past the deserted conference room and the men's room. As he walked toward the bullpen, Rita simultaneously ran toward him, though he didn't see her there. She might as well have been a pane of glass. He bumped into her, knocking the petite woman to the floor.

"Oww!" she yelped.

"Oh, hell! I'm sorry, Rita." He reached down and grabbed her hand.

"It's okay," she said as he hoisted her to her feet. "I wasn't watching where I was going."

"You all right?"

"Yeah," she muttered with a grimace, wiping imaginary dust off her bottom and her knees. She then peered up at him. "I was just coming to . . . Hey, is something wrong, Chief?"

My ex-wife killed herself today, he thought but instead of saying it aloud, he nodded. "Everything is . . . fine."

She continued to squint at him, and he wondered if his face was still blank. Was looking at him like staring at a mannequin in a department store window?

I know I may look strange, he wanted to explain, *but my ex-wife killed herself today, and I wasn't there. I don't know if anyone was there with her or on the phone when she did it. And what's worse for me than finding out she killed herself is knowing that she was alone.*

"I was headed to the festival," he said weakly.

"Oh, good!" Rita dropped a hand to her chest, looking relieved. "I was just coming to get you. Mitch said he needs assistance. He said a fight broke out on the stage between Connie and the church ladies. I think the security guys have their hands full with other stuff going on with a record number of folks there today. I was seeing if you could spare a few minutes to help him."

"What?" Was he so lost in devastation that he had heard Rita incorrectly? *"The church ladies?"*

"Afraid so, Chief."

Hearing that Connie was involved in a brawl wasn't so surprising, especially considering what she'd been going through lately. Hearing that Bernice and Mary Elizabeth were involved in one was a bit of shock.

"Why's Mitch calling for assistance?" Sam asked. "I thought Hank was there, too. He was supposed to be patrolling the festival today, wasn't he?"

"He was, but . . ." Rita paused.

"But what?"

She lowered her eyes. "He's . . . busy."

"Busy doing what?"

"He's on his lunch break."

"For *two and half hours?*"

She shrugged helplessly. "It's *Hank,* Chief," she said and it was all the answer he needed.

The myriad of emotions Sam felt finally coalesced into one: fury. His jaw tightened. He balled his fists at his sides.

"Excuse me, Rita," he said in an icy voice as he walked around her and strode into the bullpen.

"Chief?" she called nervously after him.

He found Hank sitting at his desk, as always, doing a crossword puzzle in the *Mammoth Falls Gazette* and loudly guzzling a Big Gulp through a straw.

"What the heck do you think you're doing? You're supposed to be patrolling the festival," Sam said, narrowing his eyes at the sergeant.

Hank's stubby pencil stilled. He slowly looked up from his

crossword puzzle and cocked a white, bushy eyebrow. "What does it look like I'm doing?"

Sam nodded thoughtfully and faked like he was about turn around and head back to his office, but then he leaned down and wrenched the Big Gulp out of Hank's stocky fingers.

"Hey!" Hank exclaimed, groping at empty air, just as Sam tossed the oversize plastic cup into a nearby waste bin, making Pepsi explode over the rim and spill onto the side of Hank's desk and the bullpen's linoleum floor.

"You can't do that!" Hank shouted, shoving himself to his feet, looking a lot like a slumbering bear that was startled awake by poking it with a stick.

"Just watch me!" Sam challenged before promptly shoving Hank into his rolling chair, sending it and Hank sailing back five feet until he and the chair bumped into the adjacent wall, knocking down a bald eagle calendar and making it tumble to the floor.

Rita's mouth fell open in shock. Several faces appeared in the police department's doorway; many of the people were from the surrounding offices in City Hall.

Hank made like he was about to rise out of his chair again until Sam charged toward him.

"Don't hit him!" Rita yelled just as Hank shielded his face.

"Now you listen to me, you sack of shit," Sam barked, jabbing his index finger into Hank's doughy chest, "you want to sit around watching your fat ass grow wider, you do it on your own time! Not on the taxpayers' dime and not under me anymore, you hear me? Or I'm writing you up!"

Hank lowered his hands. His face was red. His double chin trembled. "The . . . the union's going to hear about this," he whimpered.

"Like I give a shit," Sam muttered before turning on his heel and walking toward the department door. Those huddled in the doorway scrambled to get out of Sam's way.

"Chief!" Rita yelled as Sam opened the partition between the bullpen and front office.

"Chief!" she yelled again as he let it slam shut behind him.

She chased him into the hall, grabbing his arm just before he reached City Hall's main door.

"Sam, *stop!* What the hell was that?"

He didn't answer her. Instead he lowered his gaze, feeling his anger drain out of him as quickly as it had flooded every limb in his body.

"What's gotten into you?" she asked in a whisper so shrill that it sounded like a whistle. It almost hurt his ears. "Do you realize that Hank could file a complaint against you? What if Mayor Pruitt finds out about this? You know he has it out for you! You could—"

"Rita, I don't have time to talk about this right now," he said as he shoved the double doors open. She chased after him again. "I've gotta—"

"Yes, you do!" she bellowed.

She grabbed his wrist and dragged him toward to a nearby seating area where people took smoke breaks and gossiped in nicer weather. It was deserted today—a perfect hideaway from the prying eyes on Main Street.

"Yes, you do," she said dropping her voice again. "You can *make* time." She pointed a tiny finger up at him. "Look, I've pretended with you, Sam Adler. I've pretended like what happened between us didn't happen, but I can't pretend with this! You're losing it! You've been pushing yourself hard, going without sleep. I never see you eat anymore—not anything you couldn't get out of a vending machine. And now you've cracked up!" She threw up her hands. "Are you driving yourself so hard for Little Bill—or are you doing it for *her*?"

"What? What the hell are you talking about?"

"I'm talking about Janelle Marshall! Who the hell else? I

know that you've been hanging around her, going to her cabin every night when you're supposed to be off duty."

He stared at Rita in amazement. "How . . . how did you kn—"

"Suzie Lansing stopped over Little Bill's cabin a couple nights ago to bring Janelle a casserole. She told me she saw your cruiser there. She saw you through the window drinking wine with Janelle. She said you too looked 'pretty friendly.'"

Jesus Christ, Sam thought, envisioning the scrawny middle-aged woman peering through her car window with high-powered binoculars, watching him and Janelle eat dinner.

"Suzie *just happened* to come back the next night and saw your cruiser there again." Rita crossed her arms over her chest. "You had to know word would get around, Sam. No one can keep a secret in this damn town!"

So now thanks to Suzie Lansing, half of Mammoth Falls could be gossiping about him and Janelle?

"But I can't believe you would do this . . . that you would mess up your goddamn life and reputation for some . . . some *woman,*" she said with apparent disgust, "that you barely know . . . who's probably going to break your heart just like your wife did!"

At the reference to Gabriela, he stiffened like he had been doused with a bucket of water. He remembered why he had been so angry at Hank, why he had wanted to lash out at someone, *any*one. Feeling that anger had temporarily overwhelmed the desolation he felt inside. Now the desolation was back. A chill swept over him.

"What if Hank does go to the union? Huh? And if they come to me and ask what happened, what should I say, Sam? What should I tell them?"

"You do what you have to do, Rita," he answered in a voice that was cold and bare. "Frankly, I don't care."

And he didn't. He had thrown away his life before on a whim. It had been almost a decade, but he could easily do it again. No more police chief. No more Mammoth Falls. If that was the twist that life was going to send him, so be it.

Was that the feeling that Gabby had before she took her leap? Was she in a manic episode or a deep depression, or had she just stopped caring?

"You don't mean that." Rita's voice choked. Tears were in her green eyes. "The Sam I know wouldn't say that. He wouldn't . . . he wouldn't do any of this."

The Sam she knew?

And that's when he realized it. She was in love with him. All this time she had been in love with him. This was yet another woman he would have to disappoint—like he had disappointed Gabby and like he would probably disappoint Janelle, too, in the long run.

"Don't hang your hat on me, Rita. I'm not the right man," he said before turning around and walking down the sidewalk in the direction of the festival. He didn't look back as his swift gait morphed into a run.

CHAPTER 24

It was hot on stage. Even though it was fifty-two degrees outside with a high of fifty-five expected, according to the forecast on television that morning, Connie may as well have been wearing a bikini and stretched out on a deck chair in a cabana for all the sweat that was pooling under her armpits and trickling down her back. She suspected it was because of the stage lights overhead, blaring down on her like the sun in a cloudless sky over the equator. Or maybe she could be working up a sweat because of all the tussling she was doing with Bernice over the microphone.

The older woman had to be nearly twice her age and as willowy as a tree branch, but she had all the strength of a WWE wrestler.

"Let go! I said let go!" Bernice yelled.

Connie suddenly felt something hit her shoulder, then the back of her head, sending her dark hair tumbling into her face, momentarily blinding her.

"Ouch!" she yelped over the sound of a clanging tambourine. She tried to shield her head as Mary Elizabeth struck her again.

The throng gathered near the stage had increased from the twenty or so people who clapped their hands as Bernice sang hymns and Mary Elizabeth played acoustic guitar to almost a hundred or more. The crowd seemed to be multiplying by the second. They all stared at the brawling trio, slack-jawed. A few even rooted them on with shouts and fist pumps.

"Look at that crazy Injun!" an old man with white hair and missing teeth yelped below.

"Is this part of the show?" a bemused woman asked, letting a popcorn kernel fall from her mouth to the ground.

"That old chick is wailing on her!" another shouted.

"Go get 'em, Connie!" another yelled.

Out of the corner of her eye, Connie could see Officer Mitch Engel talking into his radio and madly shoving at the people around him, trying to make his way through the festival crowd to the stage. He hopped up and down like a grasshopper on an open skillet. By the time Engel finally made it to the stage, Connie knew she would probably be arrested. But what did it matter?

She had lost everything; she had nothing left to lose.

"Connie!" Janelle yelled as she climbed the stage stairs and dashed toward them, raising the hem of her taffeta-and-crinoline dress as she ran. "Connie, what are you doing?"

She stepped forward to separate the women, shoving her arms between them, but that also earned her a hit on the head with the tambourine. She jumped back, shielding herself.

"Don't you hit her, you old bitch!" Connie barked.

Mary Elizabeth glanced at her tambourine guiltily and lowered it to her side.

"Connie, Mary Elizabeth, and Bernice, you all end this right now! And that's an order!"

The three women abruptly stilled in the wake of the booming male voice. Connie looked down and saw Sam standing at the foot of the stage behind a metal barrier between the stage foreground and the crowd.

Where did he come from, and how had he beat Engel?

"You stop it now . . . or I'm placing you all under arrest!" he shouted over the jeering of the crowd as he shoved the barrier aside. "You hear me?"

Janelle walked toward the edge of the stage. "No, Sam, please don't arrest her. It's just . . . it's just a b-big misunderstanding. She was—"

"Stay out of this, Janelle!"

Janelle flinched and took a step back, and Connie knew why. It wasn't just because of the command Sam had made or his tone, but his face. His entire face was . . . off. He didn't look human anymore. No emotion registered on any of his features.

It was the same look that Connie had seen on his face only once, more than twenty years ago, when Sam had run track back in junior high. Connie had stood in the wooden stands, pregnant and about to burst, watching the track meet with most of the town. The Mammoth Falls track team had been set to win the finals, but Sam had missed the baton hand-off during the hundred-meter relay, costing the team its win and top ranking.

Sam had lowered his head when he did it. He already seemed devastated knowing he had been the reason for the team's loss. But as the crowd slowly cleared the stands and the teams walked off the field, Sam's father had marched him right back down to the track and made him practice the hand-off over and over again, all the while barking at the boy like some rabid dog.

Connie didn't know why she had lingered behind to watch Sam as his skinny, tan arms and legs pumped like a racehorse and his maroon uniform was pasted to his body soaked with sweat—but she did. The whole time she had been thinking, *Someone needs to stop this. Someone should say something,* but no one said anything. The few remaining had sat in the stands watching the spectacle of Sam running a one-man race and his father shouting at him. Around and around Sam went, until he had finally collapsed to the track out of sheer exhaustion. Tommy had yelled at him to stand up. After some time, Sam had pushed himself to his knees and then to his elbows before finally standing upright, trembling all over. He had stared at his father, and she had thought he would be crying or angry after enduring something so cruel and humiliating. But there was nothing on Sam's face as he listened to his father shout at him about not being fast enough, not having enough discipline. It was like Sam had been poured out. He was completely empty.

And today, he looked empty all over again.

I pitied you once, Connie thought, glaring at him. *I felt sorry for you, but not anymore.*

Tommy Adler wasn't the best man, but at least he had lived up to his responsibilities. He never would have let Tyler off the hook so easily. He wouldn't have rested until he had found Bill and made sure whoever had harmed Bill paid the price for it.

Your father would be rolling in his grave if he could see you right now, Sam.

Defiantly, Connie gave one more yank to the microphone. Bernice was no longer paying attention, so it was easy to wrestle it out of her hands.

"You're really going to arrest me, Sam?" Connie barked into the mic. Her piercing voice echoed down Main Street. She didn't remember her voice sounding so high-pitched and loud, but it seemed to catch everyone's attention as far back as the festival gates.

Several heads perked up, turning away from the wares on sale at the stands. She commanded their attention—from the rodeo clown who was making balloon animals to the four men in the six-shooter competition. They all turned around to look at the stage where Connie stood.

"*I'm* the one you're going to arrest?" she asked.

Sam didn't respond, but those dead eyes continued to stare at her.

"Hey, everybody! You hear that?" She looked into the crowd and locked eyes with some of the faces that peered up at her. "Police Chief Sam Adler wants to arrest me because I wanted to get on stage and make a speech about my man, about Little Bill, who disappeared a week ago, but these . . . these sanctimonious, snooty little bitches wouldn't let me! Is that what you really want to do, Sam?"

The jeering crowd had fallen silent. Officer Engel finally reached the edge of the stage and lunged forward, but Sam reached out, grabbed his shoulder, and stopped him. The police officer stared at him, perplexed. Sam shook his head.

"That's all I wanted to do, to talk about Bill, to dedicate this . . . this fashion show to him because he, of all people, deserves it. I . . . I didn't have any big dreams for myself until I met Bill," she rambled. "He was the one who talked me into opening my shop. He was the one who told me I could get my life together. He was the one who made me believe I could do . . . do *anything*, and . . . and now he's gone."

Her voice choked at the end. Her eyes began to water.

"Bill deserved the best and I wish . . . I wish I had given it to him."

She wiped away a tear and let her gaze travel over the sea of faces below her. Some looked confused, but most looked solemn. They were with her. They understood. Finally, everyone in town understood what she was going through. She felt her burden lift a little until her eyes settled on one face in particular: Yvette.

Connie stared in surprise. She hadn't expected her daughter to be here, not at the fashion show. But the young woman stood maybe twenty feet away with her lips pursed and her eyes narrowed. Someone in the crowd shifted, and Connie could see that Tyler was at Yvette's side. He had his arm looped around her shoulder. A smile was on his lips. No, it was more like a smirk.

She started trembling all over.

"Yeah, Bill deserved a lot more than what he got," she continued, scowling at her daughter and Tyler. "He led a good life and deserved a respectable end."

How dare Tyler Macy smirk at her? How dare he rub it into her face—here, of all places, and at this moment? And he was taunting her in plain sight of the cops—not that it mattered. Sam wasn't going to do anything, nor was Mitch Engel. They seemed unaware that a murderer was in their midst.

And what was worse than Tyler's presence and the cops' obliviousness was Yvette standing at Tyler's side.

A Brutus in leather, skin-tight pants.

But Yvette had always done that, hadn't she? She had always chosen others before her own mother, siding with Tyler, her friends, and her daddy. It hadn't mattered the years of sacrifice Connie had endured, or how she had tried her best to do right by Yvette. It wasn't enough. *She* never was enough.

"He was a good man with a kind heart who understood loyalty. You hear me? Loyalty! Bill didn't deserve to be . . . to be driven off the road, dragged out of his truck, and . . . and have the shit kicked out of him!"

Her words increased in speed and vehemence. Janelle stared at her in disbelief.

"He didn't deserve that!" Connie screeched at Tyler, making several people jump in alarm. "And he certainly didn't deserve to get taken out by some . . . some piece of shit ex-con who wasn't worth dirt on Bill's shoes! But there he is, the man who killed my Bill!"

She jabbed her finger at Tyler, and several men around him took a step back, one holding up his hands and furiously shaking his head in denial.

Tyler's smirk disappeared. He dropped his hand from Yvette's shoulder.

"So is this what you call justice? Is this all Bill is going to get? Meanwhile, this son of a bitch gets to walk around doing whatever the hell he wants! Is that what we let happen in this town, Sam?" she cried hysterically. Her cheeks were wet. She realized hot tears of rage were streaming down her face, sliding down her neck, pooling near her collarbone. "Is no one going to do anything? *Anything?*"

CHAPTER 25

After Connie screamed her question, the entire festival—young and old, men, women, and children—seemed to fall into an uncomfortable stillness. Janelle could even hear the faint sound of a car engine in the distance.

She was stunned. Even Sam was shaken out of whatever dark spell he had been under that made him look like some kind of cyborg. When Connie had bellowed his name, he had twitched like someone had zapped him with a buzzer. Those cerulean blue eyes were no longer vacant. They were tense and alert now.

Meanwhile, Janelle remained bewildered by Connie's allegations. How did she know Pops had been driven off the road, let alone had "the shit kicked out of him"? And how in the world did she know Tyler had done it? Where had she come up with this?

Janelle stared at Connie, disturbed to see the woman's soft features made blunt and gaunt by intense hatred and anger. But what was more disturbing was that several people in the crowd seemed to agree with Connie, from the looks of outrage on their faces and the growing whispers that sounded like a nest of buzzing bees.

"That's not justice!" someone shouted. Janelle couldn't see his face, but it was a man's voice, thick and husky. "Connie's right! Tyler Macy should be arrested!"

A few more murmurs erupted. Several people nodded in agreement.

"You guys found Bill's body and you haven't done a thing, Sam!" a woman toward the front of the crowd shouted, shaking with rage. She clutched the hand of a preteen girl who wore a One Direction t-shirt, who looked horrified and embarrassed. "Not a damn thing!"

"When's Bill gonna get some justice?" someone else yelled.

"He didn't deserve to die in a ditch!"

Sam held up his hands. "Look, folks!" he said, trying his best to be heard over the shouts from the throng beyond the metal barrier. Those shouts were slowly turning to a wave of rising, unintelligible sound. "We didn't find Bill's body! We found *a* body which we haven't identified yet! There's a big difference!"

"Bullshit!" someone screamed. "You know it's him! Stop pussyfooting around, Sam!"

"No, we don't!" Sam shouted back.

Janelle watched his Adam's apple bob above the collar of his uniform as he swallowed. She could see him fighting to keep his cool, fighting to keep his tone even. "Look, everybody, just . . . just let the medical examiner's office do its job. Wait for the body to be identified. Everyone just calm down, all right?"

"No, I'm not waiting anymore!" Connie screamed into the microphone. "I'm not waiting for the medical examiner or the cops! I've waited long enough!"

"You know where Tyler is!" someone shouted. "He's right here standing in front of you! We all know what he's done . . . what he's capable of!"

"He's no angel. That's for sure," an old man muttered. He

stood toward the front of the crowd, leaning on a cane. "Stole a car last year, didn't he?"

"Everyone," Sam said, trying again and sounding desperate, "please calm down. I . . . I know you're all upset, but don't do this! This is *not* who we are! We—"

"We just want justice, Sam! We want justice for Bill!" a woman yelled.

"Just lock him up! Throw him in jail and throw away the key!" someone else called out.

"Lock him up! Lock him up! Lock him up!" several in the crowd began to chant. The chants became louder and louder. They seemed to take over the entire festival.

What the hell is going on?

Janelle looked around her, wide-eyed. Was this what a mob looked like?

She glanced again at Sam, who was slowly shaking his head. His jaw tightened.

"All right!" Sam shouted. He grabbed the side of the stage and hoisted himself up, not even bothering to take the stairs. He rose to his feet and made a slicing motion with his hand. Janelle could barely hear him now above the chanting. "This show is over. I'm shutting this thing down!"

But the chanting continued. It became even louder.

"Get off of me! Don't you fuckin' touch me!" a man shouted.

"He didn't do anything! Let him go! Get off of him, you son of a bitch!" Yvette screeched.

That's when things took a turn for the worse: the mood, the voices, and the people. Loki waved his magic wand and the five blocks of Main Street between Poplar Road and Abbey Lane in the scenic mountain town of Mammoth Falls descended into complete chaos.

Everyone had been standing elbow to elbow only a few seconds earlier. Now they pushed and shoved at one another.

Janelle took a step back as the crowd surged forward, causing the metal barrier to clatter to the ground. The security guards who had managed to make it to the stage perimeter were powerless against the human tide and, instead, were crushed against the stage themselves.

The stage started to buckle in some spots. The metal ballasting system couldn't withstand the collective weight of all the bodies pressing against it. Janelle felt like she was in the middle of an earthquake and the ground was bucking and dipping beneath her.

Connie was knocked off of her feet. One of the other women—the taller half of the gospel duo—looked like she was in the middle of a rollicking heavy metal concert and had decided to stage-dive into the crowd. She landed on the writhing mob, her dress flying over her head, revealing her cotton panties beneath. Her cry of pain was smothered by the collective yells and shouts around her. Her friend started to wail like some horror movie scream queen.

"Shit!" Sam shouted, looking like a surfer who was trying to regain his balance on his surfboard in a massive wave. He quickly turned to Janelle. "Take the stairs. Get out of here! Get the hell out of here!" he barked at her before reaching for the radio on his shoulder and shouting for more police assistance.

"Connie!" Janelle shouted, gathering her skirts and grabbing Connie's hand. "Connie, we'd better go!"

The older woman nodded vaguely, looking dazed. The two women made it down the stairs, which seemed on the verge of collapse. Most of the other models had already fled, leaving behind hairpieces and rhinestone earrings in their wake.

Connie teetered on the last step. Just as Janelle reached for her hand to help her regain her balance, Connie was knocked onto the pavement. She landed on her rear and clutched her face like someone had hit her. Connie dropped her hand and revealed a trickle of blood coming from her left nostril.

"Oh, my God! Connie! Are you okay?" Janelle reached for

her but was shoved aside again, almost falling herself as she tripped over her hem. Her cowboy hat was knocked off her head and kicked into the crowd.

"You bitch! You fuckin' bitch!" Yvette yelled. "How could you?"

Janelle turned to find Yvette holding up her bloodied fist. Janelle realized in horror that she had been the one who had hit Connie.

"You told everyone it was Tyler who did it, you lying bitch! You want to act like the grieving widow? You really want to do that when I know what a fuckin' whore you are!" Yvette shouted, lunging for her mother again. Janelle jumped between them, holding up her hands.

"Evie, stop!"

Yvette lowered her fists. She shook her head in disgust.

"Bill isn't dead, Janelle. He just ran to get away from this cheating bitch!" she shouted, jabbing her finger at Connie, who was still huddled on the ground. "He wanted to get away from you, you slut! You whore!"

Janelle turned to Connie. The older woman's flush of rage had disappeared. She now looked extremely pale, like all the blood had been drained out of her.

They heard the police sirens then. The assistance Sam had called for had finally arrived.

Yvette glanced in the direction of the approaching cruisers, looked back at Connie and Janelle, shook her head again, and then ran off in some unseen direction, getting lost in the melee. Janelle turned back to Connie who was still sitting on the pavement, getting knocked to and fro by random knees and feet.

She was on the verge of getting trampled.

"Connie, honey," Janelle said, reaching for her yet again. "Please! We can't stay here!"

Connie hesitantly reached up and took the hand Janelle held out to her. She shakily rose to her feet.

"Hold onto me," Janelle ordered, feeling her panic rise with each passing second. She flinched when she heard glass shatter. Was that a store window? Someone else was screaming now. It sounded awful. In the corner of her eye, it looked like something—one of the vendor stalls—was ablaze. She didn't know how she was going to run in this dress, in these uncomfortable shoes. How was she going to lead Connie out of this? She didn't know the answer for sure, but she would damn well try.

"Don't let go. We can—"

Janelle was stopped midsentence when she felt herself being yanked. It felt like someone had gotten tangled in her dress and was pulling at the fabric. She heard the side seam rip. She tugged at her skirt to free herself but then she felt someone wrap an arm around her waist. She was lifted off of her feet.

"What are you doing?" she yelled. "Stop! Put me down!"

She was being dragged—physically dragged—by some unseen person away from Connie. The two women lost their tenuous grip. Hollow-eyed Connie was shoved in one direction and Janelle was carried in another.

The *Titanic* was sinking and they were lost at sea, being ripped away from each other by the vicious tide.

Janelle started to yell and kick. She clawed at the arm around her waist. The unseen person dragged her for several more feet before dumping her unceremoniously on the sidewalk in front of Mason's Grocery. She landed on her hands and stomach on the cold cement. Janelle quickly scrambled to her knees and looked over her shoulder to find Sam standing over her.

She stared at him in shock.

"I told you to get the hell out of here," he said sternly, before turning on his heel and marching back into the fray.

Here she was thinking that she was being kidnapped and instead, she had been carted to safety.

Sam saved *me*.

Janelle wanted to shout for him to come back, to stay with her—but she didn't. He had work to do, and she needed a place to hide while the mob had its fill. She reluctantly took Sam's advice. She looked around her and saw people scrambling in all directions. Several were running toward her. She was in danger of getting trampled again. Janelle yanked open the door to Mason's Grocery. She found nearly a half dozen people standing around with shell-shocked looks on their faces, including the shopkeeper, Agnes.

"Let's all go to the back," Agnes whispered, shuffling across the linoleum tile. "Come on!"

They followed Agnes and took refuge behind metal shelves and freezers, crouching low or kneeling on all fours, waiting for the riot to end. Thankfully, they didn't have to wait for long. Just as quickly as the chaos had erupted with all the spectacle of an exploding Mount Vesuvius, it fizzled out like the last sparkler at a Fourth of July parade.

After two hours, the crowd dispersed, leaving Main Street quite different from the way they had found it. Several car and shop windows were broken, including Hot Threads & Things, and shards of glass glittered in the light from the overhead streetlamps. Tents and stands were either tilting at odd angles or toppled into the street. It looked like the first annual Black Hills Wild West Festival had come to a climatic end several days early.

Janelle emerged from Mason's Grocery along with the others and limped down Main Street, gazing around her. She dragged her tattered, dirty gown behind her and ripped off the one false eyelash that had managed to survive the riot. She wrinkled her nose at the burnt smell of the charred remains of a stand selling cowboy hats and boots that someone had either purposely or accidentally set on fire. She watched as the firemen trudged back to their truck, carrying a limp water hose on their shoulders.

A few people sat on the sidewalk and metal benches, either in handcuffs or being bandaged by EMTs. Janelle had heard that one person had to be carted off to Lead-Deadwood Regional Hospital in an ambulance, though she wasn't sure if she trusted that rumor.

After all, unsubstantiated rumors are what had gotten them into this trouble in the first place.

Janelle walked back to her rental car, which was parked a few blocks away in the lot behind Christ Church. She searched for either Connie or Sam among the dazed faces of those she passed. She wasn't sure how they had fared in the confusion, and it gnawed at her that either Sam or Connie may have been the person strapped to a gurney and rushed to the hospital.

She found Connie standing in the parking lot, leaning against the truck bed of her Silverado, trembling like a leaf in a strong wind. Her nose was still bleeding. A scratch was on her right cheek. The wind had picked up again so her long, dark hair whipped wildly around her face and shoulders. She looked shell-shocked.

"Connie?" Janelle called out to her.

The older woman slowly turned and stared at her as if she didn't recognize her.

"Do you want me to drive you home?"

Connie squinted like she was trying to understand what she was saying.

"Do you want a ride?" Janelle repeated, enunciating the words.

Connie wrapped her arms around herself and nodded.

They drove to Connie's house in silence. Janelle didn't know the directions and Connie didn't bother to give them, so instead Janelle punched in her address and let the automated, robotic voice of the car's navigational system tell her where to go.

She glanced at the back of Connie's head as she drove. It was an opaque shield of all black.

"Connie," she asked, "how did you know Tyler was the one who abducted Pops?"

Connie slowly turned from the passenger-side window and fixed Janelle with that startled gaze again, as if she had forgotten that Janelle was sitting beside her and she was being driven in the young woman's car. "Huh?"

"How did you know it was Tyler? How'd you know he did it? I mean . . . Did he say something to you? Did he mention anything about Pops's disappearance?"

"No . . . but he didn't have to. I just . . . knew."

"What do you mean you just knew?"

"I just *knew*, Janelle," she said with more vehemence. "I . . . I felt it in . . . in my heart."

Janelle frowned. "So you accused a man of murder . . . based on a feeling?"

"Sometimes that's all you have," Connie mumbled before returning her attention to the passenger-side window. She didn't say anything else for the rest of the car ride.

When Janelle arrived at Connie's house, she pulled up to the end of the driveway and peered at the two-story home with its shoddy wooden steps and porch, parched front yard, peaked roof, and pale gray siding. It looked badly in need of some tender love and care. It looked lonely.

"Do you want me to come in with you?" Janelle asked, leaning over the leather armrest as Connie opened her car door. "I can stay for a bit if—"

"No, that's all right," Connie said, lowering her bloody tissue from her nose. "Look, I'm sorry, Janelle. I'm . . . I'm sorry for everything. Please forgive me."

"Of course I forgive you."

Though Janelle suspected she wasn't the one who could grant Connie the absolution she was seeking.

Connie nodded and slammed the door shut. Janelle watched

the older woman climb the porch steps, open the screen door, and close it behind her.

Janelle arrived back at her grandfather's silent cabin less than thirty minutes later. She shut the door behind her, not bothering to turn on the lights. Instead, she lowered the zipper of her gown, which was now covered in dirt, sweat, and ripped to shreds along the hem. She took it off and let it pool at her feet then stepped out of it. She climbed onto the couch in her bra and panties, bringing her knees to her chest and letting her face rest against the plaid sofa cushion. She inhaled her grandfather's scent, seeking reassurance from it, but it was starting to fade—the smell of his cologne was starting to lose the battle to the generic mothball smell of old sofa fabric.

She wrapped her arms around her legs and closed her eyes.

Connie may have been wrong about Tyler, but perhaps she was right about one thing: Pops was dead. The realization made an ache spread through Janelle's chest.

Her father had died when she was nineteen years old and she had accepted it with a stoic resignation that seemed well beyond her years. By then, he was all but a ghost to her anyway, one that drifted in and out her life. He'd missed all the important milestones, skipping her sixteenth birthday and not bothering to call or send a card. He hadn't been standing with her mother and neighbors, taking pictures, as she climbed into the limo to go to prom. He hadn't sat in the audience at her high school graduation.

"There's nothing you or I could've done to help him, honey. But it's okay to cry," her mother had encouraged when they got the call that he'd died. "It's okay to be hurt."

But Janelle hadn't cried—even at his funeral. She had shut the door on those emotions long ago, putting them in a lockbox of "Things to be Dismissed and Forgotten," and had thrown away the key. But she couldn't put this in a box. She longed for her grandfather, and that longing would never be quenched. But she would have to let him go.

It's okay to cry. It's okay to be hurt, honey, her mother would say.

So she finally did it. She cried for the father who had walked away and for the loss of the father who had stayed and taken his place.

CHAPTER 26

Janelle heard a knock at the cabin door. Before she pulled back the gingham curtains, even before she rose from her bed, she knew who would be standing on the welcome mat. She ran across the living room and flung the front door open. Sam stood in the doorway, silhouetted by the glow of the dark night underneath the full moon and the outline of pine trees in the distance. His face looked weary.

She didn't hesitate before leaping at him and throwing her arms around his neck, like he was a sailor who had come home from a long, arduous deployment.

"Ooof," Sam replied as she slammed into his chest.

He stumbled back slightly, grabbing the edge of one of the porch posts, barely stopping them both from taking a tumble down the wooden stairs to the gravel driveway.

"Oh, thank God! You're all right," she gushed against his chest, pressing her face into the fabric of his navy blue uniform. She released him a few seconds later.

He gave a bemused half smile. "Yeah, I'm . . . I'm fine."

I'm fine. After what they had just witnessed and endured, all he had to say was, *Yeah, I'm fine. That is so Sam.*

"How are you doing?" he asked, looking her up and down. "Got all your limbs? Still have two eyes?"

She took a step back and gestured at herself. She was wearing an oversize t-shirt and silk pajama pants. Her curly hair was in a loose ponytail at the nape of her neck. Purple polka-dot, rubber-toed socks were on her feet.

"Gaze upon Janelle Marshall in all her glory! All in one piece," she said, then paused. "Well, all in one piece *physically*, anyway." She shook her head. "What the hell happened back there? How did it turn into that?"

His smile disappeared. The weariness came back to his face. "It didn't take much. Just a lot of hurt and confused people looking for someone to blame, *anyone* to blame."

"And for some reason Connie selected Tyler. I thought they were going to erect a pyre, tie him to a post, and set him on fire in front of City Hall."

"I'm sure plenty of them wanted to, but they didn't. Tyler got pretty roughed up, but he made it out alive. We don't have another body we've got to send to the medical examiner. At least there's that."

"I don't think Connie wanted it to happen like that, Sam. She got . . . caught up in the moment, I guess. She apologized to me . . . for everything. I'm sure she'd apologize to you, too, for what she said."

His face darkened. He didn't look equally convinced. "Like I said, they had to blame somebody. I guess Connie decided to cast a wider net." He took a deep breath. "Look, I wasn't trying to keep you up or rehash everything that happened today. I know you're probably tired. I just wanted to make sure you were okay and apologize for being so rough with you."

"You don't have to apologize. I know why you did it. And I told you, I'm fine!" She took a step toward him. "Thank you for coming out here. You didn't have to."

He shook his head again. "Like I said, I wanted to see if—"

"But you could have called or texted to ask that."

He paused.

"That's what I mean, Sam. You came in person, and I'll admit I . . . I wanted you to come."

She forced the words to pass her lips before she had the chance to second-guess herself. *It's now or never,* she thought as she took another step toward him and hesitantly raised her hand. She placed it on his chest, over his heart.

"I had hoped you would come tonight. I missed you, Sam."

His reaction to her confession wasn't quite what she had expected. Instead of looking shocked or impressed, he looked sick, like he had come down with an extreme bout of nausea.

Oh, dear, she thought, also now starting to feel a little nauseated. Had she read this all wrong? Had she really dismissed Connie's warning and risked her engagement over mixed signals?

She quickly dropped her hand and retreated back to the cabin doorway.

"I-I'm s-so sorry," she sputtered. "I—"

"No, I'm sorry." He yanked off his cap and roughly raked his fingers through his hair. Matted with sweat and grime from the day's ordeals, his hair stood up stiffly. He turned away from her like he couldn't meet her eyes.

"Look, I've already given this speech once today. But it looks like I'm going to have to give it again." He cleared his throat. "Janelle, I . . . I'm not good at relationships. I've accepted that. I'm not the right guy to depend on for . . . for anything."

"How could you say that?" she cried.

Being humble was one thing, but this admission was ridiculous.

"You're the town's police chief, for Chrissake! You picked me up out of a crowd during a riot and carried me across a—"

"But I'm not good for the long haul, is what I'm saying! I want to be . . . but that's just not me. I failed someone already who needed me, who needed my help. I don't want to do it again. I'm sorry."

She inclined her head and stared up at him. "Are you talking about your wife? Is that who you think you 'failed'? You mean Gabby?"

From the look in his eyes, she knew she had hit the mark. Her shoulders slumped.

"Sam, you damn near *reek* of guilt. Do you know that? You used to cringe every time you looked at me. You did it like it was painful to even *see* me. You did it because I look like your wife. I look like her, right?"

He lowered his gaze to his shoes that were now caked in soot and mud.

"I bet there are death row inmates who feel they have less to apologize for than you do. But there's no reason to apologize! You didn't do anything wrong! You couldn't cure bipolar disorder. You wanted to help, but it was beyond your control. It would've been for anybody!"

"You don't know what the hell you're talking about," he said tightly through clenched teeth.

She angrily dropped her hands to her hips. "Yes, I do! I do, Sam!"

She of all people knew what it was like to be disappointed, to feel what you believed mattered most to you slip through your fingers: your vision of your future and the person you thought you'd spend your life with. You couldn't keep grabbing for the tether once it had already broken. Why keep punishing yourself?

"We're all adults. You couldn't make things right for her. Just accept it! We all have to take responsibility for our own messed-up lives, and it is not your job to—"

"Yes, it was my job!" he shouted, pointing at his chest, making her jump. His voice echoed in the dark, seeming to bounce off the trees and the starry canopy above. "It was my job! I was her husband and I made a vow. 'In sickness and in health.' That's what I told her. That was my promise, and I broke it—and now she's dead! And I'll never get a do-over. I'll never get to make that up to her."

Janelle's heart stopped. "She's dead?"

He closed his eyes and, after what felt like forever, finally nodded. "She killed herself this morning. An old buddy of mine called me and told me."

That cyborg stare at the fashion show—now she understood. It all made sense.

"Oh, Sam, honey, I'm so—"

He held up his hand to stop her. "Like I said, I'm not one to depend on." He placed his cap back on his head. "Get a good rest. Maybe I'll see you in the morning in town, huh?" He dipped his head in a curt good-bye and started to turn toward the porch steps. Watching him, she felt her throat tighten. She started to shake.

There was no way she was going to let him walk back to his patrol car and drive home alone to sit with his thoughts and his regrets. She knew what that was like, and frankly she had had her fill of it.

Janelle reached out and grabbed his arm, making him turn to face her.

"I heard what you said. I understood and . . . and I still want you to stay. Because I've . . . I've been where you are. Okay? I thought I came to Mammoth just to find my grandfather but . . ." She took a shuddering breath and released his arm. "But I did it to save my father, too, as crazy as that sounds. I kept telling myself that I wasn't devastated when he died, but I was. No matter what he did to me and my mom, he was *still* my father! I still loved him. And I've been burdened with guilt because I didn't try to save him when I had the chance. I could have looked for him, but I didn't. I let him . . . I let him die alone. So I get it. I get it, okay?" She took another step toward Sam, drawing close. Tears were in her eyes. "But you can't save someone who's been dead for thirteen years. And I'll be honest . . . I couldn't save him even then, because he didn't want to be saved, Sam. I realize that now. And you couldn't save Gabby, either—no matter how much you wanted to . . . no matter how hard you tried."

At those words, she saw something break in him. He swallowed, and she could see tears were in his eyes, too.

"We *have* to let it go! We have to forgive ourselves."

He didn't respond. Instead, he sniffed and wiped his nose with the back of his hand.

"Do you think you can do it? Because I think . . . I think I'm finally ready."

She then stood on the balls of her feet and wrapped her arms around his neck. He squinted at her in confusion. She didn't just want to let go of the guilt—but of the past, those old rules that guided her. That told her to leave her impulses and emotions behind and lead a boring, orderly life without risk or chaos. She was done with that, too.

"I'm ready, Sam. Are you?"

He dipped his head, almost in a nod, like he had finally relented. She raised her lips to his and kissed him. He responded almost immediately, wrapping his arms around her and parting his lips. Whatever last misgivings she had fell away like the clothes they would later leave on the cabin's bedroom floor.

The kiss deepened. She inhaled his scent and reveled in the rough feel of his five o'clock shadow against her cheek. She drew him closer. Janelle felt like someone had offered her a glass of some exquisite vintage wine and said, "Here, have a sip," and instead she had decided to down the whole thing with one gulp. Sam was just as ravenous with her, shoving his hands into her hair, never pulling his mouth away.

Janelle hadn't slept with another man in almost two years and only five men in her entire lifetime, including an awkward sexual encounter on a stained tweed couch in a rec room her junior year at college. As she and Sam undressed in the soft glow of bedroom's only lamp, she belatedly realized that he resembled none of her past lovers: he was pale, hairy, tall, and blond. As they lay in bed on top of crumpled sheets, she acknowledged that the torso pressing against her own and the arm wrapped around her were both new and foreign. But the newness was exciting, enticing. She took delight in the novelty known as Sam Adler.

By the time he was centered between her thighs, she was gasping for air, feeling herself being pulled under some unseen tide. She clung to him and tried to hold on to the sensations of the moment, tried to appreciate the significance of what was happening, but couldn't as the wave crested then fell over her again and again. Finally, she relented. She took her last gasp, closed her eyes, and let herself sink under the current.

CHAPTER 27

She snored. Sam didn't know why that discovery amused him so much, but it did.

"You know, I've been told that I'm a *really* quiet sleeper," she had boasted at around two a.m. after they had made love for the second time and were nestled beneath the wrinkled sheets like caterpillars in their cocoons.

Sam had yawned in response, more out of fatigue than boredom. By then, he could barely keep his eyes open. It was the type of sleepiness that came after a hard day ended with good, sweaty sex and little to no regrets.

Her voice had sounded far away as she spoke. So did the squeak of the old bedsprings beneath them as she shifted closer to his side.

"You'll barely hear a peep out of me," she whispered into chest hairs before he drifted off to sleep.

But by six a.m., evidence to the contrary filled the cabin's bedroom. Her snores sounded like a grizzly bear hibernating for the winter in a dank cave, and it roused Sam out of his blissful slumber. Once he heard it, all attempts of going back to sleep were impossible.

She didn't wake up when he climbed out of bed, nor did her

snores subside. As he dressed and made his way to the bedroom door, they got louder. He watched her with her face partially obscured by her pillow and her mouth cocked open and he chuckled silently. He shook his head as he closed the bedroom door behind him.

How could she not know she snores?

He considered this as he made his way across the living room that was illuminated by intermittent shafts of light from the window facing the front porch. He entered the kitchen and opened and closed cabinet doors in search of coffee, *real* coffee. Not the bag of blond roast Starbucks that was sitting on the counter. He had turned away from the bag faster than if the label had said "Laced with arsenic." After shifting aside a jar of olives and two boxes of linguini, he finally found it: a half-empty bag of unexceptional Community Coffee and a pack of coffee filters. He found the coffeemaker next to Bill's old toaster near the fridge, poured in some ground beans and water, and waited for it to brew.

Hadn't anyone told Janelle she snored?

You'd think her boyfriend would have told her by now, Sam thought as the coffee began to percolate.

And just like that, the euphoria of the moment wore off. The realization hit Sam with a wallop. *Her boyfriend . . .*

This wasn't some ordinary morning after. They weren't going to sit around, drink coffee, eat buttered toast, and gaze lovingly into each other's eyes while they exchanged stories about their childhoods and joked about her snoring.

Janelle was in a relationship with another man with whom she lived in a big house halfway across the country. Meanwhile, Sam was still recovering from a divorce from a woman who killed herself only yesterday. And now he and Janelle had slept together.

He leaned back against the laminate counter and swallowed the lump that had lodged in his throat.

He hadn't made any promises last night, and neither had she. Though, truth be told, they hadn't said much of anything to each other after she kissed him. Neither had been very interested in conversation after that point. Desire, sadness, and loneliness had made them both get swept up in the moment.

Just two people dealing with a lot of shit, he thought.

He had done something like this before with Rita and immediately felt regret the morning after—but he didn't feel the regret this time around. He was at peace with what had happened between him and Janelle and hoped it could develop into something more.

The last of the coffee dribbled into the beaker beneath the filter and a loud suction sound filled the kitchen. Sam turned off the coffeemaker and opened a cabinet in search of cups.

As he pulled out two chipped mugs and set them on the counter, he resolved that he wouldn't try to brush off what had happened between them. He wouldn't pretend like it was nothing—a satisfying roll in the sheets—but he wouldn't try to paint Janelle into a corner, either. She held all the cards in this. If she wanted to end it with her boyfriend and try to give a go to whatever was going on between her and Sam, he would try his damnedest to make it work. He had walked away before from one woman he loved because he didn't think he had the strength, the fortitude to stick with her through thick and thin. He would find that strength this time around.

But if Janelle decided that what had happened was something nice but also brief to be fondly remembered but not repeated, he would accept her decision—grudgingly. He would have to.

Sam heard Janelle walk up behind him less than twenty minutes later. He was sitting in Bill's rocking chair on the front porch, sifting through his muddled thoughts, finishing his cup of coffee, and watching the sun rise. He had left an empty mug on the counter next to the coffeemaker for her.

"So this is where you are!" she exclaimed. "I was wondering where you had gotten off to. I thought you had left."

She sounded relieved that he hadn't. That meant something, didn't it?

He turned toward the doorway where she stood, and he shook his head. "No, I don't have to be at City Hall for another hour or so. I've been out here the whole time. I was going to leave soon, though. Should probably head home and take a shower, change clothes, shave."

"Oh?" Janelle asked, sounding a bit crestfallen.

For the first time, Sam wondered how he could have ever confused her with Gabriela. The two women were similar but so vastly different. It was like comparing mayo to peanut butter, the Dodgers to the Braves, or the moon to the sun.

She's different now because I know her.

He knew her, and he liked her. He more than liked her—and now he stood a good chance of losing her before he could even say definitively that he *had* her.

"Yeah, but I can stay for a little while longer. Come sit with me," he said, holding out his free hand to her.

She hesitated, rubbing her bare arms against the chill in the morning air. He could see goose bumps sprouting on her skin. "I-I don't have on a coat."

"Neither do I. Come sit with me."

She wavered a moment longer before finally stepping through the doorway and walking toward him on the porch. The floorboards creaked slightly beneath her weight with each step she took. When she reached the rocking chair, she hesitated again.

"Go ahead and have a seat," he said, gesturing to his lap. "Watch the sunrise with me."

She wrapped her arms around her middle and shook her head. She stared down at her feet. "I can't do that. I'm not going to sit on you! You want your legs crushed?" she joked, forcing out an awkward laugh.

"You didn't crush them last night, did you?"

Her gaze leaped to his face.

Even though he promised himself that he wouldn't, he was pushing her again, forcing her to make a decision.

Are we or are we not going to do this, Janelle? I'm a forty-year-old man with little patience. Show me you want this or push me away, but don't waste my time with the polite brush-off, he thought, feeling his pulse quicken as he waited for her response.

Her smile widened, and she laughed an honest laugh this time around. "Fine. Have it your way." She then plopped onto his lap and fell back against his chest, facing the vista of the mountain and trees.

The wave of relief that washed over him was indescribable.

He set down the coffee cup beside his feet on the porch and wrapped his arms around her waist. He pulled her close. She rested her head back on his shoulder and snuggled against him. They watched the dawn in mutual silence. She was soft and warm and the weight of her on top of his chest wasn't crushing, just as it hadn't been last night. It was reassuring.

How low had he been yesterday? To what depths had he fallen? And now the world had flipped. At that moment, his contentment was surreal.

"I'm about to ask you a question, and I need you to be honest with me," she said out of nowhere several minutes later.

Sam correctly guessed her question had nothing to do with the sunrise. His sense of euphoria was quickly waning.

"Okay . . . what do you want to know?" he answered quietly to the crown of her head, feeling his heart go *ka-thud, ka-thud, ka-thud* against his rib cage. She was still looking off into the distance, but he was staring at the part at the center of her head with a focused intensity that made his eyes burn.

"Is . . . is the body you guys found in the woods Pops?"

That question had caught him off guard. He hadn't thought that's what she would ask. "Well . . . I can't say for sure until they finish the autopsy, but it doesn't look like it. The body . . . its condition . . . the medical examiner said he doesn't think it's Bill."

She sighed. "Okay, so if it's not Pops, what are the chances of you guys finding him alive after all this time? Is it still good? Just tell it to me straight. I wanna know the truth."

He waited a beat before answering her question. He tightened his hold around her. "*Anything* is possible but from my experience . . . no, it's not . . . it's not good."

She sat silently for several seconds, not moving.

"I'm sorry, Janelle."

"It's okay," she whispered. "I've . . . I've been bracing myself for this. Last night before you came, I cried my eyes out. I did my mourning—so I can do what I have to do next."

He frowned. "What do you have to do next?"

"I have to go back home. I have to deal with my life. I don't think I can stay with Mark anymore, and it's not just because it's what Pops would've wanted or because of . . . well, what we did last night. I don't recognize myself anymore, Sam. I'm not . . . I'm not the same woman I was when I boarded that plane a week and a half ago."

"You don't *think* you can stay with him?" he repeated back to her slowly.

"No." She paused and raised her head. She turned to gaze at him. "What? Why are you looking at me like that?"

His lips tightened as he sat up in the rocking chair, forcing her to also sit erect. "You said you know what you have to do next, but it still doesn't sound like you know for sure what you want to do."

"I said I couldn't stay with him, that we had to break up."

"No, you said you don't *think* you could stay with him."

"Why do you keep harping on the 'think' part?"

"Because those two statements are very different. It still doesn't sound like you're sure what you want."

She bit her bottom lip. "Look, I'm trying to take more risks and be braver, but I'm not like you, Sam. I wish I were, but I'm not."

"What does that mean?"

"It means you left Mammoth Falls and started a new life halfway across the country after falling in love with someone! I bet you didn't even give it a second thought, did you?"

He thought back to the moment in April 2007 when he had decided to toss his plane ticket into the hotel room trash can after his second date with Gabriela. He had opened his hotel menu and ordered the shrimp linguini an hour later. As he waited for his meal to arrive from room service, he had called his father and told him that he was staying in the D.C. area permanently.

Sam shook his head. "No, I didn't."

"See, I could never do that! Even if I know my life can't continue the way it was, I can't just . . . just *drop* everything! I can't go down a checklist and just . . . just dump my boyfriend . . . quit my job . . . leave my house. I have to consider the repercussions!"

"What repercussions?"

"*What repercussions?*" she stared at him, dumbfounded. "Sam, I was *in love* with him and I think he was in love with me, too . . . kind of. We have a house together . . . a *million-dollar* mortgage. We were setting up a life together, and I can't just—"

He leaned forward so that they were almost nose-to-nose, and she instantly quieted.

"None of that stuff matters if all those things make you unhappy . . . if they aren't what you really want," he whispered against her lips. "What do you really want?"

She trembled as she exhaled, and he felt the heat of her

breath on his mouth. He wanted to kiss her again but resisted the urge.

"I want . . . I want to be . . ." She seemed to grasp for the right words. "I want to be brave enough to do whatever I need to do. I want to be confident that I made the right decision, and I wasn't doing it out of fear or desperation or to prove to myself that I won't have a screwed-up relationship like my parents. I want to make the best decision for me."

That wasn't the answer he had hoped for or expected, but it was an honest answer. He could see the fear in her eyes as she said it.

Despite what Janelle had said last night, what she had professed to him about being "ready," he could see now that she was still lost. She was closer to finding her way and might have even found the beacon but hadn't decided yet if she wanted to follow it. Sam had been here before, but he knew from experience that no one can drag you out of the forest. He had tried it before with Gabriela and failed. No, this was something Janelle would have to do herself. You had to find your way out on your own and trust in the direction you were going.

"Whatever you need, I hope you find it," he said and he meant it.

He then leaned forward and kissed her. She kissed him back, and he pulled her against him and held her close. A minute later, she dragged her lips away and ran her knuckles on the scruff along his chin. She gazed sadly at him.

Here it comes, he thought, feeling the weight of resignation and acceptance crash into him like a sack of bricks.

"I'm going to miss you," she whispered.

"Are you going to come back to Mammoth?" he asked, trying to keep the ache out of his voice.

He examined her face before she answered. He knew her well enough now that he could tell when she was lying. She wasn't a very good liar.

"Yes," she answered truthfully, "if by some extreme chance you have any more info about Pops. Or if Connie needs someone to clean and pack up his cabin."

"I'm sure she can get folks to help with that. You don't need to come back for that unless you really want to."

"I don't know . . . but I know I can't keep lingering like this. I don't know what purpose it would serve besides making me sad and miss Pops even more." She rested her hand on top of his and squeezed it. "You have an open invitation to visit my neck of the woods. I can reacquaint you with our nation's capital."

He shook his head. "I have too many memories of Gabby out there. It'd be like walking through a graveyard."

He could imagine strolling down some city street and stumbling upon an Indian bistro that reminded him of the one with the geriatric waiter where he and Gabriela had had their first date. Or maybe he would be walking in front of the Jefferson Memorial to admire the cherry blossoms and get assailed with the memory of the first time he had kissed her along the Tidal Basin. Those recollections of Gabriela would never disappear, but he'd rather not come face-to-face with them so soon after her death.

Like Janelle, he needed to get a little stronger first.

"I understand," she said before kissing his cheek. "Maybe we could meet somewhere in the middle. How about New Orleans? Ever seen the French Quarter?"

Will we meet up as close friends . . . or something more? he wondered, but didn't voice the question aloud. Instead he said, "Too hot. How about Chicago?"

She laughed sadly. "Too cold."

"We'll figure it out," he whispered, hoping it was true.

She nodded and slowly eased away from him. He reluctantly let her go, feeling her absence the instant their bodies were no longer touching. She rose to her feet.

"I should start packing. Maybe I can book a flight and head out today. The sooner I face my demons, the better."

"And I should get going. Gotta take that shower, and I better walk the dog before he starts filing official complaints."

He handed her his now empty coffee mug and she clasped it in both hands, staring down into its depths, tracing her thumb along the brim. "I'll walk you to your car," she said softly.

They both made their way down the cabin stairs and driveway, moving at a glacial pace, dragging out the moment. Finally, they reached his cruiser and he paused near the driver's-side door.

"Oh, I forgot to give you something."

Sam opened the door and reached inside the vehicle. He popped open the glove compartment and pulled out the gold necklace with a diamond pendant attached that she had lost during yesterday's skirmish. She usually wore it all the time, so he figured the necklace had to be of some significance.

"I think this is yours," he said, holding it out to her.

When she saw it, she grinned. "Oh, my God! I was wondering what happened to that."

"I thought you might want it."

She nodded as she gazed down at the pendant. "It's my grandmother's. I always wear it because it's hers. It's the . . . the last thing I have of her." She looked up at Sam. Tears were in her eyes. "Now I'll have to go find something of Pops that I can always wear. Something I can bring home with me that I can remember him by."

At that, Sam felt a kick to his gut. "I'm so sorry, Janelle."

It frustrated him that all he could offer was his apologies.

She shook her head and bit down hard on her bottom lip. "It's okay. I . . . I know you guys tried your . . . your best . . . it's just . . . it's just . . ."

He couldn't take it anymore. He leaned down, cupped her

face, and kissed her again and wondered if it was the last time he would ever get to do it.

"Keep me updated about the search for Pops's body. I guess that's what you guys are looking for now."

"Of course, I will."

She nodded and lingered in the driveway a minute longer, not saying anything. The wind picked up. An airplane flew overhead. A dog barked in the distance.

"I'm standing here trying to work up the nerve to actually say good-bye but . . . it's not coming out." Her voice cracked. Her gaze dropped to the necklace in her clenched fist. "So I'm just . . . I'm just gonna . . ."

She didn't finish. She abruptly turned. He watched her until she walked swiftly, at a near run, back up the porch steps and disappeared into the cabin, slamming the door shut behind her.

CHAPTER 28

Tyler was really starting to worry about Yvette. She had been crying since last night. She hadn't eaten. She hadn't slept.

"That bitch. That fucking bitch," she had kept muttering after they arrived back from the festival. "I hate her, Ty. I fucking *hate* her!"

"You don't hate her," he had countered, holding a pack of ice over his bruised knuckles. They were swollen thanks to connecting with some fat old guy's jaw. He had hoped to knock out a few of the guy's teeth, but only managed to make him bite his tongue and scream like a baby.

"Yes, I do! I hate her!" Yvette had screeched before disappearing into his bedroom and slamming the door behind her.

Yvette had had dust-ups with her mother before, but this one was different. He would like to believe it was moral outrage at her mother accusing him—her boyfriend—of murder, but he knew it was more than that. The rift between mother and daughter had little to do with Tyler, though it still shocked him that Connie believed he had killed Bill. How could she think he was capable of such a thing? Tyler Macy committing murder? He'd laugh if her accusation hadn't almost gotten *him* killed—or thrown in the back of a police cruiser.

Yvette knew the truth about him, even if no one else in town did. She knew that though he may look tough and he could brawl with the best of them, he didn't have the stomach to inflict permanent damage; he didn't have the appetite for murder.

Tyler was also in awe that Yvette loved him so much and trusted him without question. He often wondered what he had done to deserve a girl like her.

When he saw her stripping at the Silver Dollar Bar seven years ago, wearing a hot pink G-string and glitter pasties, he may as well have been staring at that Sandro Botticelli painting of Venus de Milo. While the other men in the bar had hooted and hollered, pounding on the tables, Tyler had sat in almost reverent awe as he watched her dance on the stage and swing around a pole—her then purple hair whipping around her face and shoulders. She must have noticed him staring because at the end of her set, she had descended the stage stairs and walked toward him. He had felt like his heart was going to burst out of his chest.

"You want a lap dance?" she had asked him with a smile, and he had eagerly said yes, giving her the last twenty in his pocket.

But Tyler would gladly give her that twenty again. He'd pay a million, maybe even a billion dollars for Yvette if he had it. He'd do anything for her, including violating his parole and running the risk of some serious jail time if he was caught buying weed. But she needed it. She needed something to help her chill out, to stop the tears from flowing. Coke was usually her drug of choice, though neither of them had snorted the stuff in more than a year. But today they were both falling off the wagon. Today would be a "Screw moms! Screw Mammoth Falls! Screw all of you!" bash at Macy's trailer and he was bringing the balloons and party hats.

"I'll be back. All right?" Tyler called over his shoulder, yelling to be heard over the sound of the slasher flick on the dusty eighteen-inch JVC TV perched on his dresser. He shoved his arms into his beat-up leather jacket and held open the metal door to the trailer.

Yvette nodded, though she barely looked at him or at the TV screen as she did it. Instead she kept her head bowed as she sipped from her beer bottle. She picked at pretzels he had left for her in an oversize plastic bowl, twirling one around and around on her finger. She sat on his mattress with her legs tucked beneath her bottom and her head resting on the side of the trailer wall, near one of his older brother's old Insane Clown Posse band posters. Her eyes were red and swollen.

He gave one last glance at her down the hall and let the trailer door slam shut behind him. He jogged down the cinderblock steps to the parched yard below.

Tyler looked up at the sky and winced at the morning light, not just because he and Yvette had been sitting in the dark for the past several hours watching a horror movie marathon. His black eye was still tender, and looking at bright light seemed to only make the ache worse. The cut on his upper lip didn't feel too hot, either, but he would ignore it for now. It was Yvette's pain he was more concerned with, and he had to get her some badly needed "medicine" to make that pain go away.

The Macys' Rottweiler, Missy, growled as Tyler passed her. She then let out a sharp bark that sent threads of spit flying a foot in front of her. He reluctantly dug into his jacket pocket and pulled out one of the Milk-Bones he kept for Missy. He tossed it at her feet.

The growling stopped. She licked his hand in thanks, then turned her attention to the Milk-Bone.

"Just ask nicely next time," he said to her before strolling to his Harley. He then threw on his sunglasses and tugged on his helmet. A minute later, his motorcycle pulled off with a growl that could rival Missy's.

* * *

After traveling several miles on the highway and along an isolated back road, Tyler pulled to a stop in a front yard that managed, miraculously, to be even more junky than his own. He bypassed a stack of strewn tires, a wooden trough filled with manure, several chipped ceramic pots with wilted flowers and rocks, and random boards of plywood. He made his way to the trailer's door and pounded his fist against it. He waited a minute, then pounded again. The door slowly opened.

"Hey, man!" Doc gushed. "Haven't seen you in a while! How've you been?"

Tyler shrugged. "Eh, all right."

"*All right?* What happened to your face?" Doc said, cringing at Tyler's black eye and swollen lip as he pushed his glasses up the bridge of his nose.

"It's nothin'." Tyler waved his hand dismissively. "It looks worse than it feels."

"Hey, I've got an herbal salve for that. Fix you right up." He grinned and waved Tyler into the darkened trailer. "Come on in! Say hi to Snow. Hey, Snow!" Doc shouted, tugging up his sagging pants as he turned. "Snow, Ty's here!"

"I don't need any salve, Doc," Tyler said as he climbed inside and let the door slam shut behind him. "Just some weed if you've got it?"

That was a rhetorical question. Tyler could smell the heavy musk of weed as soon as Doc had opened the door.

Tyler glanced around him, examining the space that he hadn't seen in months. The living room of the ramshackle trailer was filled wall-to-wall with potted houseplants, making it resemble a greenhouse owned by a deranged horticulturalist. Snow's overweight gray Persian, Mikey, sat atop an ancient recliner that was parked in the center of the room. It had several rip marks in the twill fabric, exposing the chair's cotton stuffing, like the cat had been using the chair as its personal scratching post. Mikey opened his yellow eyes, stared in boredom at Tyler, then closed his eyes again.

"Ty!" Snow gushed, sauntering into the room. The skinny woman smiled as she opened her arms to him for a hug. "I haven't seen in you in ages. How are you?"

"Uh, good," he mumbled as he awkwardly accepted her embrace.

Doc and Snow had some good stuff, but they certainly made you work for it.

One of the doors toward the back of the trailer suddenly opened. Tyler heard a toilet flush and then running water. He glanced over Snow's shoulder and noticed as an old black man stepped out of the bathroom, limping slightly. A dog, who had been waiting patiently for him at the door, popped up and stretched.

"Come on, boy," the old man murmured before slowly making his way toward the back room, holding onto the wall for balance.

Tyler's eyes widened in amazement. *"Bill?"*

The old man paused midstep and seemed to teeter slightly.

Tyler roughly shoved Snow aside and ran down the hall. "Bill, is that you?"

The man continued to hold onto the wall as he slowly turned. Tyler stopped a foot away from him. The two men gaped at each other.

"Will you tell these fools to let me go home?" Bill snapped.

CHAPTER 29

A little after noon, Connie heard a knock at her front door. At first she thought it was the rattling heating and air-conditioning unit in the upstairs hall. She muttered vaguely to herself that she had to finally call the repairman to have a look at it, until she heard the knock again. It was distinct the second time around: three quick raps on solid maple.

"Go away!" she wanted to shout. "Leave me alone!"

Instead, she sighed gruffly and slowly unfurled her body from the fetal position on her bed as the person knocked a third time.

She had fallen asleep on top of the sheets last night, exhausted by yesterday's events and by her own self-loathing. She was still wearing her clothes from the day before—even her soiled Uggs. Her clothes smelled of soot and sweat.

She had gotten up a few times to use the bathroom, but that was it. Her phone had rung off and on throughout the night and morning, but she hadn't answered it. Who would call her? Janelle? Her friend Linda?

"You didn't slit your wrists, did you, Connie?"

No, I didn't slit my wrists or down a bottle of pills.

She just didn't want to talk to anybody or see anyone. She would tell whoever was banging at her door as much.

Connie slowly made her way past her dresser mirror and glanced at her reflection. She looked horrid, but she wasn't surprised. The bridge of her nose now had a light purple hue thanks to Yvette's punch. Her cheek was swollen. She probably should put some peroxide or alcohol on that cut or the swelling would only get worse. She should start wearing makeup again if she didn't want to scare off small children. She picked absently at a twig that was tangled in her hair.

"How did that get there?" she murmured before plucking it out, tossing it onto her bedroom floor, and heading toward the stairs. She walked down the hall and slowly descended to the first floor, holding the railing for balance.

I'll close the shop. I'll move away, she resolved as she took one step, then the next. There was no reason to stay in Mammoth. Bill was gone, and Yvette obviously hated her. Only hate could make Yvette lash out like that, could make her want to pummel her own mother and call her a whore.

Not only did I fail Bill, but I've failed Evie, too, she thought as a feeling of self-loathing overwhelmed her.

She walked through her kitchen with her head bowed and rolled her eyes when the person knocked the fourth time.

Four knocks. This better be good.

Either it was the Mammoth Falls Police Department coming to arrest her for inciting a riot or an overeager Girl Scout who wouldn't take no for an answer.

Connie removed the deadbolt then the bottom lock, not bothering to check her peephole before she opened it with a swift yank. "Whatever you're selling, I'm not—"

Her words faded and her mouth fell open.

Bill stood in her doorway with one arm thrown around Tyler Macy's shoulder and with Tyler's arm wrapped around his waist. The two men resembled fond old buddies who had just come back from an overnight drinking binge. Bill was wearing sweatpants and a t-shirt that were too big for him. He had to hold the pants up with his free hand to keep them from falling down. A mangy mutt that looked to be a mix between a border collie and a few other indecipherable breeds sat at Bill's feet, wagging its tail merrily. It peered up at her and barked as if to say hello.

"Hiya, Connie," Bill said with a smile. "Tyler tells me a lot has happened since I've been gone. What I miss?" he asked jovially.

Connie opened her mouth again, then promptly fainted to the tiled kitchen floor.

CHAPTER 30

Janelle looked up as the seat belt sign went dark.

"You may now turn on all electronic devices," a pleasant voice intoned overhead as people began to stand from their seats all around her, filling the compartment with a chorus of clicks as they unbuckled their seat belts.

"Oh, thank God!" the woman beside Janelle shouted. She shot to her feet, wiping peanut debris from her lap. "Now I can stretch!"

Unlike the other passengers, who scrambled to remove their bags from the overhead compartment, Janelle continued to sit, unable to work up the urge to fight her way off the plane. She slowly removed her iPhone from her purse and stared at the black screen. She started to press the button to turn it on. She should call Mark and tell him that her flight had touched down, that she was back home—but she held off on doing that. She hadn't called him before she left Mammoth Falls, worried that if she told him she was returning home, she'd blurt out all the reasons why she was coming back. She would share everything that had happened to her, what was eating at her. She'd tell him that she didn't think they could be together anymore.

"You don't *think* you can stay with him?" she could hear

Sam's voice repeat back to her. "It still doesn't sound like you're sure what you want."

Maybe I'm not, she now thought. *Maybe Sam's right.*

She'd felt more certain about what she'd wanted back in Mammoth Falls, but the second her flight touched down and the gravity of what she was about to do hit her with the same force she experienced from the plane's landing—an unease started to rise within her. Things started to feel fuzzy again.

Her time away had been a little over a week in her life, and it had been an extreme week, fraught with high emotions and distressing loss. Understandably, she had made a few poor and rash decisions while she was out there. Maybe a week from now or even a month from now, she would feel completely different than how she felt today. She would want to marry Mark again. She would realize that her life wasn't that bad. In fact, she had been perfectly content with the life she'd had before her grandfather had thrown in that monkey wrench and made the well-oiled machine that was "Janelle Marshall's existence" go haywire.

But then she thought about the expression on Sam's face as they sat on her porch this morning.

Had it only been this morning?

She remembered the look he had given her when she told him she didn't know if she was brave enough to do this, to grab the wheel and steer in a new direction. She saw no judgment or pity in his eyes. He looked at her like he was waiting for something, like there was some inside joke that he knew the answer to, but she hadn't figured out yet.

What do you know that I don't, Sam?

Janelle pursed her lips. She tucked her phone back into her purse and rose to her feet as the last of the passengers exited the plane—knowing she'd have to figure this out herself.

As she stepped out of the airport checkpoint a few minutes later, she adjusted the Stetson on her curly head. It was the same cowboy hat that had once hung on Pops's wall back at his cabin in Mammoth Falls. She now wore it in honor of him, though it drew more than a few curious stares from people as she passed. She didn't care; they could stare all they wanted. Janelle came to a halt and looked around her, feeling as if she was some interstellar astronaut setting foot on another planet in another galaxy.

Though it was after eight p.m., Reagan National's main concourse was filled with the steady drumbeat of noise and traffic. The clamor, the chaos, and the energy were definitely signs that she was home, but having left the sleepy, quiet town of Mammoth Falls only six hours ago, being home was more overwhelming than welcoming.

It was warm today—the pilot had announced on landing that it was a balmy seventy-two degrees outside—so many of the flyers were dressed in t-shirts and shorts, though a few were also in business suits and military fatigues. She spotted a man flipping through an issue of *GQ*. Beside him was a woman holding up a blue "I heart DC" t-shirt to a redheaded boy with freckles who rolled his eyes to the hot halogen lights overhead.

"No, I don't wanna wear it, Mom!" the kid shouted, shoving the t-shirt away.

Flyers with short layovers stood in a line five deep at the TGI Friday's where pop music blasted. The driver of a conveyance car with two elderly women sitting on the back loudly beeped his horn as the car zoomed past a row of designer luggage shops and clothing stores.

"Pardon us! Excuse us!" screamed a couple as they dashed off the automated conveyor belt to the flight check-in desk, dragging several bags and suitcases behind them.

Janelle quickly stepped aside and came to a halt along the wall, tugging her suitcase against her. "Sorry," she murmured to their retreating backs.

More people continued to walk by, all staring at their phones, laughing with each other, or running to catch their flights.

She hadn't realized that she had been strolling aimlessly, not keeping pace with the current of bodies surging around her. It had taken less than two weeks and she had already lost the rhythm of the city that whispered in your ear, "Hurry, hurry! Move, move!"

It was best to get out of the way until she got her bearings again.

She looked around and spotted a ladies' room a few feet away. She fled to it and disappeared into one of the metal stalls while a cleaning woman mopped the floors at the other end, muttering to herself about adults who couldn't manage the task of peeing inside a toilet bowl.

Janelle emerged a few minutes later and quickly washed her hands. She wiped them on one of the dangling paper towels. She looked down at her hands. They were shaking. She wouldn't even try to convince herself that her fraught nerves were from all the hubbub around her. It was a lot more than that. She raised her eyes and stared at her reflection in the wall of mirrors.

You look scared, she thought. *You look absolutely terrified, girl.*

She was. But she would do this. She *had* to do it.

Janelle gazed at her reflection a few seconds longer, then threw her bag strap over her shoulder. She headed out of the bathroom, pointing herself in the direction of the corridor leading to the metro trains, leading toward home.

The car slowed to a stop at the end of the cul-de-sac, pulling into one of the few open spaces along the curb.

"Is this you?" the cab driver asked as he leaned to the side and gazed at Janelle in the reflection of the rearview mirror, raising his bushy brows.

She turned and tiredly gazed out the window. Was this her?

It certainly *looked* like her. Her sporty red BMW was parked in the two-car driveway. Mark's Mercedes was parked in front of her car. Her eyes scanned the towering colonial with the four Ionic columns under the portico and neatly trimmed hedges along the front. Janelle could envision her old self walking in fashionable heels from the brick mailbox up the slate walkway bordered by newly bloomed daffodils. A designer handbag would be dangling at her elbow as she chattered on the phone about their housewarming party, fretting over the buffet table and wine selection.

Envisioning herself back then was like seeing a ghost—the ghost of a woman who no longer existed.

Janelle turned from the passenger window. She watched as the driver climbed out of the car, leaving his keys in the ignition as he went to the rear and opened the trunk.

This isn't me, she finally realized, accepting this truth as she listened to the driver remove her suitcase and set it on the asphalt near her driveway. How could she have tried to convince herself differently?

She exhaled a deep breath and opened her car door.

This isn't me—and I have to tell Mark that.

A minute later and with an overwhelming sense of trepidation, she stood in front of their red French doors, digging in her purse for her keys. She undid the lock and took one step into their darkened foyer when a shrill beep pierced the silence, making her clap her hand over her ears.

"Shit!" she shouted.

She had forgotten about the alarm system. They had installed it only days before the housewarming party. What was the deactivation code?

She tossed her bag to the floor and left her suitcase in the doorway as she ran toward the flashing wall panel and began to frantically punch in numbers on the dial pad, but the beeps became louder and faster.

"Shit! Shit! Shit!" she yelled, typing more numbers.

Was it 2-3-6-4 or 3-2-4-6? What was the blasted code?

Over the shrill beeps she heard the frantic thud of footsteps. Mark's silhouette appeared at the top of the staircase.

"Hold it right there!" he bellowed, flipping on the lights along the staircase and foyer. She could see he was barefoot and wearing only his t-shirt and boxer briefs. He held the putter she had given him for his birthday high above his head, like it was a baseball bat. "What the hell do you think you're doing?"

Janelle jumped back from the wall panel and held up her hands in surrender. "I was just trying to turn off the alarm!"

"Janelle?" He gawked at her. He dropped the putter to his side and stumbled down the steps toward her. "What . . . what are you doing here? You didn't tell me you were coming home today."

"I wanted to surprise . . ." She paused, realizing she'd have to keep shouting to be heard above the beeping. "Can you turn off the alarm, please?"

"Mark? Mark, what's going on?" a woman yelled.

Janelle paused as Mark ran past her and entered in the alarm code. "Wait. Is someone upstairs?"

The foyer finally fell silent, and Mark turned toward her, pushing his glasses up the bridge of his nose. He looked anxious, and not just because of the alarm that still left her ears ringing. He sat the putter near the front door. He seemed to be evading her gaze.

"Is someone upstairs?" she repeated more slowly.

"Jay, I . . . I really wished you would've called first."

"Is everything okay?" the woman shouted again, and this time the voice was recognizable. "Are you all right, Mark? It wasn't a burglar, was it?"

Janelle looked up and saw Shana standing at the top of their staircase wearing a midriff-baring tank top, boy-cut shorts, and a silky little pink robe that was so feminine it looked like it should be covered with lace and bows.

When Shana saw Janelle standing in the doorway, she halted in her steps. She grabbed for the handrail, as if to keep herself from stumbling forward.

"Oh," she uttered, quickly closing the panels of her robe. "Oh, I . . . I didn't know you were here," she said, as if Janelle were a houseguest who had arrived early to a party they were having.

Janelle stared, struck speechless. She suddenly remembered the black sedan near the driveway. It had looked vaguely familiar but she had glanced at it and quickly forgotten it, too focused on the monumental task at hand. Perhaps she should have paid better attention.

"I . . . I can explain," Mark began quietly. He paused and cleared his throat anxiously. "Look, I didn't know you were coming home. We hadn't spoken in . . . in days, and you weren't returning my emails. I didn't know what was going on with us so I . . . so I . . ." His words faded.

"So you had sex with Shana," she finished for him.

He blinked and stared at her mutely.

Well, I'll be damned, she thought.

Janelle slowly shook her head in exasperation. A giggle bubbled in her throat. It sounded like a hiccup, but then another came after it, then another. The next thing she knew she was doubled over with laughter right there in the center of the foyer, holding onto the door frame to keep from falling to her knees.

Mark looked at her uneasily. So did Shana, who still stood at the top of the staircase, pivoting from foot to foot like she wasn't sure what she should do next.

"Jay, are . . . are you all right?" he asked.

She continued to laugh. Tears were running down her

cheeks. Her stomach was starting to ache. But she couldn't stop laughing.

"I know this has to be . . . quite . . . quite a surprise. Very shocking for you, after all you've been through," he continued in a measured voice, like he was talking to a crazy person. He placed a hand tentatively on her shoulder. "If you need to sit down, I can explain—"

"All this time. All this time, I've been agonizing over what I was going to say to you and what I was going to do—and I run in on this?" Janelle's laughter finally tapered off. She wiped the last tears from her eyes and gazed at the couple again. "I've been trying to work up the balls to tell you the truth and this whole time you've been . . . *been cheating on me*? You . . . you made it seem like I was being paranoid . . . like I accusing you of something you didn't do, when this whole time . . ."

She couldn't finish. She gritted her teeth and sniffed, feeling a mix of pain and disappointment. She reached down for the cowboy hat that had fallen off of her head and turned toward the open door in disgust.

"Jay, please . . . please don't walk out. Not like this," he begged, grabbing her forearm. "Let me ex—"

"Don't touch me! Don't you dare touch me, damn it!" she shouted, punching his shoulder.

"Oww!" Mark instantly let go of her arm. He actually looked surprised, maybe even offended by her punch. He rubbed his shoulder absently. "Look, Jay, Shana and I only became well . . . intimate within the past few days, after you basically refused to talk to me! You—"

"Actually, sweetheart," Shana said as she held up her finger and strolled down the flight of stairs, "there was that one time in the wine closet a month ago when we—"

"Shana!" he snapped. "I don't need your input. I have it covered, okay?"

Shana immediately fell silent. She lowered her eyes.

Janelle shook her head. "I should've known, though. You've got that weird Oedipal complex going on with your mother. Of course you'd end up screwing a woman just like her!"

"Hey!" Mark and Shana cried in unison.

"Don't bring my mother into this!" he shouted, making Janelle roll her eyes. She grabbed the handle of her carry-on bag and headed to the door again.

"Look! Look, Janelle, I admit that I'm not perfect! I'm a human being. I make mistakes! I wasn't trying to hurt you!"

At that, she paused. She turned back around to face him.

"I . . . I fell in love with someone else," he said softly, silhouetted from the light behind him in the foyer. "I didn't expect it to happen but . . . it happened." He threw up his hand. "I'm sorry and I mean that. I didn't want to hurt you," he repeated. "I didn't want to disappoint you."

Janelle gazed at him, seeing him for the first time for the man he really was. She had tried to make him her rock when he was just as frail as she was. Try as she might at that moment, she couldn't stay angry at him.

"I didn't want to hurt you, either," she whispered. "That's why I agonized about telling you the truth."

"The . . . the truth about what?"

She sighed. "I cheated on you, too."

His mouth fell open. So did Shana's. "W-what?" he sputtered.

"While I was in Mammoth Falls, I . . . I slept with another man."

"I don't believe you. I don't believe you!" He squinted. "Are you saying all of this make me jealous? To just to get back at me for what—"

"No, I'm not. It's *true*, Mark! His name is Sam . . . Sam Adler, and he's amazing," she said, even as Mark continued to shake his head in denial. "He's unlike any other guy I've ever met. I care about him. I think . . . I think I even fell in love him," she said, letting the words settle in.

"*What?* Wait! Wait just one goddamn minute!" Mark barked. "You're telling me that you had sex with some guy you met in . . . in fucking South Dakota *a week ago?* Now you're in love with him?"

She nodded and gave a sad smile. "Sounds crazy, doesn't it?"

"It doesn't sound crazy—it *is* crazy, Janelle!"

"Maybe . . . but it happened—just like what happened with you and Shana, right? That's why I know I shouldn't be too angry at you. It'd make me a hypocrite. I was wrong. We were *both* wrong, but maybe it's meant to be this way. Maybe we weren't meant to be. It's okay to admit that . . . even if hurts to do it."

This is not my life, she thought sadly, looking through doorway and around the foyer. *This may still be Mark's life, but it isn't mine anymore.*

She would handle the messy disassembly of her old life tomorrow or the day after. But tonight she would spend her time coming to terms with the fact that she was free to start a new path. This life was over.

Janelle pushed her tote bag strap up her shoulder. "Goodbye, Mark."

"Wait! Wait!" he shouted, grabbing her arm again. "I can't let you go like this, Jay! Your grandfather disappearing . . . you finding me and Shana together . . . You're obviously having some . . . some mental breakdown! I mean you had sex with *a total stranger!*" he squeaked. "Now you say you're in love with him? The Janelle Marshall I know would never do something like that!"

"Because you never knew me," she said softly, "the *real* me— and you never will."

He stared at her dazedly.

"Just let her go, Mark!" Shana called out to him, sounding annoyed.

Finally, ever so slowly, he released Janelle's arm, and she

shut the door behind herself, closing it in his face. She stood under the portico gazing around her. She was terrified and exhilarated all at the same time. It was like she had just gone over the crest of a roller coaster and taken the plunge to the tracks below, only to realize the drop wasn't as bad as she thought it would be.

The chartered car had left and the neighborhood was quiet save for the incessant chirp of crickets and trill of frogs in a nearby development's pond. She glanced at the driveway. She couldn't leave in her BMW. Mark was blocking her in with his Mercedes. She'd have to go back inside and ask him to move it and there was no way . . . *no way* she was going to do that. Not after her big exit!

She slowly walked down the slate pathway, loudly dragging her suitcase behind her. It got stuck in the cracks between each paver and she had to yank it a few times before she finally reached the sidewalk.

"Where am I going to go? What am I going to do?" she mumbled.

"How about New Orleans? Ever seen the French Quarter?" she had asked Sam that morning as they sat in her grandfather's rocking chair on his porch.

"Too hot. How about Chicago?"

"Too cold."

Janelle removed her cell phone from her tote bag to first get an Uber to take her to a nearby hotel. Then she would call Sam and tell him that she could meet him wherever, whenever. Chicago, Los Angeles, the Bahamas. As soon as he was available, she'd meet him. She was officially free now!

She pressed the button to turn on her cell, nervous and giddy as she did it.

When she did, she frowned. Her screen showed that she had seven voice mails and a dozen text messages.

"What the . . ." she mumbled, then jumped when her phone

began to ring. She almost dropped it. She saw the number on the screen and quickly pressed the green button to answer.

"*Sam?*" she nearly shouted.

"Janelle?" he answered back, making her shoulders sink with relief. Hearing his voice was like having him reach through the phone and wrap an arm around her shoulder.

"Oh, Sam," she groaned, just wanting to sink into him.

"Are you all right?" he asked, worry tingeing his voice.

She laughed and gazed around her again at the empty cul-de-sac. "Oh, I'm fine! I'm just standing in front of my house on the curb with my luggage. I walked in on Mark with another woman. I'm not torn up about it, but . . . my car is blocked in and now I can't leave."

"Well," he said with a warm chuckle that made her smile despite how bemused she felt, "sounds like you've had quite a day."

She nodded, set her suitcase flat on the ground, and plopped on top of it. She rested her elbows on her knees. "You have no idea!"

"And it's about to get a lot more interesting," he said, making her brows furrow.

"Huh?"

"I've been calling you! I've got somebody here who wants to talk to you."

She heard a rustling sound and then Sam muttering, "Go ahead," in the background.

And then a voice came to her, seemingly across the universe, across time, and from the dead. It spoke through her phone and into her ear.

"Hey, baby girl!" Pops answered. "How've you been?"

CHAPTER 31

After 8-Day Search, Mammoth Falls Man Found Alive

Police Say Man Was Held by Area Couple, Kidnapping Charges Pending

May 5, 2016

By Laurie Spencer, *Mammoth Falls Gazette*

Bill Marshall of Mammoth Falls, whose damaged Ford truck was discovered dangling over a ravine off of Cedar Lane on April 22 and who was declared missing by police, was found and rescued from a Spearfish couple. His rescuer was 27-year-old Tyler Macy, another Mammoth Falls resident.

"Tyler is definitely a hero," said Mammoth Falls Police Chief Sam Adler. "If it wasn't for him, who knows what would have happened to Bill or if we ever would have found him."

"It's not like I was looking for [Bill]," Macy said, who explained that he had visited Donald Holler and Alice Kennedy of Spearfish because they were "acquaintances of his."

"I just happened to be there that day. I hadn't planned to be. I'm glad I was, though," he said.

Holler and Kennedy are now facing kidnapping charges in connection to Marshall's disappearance. They are currently at large and police have issued a national alert to help place them under arrest.

"We went to their trailer to arrest them a couple of days ago, but it looks like they pulled up stakes," Chief Adler said. "They probably got wind that we were looking for them."

Marshall said that the couple did hold him in their trailer in an isolated four-acre lot for more than a week against his will after they discovered him on the side of the road. But he said that they did it to nurse him back to health and he holds no ill will against them.

"It was just a big misunderstanding," Marshall said. "I know how that goes . . . when your good intentions go to hell. Pardon my French. I just hope when and if the cops finally do find them, the judge will go easy on them. They're good people. Just stupid and crazy, I guess."

The kidnapping charge will be the first criminal charge for Kennedy. But Holler has previously faced possession of a controlled substance and marijuana distribution charges. In 2009, he served a two-year stint in a California prison for drug-related charges.

"We can't go light on them just because they had good intentions," said Lawrence County State's Attorney Chance Stanton. "Whether they go to jail or go free is up to a judge or jury to decide."

Marshall's rescue brings an end to an eight-day search that included the Mammoth Falls Police Department, the Lawrence County Sheriff's Office, several other police departments, and four search and rescue teams. Trackers surveyed ten miles' worth of forest in the Black Hills, even recovering the remains of a hiker who had disappeared three years ago.

Macy will receive a commendation from the mayor of Mammoth Falls and town council for his heroic action during a ceremony at City Hall on May 8.

"It's crazy," Macy said. "I heard they're giving me a key to the city. My picture has been in the paper and on TV. And it's not even my mug shot."

Little Bill sat on his front porch, rocking listlessly in his chair, hearing the wood give against metal screws and crack and creak beneath him. He waved away a gnat that circled near his ear as he listened to The Mutt snore at his feet.

Neither he nor the dog had budged from the front porch for almost an hour. They had done a few scratches here or there, but that was about it. Since Bill had left Doc and Snow's trailer, he couldn't stand to be confined in any space for long—including his own cabin. He had to get out, to feel the wind on his face and peer at the clouds overhead. He'd take walks on well-worn trails with The Mutt at his side, even though he still hadn't fully recovered and it somewhat pained him to limp along the parched earth. But the walks and the solitude helped to bring him peace of mind, and some days that was in short supply.

By the time the tepid weather of May had given way to the burning heat of June, Little Bill had gotten sick of television cameras, boom mikes, and those little mike packs and wires that hang from your belt like fanny packs. He had started to loathe all the reporters, producers, and dumb questions.

"So what was the thought going through your mind when your truck went off the edge of that cliff?" one dunce on *Good Morning America* had asked him.

"Were you afraid of your captors?" the local TV anchor had asked during a one-on-one interview.

"It's your own fault," Mabel would say in his head every time he'd wanted to rip off his mike and march out of those TV studios. *"You're the one who created this mess!"*

That was true. A little plan he had hatched at a casino bar to keep Janelle from getting married to a man unworthy of her had had ramifications far beyond what he had anticipated—but not all of the outcomes had been bad.

Sure, a few of the shop windows along Main Street still were boarded up from the riot that had taken place three months ago in his absence. (Though he still didn't understand how his disappearance could lead civilized people to decide to break windows and set part of the town on fire.) And Doc and Snow had closed shop in their dilapidated trailer and disappeared—something that he still felt bad about.

They hadn't quite kidnapped him, like the news stories claimed. "Kidnapping" was such a harsh word. And they had seemed like decent folk. He fervently hoped that they had gotten away.

Little Bill gazed at the pine trees on the other side of his yard, imagining them as swaying palms, the gray gravel as a white sandy beach.

Maybe they were living in Tahiti, wearing sarongs and smoking reefer. Or maybe they were living in some forest in Costa Rica, practicing their holistic healing. He even hoped that the fat Persian cat, Mikey, was happy.

But again, not all the outcomes had been bad; some good had come out of all of this.

See! I didn't make a complete *fool out of myself, Mabel.*

"No, *not a* complete *one,*" she conceded.

Bill tore his gaze away from the trees when he heard footsteps coming toward him. At the same time, The Mutt's ears perked up and his snoring abruptly ceased. Connie stomped onto the porch with hands on hips, letting the screen door slam shut behind her.

"They still aren't here?" She raised her hand to shield her eyes as she peered down the driveway.

"It's just five thirty," he said, waving at the gnat again. "We've got time."

"We should've driven there ourselves," she muttered irritably. "I have my own truck. I could've—"

"They wanted to be nice . . . to do a favor. Let them do it."

"But now we're going to be late!"

"Well, it ain't like we've got dinner reservations at the Ritz, honey! It's just something Janelle's cooking up."

Connie balled her fists at her sides. "I *knew* I never should've let you talk me into . . ."

Her words tapered off, and she unclenched her fists when they both heard the loud rumble of a truck engine. Soon, a red F-350 with sparkling chrome that caught the light overhead came into view intermittently through the line of trees, bobbing along the unpaved road. A few seconds later, it pulled to a stop in front of the porch, kicking up gravel in its wake. One of the doors flew open.

"Hop in!" Tyler called out, waving them forward.

Connie sat on the leather seat, surrounded by new car smell, with the truck door on one side and her daughter on the other. At that moment, the prospect of hurling herself out of the moving vehicle to the black asphalt now racing past her car window seemed less intimidating than continuing to sit beside Yvette in strained silence.

Bill and Tyler weren't silent. They were laughing and talking in the front of the cab. Bill was regaling Tyler with some bawdy tale as he gesticulated wildly. She wished he would shut up.

Connie stole a glance at Yvette, gazing at her daughter in profile—the long green hair, the stubborn set jaw, and those big, dark eyes that she had inherited from Connie's mother. Just when it seemed like Yvette could feel Connie's eyes on her and was about to look in Connie's direction, Connie turned back around to gaze out the window.

Mother and daughter hadn't spoken to each other since that day on Main Street, when all hell had broken loose and Yvette had slugged Connie in the nose. Or, at least, they hadn't spoken directly. Oddly enough, Little Bill and Tyler had become their intermediaries, their mouthpieces. The two men had become fast friends since Tyler had rescued Bill from his captors. They spoke almost daily.

"He's a good boy, Connie," Bill had confided one day. "You might like him if you gave him a chance."

"I highly doubt that," she had muttered in reply.

"He wants to get you and Evie back together," Bill had said, giving her pause. "That says something about him, don't it? He can't be *that* bad! Maybe he could help."

And so began a series of maneuvers—some subtle, some not—to get Connie and Yvette to make up, to end the Arctic freeze that had formed between them.

Ty says Evie misses you, honey.

Ty and I agree that this nonsense has dragged on long enough. One of you has to be the bigger woman.

You can't stay mad at her forever!

Even Janelle seemed to have gotten in on the act, inviting both Connie and Yvette to dinner at her and Sam's place, not letting them know that the other also was coming until it was well after it would have been possible for either to politely back out.

"But you have to come, Connie! I'm going to have all this extra food. I'm even making your favorite dish."

Connie wasn't aware that Janelle even knew what her favorite dish was.

"Please come!" Janelle had pleaded. "It wouldn't be the same without you."

And then came Bill's whining about how her Silverado didn't have enough leg room, aggravating his injured back and leg. Tyler had offered to give them a ride in the new pickup truck he had purchased with the generous reward given to him for finding Bill. It had plenty of leg room, according to Bill.

Finally, after so many hints, cajoling, begging, and bullying, Connie capitulated.

This is how she found herself sitting next to Yvette, sliding on brand-new leather car seats, struggling to figure out what to say to her own daughter.

"How . . . how've you been?" she ventured, turning again toward Yvette.

"How do you think I've been?" Yvette mumbled sullenly in reply, staring at the headrest in front of her.

The two men sitting in the front seat quieted.

"I think you've been angry at me."

"Why whatever made you think that, Mama?"

"But I'm not mad at you," Connie continued undaunted, ignoring Yvette's sarcasm.

"And why the hell should you be?" Yvette shouted, whipping around to glare at her mother. Bill and Tyler glanced uneasily at each other. "*You* were the one who—"

"I hoped hitting me made you feel better. I hope it helped you get whatever you wanted to get off your chest."

Yvette fell silent. She uncrossed her arms and let her hands fall to her sides. She stared at her mother uneasily, like she was staring at a waiting bear trap. "What do you mean?"

What did she mean? There were so many things she wanted to say. Decades' worth of emotions and heartbreak and disappointment about her own childhood, about the childhood she had given Yvette that she wanted to offload, but it all seemed futile now. Dead weight that she had been carrying around for way too long.

"That day I could see so much hate in your eyes, all that anger that you kept bottled up, and it finally boiled over. But you got it out, Evie. It's done. Let it go. We *both* need to let it go." She pursed her lips. "We've been going like this for years. This back and forth, tit for tat . . . but it's gotta end. The only people we're hurting are each other . . . and I don't want to hurt you. You're the last person in this world that I want to hurt, honey." She stared beseechingly at her daughter. "Can we end it?"

Yvette didn't reply. Instead she stubbornly turned away from her mother and stared out her passenger-side window.

Connie sighed in defeat. Bill and Tyler shifted uncomfortably in the front seat. Connie looked down at Yvette's right hand. It lay on the leather seat between them. Slowly and with great trepidation, she reached out and touched Yvette's outstretched fingers. Her daughter didn't pull away as she had expected. She held Yvette's hand and squeezed it. She felt Yvette's fingers shift—unclench then fan out—so that they linked through her mother's. Finally, Yvette squeezed her hand back.

Tears pricked Connie's eyes. The two continued to sit hand-in-hand, not saying anything, listening to the sound of the rumbling engine as it filled the truck's compartment, as they made their way through downtown Mammoth Falls to their destination.

Janelle set the last plate on the dining room table. She heard Sam's heavy footfalls in the living room followed by the *click-click* of Quincy's claws on the hardwood floor.

"We're back!" Sam shouted. The door slammed shut behind him. "I'm gonna take a quick shower before everyone gets here!"

"All right! I'm still setting up," she called back, placing a wineglass on the table.

"I'll help when I'm done!"

Janelle had had to rummage through Sam's pine cabinets and drawers for decent tableware for tonight's dinner, battling a level of disorder that still left her confounded. Water glasses were on the same shelf as cartons of trail mix and Frosted Flakes. Forks and knives were commingled in the shallow plastic slots meant to sort silverware according to kind. She found the matches and candles under an opened pack of batteries, old DVD player's instructions, and car wash flyers. But she supposed she should be used to Sam's brand of household chaos by now since she had been staying with him for more than two months. He had even ceded real estate to her in his house, giving her a section in his closet for her clothes, a side of his bathroom sink for her toothpaste, hair spray, and mouthwash.

She was living with Sam because she hadn't wanted to push Pops out of his bedroom and didn't find the cushions of his plaid living room couch very inviting. She could have rented a room instead; the price at the local bed-and-breakfast on Poplar Street for a queen-sized bed with en-suite bathroom wasn't expensive. But now that she had quit her job at Bryant Consulting (Lydia had almost hyperventilated when she told her by phone) and had no immediate job prospects, she couldn't imagine spending the bulk of her savings on an indefinite hotel stay.

"Save your money," Sam had said to her in bed one night soon after she had arrived back in Mammoth.

They had been staring up at the ceiling, listening to the crickets outside his bedroom window.

"Bunk with me," he had offered.

Though in the end, saving money meant little to her; her savings would receive an influx of cash soon with the proceeds of the sale of the house she and Mark had purchased together. Now that they had broken up, he said he no longer had interest in keeping their 3,500-square-foot home.

"Shana said she prefers a condo closer to the city anyway," he had divulged by phone.

"I'm sure she and Brenda will have fun decorating it!" Janelle had replied cheerfully.

Though she had intended no malice behind that comment, maybe she shouldn't have mentioned his mother in light of what she had last said to him. Regardless, Mark had rushed off the phone soon after.

Mark still didn't believe her when she said she wasn't angry that he had cheated on her. He thought she was putting up a brave front when she told him that she was content with how things had ended between them.

I know I hurt you, Janelle. I'm ashamed at how I behaved, he had written in one email. *It was the last thing to push you over the edge. You had to be devastated.*

She initially wanted reply that *he* seemed more devastated by their breakup than she did! But instead, she sent him a selfie of her, Sam, and Quincy hiking on Overland Trail, a fine sheen of sweat on their brows, smiles on their faces, and a silhouette of the mountains set against the rising sun in the picture behind them. The caption read: *Does this look like a woman who's devastated?*

She hadn't meant to gloat. She just wanted to prove to Mark that she really was okay.

So it's because of your mountain man? Mark had written in a terse reply to her. *Your cowboy?*

She could practically see his condescending sneer in the email's Helvetica type.

His name is Sam, she had written back, *and no, it's not* just *because of him.*

Though being with Sam certainly helped. It was hard to

mourn the loss of one relationship when you were acquainting yourself with another one, discovering a new lover's idiosyncrasies. Every day she was learning new facts about Sam, like, for instance, he had played football in college and flirted with the idea of playing for the pros until he injured his knee, he liked to eat his toast slathered with chunky peanut butter, was a total slob who also sang loud and off key in the shower, and was a registered Republican.

She didn't know what to make of that last revelation. Though she told herself that Sam may be conservative politically, at least he was a liberal in the bedroom: free thinking, always equal opportunity, and willing to put the needs of his fellow man before himself.

And despite their differences, Sam still fit her much better than Mark did. With Mark she had been a square peg shaved and battered until it fit into a round hole. With Sam, she was the uneven puzzle piece that seemed to find its equally uneven match.

She cared for Sam. She even loved him and suspected he loved her, too—though they hadn't exchanged the declaration out loud yet. Some women would be eager to use the "L word," to ask what all this meant and what their future held, but Janelle was more comfortable with ambiguity now. In the past, everything had to be clearly defined and rigidly constructed. But now she took pleasure in her new imprecise existence. Maybe she and Sam would ride off into the sunset; maybe they wouldn't. Maybe she would get another job in HR or start another career. Maybe she would stay in Mammoth Falls permanently; or maybe, she would strike out on a new course, use the proceeds of her house sale to buy a place in California or spend a year in Europe or sail along the African coastline.

"How the hell did you come out of this more confused than before?" Pops had exclaimed a few days ago when he had stopped by early one morning for an ambush, to pin her down.

He had asked her about what was going on between her and Sam, about her plans for the future.

"I'm not confused, Pops," she had answered between bites of bacon. "I know what I *don't* want. I know what I'm *not*. I just see more possibilities now. That's all. Because that's life, isn't it?" she asked, feeling philosophical. "Not a quest to find the right door, but the realization that a series of doors are open to you. There isn't a 'right' choice; just the best one for *you*."

Pops had rolled his eyes in exasperation and turned to Sam. "Boy, are you listening to this nonsense?"

Sam had nodded and smiled. "Yep, I heard her."

"Your woman could wander off at any moment! She could pack up her bags and head off to 'possibilities' somewhere!"

"I wouldn't just *leave!* I'd tell you guys where I was going and . . . I'd ask Sam to go with me—if he wanted to go."

He might say no, but she suspected he would say yes. They were linked now. In fact, they would be headed on their first trip together later that week. They were going to Virginia to pack the last of her things since the new buyers were set to move into the house later that month. They also would visit the cemetery where Gabriela was buried to lay flowers on her grave. It was a journey that neither wanted to take alone—and they wouldn't have to.

"You're all right with all of this, boy?" Pops had asked Sam, raising his brows. "You're okay with her being so lackadaisical about everything?"

Sam had shrugged. "Hey, she said she'd ask me. What can you do?" he had said before bringing his coffee to his lips and giving her a meaningful look.

It was a similar look to the one he had given her that day on Pops's porch before she left to head home to Virginia.

But instead of the look saying, "I know something you don't know," it asked, "Do you get it now?"

Yep, she had thought, as she stared back at Sam, *I get it.*

"More toast, Pops?" she had asked, offering a platter to him.

Her grandfather had grumbled in reply before reaching for a piece of buttered multigrain and tossing it onto his plate.

Janelle now closed the oven, dropping the last roll into the bread basket sitting on the counter. She set the basket in the center of the dining room table, stood back, and gazed at her handiwork, checking every detail before their guests would arrive for the last dinner they would have before heading to Virginia tomorrow.

None of the plates on the table matched; it was a hodge-podge of colors, patterns, and sizes. Some of the glasses were chipped and she was short one salad fork. The tablecloth had a brown stain along the hem, even though she had bleached it twice. The taper candles were from Christmas; both were red with little snowmen on them.

A table like this would have made her insane a few months ago, yet there was something comforting about it today. She could see beauty in the disarray.

"Quincy! Quincy!" Sam shouted as the Lab galloped into the room.

Janelle jumped aside, almost getting sideswiped as Quincy plopped his front paws on the table, dove face-first into the bread basket, grabbed two rolls and ran off, knocking over a water glass in his wake. It left a pool of water on the tablecloth.

Sam ran into the room soon after, with his hair still wet from his shower and the fly of his jeans still open. He glanced at the table. "Shit," he muttered to her, stifling a laugh when he saw the annoyed expression on her face. "Sorry," he said over his shoulder, before running after the dog. "Dammit, Quincy, get back here!"

Janelle reached for the turned-over glass just as the doorbell rang. It was followed by a knock. Their guests had arrived.

She sat the glass upright then glanced back at the table—the pooling water, the mismatched plates, and the upturned bread-basket—and shrugged.

"Coming!" she shouted, before walking out of the dining room, toward the front door.

BETWEEN LOST AND FOUND

Shelly Stratton

ABOUT THIS GUIDE

The suggested questions are included
to enhance your group's reading of
Shelly Stratton's *Between Lost and Found.*

Discussion Questions

1. Pops develops an elaborate scheme to get his grand-daughter, Janelle, to Mammoth Falls, South Dakota, to try to convince her not to get engaged because he thinks she will respond differently to him there. Do you think his motive is just to prevent the engagement/to get her to break up with her boyfriend, or is there a greater motivation at work?

2. When Janelle hears that her grandfather has disappeared, she starts to reflect on her own father's disappearance more than a decade earlier. What parallels exist for her in both experiences?

3. Is there any metaphorical significance to the name Mammoth Falls? Do the Black Hills also play a thematic role in the book?

4. Sam has an almost visceral reaction to Janelle because she reminds him of his ex-wife. He feels himself simultaneously attracted to her and wanting to distance himself from her. Do you think this is a normal reaction?

5. Connie and Yvette have a challenging mother-daughter relationship. Connie said she can see herself reflected in her daughter. Do you think reflections on her own life are why she's so hard on Yvette?

6. We find out that Pops is alive but he's being simultaneously held hostage and healed by the hippies, Snow and Doc, in their trailer. What meaning do Snow and Doc serve in this narrative?

7. Sam also sees parallels between Pops's disappearance and his ex-wife's battle with bipolar disorder. What parallels are there?

8. Janelle's inability to find her grandfather starts to make her unravel both on a mental and spiritual level. When she expects Mark to come to her rescue and reassert stability, he fails her. What ramifications does that have for her and for her "journey"?

9. Connie is plagued with guilt for the affair she had during her and Pops's engagement. Why is she still unable to let go of the guilt, even though he's forgiven her?

10. Sam and Janelle quickly develop a friendship that they both suspect may be turning into something more. Do you think the tense situation and heightened emotions are playing with their heads, or are they legitimately falling for each other?

11. Connie loses it when she gets word of the body found in the forest. She also starts to rethink her view of Sam and discourages Janelle from developing any romantic relationship with him. Besides not wanting Janelle to cheat, what are her other motivations?

12. Sam gets news of his ex-wife's suicide and emotionally shuts down. Connie observes that she has seen him do this before but in another context. How are the two situations related?

13. The tranquil, friendly town of Mammoth Falls erupts into chaos during the Wild West festival. Do you see any parallels to current events?

14. Janelle's acceptance that she will never find Pops leads her to the acceptance of another thing she hasn't realized she has been grappling with for years. What is it?

15. Sam and Janelle argue and realize that they both have been

undergoing similar emotional journeys with guilt and responsibility. They conclude that is this why they've felt such a strong connection to each other. What issues were they both tackling?

16. Janelle returns to Virginia and finds Mark with Shana. Were you surprised by this discovery? Why or why not?

17. Have all the characters been found by the end of the book? Why or why not?

Connect with Us

Visit us online at
KensingtonBooks.com
to read more from your favorite authors, see books
by series, view reading group guides, and more.

for sneak peeks, chances to win books and prize packs,
and to share your thoughts with other readers.

facebook.com/kensingtonpublishing
twitter.com/kensingtonbooks

Tell us what you think!

To share your thoughts, submit a review,
or sign up for our eNewsletters, please visit:
KensingtonBooks.com/TellUs.